THE PACHINKO

WOMAN

THE
PACHINKO
WOMAN

HENRY MYNTON

WILLIAM MORROW AND COMPANY, INC.

New York

Quotation from Joseph Conrad's *Under Western Eyes* is from the Penguin
Twentieth-Century Classics edition, edited by Paul Kirschner, 1996.

It is the policy of William Morrow and Company, Inc., and its imprints
and affiliates, recognizing the importance of preserving what has been
written, to print the books we publish on acid-free paper, and we exert
our best efforts to that end.

Library of Congress Cataloging-in-Publication Data

Mynton, Henry.
The Pachinko woman / by Henry Mynton.—1st ed.
p.   cm.
ISBN 0-688-16170-7
I. Title.
PS3563.Y6P33   1999
813'.54—dc21   99-18700
CIP
Printed in the United States of America

First Edition

1 2 3 4 5 6 7 8 9 10

BOOK DESIGN BY CATHRYN S. AISON

www.williammorrow.com

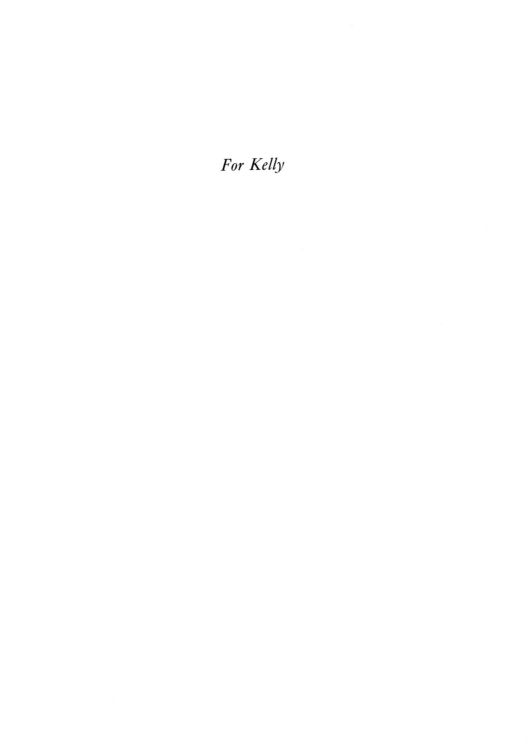

For Kelly

ACKNOWLEDGMENTS

To Jed Mattes, my literary agent, and Fred Morris, his associate, my appreciation for their encouragement and support.

My great thanks to Betty Kelly, editor at William Morrow, for understanding the effort and the end.

I was also fortunate to have Richard Marek as my editor—his patience, insight, and genius taught me more than a hundred courses in the magic art of writing.

To the many Japanese and Korean nationals who contributed their knowledge and time to my understanding of their pachinko world, a special thanks. I should like to mention particularly Cecilia Kim and "The Horse" for pointing the way.

I am also indebted to my good friend Ariana, who provided access to A. Vespa's fascinating autobiographical account of life in Harbin, China, in the thirties, which was useful as background.

The unselfish and the intelligent may begin a movement—but it passes away from them. They are not the leaders of a revolution. They are its victims.

Joseph Conrad
Under Western Eyes

PROLOGUE

July 18, 1941

This may be the last entry in my diary. I cannot bear to write the unspeakable truth anymore. I met the American girl again yesterday. She has beautiful yellow hair and eyes the color of the sky. Around her neck is a chain with a gold cross. She is Christian like me. I think they have drugged her, because she does not show any emotion, and there are strange marks on her arm. Her Chinese speech is slow and her eyes do not focus.

I met her in the hall and there was a male orderly who became angry when I tried to speak with her. I only asked her what her name was.

"Elizabeth," she said slowly in her soft voice.

The orderly grabbed her arm and hurried her away.

Yesterday afternoon, I tried to escape but was caught and beaten and tied, so I could not write secretly in my diary until now. Perhaps I will die and the Japanese will find this and then it will not matter anyway. But I am writing in the hope this record can be saved; I want others to know what was done to us. Not only us Korean women but to an American woman as well!

The room they assigned me is only six tatami mats in size. When the first Japanese soldier came in, a strange hot wind blew through the open window. It fluttered the loose blue yukata that I had been ordered to wear with nothing underneath. I could not bring myself to look at the man's face but simply pointed a trembling finger at a place on the floor and watched a rough hand place the ticket in the small box that I had been given for that purpose.

As the man came toward me, the room started to spin. In my fevered brain, I saw my mother and asked for her forgiveness. I prayed for death. Every night, I will say the same prayer.

PART ONE

Only when people refuse to do some things
are they capable of greatness.

Korean proverb

1 : THE GAME Tokyo: Sunday, 6:00 P.M.

STEIG SPENT AN hour getting to the gambling place that Japanese call a pachinko parlor. The drizzle had stopped, but not the Tokyo humidity; he was sweating in the June evening heat. Following his training, the German had doubled back twice, changed trains, taken a bus, broken his profile by putting on a cap and jacket, changed pace frequently, and finally strolled the open space near Meiji Park. This allowed him a good look to see if he was being followed. Two couples in cutoff jeans and rapper hairdos were heading the opposite way. Nobody else. He was clean.

The pachinko parlor was crowded with players—a large three-floored casino filled with hundreds of shiny upright machines, miniskirted attendants, flashing lights, blaring music from *Rocky*. Steig worried all the winning machines might have been taken.

Above the whirling of steel balls and thunder of howling music, displays of flashing lights exploded in dizzying streaks. One wall was fifty TV screens writhing with Japanese soaps, the first inning of the Yomiuri Giants baseball game, and erotic foreign films. The noise and excitement were cataclysmic. A sense of place prevailed as if this were the eye of the storm.

As the steel balls collided crazily, as the lights flashed, as pinwheels spun, as flippers snapped and tulips cracked open or shut, all players sat mesmerized. Jackpot caves winked seductively, urging them on.

At the outset, his handlers had told Steig that pachinko, Japanese-style pinball, was a huge business. That the "casinos" or "parlors" were crowded day and night. Thirty million Japanese played the game and spent as much on pachinko as the government did on national defense. Therefore, Steig's job would not be easy.

To Steig's German mind, the Japanese had always been a conservative, clannish, no-frills people. Now he was being told they were a society of pachinko addicts. Go figure, Steig thought. His handlers had no clear answers. But Steig soon reached his own conclusions.

When he had arrived at his first pachinko parlor three months ago, he had seen that there was not one reason but many. Japanese men came to escape the stress of their office environments, or for the money, or to pick up women, or just for the fun of it. You could win big. It was the most widely available public gambling in Japan.

The miniskirted attendants brought Pepsi, solved machine problems, and high-fived announcers when you hit a jackpot. They did not mind being asked for a date. Hovering near cash registers were the yakuza, the gangsters with their punch-permed hair, who handled security, heightening the atmosphere of risk.

Still, Steig did not understand the real attraction of pachinko until he had played for several weeks and talked to a number of addicts. It was a loner's game requiring intense concentration, skill, a mathematician's eye for detail, stamina. It pitted the individual against the machine.

For Japanese players—who lived in crowded homes, whose careers were spent in company groups, who commuted on the most crowded transportation in the world, who were continually being reminded of the need to harmonize with fellow Japanese, and who could never find the mental and physical space a Westerner knew—being "alone" with a pachinko machine was a supreme luxury.

That was why the thirty million Japanese played, Steig concluded. To get away from each other. The Japanese were human, after all. Steig began to like them—and their game.

STEIG HAD LEARNED how to win at pachinko by stalking the "pros" who hung out at the casinos. He watched what they did and asked why they did it. These were players who made their living at the game, in some cases earning hundreds of thousands of dollars a year. But the pros could not win every day. Steig knew from watching them that even the best lost two or three days in ten.

As he looked around the parlor selected tonight by his controller, he did not hear the thunder of the balls, the shriek of the music, the sirens announcing jackpots. Nor did he notice the stifling air, the clouds of cigarette smoke. He was selecting a specific machine. Distinguishing an "asobi-dai," a machine that would not be profitable, from a "kamban-dai," one that clearly favored the player. This selection process, he knew from experience, was the key to winning.

Each machine was periodically "set" by a "kugishi"—a nail doctor—to be easy or hard. Most machines at any casino were nonwinners. Only one in ten was set to be easy, to encourage the myth that anyone could win. Figuring out which ones were "givers" rather than "takers" required skill that most players did not have.

First, Steig checked the ashtrays at vacant machines. Five or six butts in an ashtray meant the previous player had been there thirty or forty minutes. Steig found a vacant machine with six butts and considered the implication. Thirty minutes on the machine meant three thousand balls played, since an average player shot one hundred balls a minute. Cost of rented balls was one hundred yen for twenty-five. Therefore . . .

Steig calculated that the previous player's winnings were seven to ten thousand yen, for few Japanese players were willing to invest over twelve thousand yen in thirty to forty minutes of losses. They would get up and search for a better machine or leave.

He sat down, checking the butts to make sure they were all the same brand and not left by several players. Good. Now he examined the upright face of the machine in front of him. It was glass, about three feet high, a foot and a half wide. Its colorful, complex veneer board was made of Japanese beech and bristled with approximately 250 golden nails. These protected eight scoring holes or "slots," and a central "generator" slot. There were pinwheels, flippers, and tulips to guide the eleven-millimeter, 5.5-gram steel balls into or away from slots. If a ball hit a V-zone in the "generator," flippers opened increasing sizes of slots and winnings soared.

Basically the game was simple. Players shot the steel balls up to the top of the board, hoping they would bounce off the nails in the right directions to land in slots that rewarded the player with up to thirteen new balls so he could keep playing. Or he could exchange the balls for prizes or money—two to three yen per ball. Predicting how the balls would ricochet was therefore critical.

Steig tried the handle for its "feel." It was connected to a spring-based shooting device. Consistency was critical, he knew; a quirky spring could vary the arc of shots up and onto the nails and make accurate aiming impossible. This spring was strong and consistent.

Next, he looked at the nail alignment.

Although to the uninitiated all nails appeared to be at a ninety-degree angle to the board, only a few really were. He focused on 25 percent of the nails only—the ones nearest the four highest-scoring slots—since these would most influence the fall of each ball as it bounced down the window in front of him.

If a nail was pointing slightly upward it would slow and deflect the ball left or right. This was considered good above a scoring slot, while a downward-pointing nail was not good since it would deflect the ball away from the board's surface.

Similarly, a nail pointing left or right would deflect the ball one way or the other, depending on the trajectory at which it was falling.

None of the slots was "blocked," he decided. The machine was fair. It would be up to his hand-eye coordination then. Fine.

Steig sat up straight, finally ready. But first he looked around at the other players, the attendants, the protection. Already, he was timing his move. So far, the real heavies had not arrived. They would come later in the evening perhaps, when the final take was counted. That was why he always came at six o'clock. He would play for an hour or so. Get the feel of the place. Then make his move.

Steig inserted a cash card into the machine. He set the gaudy knob that determined the speed of each ball and the height of its arc inside the case, pushed a button that set the machine in play, and watched. The balls erupted like a fountain over the forest of golden pins that guarded each jackpot hole. He adjusted the shooting knob once, then sat back, satisfied.

The more balls that could be dropped into that golden forest, the greater the chance of finding the hole that would release an ecstatic deluge of new balls into the winner's cup. The erotic connotations of the game were obvious; a shrink could have a field day.

It did not occur to him that pachinko might change his life forever. Gunther Steig had come to Japan as he had gone everywhere else in his thirty-three years of life—without considering the consequences.

HE WON EIGHT boxes and quit. No big jackpot, but enough small ones to give him a satisfactory night: 3,000 yen per box or nearly 350 German marks. He patted the machine. It glowed at him, and he grinned. Things had been tough before he came to Japan. It was good to be winning again.

A Japanese girl at the machine next to his stared enviously at his winnings. Steig knew he was not handsome, but women were attracted by his smile—and by his eyes. They were light blue, almost colorless. Ice-blue, like a wolf's.

He had arrived in Japan nearly three months earlier. So far his visit had been a success. Six targets in the past month. All successful. He was being paid well, and the client contact had been professional. He knew better than to ask questions. He still had no clue as to his client's nationality or true objectives. He only knew that his controllers were Asians.

Careful people, he could say that for them. They required a system of cutouts and drops for identification of targets and communication. Chalk marks on specific walls or poles or benches to signal when a drop was ready and when it had cleared. He didn't know their ideology. He didn't care. So long as they paid him well. He had long ago emptied himself of prejudice. All of the targets had been Koreans.

He took his winnings to the gift corner. Pointed at the Rémy Martin brandy and a Seiko watch. Plus cigarettes. They were handed to him in a plain plastic bag with a polite bow. Thus, technically, pachinko was not gambling, since no cash had changed hands on premises. But Steig knew that at a store or vendor nearby, ryōgae prizes could be exchanged for cash. The exchange place was not owned by the parlor, and no connection to the yakuza had ever been proved by halfhearted police efforts. Pachinko had become too ingrained in the Japanese soul to change things now.

The manager's office was in back. Steig walked by it to a men's room, noting where the second door was located. A manager's office usually had two doors, the second allowing escape to an alley or corridor or to a busy street.

His research nearly complete, and his winnings under his arm, Steig headed out the front door of the parlor and turned left, then left again at the corner. He reached a back street behind the pachinko hall and walked toward the alley he wanted, the one the manager's door led onto. Two pretty girls emerged from a bar across the street, and he waved at them. They giggled and put their hands over their mouths. He pointed to another bar up the street with a sign that read "Telephone Karaoke Club." In his passable Japanese he said, "Would you mind keeping this for me?" He held out the bag containing the Rémy Martin. "Ten minutes, then I will buy you both a drink. I have some business to do."

One of them was tall and fashionable, dressed in an expensive business suit. She peeked into the bag. They were both clearly office girls, out for some fun. Their cheeks were rosy from drink. Again they giggled, looked at each other. Steig grinned disarmingly. The tall one nodded and took the bag.

Steig was a technician in everything he did. He knew that in Japan, where people were taught to be polite, someone asking for assistance was not considered threatening.

He liked Japanese girls. They had pretty faces and slim figures, a pleasant change from East German women. They thought nothing of taking long exotic baths together with men they favored, and as a matter of form they often apologized for being inadequate after sex.

He reached down as if to adjust his shoe, and his hand brushed the handle of the long knife in the ankle sheath beneath his pant leg. He straightened up. "Good, then. We'll meet at the telephone club. I won't be long—just an errand for a friend."

2 ⁝ THE CHOSEN ONES Tokyo: Sunday, 8:15 P.M.

LOW CLOUDS HOVERED over Tokyo. Smoky plumes backlit by flickering light from the huge entertainment district looked like a firestorm from another war. In a way that was true.

Chief Inspector Tetsuo Mori of the Public Security Bureau arrived at the pachinko hall. Five precinct police cars were already double-parked, red and blue lights flashing.

The shrill siren of an ambulance competed with a police loudspeaker warning spectators not to cross yellow-tape lines isolating the pachinko parlor. Mori was short for a Japanese, but his wide-set eyes showed a confidence that belied his size. The knuckles of both hands were permanently disfigured from years of pounding karate boards in police dojos. His face was unlined. The only sign that he was approaching middle age was thinning hair, which his wife, Mitsuko, attributed to his love of sakè.

He slapped an OFFICIAL POLICE card against the window of his car and got out. Another Korean down. The office had reached him as he was gulping a bowl of tempura udon at a shop the cabbies and truckers frequented. Although it was a Sunday, he had been checking pachinko halls in areas of Tokyo where stabbings had occurred over the past four weeks. Four in Tokyo. Two in Kansai. It was becoming an epidemic. Stab wounds by the same long thin blade.

After taking the call, he slurped down the last of the noodles and tilted the delicious soup into his mouth. Several drops dribbled down his chin. He always got the no-win cases, Mori told himself. His boss, Aoyama, saw to that.

He waved at the owner, who once had been a decent flyweight. The owner waved back. "How's the right, Inspector?"

"Can't complain."

"Go a few rounds next week?"

"Sure. You have insurance?"

It was a standing joke that the owner repeated each time Mori came. He also called Mori if he heard anything interesting around the counter. In return, Mori had helped him get a liquor license. It was called "giri," obligation relation; that was how business was done in Tokyo.

Outside, he tilted his nose to savor the thin strands of rain. Almost a mist, it tasted of charcoal smoke from a nearby yaki-imo cart and smelled of the green hedgerows of nearby Asagaya, where he had grown up. In his childhood, he would go out walking in such rain when his mother worked nights and he was feeling lonely. He would pretend the raindrops were arrows from the gods who had taken his father. "Remember, we are of the Satsuma Clan," his mother told him. "Remember that your father was known in every city and town of Japan for what he did for his country. His death was honorable. One cannot ask for more than that."

On his way to the pachinko parlor, Mori thought about the Korean community in Japan. Had the Koreans gone berserk? Initially, he'd assumed the obvious—a yakuza turf war had erupted. But so far all his contacts had denied any connection to the killings. Either this was the truth or a lot of money was being spread around to keep it quiet.

Maybe it was a feud among the Koreans themselves? The North Koreans in Japan didn't like the Southerners, but there'd never been anything like this before. So far, those were his two options. Otherwise, the killings didn't make sense. He pushed his way through the crowd toward the pachinko hall.

The officer on the door stared at Mori's ID and saluted. The ambulance had pulled up over the curb, back doors yawning open. The crowd, mostly eager young college kids excited by the violence, had gathered expectantly, ignoring the rain. There was very little violence in Japan, and anything in scarce supply still attracted an audience.

Mori noted that the pachinko hall was in a good location, another high-volume business. He fixed his eyes on the policeman. "What do we have tonight, Officer?"

"A stabbing, sir. Same as the others. And a garrote." His name tag read Officer Takehashi.

"Any other clues?"

"None, sir, but it was the Chosen Ones sure as I'm standing here."

Mori smiled politely. "Chosen," pronounced "Cho-sen," meant "Korean" in Japanese and was usually uttered with a little smirk. "Chosen Ones" was police talk for Koreans who lived in Japan. Korea had been occupied by the Japanese Imperial Army from 1905, an occupation that lasted until the end of World War II. Korea had been a colony, Koreans the Japanese's slaves. In the thirties, many Koreans had been forced by the Imperial Army to immigrate to Japan, where they were assigned the dangerous jobs most Japanese workers refused to perform.

Takehashi gestured toward the inside of the hall. "They're screwing up our country, the fucking Koreans are, sir."

"Who is it this time?" Mori asked. "Owner again?"

"Yes sir. Same as the others. Done very neatly. None of the players saw a thing."

"Take the money, did he?"

"All the money, yes sir." Takehashi stared inside the pachinko hall. "Owner's not dead yet, sir. They're bringing him out now."

A team of paramedics rushed past them, carrying a figure on a stretcher. Blankets covered all but the ashen face. Mori went over, flashed his badge. "Can he talk?"

The paramedics shoved the stretcher into the vehicle and jumped in. The vehicle started to move, the siren blared. One of the medics shouted to Mori, "No! Puncture wound to the heart. Don't think he's going to make it. Lost too much blood." The doors swung shut and the ambulance careened off, the wail of its siren trailing into the night like a dying scream. Mori watched the ambulance until it disappeared from sight. One more chance lost, he thought. The crowd began to disperse.

Officer Takehashi came up to him. "Forgive me for saying so, sir, but these people are like animals. Kill each other over the slightest insult. There's some kind of war going on between the North and South Koreans in Tokyo, if you want my opinion. They're just trying to make it look like a robbery. And this one is like all the rest. No clues. Like some ghost is doing it."

"Or somebody very professional," Mori said as he started inside the pachinko hall.

"Oh, it's a Korean, all right!" Takehashi said after him. "No Japanese would use a knife and a garrote. No Japanese would do that. Monsters is what they are."

3: THE TV EXCHANGE Los Angeles: Sunday, 11:00 P.M.

HELIM KIM INSTRUCTED the well-dressed, middle-aged Korean to pull into the drive of a large stone house on the outskirts of Los Angeles. She did not wait for Park Chung Il to open her door, and he had to hurry up the walk after her. The rain had started to come down harder.

At the door, she turned to him. "My father's out of town tonight. We'll have the entire place to ourselves, but don't get any ideas. I have a boyfriend."

Park didn't answer. He already knew that. The boyfriend's name was Steve Juric, and he was a problem. A shame she wasted her beauty on a foreigner.

An Asian maid opened the door and stared at the Korean man behind Helim. Park was elegantly dressed in a tailored suit and silk tie. He brushed the rain from his shoulders as they entered the house.

Helim spoke in Korean to the maid, and she disappeared into the kitchen to fix tea. It was nearly one in the morning, but Park felt antic- ipation, not fatigue. The flight from Europe had been tiring, but that was the least of his concerns.

Tonight, Park would review the diary. Tomorrow he'd call DeCovasi.

The house was elegantly furnished. Helim's father had prospered as manager of a Korean bank branch. A red lacquer chest covered with brass metalwork faced the front door. In each room art objects from different periods of Korean history were softly lighted. Intricate brush paintings on the walls, vases, plates, and pottery on shelves. Park felt a touch of nostalgia. He hadn't been able to return to North Korea for five long years.

Helim gave Park a quick tour of the house. In the library, she explained that she didn't have enough room at her small Westwood apartment for all her articles and books on rights for Asian women. He figured she had become addicted to such nonsense when she worked at the UN. She'd been a translator there for four years before setting up her own translation and consulting firm in Los Angeles. Her clients were mainly from the Korean community or the UN. She was also a consultant to Allied International, now the largest pachinko firm in Japan, in which her grandmother was part owner. Helim traveled often to Asia and was respected by the pachinko industry.

Ten days ago, she'd returned from a UN client contract in the city of Pyongyang and provided Park with useful information about conditions inside North Korea. She was a key piece on his chessboard. The queen, Park liked to tell himself. She had her mother's beauty and strength of character, her father's brains, and her grandmother's shrewdness. A stunning combination, Park thought. Best of all, she was well connected to both pachinko and the UN.

She ended the tour in the living room, pointing out a piece of Silla pottery a thousand years old, wall hangings that the Los Angeles County Museum of Art had asked for and her father had promised in his will, lacquer boxes hundreds of years old in perfect condition, porcelain plates in reds and blues from the seventeenth century, celadon from a contemporary potter now living in Seoul. So much wealth, Park thought, when many of our countrymen are starving.

Two million people had already died. Unrest was spreading. Which was why nine months ago Park had formed Koreans for Democratic Action. The KDA sponsored indirect actions aimed at destabilizing Pyongyang and liberalizing North Korea.

Until five years ago, Park had been a senior member of North Korean intelligence. In one of the hard-liners' periodic purges, he'd been stripped of all powers and exiled to Helsinki for being too liberal. The tribunal that had handed down his verdict had also banned him from ever returning. At the time, there had been many who whispered that Park's life had been spared only because he was related to the current North Korean leader, Park Tai Jin.

But times had changed. China was pressuring Pyongyang to open its markets to the West. Hard-liners were losing support. His best chance to return was now, Park decided. It was time to play his queen.

Helim was showing Park an old picture of her father, a slight but intense-looking man, a banker dapper in a suit and tie. Next to him was a beautiful woman. Her mother, Park knew, since he'd met her long ago. The picture reminded him of her proud eyes and unyielding strength of character.

"Your mother?" Park asked, since Helim knew nothing of that meeting.

"The last picture of them together," she said.

Park studied the beautiful face. Not unlike Helim's. "What a pity she disappeared before you grew up." Her grandmother had raised her in Tokyo, Park knew. That explained Helim's complex character. She'd been raised in a pachinko hall, friends joked. She understood the thrill of high-stakes games early in life.

"Yes." Helim shrugged. "I felt abandoned at the time. I was only seven." She stared at him a moment as if reading his thoughts. "I'll get the diary. It's what we came for." She excused herself to go upstairs as the maid entered with ginseng tea.

Rain pounded against the windows.

He had one reservation about Helim Kim. Like many Westernized Koreans, she'd shortened her name and used the Western order to please Americans. True Koreans introduced themselves by birth names, surname first. Was she strong enough for what he had in mind?

Park considered the gamble he was making. It was huge. Eight months ago he'd contacted the FBI. They were concerned about money-laundering. He could deliver the largest laundering operation in Asia, he told them. Blackmail from Japanese pachinko companies in the billions of dollars was being shuttled through offshore banks from Japan to North Korea. Someone inside the Japanese government was involved. He couldn't take the information to them.

You should have been a novelist, they said. Show us some evidence. So he had.

Bank telegraphic transfers and deposit certificates placed in a Hong Kong safe deposit box during his last days with North Korean intelligence. Account numbers in Vanuatu, BVI, Antigua, the Seychelles. Tokyo company accounts of known yakuza organizations. Secretly taped interviews with pachinko owners. All money flowed to Pyongyang, owners said. It was the major source of foreign exchange for the North Korean government.

"And you think you can stop this?" DeCovasi was his control, marketer, defender, security blanket, and confessor—the one man who had almost as much riding on Park's success as Park did.

Yes, he said, and told him how.

His pro-democracy group, the KDA, had persuaded ten large pachinko chain operators, controlling half of all the parlors in Japan, to file for Japanese stock exchange listings. Public listing in Japan demanded transparent accounting, stringent auditing, and recording of all funds transfers abroad. Japanese ownership and auditing would prevent extortion payments, dry up the money source, decimate Pyongyang's foreign exchange. And force open its markets. The projected cost of the operation was insignificant compared to possible gains.

Scoffers at the Hoover Building argued that Park's claims were wildly optimistic. Listing wouldn't stop extortion, they said. However, DeCovasi lobbied his friends, called in his chips, insisted the downside was minimal. Approvals for the KDA to proceed were finally granted. One condition. No violence.

When killings of pachinko owners erupted, DeCovasi was livid.

But Park sounded pleased when DeCovasi called him in a fury.

It proved Pyongyang was worried. It proved Park's worth to American intelligence.

Pyongyang was trying to frighten firms away, Park declared. But it had not. All those killed were his people, Park sighed. Owners or managers who had filed for listing. Then he added the kicker. The stock exchanges had turned down *all* listing applications. Clearly a Japanese politician was pulling strings to help the hard-liners in Pyongyang.

"Politician? Who?" DeCovasi demanded.

"No idea. Near the top is my guess. Very near. Perhaps you should make a trip to Tokyo."

"I'll consider it. Your North Koreans then? Who are the people in Pyongyang who want the listings stopped?"

Park named two hard-liners: Alpha, head of North Korean intelligence, and General Myun Chun Kuk, former head of the tribunal that ran North Korea, the very tribunal that had banned Park forever. When DeCovasi asked for specific proof, Park didn't have any.

"Can't help if you don't have them cold," DeCovasi admonished. "You're talking high-stakes poker. We don't play unless we have a winning hand." He paused as if checking his cards. Then DeCovasi made what was to later prove one of the major mistakes of his career. He promised that if Park could get proof of the two hard-liners' involvement in the listing killings, the American government would act.

Park moved quickly. He wanted revenge. And implicating Alpha and the general would hinge on flushing the Japanese pol who had maneuvered the stock exchange turndowns. To shake that tree, Park had to play his queen.

Helim had literally been raised in a pachinko hall. She'd helped parlay her grandmother's chain into one of the largest pachinko groups in Japan. She was the expert. The trade called her the Pachinko Woman.

With her, however, came a problem—the boyfriend. Steven Juric, recently divorced, Asian legal experience. Her lover. How much was Helim telling him? Park worried. Particularly after she credited Juric with the idea of using Japanese TV to reverse stock exchange turndowns.

However, the lawyer's concept intrigued Park, for it could also be a way to flush the Japanese pol protecting laundering to North Korea. And topple his hard-line enemies in North Korea. Claiming it as his own, he'd presented the idea to DeCovasi. "We take the turndowns to the Japanese public through TV. Shout extortion and laundering. Wake up the mass media to the fact that pachinko is financing weapons of mass destruction. Long-range missle research. Explain how listings can stop it."

"Why should the Japanese old-boy network care?"

"We'll put it to them in black-and-white. They either list the Korean firms or admit that the exchanges and the government are backing extortion and indirectly financing Pyongyang."

"How do you get airtime? We're certainly not going to buy it."

"Do an exchange for airtime. Use talk shows. No airtime costs there."

"What kind of exchange?"

"A diary. I'm flying into L.A. this week to see Helim for details. If you agree."

"We're always willing to listen."

"STEVE'S THE ONE with experience listing companies in Japan," Helim said, fingering the fragile yellowed book she'd put on the table between them. "Not me. Two years ago, one of his semiconductor clients got turned down like us. Reasons given were the usual technical bull. What really happened was that local competitors paid off a Ministry of Finance official. Steve learned about the payoff and negotiated an exchange—airtime on a major TV network to promote his client's listing in exchange for details of the MOF bribe."

Park knew Helim's enthusiasm was not entirely patriotic. She owned shares in her grandmother's company that would be worth millions if they were listed and sold. She'd be able to afford a few baubles for herself as well as support for her causes. "So this diary's your bribe?"

"My grandmother's diary," she corrected him.

"Which TV shows?"

"Hideo Katano's, for openers. He forced a prime minister out a couple of years ago."

"The trucking scandal—yes, I remember."

"His TV news show is the highest-rated in Japan. Thrives on exposures and scoops that tweak the old-boy network. Steve's case was picked up by other stations. Eventually steam-rollered nationally. Got his client's listing."

"So you offer Katano a spicy bit in this diary?"

"Exactly."

"And in return get time on his show to talk about pachinko."

"Right. And other shows, we hope."

"What's in this diary that's so interesting?"

"I'll read it. Then you'll understand."

"Why don't you let me read it? Faster."

"It's written in Japanese. My grandmother was educated during the Japanese occupation. All Koreans were forbidden to write their own language then. Schools only taught written Japanese. That was all my grandmother knew."

"Of course," Park said. "Stupid of me. How old was she when this was written?"

"Eighteen."

Helim began to read in a low pure voice that wrapped Park Chung Il in the cocoon of the past.

July 12, 1941

The world is now ending. Yesterday I arrived in Harbin, China, a dusty city full of arrogant Japanese soldiers and frightened Chinese civilians. I was ordered to a medical tent to be examined again by a Japanese officer, a colonel.

"First about your name, Jonquil Kim. Jonquil isn't Korean, is it?"

"It's my Christian name, the English name of a narcissus flower. My Korean name is Choon Sil, but my parents . . ."

"We'll use Choon Sil on our medical records then." He wrote this down.

The examination was cursory and it was here that the way in which I was to serve the Japanese Imperial Army was made clear. For the first time I realized I would not be a nurse as I had been told in Pyongyang.

"You will be a 'comfort woman,' " the officer said. He was quite fat and jolly, as if he considered everything a huge joke. "This is a great honor," he added, lest I misunderstand, and he stared at me, first at my face, then at my body. "You are honored, yes?"

"What does this . . . 'comfort woman' . . . do?" I could hardly find my voice.

"You mean no one has told you?" The medical officer laughed until his double chin bobbed up and down. Then he picked up something from his desk. It was odd-shaped and made of plastic. "The men will use these, so you need not worry. An Imperial condom. Very high quality. Japanese products are known for quality, you see." He put the object down. "Furthermore, you will be examined by me every month. Just to be sure." He smiled queerly at me and picked up a printed piece of paper. "Now, you are a smart girl and can read Japanese. This is an instruction. You will be given the right to raise any problems you are having with me or your manager. We are attempting to improve the system, make it more efficient. Your suggestions are welcome. We all must work together.

"Your pay will be deposited to a local bank. Less deductions for your food and room by the manager of the franchise, of course. He is a Korean like you. Very nice fellow."

When I did not speak, the colonel continued, "It explains the procedure, which you will strictly follow. Each man must have a ticket, which you will collect when he comes into your room. Every day you must collect twenty-six tickets and turn them in to the manager downstairs. Then you may clean your room and take your leisure. There is a time limit of thirty minutes for each man. If he has not achieved an ejaculation in that time, you will be accountable. So you must be efficient. Do you have any questions?"

July 13, 1941

A foreign girl was assigned the room next to me today. She has curly blond hair that bounces on her shoulders when she walks. But her

eyes are vague and she speaks only a little Japanese. I found out that
she is an American who was working for the Red Cross in Harbin.
Japanese soldiers arrested her on charges that she is a spy. She has
a boyfriend but he has not been able to contact her. After Japanese
officers interrogated her for a week, they sent her here. Like myself,
she's been raped repeatedly. When she explained this and started to
cry, my heart went out to her. For a moment, my own problems
seemed less important than this beautiful American girl's.

Park saw that Helim was not turning the pages of the diary, nor was
she reading the words. Her eyes were staring into the distance as she
recited. She knew it by heart.

4: CABARET GIRL Tokyo: Sunday, 11:10 P.M.

HALOS SURROUNDED TOKYO'S streetlights. A glitter-glass sidewalk was filled with homeward-bound girls under pastel umbrellas and men carrying their suit jackets. Mori double-parked in Shinjuku near Tomi's club.

The pachinko hall owner had died on the way to the hospital. Although everyone in the hall had been questioned, no one had seen or heard anything useful. One player thought he'd glimpsed a foreigner checking out the manager's office shortly before the killing. But no others had seen him, and the player couldn't describe the gaijin or provide any other details. Foreign faces were difficult to remember, the man complained. They all looked alike. Mori had agreed and dismissed the witness.

Like the others, it had been a very clean job. A forensics team had found no prints or traces. There was a back door leading onto an alley, but it was locked. No clues had surfaced in the alley or on the lock. Mori theorized the killer could have entered that way and locked it again on the way out. But only a highly skilled expert with locks could have performed that trick. In which case it was not a common criminal that they were dealing with. And the yakuza would have done it differently—slammed a hole in the door and forced their way in. That left only the North-South hypothesis. Something political. Mori was hoping Tomi could help.

Mori admired Tomi. Unlike most Koreans born in Japan, she never tried to hide the perceived defect of her Korean race. She told newcomers straight off that she was a Korean, as another might explain an incurable disease that was not contagious.

As a high-ranking member of the North Korean Association in Japan, Tomi was easily the best of his Korean informants. Over the five years he had known her, she'd rapidly moved up in the association. It was through Tomi, for example, that he had learned that all the recently murdered Koreans were of North Korean descent.

He considered how to approach her tonight. Obliquely, he decided. Wouldn't do to let her know he had no clues at all. It was nearly eleven-thirty, and the club was emptying; the commuter trains stopped running in another hour. A girl with good legs in mesh stockings waited for his order; he requested a Suntory-water at the special rate.

"It's my pleasure," she said, backing away like a skittish colt before it breaks and runs.

The "special" was a bargain weekend rate for the off-the-rack crowd. Five thousand yen if you left within one hour. One drink and one girl included, with a polite reminder not to forget the time. The club's heaviest nights were weekdays, when the businessmen were entertaining clients. Weekends were for solos and sponsors of the girls. Mori was both.

Bit nervy tonight, Mori told himself as he watched the girl hurry away. She stopped by the manager's desk to speak with the captain, who glanced in Mori's direction. Of course they would know who he was. The club was owned by a Korean yakuza notorious for his temper. The owner was suspected of having connections with North Korea and cheating on taxes. So were the girls. Each girl at Club Reo went by a false name and an assigned number, like a Swiss bank account. They didn't like to see anyone from the government on premises.

Tomi had been working various Korean clubs part-time since Mori had met her five years ago. He had no illusions about her loyalty. In his business one assumed that she reported parts of their conversations to her North Korean superiors to keep them happy. However, she was a channel—a useful means of communicating with the North Koreans in Japan. Occasionally she did something dangerous and secret for him. Tonight he would make one of those requests.

At times, in the past, Mori would take a day off, take Tomi and her child to Marine World, or on special occasions, like Korean Children's Day, to Disneyland in Chiba. The boy would be four this September.

He blew cigarette smoke into the arrows of light from a revolving mirror ball. Under it, a small band had just finished a break. She'd once claimed the boy was his, but that was an old trick, and Mori wasn't fooled. All the cabaret girls collected from as many clients as they could when they became pregnant. With abortions so cheap and accessible, their motivations in having a baby were obvious. There were stories of girls from

the legendary Madame Cherry's Copacabana purchasing apartment buildings, art galleries, stables of horses from just one child. Of course, those
children weren't half Korean.

"GOOD EVENING, MORI." Tomi was tall, with long luxurious legs he'd
always loved.

Mori flicked his cigarette in the ashtray. "You're looking lovely,
Tomi."

"We're in a good mood. You must want something." She slipped into
the seat next to him. Her hand rested accidentally on his thigh.

"You should trust me more," Mori said, removing her hand.

"A trail through the mountains becomes a path if it is used." She
looked at him with warmth of knowledge and turned on the red table
lamp that alerted a waiter. "If unused it becomes blocked by grass. Is
your heart blocked with grass, Mori-san? You could at least give me a
kiss."

He did, and afterward could taste her lipstick. Memories, he thought.

"So, what is it tonight? You need more information? You wish to use
me? Or will it be just sex?" A waiter appeared, and she ordered a "regular," which meant cold tea that would have been charged as a fifty-dollar
alcoholic beverage had Mori not been on the special.

When the waiter left, Tomi took out a tissue and wiped away the
lipstick on Mori's lips. He felt the tissue caress his skin and inhaled its
scent. Her scent. He missed her.

He collected his thoughts. Business first. Start with a compliment.
Koreans were emotional people, like Americans. And the issues tonight
were sensitive.

"Nice earrings," he said.

"You really like them? Oto got them for me."

"Oto" meant "father," slang for an older male friend. It was the name
Tomi used for her sugar daddy. The earrings were in the shape of reindeer.

"Nice. Very nice." He knew everything about Tomi that he needed
to know: the names of her regular customers, the birthday of her illegit-
imate son, that she rented two flats paid for by someone else, that the last
time she left the country (a harmless splurge to Phuket) was with a Korean
banker named Kim. For the past three years, she had been kept by a
secret sponsor, a gentleman who saw to it that her bills were paid, her

clothes fashionable, her jewelry adequate. Mori hadn't probed further. Everyone had a right to some privacy, even one of his Korean informants.

"They're pure gold."

"But reindeer? Isn't it a bit early for Christmas?"

"Nothing to do with Christmas! They're symbols for those of us who want a democratic reunited Korea. Our ancestors believed the sun, which bathes all Korea, was a golden reindeer. Now what is it you wanted?" Her voice had lost some of its early warmth.

Mori looked into her eyes. "Another Korean was murdered tonight. I wondered if it was a Northerner. Have you heard?"

Tomi returned his stare. "If it were Japanese being murdered, the newspapers would be full of it and a hundred-man task force of detectives assigned."

"I know," Mori said patiently. "For everyone there are things we cannot bear. It polishes our souls."

"It is because a Korean death is unimportant, because formerly you occupied our country and looked down on us as slaves. Some in Japan still do."

"I am aware of such things," Mori sighed. The important lies must be interlaced with kernels of truth to be believed. "But the majority of Japanese are sympathetic to the Korean cause. I am one of them, as you know, and I need information if the number of deaths is not to reach eight."

Tomi's lips had fixed in a pout, and she was carefully examining her fingernails.

"C'mon, Tomi. What is going on among Koreans in Japan? I need a specific motive. Could the killings be connected to your reindeer?"

She looked up. "What do you mean?"

"Connected to a democracy movement or reunion of the two Koreas. Or some other political issue."

She shrugged. "Who knows?"

Their drinks came, and Mori toasted to a democratic reunited Korea. He was used to handling difficult sources. "Assuming the one murdered tonight is a Northerner, I figure South Koreans are behind it."

Her eyes divulged nothing.

"Okay." Mori put his glass down. "There are two associations of Koreans in Japan, one for Northerners and the other for Southerners. How many members are in each?"

"I don't know."

"Of course you do. Each has approximately half a million. The North Korean association is controlled by Pyongyang and the South by Seoul. They hate each other." He waited, but she still did not speak.

"So don't help," he said. "Maybe the number of deaths reaches a hundred. Police don't care; fewer Koreans sells here."

He saw her eyes begin to tear.

"Okay, sorry. I went too far."

She sighed. "North Koreans and South Koreans in Japan don't get along, you're right, but the rest of your hypothesis is wrong. We are controlled by no one."

"Okay," Mori agreed. No Korean he'd ever met had admitted that truth. "Just tell me this—is the feeling very strong about liberalization and reunion?"

Tomi looked at her nails again. "Most Southerners want more democracy in the North before they discuss reunion. Our association is divided between those who want it and those who do not."

"Deeply divided?"

"There are some things it is better not to talk about."

She'd folded her arms. Her body language was saying: don't come near me.

"Let me guess, then. The North Korean military doesn't support liberalization, right?" The old-timers were the hard-liners, more interested in war than in peace.

"How should I know? I'm not a general."

"But you must hear things."

"Some things it's better not to hear."

"What are you afraid of?"

"They're violent people."

"Those who oppose liberalization?"

She nodded.

"Do pachinko owners support it?"

"They support democracy." She took his hand in hers.

Mori felt the warmth of her hand. Now they were getting somewhere. Pachinko money could figure in the North Korean political equation if it was backing or opposing the communist government. If it was opposing, then Pyongyang's supporters could be behind the murders. "So there's a group that opposes the government in Pyongyang?"

"Not exactly. There is a political split within the North Korean government itself. Between all our beautiful young technocrats who wish to open our markets, become like the West, eventually reunite—and those who do not."

"All right. Maybe you've given me something." Interesting, he thought. A deep-seated battle for North Korea's soul.

"That's all you think about, isn't it?"

"C'mon, Tomi, I just came from the murder scene. Okay?"

Tomi shifted in her seat. "I'm glad you came tonight, Inspector, but I've been thinking. Maybe it's time we said goodbye."

Mori examined his watch. "I have another five minutes."

"That's not what I meant. Our relationship. Maybe you should not come here again. Or call me."

Mori lifted his Suntory-water and wished he'd ordered something stronger. "I see. Please tell me what I've done wrong."

"Nothing." She twisted a ring on her finger, a ring Mori had given her two years ago.

He stared at the ring. She was scared, but he didn't know why. "It must be something I've said," Mori insisted.

"You still don't understand me. I'm surprised."

"Okay, I won't ask any more questions for a while. You're upset."

"You'll get me killed one day, Inspector. And for what, I ask myself. For an old lover who doesn't care for me anymore. Who maybe never loved me anyway. Who just uses me. I must be crazy."

"We pay you well, Tomi. Anyway, it wasn't like that at all. I cared about you very much."

"I am not interested in your money, and don't lie to me!"

"Why're you so upset? What's wrong?"

"I tell you the truth. 'Intelligence,' you call it, but pimps work the same way. Get a string of girls to fall in love so they can use them. Is this what you did with me, Inspector?"

"You were the only one, Tomi, while . . . I swear."

"Bullshit."

"We broke up three years ago, when you became Oto's mistress. He pays your rent. I can't afford it. What did you expect, Tomi?" Mori began to collect his things.

"An old man who is rich and likes toys. Who never makes love, just requires me to entertain his friends."

He ignored that. "You people don't want the police involved in anything Korean? Fine. You think you can take care of it yourselves? Okay. Go ahead, be my guest. Get your fucking head blown off."

"Do you love me?"

Mori's mouth gaped. "I have a wife, for God's sake. You have Oto."

"It didn't matter before. Anyway, wives are chattel in Japan. For appearance only. No one loves his wife."

"We've had some good times, Tomi. You know I've always cared about you."

"For me it was more than that."

"Where is this going?" Her occasional fling was business. He'd accepted that. She had to keep clients happy. Until three years ago, they'd both agreed they were in love. He welcomed a night with her and would lie about anything to make it happen. But he'd never been a big-time sharer. The sugar daddy—that made it different. At least for him.

"The way it used to be."

"Tomi, why are you bringing this up now? Why tonight? Did Oto cut you off?" He suddenly wondered if she was in some kind of trouble, or had been offered a better deal by another service. The PSB had never been that generous.

"You ask dangerous questions."

"I'm just trying to help find out who's murdering your countrymen."

"North Koreans don't need your help. Leave us alone. We'll find the killers and deal with them ourselves. I want to talk about us."

Mori had rules. One was that he had only one woman on the side at a time. Not like some of his married friends who slept around. And bar girl or not—sleeping with clients or not—he'd expected her to understand that. Was he stupid? Yes, he told himself. Must have been nuts. "Tomi, there's something I need to know. Do you still visit that North Korean boat each month when it comes in?"

"Yes, I do. But don't change the subject. What about you and me?"

"I came tonight to talk about a wire job. The boat arrived two days ago. Can we talk about that?"

"Is that your answer?"

"Look, I don't know what is going on here, but I am sure as hell going to find out. Whether you and your countrymen like it or not!"

"Then it will cost you much more this time if it is strictly business. Just money from now on." Her beeper chirped. Another table was calling. "I have to go now." She sounded out of breath. "In a little while, I come back . . . wait. We will talk money for the boat."

"It has to be done tomorrow or the day after. The boat leaves Wednesday. I need your yes or no. Now."

She thought a moment. "Call me at home then, later tonight. We'll arrange details. But I won't be cheap. This I can promise. Now I go."

Signaling the waiter, Mori pondered this latest change of her mood. Something had happened. He wondered what. Eventually, she'd tell him, he decided. Maybe Oto *had* left her. At least the night had not been a complete waste. She'd given him a rift between liberal technocrats and militant hard-liners who didn't mind knocking off a few Koreans in Tokyo if it kept the rest of the boys in line. So now he was hunting for North Korean government types. Great. Was it another dead end? He'd have to talk with his uncle tomorrow.

5: OVERSEAS CALLER Los Angeles: Monday, 10:15 A.M.

THE WELL-DRESSED KOREAN showed up in the morning of the second day of his Los Angeles visit, paid cash, and used one of the phones for over two hours.

The room had been rented a week earlier by a twenty-five-year-old computer hacker named Osborne who'd paid one month's rent using a credit card number sourced through underground software known as Card Magic and sold on the Internet. The card was not in his name. He'd then rented five desks and bought the push-tone phones.

Park Chung Il's last and longest call was to a secure number in Washington, D.C.—to the FBI.

"DeCovasi speaking," a voice said.

"I met the Pachinko Woman last night and am meeting her again after I hang up."

"Are we secure?"

"Yes."

"What're the details?"

Park went through Helim's operation, putting as favorable a spin on it as he could. "I hope you'll let her proceed," he concluded.

"A moment." The phone went on hold.

Park guessed that he'd been on speaker, and DeCovasi was conferring with other associates in the room. DeCovasi came back on. "Agreed that she proceed. The pachinko company listing will benefit everyone."

"Right," Park agreed too quickly, wondering who "everyone" included.

"We're hoping it'll force those who are behind the Japanese protection of this illegal money flow to reveal themselves so that we can prosecute and destroy them."

It sounded like a prepared statement, Park thought. Good. At least, they would back him. "I'm sure someone in the Japanese government is involved. And that they're working with Alpha, the head of North Korean intelligence. Like I've told you many times, he and General Myun Kuk are behind the killings in Tokyo and the flow of illegal money. I'm sure of that."

"One more time, my hands are tied on those two until you get me some hard data. But tell your Pachinko Woman to proceed, Park. I'm impressed." He paused. "When the hell do I get to know her real name?"

"Today. In exchange for two things."

"As long as money's not one of them."

"Not money."

"You've my undivided attention."

"The background on an American male who's close to the Pachinko Woman."

"I can handle that. But we're going to need her name. And his."

"I'll provide hers on condition no others are given it. Even within your esteemed organization if you don't mind."

"Agreed."

"So take your phone off speaker and get that team the hell out of your office."

"Don't trust anyone, do you North Koreans."

"Not in my position." Park heard a click. The phone went to hold.

"Okay, it's off speaker. Everyone's gone."

"Name is Helim Kim."

"Give me some background. She's Korean?"

"Naturalized American. Has her own translation company. Loves America. Worked at the United Nations. Supports women's causes. Still does the odd job translating for UN teams that visit Pyongyang. Has a high-priority clearance. Just got back ten days ago."

"Sounds classy. What about her psychological profile?"

"Born in Tokyo, parents of North Korean origin, moved here to attend college ten years ago. Mother disappeared when she was seven. Grandmother raised her."

"What's Granny like?"

"It's her diary."

"Jesus. Her grandmother was a comfort woman?"

"Yeah, but she's one helluva lady. Made a fortune in Japanese pachinko halls. Helim was raised in one."

"Sounds like your girl's a triangle: American, Korean, Japanese background."

"She's American as apple pie. Loves American pizza, boys, football. A charger all the way. In Korean we call her type 'chumoktajim.' 'Go-for-it' personality."

"I can live with that. Point her in the right direction, she'll score a touchdown."

"And willing to take risks. Her Korean side is fatalistic. She was raised with shamanist superstitions. Granny is a real shaman, but Helim's a modern woman. She's not afraid of anything."

"What about the Japanese background? That dent her any?"

"She's overcome everything, including the lack of self-esteem from being a Korean raised in Japan. Kept her expensive tastes."

"So she's a spender. What woman isn't? How steady is she?"

"Seen her in a couple of tight spots. Never blinked."

"She's not to be put at risk in future. She's an American citizen, right?"

"Understood." Park let out his breath. DeCovasi had bought her. It was vital they believe her totally. Helim was his queen. He was putting her into play. Let them discover the truth later when it didn't matter. She would be sacrificed, but that was what queens were for. To allow the kings to win.

"So what's her thumbscrew? Where's her soul?"

"Crusader," Park chuckled. "Equal rights for Asian women. Elimination of child labor. Antislavery. Find all the landmines. Waste of time."

"Maybe she'll get lucky. Sounds like an Asian Joan of Arc."

"In the seventies, Granny formed a comfort-woman association. Goal was compensation from the Japanese government. Helim got involved recently. Used the Internet. Membership soared. New members are every race, social level, creed, worldwide. Fancy name directors. A perfect fit for my pro-democracy movement. Most of her Korean members have joined the KDA. We work together."

"She sounds almost too perfect. There must be a hole in her armor somewhere. But back to this American male you don't like. What's his name and why information on him?"

"Steven Juric. Her lover."

"You got the hots for her? Need more than that, Park."

"I'd like to know how much he knows. He's an international lawyer. Suggested the use of Japanese TV media to her. Without knowing what was really involved, she's assured me."

"Shit, Park. You have to control your people. Or use a cutout. I can't do that for you."

"It was quite out of my control. She's headstrong, like her grandmother. And in her defense, the lawyer boyfriend came up with some excellent ideas. I can only hope she hasn't told him about me. You understand we can't allow a third party to find out about me. Too much is at stake and too much can go wrong."

"She doesn't know about your contact with us, I hope."

"No. I've been very careful."

"I certainly hope so. What's this Juric's address?"

Park read out an L.A. address, on Lincoln Avenue.

"Okay. Need a day or so. What's your other request?"

"Helim occasionally works as translator for the IAEA."

"International Atomic Energy Agency. Good group."

"She recently worked for them in Pyongyang. Told me they came out with a small sample of plutonium. Leader of the team was a fellow named Tomás Velaquez. Costa Rican."

"And?"

"That's it. Don't you think it strange? We never got a sniff before. Suddenly North Korea is generous. Why? They didn't think a small sample could be tested. Got careless. At least that's the story circulating."

"You don't buy it?"

"Let's just say I'm very curious. It's too pat. When they realized what happened, that enough was handed over for reprocessing dates, heads rolled at the facility. That's what I heard. So I make a check. Nobody's gone. Business as usual."

"All right, so where you going with this?"

"Velaquez stopped in Hong Kong on the way back. Took two or three days to get permission for entry of plutonium to the UK. London hadn't expected the sample for testing. Still hasn't been tested, matter of fact. All sorts of UN red tape."

"Right. So—?"

"Whisper is the sample was switched in Hong Kong. After Velaquez arrived."

"By whom?" DeCovasi's voice rose.

"Don't know that part."

"But you'd like to guess."

"Helim was there, translator, but she's the one who told me about it—about the plutonium sample being released. She also suggested this listing idea. Wouldn't make sense. I've ruled her out."

"Who's next?"

"I like Velaquez."

"Why him?"

"He's Costa Rican. Helped overthrow the generals. No money. Loner."

"Pretty thin."

"I'm not as smart as you people. Just providing a starting gate."

"Why should we even bother?"

"Because it could destroy the peace negotiations, the clean nuke reactor deal, the softening of lines between North and South, turn the Korean peninsula into a flashpoint. Last thing anyone sane wants."

"We'll see."

"And tell me what you find out. Okay?"

"Why'd you want to know?"

"Can't give you details, but I think it's connected to the pachinko killings." Park chuckled softly. "May God help you in the cause of freedom." He hung up the phone.

JOHN DECOVASI SLOWLY replaced his receiver. Cocky son of a bitch. The plutonium could be major points with State and the White House, however. Park knew it. Some serious homework first. Park could have screwed up his facts. He was getting to be pretty demanding on payments, too, perhaps because the bastard knew how important he was to De-Covasi's position.

DeCovasi stared at the power wall behind him. Pictures with key figures in his career. Of himself with the president. In front of the big Buddha at Kamakura with Japanese staff of the Tokyo office during his reign there. Others with members of the Senate Select Committee on Intelligence, with the chiefs of staff, and with several of his friends in the National Security Agency posing near a large satellite dish at the antenna farm in Virginia. But centered in place of honor was one of himself with the current director, Frank Murphy.

Some people liked their bosses. DeCovasi revered his. Murphy was a career FBI man. An agent's agent, and a man who was totally honest and dedicated to the United States of America. A family man, with two beautiful children. A man who would stand up to anyone. Including the president. He'd already proved himself on that one.

The director had personally selected DeCovasi four months ago for the most significant opportunity of his career. Assignment to the coveted number two slot at Special Investigations Group. With it came the broad hint that the top job was his if he didn't fuck up.

SIG dealt with special situations that weren't strictly traditional FBI business. Like Park Chung Il. And Park was DeCovasi's alone. No one else allowed near. Yes, Park, DeCovasi knew, had been his ticket to this promotion.

A phone call eight months ago in Tokyo. "Park Chung Il is my name." He was North Korean and wanted to defect.

A "walk-in" was immediately suspect to any intelligence service, particularly if it was a North Korean. North Korean intelligence had been cold-war-trained by the former KGB, masters at the art of "plants," defectors who in reality continued to be loyal to homeland governments.

Still, DeCovasi had met with Park. Danced him around Tokyo for eight hours using every trick he knew to determine if the man was under enemy control. And he'd listened to Park's story.

Park said he'd been born in a wealthy Pyongyang suburb, the child of a government official who was distantly related to North Korea's former leader Kim Il Sung.

He rose quickly through the ranks of North Korean intelligence. His main rival's name was Kim, but everyone called him Alpha after his heroics in the Burmese temple bombing that killed a number of South Korean officials.

Alpha recognized Park as his chief adversary for the top position in the intelligence service and plotted continually to embarrass Park and destroy his career. Alpha was Russian-trained and close to several KGB operatives who controlled North Korean intelligence in the eighties. One of these men was Aleksei Romanov, the current commercial counselor at the Russian embassy in Tokyo.

Unlike Alpha, Park chose to ally himself with the technocrats he believed were the future of North Korea. Park had secretly sought out liberals inside the Pyongyang cliques and found a number who were close friends of the current leader. The problem, Park knew, was the opposition of the generals of the old regime who ran the country after Kim Il Sung's death.

Park understood that the present leader was a figurehead, not trusted by many of the senior military men. This meant continued isolation from the West. However, gradually the older men were being replaced by younger officers, some with more liberal views. The leader's power base was growing.

When Park's liberal views eventually became known, Alpha challenged him openly. In a closed hearing after a narrow vote, Park was exiled for life to an impotent position with the North Korean consulate in Helsinki. However, he managed to keep his lines inside North Korea. That he had not been assassinated, he knew, was due only to his blood relationship to the present leader.

"Why do you want to defect?" DeCovasi asked.

"Because working alone, I can't influence events in North Korea."

"What if you had our backing and funding? This isn't an offer. Merely a concept."

"Then I would be very interested. I have already formed a pro-democracy group, the KDA, but it needs money to function. We are trying to disrupt a huge laundering operation being run out of Japan by North Korean intelligence."

DeCovasi understood that Park could be a major asset if his story was authenticated. He sent a message to Washington outlining Park's vitals and recommended that Park be persuaded to remain in place with U.S. funding.

The next morning, DeCovasi received authorizations to offer Park a financial package to remain in place. It was agreed he was worth much more to them in Helsinki than as a defector living under an assumed name in the United States. Skeptics doubted Park's potential, since he wasn't trusted by his own government and lived abroad. But DeCovasi had convinced the two men that counted—his immediate boss, Joe Pipe, and Frank Murphy. Privately to both men, DeCovasi guaranteed that Park's lines inside North Korea would pay off. They had already begun to.

Besides telling them about the pachinko laundering racket, Park had recently given them information about a widening rift in Pyongyang. This had attracted attention at the State Department. As Park's information hardened—that North Korean intelligence was behind the killings in Tokyo and the flow of illegal funds to North Korea—this had spurred the Intelligence Oversight Committee to order a list of options to stop both.

DeCovasi leaned back in his comfortable chair. He had no doubt that he had been anointed number two over hundreds of other candidates because of Park.

DeCovasi understood his position was not without risk. While Park had made DeCovasi a star, Park could also destroy him with one wrong move.

The FBI officer checked the names he'd underlined on the legal pad in front of him. Steven Juric. Helim Kim. Tomás Velaquez. Then he picked up his secure phone. "Get me our Vienna office. Then Los Angeles. I have some names I need to have checked out."

6 SNOW WHITE Tokyo: Monday, 12:30 P.M.

THE BAR WAS down the hill from Meiji Park in Shibuya. It was twelve-thirty as Steig neared the location he'd carefully memorized. He walked through the crowds and lingered by the Akita dog statue in front of Shibuya Station. He had heard the story. The dog used to come to the station every evening to greet his master, who suddenly died. The family then moved away and abandoned the dog. Until the dog died, he continued to wait for his master at the station each night. Loyalty exceeds holiness in Japan, the statue said. Even when it is fruitless.

He did not know if it would be his last meeting with these people today. But there would always be a market for his skills; if not here, somewhere else.

He pushed open the door of the bar and went inside. There was too much air-conditioning, and the cold air made the sweat on his back feel like ice. Like most Japanese bars, it was tiny. Six tables, all full with a lunch crowd; he could smell food cooking. But the bar itself was empty. The theme was clearly Korean, for the walls were full of posters of Cheju Island, Seoul's Gates, Sorak National Park. And hanging from pegs were Korean snowshoes, straw winter boots.

Behind the bar were bottles of soju, distilled from sweet potatoes, milky white makkoli and popchu wine. Steig crouched onto the stool. Carefully, he put a *Japan Times* on the smooth surface of the bar under his right hand.

"OB beer," he said.

He continued to study the interior. There were shelves on one wall stacked with boxes of ginseng, celadon teacups with cranes brush-painted on the sides. Symbol of longevity, he reminded himself. Perhaps he should order a dozen. Also there were statues of golden reindeer, shells of giant sea turtles. From a tiny kitchen in back of the bar came the odor of kimchi.

The barman returned with the opened bottle of beer, and the German lifted his glass, following the Korean custom. The barman filled it expertly, the foam just cresting the rim. He noticed Steig looking at the ornaments. "From Korean history," the barman said in Japanese. "You into Asian history?"

"No," the German responded. "I wish I had the time."

"You work hard, get rich, then study, right?" The barman looked at Steig's clothes. A short-sleeved shirt, slacks, a jacket he'd put on the shelf under the bar. Neither rich nor poor. Utilitarian. A man who thought about purpose rather than style.

A heavyset Asian male with punch-permed hair and violent eyes slid into the seat beside Steig and ordered an OB. Steig glanced at the left hand. It was holding a folder with airline tickets. The man had checked the *Japan Times* under Steig's right hand.

"Congratulations on your excellent work." The voice was low, and the face did not look at Steig, just stared straight ahead. "Your contract is completed."

"I will be heading back to Europe."

There was a pause. "You are formerly with the Stasi, I understand."

Surprised, Gunther Steig glanced at the man a moment to determine if there was anything more to the question than curiosity. To his pleasure, he detected a deference in the Asian man's eyes. "Yes," he said. "Before . . ."

"A shame the wall came down."

"An obscenity," Steig hissed. "You have my tickets?"

The man slid a folder across the bar.

Steig looked up. "This is not to Europe. And a five-o'clock flight today?"

"We thought you would be pleased."

"But it is to the United States."

"Yes. Your work here has been excellent. They want you to fly to Los Angeles immediately. A job there of some importance."

"How much?" Steig did not like abrupt change. Had an emergency arisen? Or did they wish to sever all connection to the killings—including him?

"Double what was paid for previous targets. Monies deposited as usual."

"The objective?"

"A woman. She has an unfortunate fervor for democracy and pa-chinko. Terminal, I suppose one could say. Rather attractive, I'm told. And quite an expert at the game."

"How will I recognize her?"

"I can show you her face. But only once. Please memorize it." The Asian removed a picture from an envelope and held it up.

Steig stared at the picture. Eurasian. A beauty mark below the corner of her mouth. He would have no trouble remembering her. What a waste, he thought.

"Her Los Angeles address and particulars are included with the ticket folder. Also your hotel reservation. Once you reach L.A., you are to go to this restaurant in Koreatown." The man handed Steig a slip of paper with an address in downtown Los Angeles. "You will be contacted there by an American who will give you the final briefing. I assume you can do the rest. The woman will be referred to in all future contacts as Snow White."

"Good. I am a Disney fan."

The man didn't smile. "Any questions?"

"None. Don't worry about a thing."

7: HELIM KIM Los Angeles: Monday, 2:30 P.M.

BRADLEY TERMINAL AT LAX was busy this afternoon. Helim waited at the self-serve restaurant near the departing passenger luggage check. Park was never punctual, and she'd opened a file to read.

When Park arrived he bought a coffee and a sweet roll, then strolled casually over to her table. He was wearing a white turtleneck and black slacks.

"An apple juice," he said. "So that's how you keep in such good shape, Helim."

"I also run."

"You run." He wrinkled his nose. "There are times when I feel I don't know you at all." He put several pages on the table. "For example, I've been thinking about the diary. Extraordinary that your grandmother was able to accomplish so much after such a start. She raised you, I understand. After your mother . . . disappeared."

"Yes. They told me my mother was dead. I can barely recall what happened. It was so long ago." Liar, she scolded herself. She remembered the day they told her as if it were yesterday.

HER FATHER HAD been moody since her mother had gone on the trip. Then one Sunday he'd packed a bag with Helim's clothes and taken her on a tram ride to a crowded section of Tokyo. They'd finally arrived at a place that had a wonderful sign with blinking lights and, over the glass doors, a marvelous green globe lit from the inside like a lantern. When her father opened the doors, a wave of noise washed over her, and for a moment she'd been frightened. But as she looked around, she saw beautiful flashing lights and hundreds of people sitting in front of colorful upright machines with glass windows. Inside, cascades of metal balls fell like silver snow.

A girl came over and greeted her father. "You must be Helim," she said.

"Say hello," her father prompted.

"Can I stay here for a while?" Helim asked her father. She wished she could be like this girl. Work in such a fascinating place.

"Maybe. Come on—we'll go see if grandmother agrees."

The girl led them up the wonderful aisles, and they entered a cluttered room. Her grandmother was sitting at a desk full of papers.

Her father nudged her, and Helim went over and bowed as she'd been taught to do each time her grandmother visited.

Her grandmother lifted her up and sat her on the crowded desk. "What a polite child you are. How good to see you."

"Can I stay here for a while?" Helim repeated.

Her grandmother sighed. "You didn't tell her, then?"

Her father shook his head.

"From now on how would you like to stay with me, Helim? My apartment is just across the street. You can play here every day after school too. Would you like that?"

"Yes."

"We have nothing to be ashamed of," her grandmother said to her father.

"When Mother comes back, will she stay here too?" Helim asked.

Tears welled in her grandmother's eyes, but she blinked them back. "Your mother isn't coming back. I'm sorry." She put a comforting hand on Helim's tiny shoulder. "She is with the sky-god who is a friend to all of us and lives in the clouds. She has decided to stay with him."

"That's all right," Helim said, not knowing what else to reply. She was too frightened and confused.

"There was an accident while she was on her trip," her father said. "There was nothing we could do. But you'll be all right, Helim. We love you, and we'll take care of you. We know she misses you very much, and she'll always be watching over you."

PARK FLATTENED THE pages of a schedule on the plastic tabletop. The Korean had added an extra dose of aftershave today. Christian Dior was his favorite, Helim recalled. Last Christmas she'd given him a bottle. She had wondered then if she was being too intimate, but Park was someone she needed on her side, and he was a man with expensive tastes.

"Well?" She waited.

"TV contact is approved. Hideo Katano's show, didn't you say?"

"Wonderful." Helim squinted at a clock. "I'll call him after his evening show . . . which would be about six o'clock tomorrow morning our time."

"The main thing is they must agree to interview time in exchange for the diary. No money."

"That was the idea. I give Katano the diary, he interviews me. Then I'll tell the Japanese public how money is being extorted from pachinko hall owners. And laundered to North Korea. How listing of our companies will stop it."

Park downed half his coffee. "This could help us find out who's killing our countrymen too."

"How?"

"My sources tell me the killer is one man working alone. Probably a professional. We'll never catch him. Behind him must be a Japanese politician, however. Working with the masterminds in Pyongyang."

"Perhaps," she said. "But isn't that a job for the police? How can we catch a corrupt politician?"

"Let Katano think you know more than you do. That you have something juicy. A Japanese pol involved in pachinko protection rackets. See what happens. The human mind is a wonderful instrument. Hit the right notes and the pol will come to us."

Yeah, right, Helim thought. With yakuza knives and guns. She'd call Katano. Go to Japan if necessary. But she wouldn't be the tethered goat for Park's Machiavellian mind games. "When shall we meet again?" she said, anxious to leave now. It wasn't pleasant to have doubts about people you wanted to trust, but if you were smart, it came with the territory.

"Thursday, in San Jose. You'll have phoned Hideo Katano by then. If it is go, I'll have cash for your trip."

"No one's said anything about a trip yet. Stanford Mall?"

"Yes. Usual place there. I hope you'll have good news for me."

"I will."

Park's cellular phone beeped. He let it ring. "One last thing. This boyfriend of yours, Steven. Not telling him too much, are we? Must keep our secrets safe from outsiders."

"Why is it that after all I have done, you don't trust me?" Helim held her temper.

"Trust isn't the issue." Park's cellular phone continued to beep urgently, and he pulled it from his briefcase. "Yes? . . . Just one moment." He motioned apologetically at Helim and walked outside to speak privately with one of his contacts.

Helim watched him go, knowing he would have forgotten her question when he returned. It mattered to her that Park didn't trust her. That was why she was losing trust in him, she decided. So different from Steven, she thought. Steven was the most straightforward person she'd ever known. Maybe that was why she loved him.

HELIM AND STEVE Juric had been formally introduced at the Korean Association offices in late March, just when the Santa Anas were beginning to blow from the desert, less than a week after Helim had decided that her two-year affair with Tomás Velaquez must end. Tomás lived in Vienna and had never hinted at her moving there. Now she'd decided she wasn't going to leave L.A. for any man.

Steven had shown up in a weathered sport jacket and jeans, loafers, no socks. She first saw him talking with one of the directors and noted his strong shoulders and strapping chest. Someone introduced them: "Helim, this is my lawyer, Steve Juric. He's volunteered his services. Isn't that great?"

She noticed how tall he was. Her eyes scoped his hands as they shook—no rings. When their eyes met, she liked their self-restraint. A modest lawyer, not a trumpeter. That was a relief.

They spoke briefly; later she couldn't recall what was said. But she did remember he had the habit of wrinkling his brow when he spoke, and that his voice was deep. He used words carefully—a sign of honesty, her grandmother had once told her. Part of her shaman teachings had been the mental states of the six kinds of animals and men—ruled by Greed, Faith, Hate, Intelligence, Delusion, or Discursiveness. Which was Steve? She wasn't sure yet.

She could see he had spent time in Asia, for he had the habit of exchanging meanings not only with words but also with what was not said. He had a simple lifestyle, according to the friend who had introduced them. Little money. Recently divorced. Worked for himself. Raised by his mother. Athletic and had played everything in high school and college.

Big on water sports. Sounded normal, she mused. But somehow he wasn't. That intrigued her.

They met again the next week by chance at the association's library. She had just stopped by to check a fact for a client and had on no makeup, tight washed jeans, a loose shirt. Her hair was a mess. To her bewilderment, he was suddenly standing not five feet away absorbed in Ishiguro's *A Pale View of the Hills.*

For a moment, she thought about slinking away. Then decided what the hell, go for it. "Good book," she said.

Juric looked up. "Helim, isn't it? Caught me goofing off." The calm eyes that studied her still belied ambition. No jacket today, she saw, and his muscular arms were tanned and powerful against a black polo shirt.

"You like the book?"

"Yeah. Wish I had his insight into the female character. Like Márquez."

"If you want to take it out, you can use my card."

"Sure it's no bother?"

"Come on. I'll show you to the checkout desk." It was desperate stuff really, and she felt slightly silly practically dragging him over. "You sound like you read a lot. I thought lawyers didn't have time for novels—too busy poring over contracts."

He shrugged.

Helim blushed. "Oh, I didn't mean . . ."

"That all lawyers are narrow-minded and greedy?" They paused at the checkout desk.

Helim was blushing furiously. All avenues of escape shut down.

Steven seemed not to notice. "Guess I'm atypical. My spare time is invested in trying to keep a whacked-out Dodge running. Used to write as a hobby, but not lately. Can't take the time."

Helim rode bravely forward. "Maybe you should write a book someday. Look at how well lawyers do as writers."

Steven's agreeable silence provoked her to another try.

"I mean, why do we have to do just one thing all our lives?"

"Right now, I'm just trying to keep my head above water. Anything will do."

She stared at him, trying to interpret his self-deprecating style. Her rich Asian friends would have said that as a matter of form. But not this tall brawny man, she decided. Was this his first admission of interest? She hoped so. "You're very candid for a lawyer."

"Candid?" he said. "All I did was admit that I'm a struggling lawyer."

"Lots of people here try to put on a bigger suit than they wear." He had this infuriating ability to make her feel defensive. "Particularly on the first try."

"Better to be honest. I learned that the hard way."

"So now you're old and wise."

"Yeah. Grew up way out in the Valley where you'd mow the grass and find a car. Before my mom and dad got divorced, we lived casually. Dad collected old cars and things. Strangers were always dropping in thinking we were holding a yard sale."

Helim laughed and felt it relieve her tension. "You don't expect me to believe that."

"In law school they teach you to exaggerate. Gets your point across better."

"Sorry. You're not my image of a lawyer."

"I was once. After I got a law degree, I got married, joined a firm, bought a house, fancy car, closetful of suits, worked twelve hours a day at a big international law firm and billed eighteen like everyone else. My wife's father was senior partner. Taught me how to cheat."

"So what happened?"

"Finally I divorced the lifestyle, the woman, the cheating, and the job. Threw away the suits. I'm playing catch-up now. Suits and ties make me uncomfortable."

"My! An acute case of integrity. Different."

"Oh, I have my problems too. I'm a health freak who loves ice cream and barbecued T-bone steak. So what do you do, Helim?"

"I have a translation and consulting company, work for the local Korean community, help out on fund drives and seminars here. Dad is a director of the association. How come you volunteered your services?"

"Because I needed work. I've just set up my own law practice—figured to do some stuff for free and let people be impressed. Hoped that would lead to real contracts."

"What kind of law?"

"International. Setting up joint ventures, mostly."

"You're several years late. There are three good Korean lawyers in the association. But business is contacts, of course. And if you make some good friends, who knows? Depends on how you treat them. Here, give me the book, if you still want to check it out." She held out her hand. It was clear to her now that she had gained the higher ground.

He looked down at her outstretched fingers as if considering more than her offer. "You have time for a cup of coffee?"

Helim hesitated. Mr. Juric was not quite so uninterested as she'd first assumed. Nor, to his credit, was he trying to impress. "Okay, I could use one."

Steve met Helim's father one night a week later at the association. As manager of the Korean Merchant Bank's L.A. branch and a senior director of the Korean Association, Chul Kim was always on the lookout for good legal advisers who wouldn't charge much.

"Steve's going to do very well," her father told Helim later that evening. "He's a thinker. He's hardworking. And unlike most American lawyers, he listens."

Before the end of the first month, she invited Steve to her father's home for a Saturday lunch. "Tell him to bring his swim suit," Chul Kim suggested. "I'll have to leave after lunch, but you kids can have the place to yourselves." Then he looked at her curiously. "Just how close are you two?"

"Dad!"

"Just want to be put in the picture."

"You should know I never sleep with anyone so soon! Surely you've figured that out about me."

"You never know, these days," he said. "But I must say that I'm very happy to hear this."

Helim rolled her eyes. "Besides, I'm still not sure about Steve. He's divorced."

"I knew that. Think I'm not interested in my daughter's foreign friends?"

"You're a terrible bigot."

"I know, I know," he chuckled. "I also checked his divorce case in Orange County Court."

"Why?" she asked, trying not to sound annoyed. But she already knew. Her father wanted her to marry a rich Korean businessman. There were a number in the local community. Preferably someone who could give his bank a large account. Whatever he'd found out about Steve would be used to argue her out of a serious affair.

"I'm thinking of offering Steve some legal work. Part of the background check. Apparently Steve's wife drank and played around. She was the one that sued for divorce. Claimed he traveled too much. Which he probably did."

"Well, he's an international lawyer. What did she expect?"

"She took him to the cleaners. Maybe it was his fault—who knows? He has debts and alimony. I wouldn't get too serious."

Helim blushed. "You're really too much."

SHE LAY BESIDE him, her body heavy and drowsy. The lunch had gone well. Her father had offered Steve a contract with the bank. Alone now, they'd come out by the pool. Suddenly she'd wanted to shout at him, felt like hurting him. Hurling things. Even though she knew this feeling was not his fault. It was frustration at knowing how good this was, how tender and passionate and caring he was, yet understanding it could never be. At least her father would be pleased.

"Damn," she said, getting up.

"What?" Steve looked up at her. "Forget something?"

"It's just that I don't want commitments. I . . ." She stood tensely braced over him. "My Korean blood, I guess—we get so . . . involved, emotionally. It's so strange, but I just felt something bad. An ill omen. After . . . after we made love. It scares me."

He stood and put his arms around her. "That's not allowed."

"It's my problem, not yours."

He kissed her forehead. "Want to tell me?"

She felt her frustration seeping away. "Maybe someday. It's no big deal. Something that time will solve." If only that were true, she thought, and turned, leaving him to dress and to restore herself.

Later, when she was alone, Helim accepted the feeling of mixed joy and sorrow that had entered her soul. It wasn't perfect, as she'd planned, she told herself. That was why. You find things out in the damnedest ways. There were too many pieces of her past that could never be shared with Steven.

She could not tell him about Park.

Nor her mother.

Nor why her grandmother never returned to her homeland.

Nor the truth about pachinko.

Nor the plutonium. Never.

There would have to be so many secrets. How could any relationship ever work like that?

"SORRY ABOUT THAT," Park said, bringing her abruptly back to the present. "Now, about Steven."

"What about him?" Her anger rose. "I would also like to make one thing clear. I never agreed that you could decide every detail of my life. Understand?"

"Perfectly. A little tense, aren't we?"

"Who are these friends of yours who are always calling? You never tell me anything about them. Do they have to approve everything?"

"Need to know, Helim. First rule in intelligence."

"Oh, for God's sake, Park, don't patronize me."

"It seems to me we had the same conversation over your last boyfriend, Tomás. My informants tell me you two stayed together in Pyongyang on your last trip. Have a nice time?"

"It was strictly business. A UN contract in which I was paid to translate. We're friends now. That's all. Period."

"To the disinterested observer, it did look as though you two had reunited."

"I'm not like that, Park, unlike some people I know."

"We're after the same thing, Helim. Don't ever lose sight of that. The diary, the TV interview, the Japan trip—all are steps along a path that will lead to overthrow of the military dictatorship in Pyongyang. Isn't that what this is all about?"

"Sure," she said, recalling a Korean proverb her grandmother liked to quote. It is better to lie a little than to be unhappy a lot.

"WILL THE SAMPLE be sufficient?" Tomás Velaquez asked.

Dr. Ralph Jordan thought for a moment, then peered through the window at the lead container inside. "Oh my, yes." Then he added, "The textbooks, bless them, insist you need a large quantity. However, this new equipment requires even less than when you did the Iraqis."

Velaquez sighed with relief. The International Atomic Energy Agency representative was dark and slim and rationed his words carefully, always preferring to listen rather than talk. He had been a diplomat for the government of Costa Rica in his earlier life. As a teenager, he had fought for the democratic movement. Long ago, it seemed now, although he was barely in his mid-thirties.

"You did well to get this much. We really didn't expect anything at all." Dr. Jordan grinned wolfishly at the IAEA man.

Velaquez shrugged at the compliment. It had been luck more than anything. There'd been no formal request, or clear orders from the top to obtain the plutonium. With progress being made in replacing North Korea's dirty nuclear reactors with South Korean clean types, no one wanted to risk upsetting the North. A team of UN experts was in North Korea on a permanent basis now. There had been good progress. His orders had been to see that the rods were being inspected properly by the UN team. To make sure they were intact and hadn't been moved. Smell around a bit, something he was very good at. Keep it informal, which was the way Velaquez preferred things.

He'd obtained the plutonium sample from the North Koreans almost as an afterthought and had shown no interest in it until he was leaving. Let beautiful Helim handle the politics. Meanwhile, he stayed with the

Koreans on the drinking, kimchi, goat's milk, and overspiced food. Told naughty political anecdotes about the UN secretary-general and the U.S. president's wife. Buttered up his guides with little presents of Wedgwood they'd treasure forever. He even passed the odd dollar or two in the right moments, never thinking of them as bribes.

In short, he pretended he loved every minute in North Korea. Then at the end, he casually asked for the order, as every good salesman will do. Some scrapings, a thimble or two, because his IAEA bosses would ban him for life if he didn't come back with a souvenir. A deprecating chuckle here.

"Useless," Helim had interrupted to complain in front of everyone, playing it flawlessly to argue him out of it. The perfect scam team, because both knew what the textbooks said—and what the North Koreans believed—that you needed a railroad car full of plutonium to run a decent test. A test that would tell them once and for all whether or not North Korea was still trying to produce atomic bombs.

Yes.

Helim Kim had been the key.

USING A ROBOTIC arm, Jordan positioned the lead-lined box carefully inside the machine. He manipulated a small robot arm that opened the box, removed a glass test tube with a thimbleful of black material, poured the contents into a small capsule, and shut the top. The capsule was attached to an umbilical cord filled with wires. Jordan pressed a red switch.

In a few moments Tomás would know the results of weeks of hard work. And longer than that waiting for this damn test to take place. It had been over a week ago that he'd handed the sample to the Brits. And since then, he'd been just hanging around hoping for the red tape to clear. It was almost as if the Brits hadn't really wanted it tested. Finally there had been a United Nations request. Do the test, dammit!

The computer monitor displayed a series of bar graphs in different colors.

"Each color is an element, right?" Tomás asked.

"Yes. We'll get a readout on the spectrograph in just a second." Dr. Jordan was a strong, gruff-looking man in his fifties with a wide athletic face, sky-blue eyes, and close-cut salt-and-pepper hair. His neck was leathery from weekends refereeing in a minor football league; other days he was a professor of nuclear physics at the University of London's Imperial College.

The colored bars began to change.

"Now, what we're really interested in"—Dr. Jordan leaned forward— "is the red."

"That's the americium 241, then?" Tomás took out a starched white handkerchief and gently wiped his forehead. He knew perfectly well that it was.

"Our friend americium," Dr. Jordan agreed.

The bars stopped changing size and a blinking light appeared on the screen. "Hah! Now we have a fixed number. You see the final amount there?"

The IAEA senior asserted that he did.

"Plutonium decays into americium 241 at a known rate. The amount tells us that this plutonium isotope was reprocessed twice." Jordan punched a key, and two series of numbers appeared. "In 1975 and 1993."

"Shit." Tomás blurted this out without thinking. As if the truth disappointed him. North Korea had had no nuclear processing facilities in 1975. Therefore this plutonium had been bought by Pyongyang after 1993. And for obvious reasons, would be the UN Security Council conclusion. The North Koreans were buying reprocessed smuggled plutonium on black markets in violation of the Geneva Convention. Most likely from Russian thieves. That proved they had a secret agenda. Which meant that even if they converted their dirty reactors to the water type that didn't throw off plutonium, they could still make their bombs. He could almost hear the distressed voice of the U.S. UN representative. The American public would be outraged. It would destroy the deal to replace the North Korean reactors.

"Liars." Dr. Jordan happily punched the key that started a printout. "This is our lie detector." He was a scientist. And like many scientists he was more interested in conducting lab tests than in dealing with the political implications.

"Yes." Tomás now faced an unpleasant task. Only three countries could have secretly supplied plutonium to North Korea in flagrant disregard of the future of the Korean peninsula. China, Russia, or Japan. And it had been recently reported that North Korea was improving its Nodong missile's capacity to carry nuclear payloads. Intelligence predicted that the missile would be able to reach the United States within the year. No, he told himself. This would not be welcome news in New York.

Jordan spoke in a voice unruffled by the implications. "The Iraqis were nailed the same way, weren't they?"

"I played a small part, yes."

"Good. Saves me a lot of explanation then. I'll get the printout for you and your friends in Vienna and New York. Then you can be on your way."

Dr. Jordan made three copies of the printout. "This equipment is classified, so nothing you've seen here can be discussed. Only the findings."

"Right," Tomás said politely. He put the copy in his briefcase next to the folder that contained his flight tickets to Vienna. He made a mental note to try to reach Helim from the airport. No doubt she would be pleased by his news. There was a good possibility that the UN Security Council would be meeting shortly in an unpublicized emergency session.

9: **THE OYABUN** Tokyo: Monday, 4:00 P.M.

"IRRASHAIMASU. WELCOME." Mori's uncle opened the door and squinted into the evening dusk like an awakened bat. He was dressed in black, a flowing man's kimono that scholars favored. His appearance was fragile yet earnest: large earlobes of a Buddha, pallor of an avid reader, and skeletal body of a chain-smoker. He had once been the deputy security minister, but that had been ages ago. However, he still had access to information that most Japanese did not. After Mori's father died, his uncle had taken on the role of mentor or Oyabun, which was one of sacred trust.

The Oyabun's wife had died some years ago, and he now lived alone in a small house in Shibuya with a cockatoo and a blind cat. Mori took off his shoes and entered the house, sliding open the door of a small shuttered room off the entrance, which smelled of incense. On a low lacquered table in the middle of the room was a glass case lit by three flickering candles. Inside the case was a single object—a rusted short sword. Beside the case was the black-bordered picture of a stern-faced Japanese in a general's uniform. Mori knelt and bowed three times.

As a child, Mori had lost the only thing a child really feared to lose in Japan—his father. Perhaps that was the reason he had taken a job with the National Police.

He could remember every detail clearly even now.

It was the last day of the war, after the emperor's broadcast of capitulation. The smell of cordite from American bombings, the fierce sun the color of blood, the tears streaming down his mother's face were memories that flooded back each time he entered this room. Since that day, the short sword that his father had used for seppuku—chosen death—had never been washed. It was still their most treasured family heirloom. Even though the blood had turned to rust.

Mori rose, bowed, and closed the door quietly behind him. His uncle, who was waiting silently in the hall, then led the way toward the back of the house.

"How is your wife, Mitsuko?" They never talked about Mori's father directly now.

Mori did not answer immediately. He followed his uncle across polished wood floors to an inner room where the noises of the street were muffled and far away.

"As always, she still works too hard," Mori said. He looked around the room, a modest refuge that counted for effect on shadow rather than light. The walls, which were of neutral color, clay textured with fine sand, were filled on one side with bookcases and on the other with pictures of the island where the Oyabun had served during the war.

The Oyabun gestured Mori to enter. "You can't blame her. You spend all your time with your work, as always. You show her little emotion."

"The job is time-consuming," Mori agreed, politely skirting the issue. "There is always some new and unique problem having to do with foreigners. That is why I have come today. I need some advice."

"I never advise. You know that."

"Then perhaps you can share some of your wisdom."

His Oyabun smiled. "Few people these days call it that. Sit over there."

Mori sat where his uncle pointed, cushions on the tatami floor facing the tokonoma alcove. To his right, sliding shoji opened to a tiny garden, in Karesansui rock form style, sand raked like waves. Afternoon sunlight whitewashed the sand. The faint scent of incense reached Mori's nostrils. The cat came into the room, found the Oyabun, and climbed onto his lap. "So. What is the problem?"

Mori paused to organize his thoughts. "Koreans. I am in the middle of a murder case involving Koreans and pachinko."

"Go on."

"In Shinjuku, a pachinko hall owner was stabbed yesterday. He died in hospital. There've been a half-dozen similar stabbings recently. In Tokyo and Osaka."

"And you think it is somehow connected to pachinko?"

"Yes. The deceased were all influential owners of pachinko halls. But

I can't figure out what's behind all this. I have heard that there is dis-
agreement within North Korea. Between the hard-liners and technocrats
who wish to open up their markets to the West."

"Pachinko halls are connected to all sorts of disease, Mori. Vice.
Gambling. Money laundering. I was told pachinko is a huge business.
Over sixty percent of all gambling in Japan, and we are the biggest gam-
blers in the world. This means pachinko is the largest casino in the
world."

"How big?"

The Oyabun selected a folder from a bookshelf, then read to himself
for a moment.

"Quite a business!" he remarked, like a man refreshing his memory.
"Gross of over twenty trillion yen annual income in '97. Nearly two
hundred billion dollars American."

Mori grunted. The number seemed too high. "Can't be. That would
make it larger than our auto industry, telecommunications, and steel.
Combined."

"It's conservative," the Oyabun said firmly and turned a page. "There
are over eighteen thousand pachinko halls registered, all with hundreds
of machines, some with thousands. Plus a number that aren't licensed. If
each averages slightly over one hundred million yen a month . . ."

"Okay, okay." He paused to think. "I heard that North Koreans are
heavily involved in pachinko."

"They own eighty percent of the halls, according to this report."

"Where did the data come from?"

"A military intelligence group I happen to know the head of. They've
investigated the Pachinko Association, the National Police division that
handles gambling, and the Tax Office, which has the best records of
pachinko ownership. Highly confidential. The fact that North Koreans
control pachinko is a well-kept secret. It seems we're embarrassed by it."

"Should think so. How did Koreans take over the industry?"

"After the Great War, local Koreans got into it. Some Japanese tried
to open pachinko parlors in the sixties, but the yakuza prevented them."

"Japanese gangsters helped North Koreans?"

"Money and power," the Oyabun said. "After World War II, the
Japanese government allowed reopening of pachinko halls, on one condition: no cash prizes for winners, only merchandise. During Occupation
this was fine, since parlors offered black-market goods like stockings and
cigarettes. But when Japanese owners began to set up pachinko parlors

and compete in the sixties, they were allowed to give cash prizes. So the yakuza went to the Korean pachinko parlor owners and offered to set up exchanges near the pachinko halls—separately owned locations that would exchange any merchandise won in the halls for hard cash. The yakuza then sold the goods back to the pachinko halls for original cost plus a fee."

"A protection racket."

"That's how it started. In addition to the buy-back system, the yakuza guaranteed the halls against encroachment by Japanese or others. The system diversified. Politics got involved. A means to send money to North Korea developed. But that's where it gets murky."

"So money is skimmed by yakuza from Korean-owned pachinko halls for their own pocket and to send to North Korea? How much is involved, do you think?"

"Two or three percent."

"How much is sent to North Korea?"

"Maybe half."

"What's that in foreign exchange, say U.S. dollars a year?"

The Oyabun pulled out a calculator and did the mathematics. "Two billion dollars."

Mori whistled. "And what percent is that of the North Korean GNP? Do we know?"

"About ten percent of the North Korean gross national product last year."

Mori considered this data. "Enough to kill for, I should think."

"Yes."

"I'm not getting much support in my investigation. Aoyama, my boss, thinks we shouldn't waste time on Koreans. Thought you might know why."

"Certainly. You can see the complexity this presents us. No one in the government wants to confront this issue. No one likes to admit it exists. You see, Pyongyang counts on the pachinko industry. Furthermore, the involvement of a high-ranking Japanese official is likely. Nothing has ever been proved. All investigations have been dead ends."

"The government was uninterested?"

"Yes. There was a Justice Department inquiry into the pachinko money-laundering problem several years ago."

"I heard about it," Mori said.

"The conclusion was," the Oyabun continued, "that money leaked to

North Korea had declined to under one hundred million dollars from a previous high of six hundred million annually."

"Really!" Mori scoffed.

"They're afraid of North Korea," the Oyabun added genially. "They've stuck their heads in the sand."

"Yes sir."

His uncle sucked air softly between his teeth and squinted at the raked sand. "There is a fight for power over the Korean peninsula going on now. More vicious since the financial turmoil there." He smiled, showing teeth yellowed by tobacco. "The road to power is an unclean one."

Mori nodded and considered the implications. Pachinko made huge amounts of money and was very likely connected to politics, here and on the Korean peninsula. His uncle had provided a valuable link. If large amounts of pachinko money were passing legally and illegally to North Korea, it could be connected to the split inside North Korea that Tomi had hinted at. Between those favoring an opening to the West and those opposed. Between those favoring reunion with the South and those opposed. But where did he go from here?

The Oyabun crushed out his cigarette. "Remember what the Americans never learned. That there is no such thing as a final victory."

"Could the Americans be involved?" His uncle had implied that pachinko was part of a fight for power over the two Koreas. A lever to control North Korea, perhaps.

"They are always involved."

"How?" A coil of smoke spiraled up from the ashtray.

"On one side or the other. I do not underestimate the North Americans as some of our leaders do, particularly if they get angry. The North Americans perform best when they are angry. I believe we learned that lesson once."

"I'll keep an eye on them."

"Do that. There is a deadly game for regional and world power still going on. Many have been lulled to sleep by talk of peace, of one world. But hegemony over the Korean peninsula is a prize all the big powers covet. They call meetings and discuss it among each other, but all that is superficial. The U.S., China, ourselves, the Russians—all want control. Remember, it is the silent wars that are the most dangerous. Whatever you do, show no one your mind."

Mori rose to leave. He did not want to tire his uncle, and they had talked enough. His Oyabun's strength lay in his formality, Mori decided.

His distance. He had been verbose today by past standards. No doubt because he felt strongly on the issues involved.

Mori slipped into his shoes. "I will think about what you have said. In particular, about the Americans. Something is going on that is not good. I will try to find out what it is."

"Watch yourself, my son. Do nothing rash."

"I will be careful, uncle."

His uncle turned. "By the way, do you happen to have any good yakuza contacts? The Ichiwa-kai in particular." This was the fastest-growing yakuza association in Japan.

"One top-level. In Kobe. Why?"

"It might be useful to have a little chat with him. Soon. I have heard what might be only a rumor, but one can never tell."

THE HOUSE WAS in the Kitano-cho section of Kobe, an area of low hills and expensive dwellings. Foreign traders of the Meiji and Taisho eras had built European-style houses there, and a number had stood through the earthquake, saved by the solid rock. In fact, Mori noted, the hill area had been left surprisingly untouched.

A police captain escorted Mori to a street where blue police armored vans were parked over curbs like beached whales. Only one lane of traffic could get through. Beyond the street, Mori could see the lush green forests of the Rokko mountains outlined by a bright moon.

"Some local business," the captain said, gesturing at the vans. Mori walked the rest of the way alone.

A fragmentation net made it easy to recognize the address. A man answered the door, took Mori's card, and showed him inside. Everyone protects everyone, Mori thought. This is the Japanese system, and it is foolproof.

The head of the Ichiwa-kai was named Kumamoto. He came into the room after Mori had waited only three minutes, a sign of respect. Kumamoto was resplendent in a silver men's hakama with black underrobe, and his silver hair gleamed with recent brilliantine. He looked like a company president.

"We apologize for the inconvenience outside." Kumamoto seated himself opposite Mori, who had been given the place of honor. There was a decent bonsai in the tokunoma and a flower arrangement in a converted hibachi, the way the foreigners ordered them these days. Kobe still considered itself the most European of Japan's cities.

"Grenades?" Mori asked as a girl served tea. He noticed that she was much too pretty to be a servant.

"A rocket launcher fired with great inaccuracy from a passing Nissan," Kumamoto sighed. "A home run was scored on the house next door. Fortunately no one was in it." Kumamoto smiled as if he'd already exceeded his quota for the day. He had the yakuza predilection for blunt grammar, the oversolicitous manner of the dispassionate, and the quick temper of those who can back up their words with more than money. The press had taken quite a liking to him.

"In the old days," he said, "differences were settled with greater skill." The girl returned with sembei crackers in shiny cellophane wrapping. Mori remembered that this address was home of the Ichi-go-san. Number One Mistress. Kumamoto continued, "They've shot at this house at least forty times without hitting it. There is no real commitment anymore. I have set a new group to recapture the old way."

"Commendable," Mori agreed. "Although I imagine it has disrupted real estate values in the area."

Kumamoto grunted. "The earthquake took care of that, I am afraid."

"Yes, of course. My apologies. I was rude."

Kumamoto waved his hand. "You are here on business, not to discuss property prices."

"True."

"And you flew down here giving us only several hours' notice. We agreed to meet, since I consider your father one of the true heroes of the Great War. A pity that we lost him."

"Thank you for your respectful thoughts."

"So I am willing to help you in any way, despite a tight schedule."

"Understood and appreciated. For my part, let me tell you that I sympathize with our North Korean friends who are currently being criticized by the West for not living by Western standards—Rule of Law being only one of them."

"The West is led by a declining power," Kumamoto said. "A shame so much time has been lost trying to educate the United States to our ways."

Mori's voice was soft. "I want to assure you that I personally am not an adherent of Rule of Law."

"Inspector, your reputation, may I say, is well known and admired here."

"Thank you. So I want you to know that I have not flown down to Kobe to attach blame to any events that might have occurred in Tokyo or Kansai. For example, the unfortunate North Korean deaths."

Kumamoto was impassive. "Not that it matters," he declared, "but I think you should know it was not our hand that did the Koreans in, Inspector. Of that I can assure you."

"Nor am I here to make that inference, Kumamoto-san. I am here instead to ask your help in righting whatever wrongs these deaths were meant to solve."

Kumamoto chuckled. It was then Mori knew he had been right in coming. That his uncle knew more than he was saying. Mori held out his hands as the emperor did in blessing the masses on his birthday. "I am here to learn from you anything I can about the repugnant people who are trying to move North Korea together with the South. To Westernize."

An expectant fire ignited in the yakuza's eyes. "It is what I have been telling anyone who will listen," Kumamoto began. "There are two groups who are split on a change of government in North Korea. Also they are divided on reunion of the two Koreas, which is a dangerous idea. Same as opening markets. It has pitted brother against brother."

"I am sorry to hear this." Mori adopted the tone of the professional mourner, conveying regret and sympathy simultaneously. The attacks on this house were symbols of the disagreements, no doubt, Mori decided.

"There is great irony if one can appreciate such things." Kumamoto lifted his tea and sucked noisily to relieve the heat. "The deaths are being blamed on my group. Hence the iron net outside. We have investigated ourselves, and it appears an outsider has been brought in. To avoid just such problems."

"Yes, I agree that is a nice irony."

"Japanese are not involved."

"It relieves my soul," Mori admitted. "A foreigner then?"

Kumamoto walked across to a bookcase lined with texts on Bushido and Buddhism and other Asian religions. He pressed a button and the front of the bookcase swung open, revealing shelves stocked with liquor.

"You like brandy?" Kumamoto held up a one-hundred-year-old bottle of Rémy Martin.

Mori was not used to such luxury. "Thank you. Then I must be leaving."

Kumamoto poured two ponies and handed one to Mori. "What is your hurry? You have only just arrived. I can arrange hotel and a woman."

"Most kind of you, but I must return to Tokyo tonight. Tomorrow I visit a Korean ship. But I thank you for your time. You have provided valuable insight." Mori lifted his glass. "Kampai."

"Thank you. We understand the foreigner is European and very . . . qualified."

"Assuredly so. He has left no clues. Is there anything else you can tell me?"

"I know of several generals in Pyongyang who are angry at certain people in our government. For example, the current prime minister. They would think nothing of shooting one of their Nodong rockets at the Diet Building." Seeing the look of disbelief on Mori's features, he added, "The threat is not idle."

ON THE FLIGHT back to Tokyo, Mori considered his new information. A witness at the last murder scene had claimed he saw a foreigner. Kumamoto had been more specific. What nationality was this foreigner? Mori wondered. He pulled out his appointment book and checked tomorrow's schedule. A morning meeting with an old friend from the FBI. No objective stated. Mori had assumed it was a social call. Now he wasn't so sure.

10: THE PHONE CALL Los Angeles: Tuesday, 5:45 A.M.

STILL IN HER nightgown, Helim sat in the kitchen of her Westwood apartment. She'd eaten no breakfast. She wasn't hungry. She was staring at the clock.

Fifteen minutes more and it would be 10:00 P.M. Tokyo time. The telephone was on the kitchen table in front of her, along with a legal pad on which the TV station's number was written and a ballpoint pen. She did not want to consider the risks. Or the possible rewards. She was nervous, so she thought about Steve. That helped. If not for Steve, she told herself, she would not be making this call.

SHE HADN'T PLANNED to tell Steve about pachinko. But the problem had been on her mind since the Japanese stock exchange commission had turned everyone down. Helim knew why. No company owned by North Koreans had ever been accepted for listing by a Japanese stock exchange. Nothing to do with their financial statements, which were blue-chip. It was a rights problem. That was why she had decided to ask Steve's advice. He was a lawyer, after all. Had worked in Japan.

She'd started by telling him about her life in Tokyo before she came to Los Angeles. Both her parents had been born there, children of Koreans who had found themselves in Japan at the end of World War II.

Since she'd never talked about her past before, he realized some kind of breakthrough was taking place. "So how come they were in Japan?"

"Complicated question, but one I'd expect from a legal mind."

"You don't have to answer. You can take the Fifth Amendment."

"The short version is that the Japanese occupied Korea in 1905 and we were their slaves until the Allies defeated Japan in 1945. The Japanese ordered my father's parents to Japan to work in a munitions plant there. It wasn't something you argued about in 1936. Those were the days when Japanese soldiers still liked to lop off heads."

"Uh-huh. What part of Korea are they from, your father's parents?"

"The North, a suburb of Pyongyang."

"How about your mother?"

"Also Northerners. Of course, no one made much of that until the fifties, when the Korean War divided the country. My mother was born in Japan because her mother, my grandmother, was . . . forced by the Japanese military to work for them in China during World War II."

"Wow. She must have a story to tell."

"She was captured by the Russian Red Army in Harbin. She escaped to Shanghai and decided not to return to Korea, for various reasons. But Shanghai in those days was unstable and dangerous. Nationalist Chinese forces and communists were at war. She bribed Nationalist Chinese soldiers to put her on a military hospital ship headed for Japan. She figured she could get to the United States from there. But she got sick on the way. Malaria."

"She had it rough, then."

"She nearly died. In Tokyo, Koreans took her in, thinking she was going to die. Many people did in those days from lack of food. She had high fever and delirium, during which she said many things she could not have known. Korean elders came to listen and decide what should be done. The wisest of the elders realized she was going through the Transition. She was being reborn."

"What does that mean?"

"North Koreans believe that shamans are selected by divine calling. It's a chaotic process involving hallucinations, clairvoyance, often high fever, and eccentric behavior until the divine powers are recognized. In South Korea, shamans inherit their roles through family lineage. Fortunately, these were North Koreans she was staying with."

"So they believed she was becoming a shaman?"

"Yes. The elders told the others that the gods were doing this to manifest their sorrow for her suffering during the war. For she spoke of horrible tortures of the body and soul."

"What kind of tortures?" Steve asked quickly.

"It was war," Helim said evasively. "Things happened."

"Sure."

"So it was agreed," Helim continued, "that if she recovered, she should be sent to live with the highest shaman priestess in Japan. She would teach my grandmother the ways of shamanism, an inheritance decided by the gods."

"When she got better she adopted this . . . religion?"

"Not so much a religion as a belief. She was a devout Christian. And when she heard they had decided she must become a shaman, she was upset. She didn't tell anyone, because she was afraid of being turned out. When she was sent to the old woman and learned about shamanism, she realized it could be used for healing. She became a believer and a practitioner. A very good healer, in fact."

"So shamanism is a belief. You don't have to give up your religion to practice it?"

"To some it's a religion. To me, shamanism is a belief."

"Okay, what happened to your grandmother?"

"In order to support herself after she recovered, she worked in a textile plant. There she met a Korean man who was setting up a factory to make pachinko machines. You know what pachinko is?"

"Yeah. Great game. I played it a couple of times on my trips to Tokyo."

"Okay. Well, in those days pachinko halls were starting up again. The Japanese military had banned pachinko during the war, of course. An American officer my grandmother later married lent her money. She bought one machine and persuaded the plant manager to let her install it in the recreation room. By this time, she had become a shaman healer and was called on to travel to Korean communities near Tokyo on weekends and holidays. Soon she was using these trips to sell pachinko machines to other Koreans. And after several years she had enough money for a parlor."

"So she became a shaman and got involved in the pachinko business too," Steve said, intrigued by the curious mixture. Psychic power and a pinball game. "What happened to the American she married?"

"They had a child, my mother. When the Korean War started in 1951, his reserve unit was called up. He was killed near Seoul by a grenade a year later. My mother was three years old when it happened. So I never saw him."

Steve took her hand. "Ironic that he was killed in the Korean War."

"If you mean fighting the North, where his wife's parents were from, yes. But my life is full of ironies. I lost my own mother when I was seven years old." She stopped, because she could suddenly remember her mother's smell, her soft caressing voice, and the white dress she'd worn the last day Helim had seen her. Recently, she'd dreamed she was holding on to her mother's dress walking through a crowded street in Tokyo. When she awoke her hand was clutching her bedsheets. For some reason she could feel tears on her cheeks.

Steve looked across at her. "You okay?"

"Sure." Helim folded her hand as if crushing the thought. Destroying it. "I keep a picture of her in here," she said, and clasped the gold locket on a chain around her neck. "Her spirit is inside, my grandmother told me. It keeps me from harm. This is what shamans believe."

"And do you?"

"Yes. But don't worry. We don't try to convert others. Shamans are mainly women in Korea. They perform healing mainly for other women. Females are the ones who call on them to perform a 'kut' in their homes. A kut is like an exorcism. The reasons you can guess: illness, husbands who squander their earnings on mistresses, marital disagreements, a husband's drinking problem, and so on. In Korea, it's a way to counter the chauvinistic society Korean women are forced to live in. A safety valve."

"And what do you believe?"

"It's quite simple—that all humans possess powerful spirit energy, but only a few are able to recognize and utilize this energy. My grandmother is one. When our bodies die, a part of our spirit energy enters someone whom we love. It intertwines with the loved one's energy and helps them to a happier life."

"That's a nice idea."

"You can find it in the Bible as well. In shamanism, the maintenance of one's personal energy is the essence of well-being and health. The shaman shares her special powers, sacrifices her energy to heal others. She calls up a matching commitment from the patient's deepest subconscious, an obligation, to work with the shaman to save oneself."

"Then it's less a religion and more a kind of alternative medicine."

"Call it what you like. It works. But you don't just become a shaman. You have to prove worthy. The status can be conferred only by those you help with your healing power."

"And your grandmother?"

"After her husband died, she never loved another man. She loves the sky. Trees. Rocks of certain shapes and colors. Animals."

"What did you do after your mother died?"

"I went to live with Grandmother. As a child I used to play among the machines. On holidays, she would sometimes take me into the mountains away from the pachinko halls. To think. To seek answers. To watch the way the wind shaped the trees and to enjoy talking with the spirits of the animals and the birds. She lives with the objectivity one can enjoy in life when one does not participate emotionally. I once put it down to some defect of her character. Actually there were other reasons."

"Like what?"

"Things that happened during the war. What I'm leading up to— why I've given you this long background—there is something you might be able to help me with. It has to do with my grandmother. She wants to get her pachinko company listed, but the Japanese stock exchange turned her down. Others that applied were also refused. We need a way to get around the damn Japanese system so we can get our companies listed. Think about it, will you, Steve?"

"Sure. But I'm curious about one thing. Why does she want to list? I mean, your grandmother sounds very successful. Why go public now?"

Helim's eyes went blank as if she was searching deep inside herself for the answer. "Very simple, really. She set up an association years ago. I help her with it now. An association to support various causes: to eliminate abuse of Asian women's rights, eliminate child labor, child prostitution, things like that. The money she gets will help finance our activities."

A week later, they'd met for dinner. Steve had several very practical suggestions.

HELIM'S EYES WENT to the clock on the kitchen wall. Ten o'clock in the evening Tokyo time. Katano's news show would be ending. She should call now.

She took a deep breath. This would be irrevocable, she told herself. Terrible things could happen if it went wrong. Do it, she commanded herself. Do it! She began to dial.

HIDEO KATANO, JAPAN'S most popular TV news anchor, leaned into the camera and asked his nightly closing question: "What on earth is happening to Japan?"

With that, the "On" sign went to "Off," the red camera light disappeared and the screen was filled by a montage of a whale and other objects floating through Tokyo's skyscrapers. The network went to its eight-minute half-hourly commercial break and the sound of scattered applause issued from the staff and onlookers around the studio. Katano turned off his microphone and bowed to his attractive female assistant and the Tokyo University professor who had been his analyst tonight.

Tanaka, his producer, called over the studio speaker, "Nice job, everyone. Katano-san, you have a long-distance call. Urgent and female, of course."

There were chuckles from the crew and cameramen as he headed for his dressing room. Katano was known as something of a roué. But Katano was sure the call wasn't personal—all his friends had strict instructions not to call him at the studio. It must be business, then. Before picking up the phone, he attached a line from his recording machine, then flicked the recorder on. He could use a good piece of material.

Calmly, he lifted the instrument. "Katano speaking. What can I do for you?" He had people calling him with tips, threats, proposals every day. For the most part they were cranks and opportunists. But one such call had provided information critical to the downfall of a prime minister. So he tried to take every call personally.

"My name isn't important." The speaker was a woman, her Japanese fluent, with just the slightest accent.

"Fine, no names," Katano replied. "How can I help you?"

"I have a diary."

"Content?"

"A diary that describes shocking actions of the Japanese Imperial Army during the war."

Katano inwardly groaned. "Not comfort women, darling. Or the Nanking atrocities." He said this as kindly as possible. "We've already done that."

There were three beeps on the line, indicating this was an international call. Quickly, Katano flicked a console button that traced numbers.

The female voice said, "I will send you one page, and you can judge." The voice was tightly controlled, which intrigued Katano more than the words the woman had spoken. Perhaps he had better make sure.

"How much you asking?"

"Nothing. No money."

"That is very generous, isn't it? Something else then?"

"If you use the diary, you must guarantee you will air information about the Japanese pachinko industry I will give you. One half hour on the pachinko industry for the diary. If it generates audience interest, over a ten share, I want a series done. That is my price, and it is not negotiable. You are the first network I have contacted, and I will not contact any others until you answer. Within one week, let us say. All I wish is for Japanese people to know the truth."

Katano paused a moment. "Okay, send the fax, but I can't guarantee you anything."

"One half hour airtime on pachinko for the diary. A ten rating and we do a series on the Korean pachinko issue. No money." The voice was silvery, intriguing. A good TV voice. Katano wondered if the face was as enticing. "What is your fax number?" the woman's voice continued. "I will send the pages now. You decide."

He gave her the fax number and disconnected. A strange call, he thought, but not one that would amount to anything.

THE PROFESSOR WAS talking with Tanaka when Katano emerged from his dressing room, freshly showered and changed. Tanaka held a fax tightly in his hand. Tanaka led Katano to an empty office, and they both sat down.

"I think we have something here," Tanaka said.

Katano studied his producer for a moment. Tanaka was bespectacled, pudgy, intense, and, at the moment, beaming with excitement. "What is it?"

"You got a call, right?"

Katano scowled. "Just another comfort woman. Japanese don't want to hear about that anymore."

Tanaka handed the fax to Katano. "Read this. Not just another comfort woman. This is news!"

Katano took the fax. After a minute he put it down. "I don't believe it! Buddha loves us again."

"Thought you'd like it."

He stared at his producer. "The PM's going to shit. An American comfort woman!"

"The show could use a lift. Don't you think?"

"This is great. An American comfort woman!" Katano repeated, thrilled at his good fortune.

"It gets better. We'll ask for a meeting with the American embassy.

Insist on a spokeswoman. Not tell her exactly what we have. Just the comfort woman issue. USA viewpoint. What their thoughts are, see. Then in the live interview, lower the boom. Americans don't give a damn if it's just another Asian, right? But if an American girl was being forced to have sex in a Japanese military brothel while we were bombing Pearl Harbor!" He paused. "How much are they asking, by the way?"

"It doesn't figure." Katano shrugged. "Just publicity on the pachinko industry. A half hour airtime. Maybe a series if it generates interest. Can you handle that?"

Tanaka squinted behind his glasses. "You didn't promise prime time?"

"Of course not. God knows why she wants publicity for the pachinko industry."

"She must have an ax to grind, but who cares? It's your call on the American comfort woman."

Katano considered his decision. He would be responsible ultimately if they ran the story and something went wrong. "My only concern is if it's a hoax." A competitor trying to hit us in the ratings by making us look silly, he thought. "I used my phone tracer, and this call was from a Southern California number. Speaks Japanese almost perfectly. I'm getting the person's name and address checked."

"They're Koreans, I'll bet. Ex-pats." Tanaka was grinning. "A zillion live in L.A. So what should we do?"

Katano thought a moment. "Let's go for it! Invite her here soon as possible. Before she changes her mind. This next weekend is open. Try for that. Have her bring a page of the original for aging authentication. Maybe we can get more than the diary. We'll give her airtime for her pachinko story and I'll tape the interview in Atami Sunday and Monday. Quiet hotel there I know called the Shimizu Inn. Pick her brains clean on the American comfort woman. And who knows, her pachinko interview might be interesting too. I've heard some rumors lately, and she may be able to confirm them."

11: THE CASH CARD Tokyo: Tuesday, 10:15 A.M.

THEY HADN'T MET for over ten months.

The last time had been when John DeCovasi was assigned to the Tokyo office as station chief. His name then had been Alex Rayburn.

Mori stared at his card: Deputy Director SIG: Federal Bureau of Investigation. A Washington, D.C., address. He'd been promoted.

"Most people just call me John these days," DeCovasi chuckled as Mori stumbled over his last name.

"What does SIG stand for?"

"Special Investigations Group. We do special assignments. Go anywhere. Actually, I'm on my way to Vienna. Got an evening flight."

"Vienna?"

"Yeah. We've been growing our overseas network. Be in seventy countries soon. Two years ago we were in half that number."

"So," Mori muttered. "The FBI is expanding its overseas operations."

"I won't say we've enjoyed the CIA's recent problems," DeCovasi added. "In fact, we've shared them, but it certainly hasn't hurt our overseas growth. Of course, we're careful not to step on anyone's toes. Our focus is on terrorists, criminal organizations, laundering, and drugs."

"So what can I do for you, John?"

DeCovasi grew serious. "We've got a little operation coming up in your Niigata Prefecture. I'll need some assistance from the local police."

"The chief's an old friend," Mori said, pleased the favor was so easy to perform. "Captain Homma. Use my name. I'll let him know you'll be in touch. Your people still have that compound on the outskirts of Niigata City?"

"Sure do. You're welcome to use it anytime."

The compound had tennis courts, a swimming pool, and one of the most unusual shooting ranges in Asia. "Anything else?"

"Matter of fact there is." DeCovasi leaned forward. "My friends on our Asia desk have been analyzing the North Korean problem for some time. Basic things, you know, like the North Korean economy. Funds inflow and outflow. Official data. They discovered nothing adds. The North Koreans, according to what they sell and make and buy and spend, should have been bankrupt even before the floods hit them in '96. And those floods were followed by a drought and typhoon that totally disrupted their economy. Doesn't figure. Their T accounts just don't balance." He paused as if a sudden idea had occurred to him. "Unless, of course, someone's keeping them alive. And it isn't the Russians or Chinese, according to our contacts."

Mori felt a tingle at the base of his spine. "There are a number of joint ventures supported by . . . Japan's Korean residents," he suggested. "You know, a company name in Pyongyang with only a mailing address. An excuse for the Chosen Soren, the local North Korean Association, to send more money. A number of different gimmicks like this are used to maximize the funds legally sent there from Japan."

DeCovasi snorted. "That's pissant stuff, Mori, we both know it. How about some major money-laundering? Any ideas?"

Mori hesitated. "Not really. Although I've thought about that recently."

"Bet you have. Like the cash card program your National Police supported for all pachinko parlors in '93. You guys tried to use the plastic to monitor income, stop the unaudited cash flow to Pyongyang, but it didn't work. Yakuza counterfeited the cards and Sumitomo and Mitsubishi lost a half billion dollars." DeCovasi's tone grew harsh. "Some of us think it was a halfhearted punt, Inspector."

Mori cleared his throat. "What's this leading to?"

"The amount of money going into North Korea from Japan is several billion dollars a year. That is about ten percent of their GNP—enough to finance their military and armaments industry. Now I know that your government will insist that only a piddling fifty to a hundred million dollars annually is getting through—mainly in bogus companies like you just described. We say bullshit." DeCovasi glared at his friend. "For example. There's a North Korean boat that docks every month in Niigata City. Visitors are allowed on board. They bring boxes of food for their relatives in North Korea. Some of the boxes are filled with checks and money orders."

Mori recalled his Oyabun's warning. A silent war was going on for the Korean peninsula. Americans were involved. How were Americans connected to the Korean murders? he wondered. And just what was the FBI objective in Niigata City? "How much can be carried in boxes to a ship?"

"Not what I'm talking about." DeCovasi grimaced. "The visitors to that boat set up the really large amounts that are sent from banks here to dummy accounts in Switzerland, the Caymans, Luxembourg. Many streams feeding a river, creating an ocean of laundered cash flowing from Japan to North Korea. And it was this hard cash that funded their nuclear bomb project, and is keeping the North Korean economy alive. Our friends at State say it's preventing serious efforts at compromise and possible reunion of the two Koreas."

Mori was silent. He could not disagree with the American but could not admit this.

"I need more than your silence, Inspector Mori."

"I am not involved in the case. Much as I would like to be."

DeCovasi spoke softly. "I know better. And I am here to tell you we are not going to sit on our hands if your team can't handle the Koreans."

"Is this what your Niigata operation is about?"

"Yes."

"But you just said you were going to Vienna."

"It's connected."

"What kind of operation, John?"

"We figure most of the laundered money is from pachinko companies owned by North Koreans in Japan. So the key is to take the companies out of the hands of North Koreans."

Mori's eyes flickered. "How?"

"Simple. By taking them public. A few huge cooperatives and companies dominate the pachinko industry. North Korean–owned, of course. All the managers are terrorized by Korean yakuza and do what they're told. Huge amounts are paid as protection money. This is what is being laundered, we guess. If, however, these firms are listed on Japanese stock exchanges, they won't be able to hide their profits."

It was a terribly simple idea that had not occurred to anyone else. Those were always the best ones, Mori told himself. "How'd the FBI suddenly get so smart?"

"We didn't. But we've developed a good source. North Korean."
DeCovasi looked out the window. "He's been in contact with a number
of large pachinko groups in Japan that want to get themselves listed on
the local stock exchanges. Some want to cash in for retirement. Others
are frightened and want to attract Japanese management. But in all cases
they want to avoid paying extortion money to the yakuza. Problem is the
Japanese stock exchanges aren't cooperating. Seems they feel pachinko is
an unethical business. I believe someone in the Japanese government has
passed the word. They don't want any listing to go through."

"Why would a Japanese government official care?" Mori tried to
sound offhand.

"C'mon." DeCovasi smirked. "We all know about your politicians
and their ties to the yakuza."

Mori was silent.

"So," DeCovasi continued, "we've been sponsoring a movement."

Mori said, "What kind of movement?"

"Call it pro-democracy. Can't give you too much more on that. Washington is paranoid about leaks. But I can tell you that we're funding a
North Korean dissident group led by an individual who lives abroad and
has established close connections to owners and relatives of important
North Korean pachinko operations here. He has several good people
working under him. One woman in particular. That's the main reason
why I'm here today."

"Woman?"

"She looks almost too good to be true. Now we think she may be.
We need your help on a background check."

"How come?"

"She's trying to persuade a Tokyo TV station to run an interview
about the pachinko industry to help change its image, get approvals from
the stock exchanges, and promote more pachinko companies to apply for
stock exchange listings. This will put pressure on the laundering pro-
grams. Doesn't know her boss is funded by us, of course."

Mori scratched the back of his head. "Why do you need my help?"

"Troubling information has come to our attention."

"Information?"

"Top-secret stuff. All I can say is, recently we developed knowledge
that makes us suspect this woman is a double. That she's actually working
for North Korean intelligence as well as our man. Has to do with a recent
trip she made to North Korea and Hong Kong as a translator under UN

sponsorship. And some plutonium. That's all I can say, but it's why I'm going to Vienna."

Mori tried to reconcile that. "And she doesn't know her dissident friend is working with the FBI?"

"No. Since she was born and raised in Japan, I'd like to ask if you could run a check on her. Find out what you can."

Mori thought a moment. He could cover that, certainly. It would help him find out what the Americans were up to. No one needed to know. "Okay, agreed. Give me her name and I'll check her out. But I can't do it this week. As soon as you leave I'm heading for Niigata City."

"Appreciate it. But do it soon. If what we think is going on, it's very big. Helim Kim is her name. She could be involved in a North Korean operation that jeopardizes the entire Asia region. Next to it, the recent economic turmoil here will look like a Japanese tea ceremony."

PART TWO

It is often necessary to make a decision on the basis
of knowledge sufficient for action
but insufficient to satisfy the intellect.

Immanuel Kant

12: **THE BOYFRIEND** Los Angeles: Tuesday, 5:30 P.M.

LOCALS COULD NOT remember a rainier June in sixty years. Underpasses in Orange County filled with water, drivers had to be rescued, and five rivers overflowed that had never done so before in the history of the county. People told jokes about how it was more dangerous to drive to Northridge on 101 than through North Hollywood late at night.

On a Tuesday afternoon in the third week of June, Steve Juric spent nearly two hours driving from Thousand Oaks to the cracked three-story earthquake survivor near the Rose Bowl that housed his one-man office.

He parked in the litter-flooded space behind the building and sat for a moment, staring thoughtfully at the rivulets washing down his windshield like a Zen priest meditating under a waterfall. Things had certainly changed in the three months since he'd met Helim Kim. Decidedly for the better.

Thanks to her father, his business had grown. He would not have to work at this godforsaken office much longer. He gripped his attaché case in one large sinewy hand, dashed through the rain, and bounded upstairs to his third-floor walkup. Fortunately, neither of his new Korean clients had insisted on seeing his tiny offices. Helim's father, Chul Kim, had been instrumental in that. Kim's introductions had guaranteed Steve's credentials, no questions asked. In the intricate network of the local Korean community, Steve had quickly learned that introductions meant face, credibility, quality—everything.

The office door was locked, a sign that his legal assistant, paralegal, and secretary, Angie, had left for the day. He unlocked the door, set his attaché case down, eyed the stack of correspondence in his in box, and pressed the play button on his answering machine.

The first message was from Ron Uemura, one of his oldest friends. They'd gone to high school and law school together, before Ron opted for a career with the FBI. His message asked Steve to call back. Ron had been assigned to the Los Angeles office over a year ago, and they had drinks together once or twice a month. Occasionally they took a day off and went surfing. Like the old days.

The second message was from Edie's lawyer, asking if his alimony check had somehow been lost in the mail. "Screw you," Steve replied happily to the machine. The third was from Helim's father, inviting him to lunch at the Korean Club tomorrow; he jotted a note to call and accept. The fourth was from Helim herself:

"Hi. I'm at the Korean Association until six tonight. Come on over if you get back and can spare the time. I have some exciting news!"

Steve looked at his watch. Five-thirty. Exciting news probably meant she'd wangled another trip abroad. He picked up the phone, dialed the association number, and finally got through to her. "What's up?"

"I'm off to Japan this weekend."

"What is it this time? Meeting the emperor?"

"Our pachinko company listing. Remember?"

Steve squinted. "Oh yeah."

"No you don't. You gave me some advice and I took it. Now I need some more. You have any time tonight?"

Steve let out his breath. "I've got a ton of work here."

"When's the last time you relaxed?"

"Don't ask."

"You've got to step out of that brilliant brain some time. Just let go."

Steve sighed. Helim Kim was a difficult woman to resist.

Besides, she had a point. He tended to get neurotic, too self-absorbed, when it came to his work. Helim had helped him remember there was more to life than painful memories, alimony checks, and trying to get back on his feet professionally. Much as he hated to admit it he knew he would never be able to resist Helim. Her power over him was complete— and it was much more than physical, despite what his friends liked to think.

"How about later?" he asked.

"Fine. My place, whenever you can get there."

13: THE WIRE Niigata City: Tuesday, 8:00 P.M.

A LARGE WHITE ship under the red-and-black North Korean flag was tied up at the largest berth of Niigata City's harbor. Three men and a woman strolled unhurriedly from a tiny customs and immigration shed toward the gangway that led up onto the Korean vessel. Separating the sheds from the surrounding area was a fence posted with signs, the only indication that this was an international entry point.

Before she stepped onto the gangway, the woman stopped and looked around, then up at the face of the gray sky. A shudder ran through her body, and she walked up and onto the ship.

In an unmarked police car parked near the dock, Chief Inspector Tetsuo Mori of the Public Security Bureau tried not to show the tension he was feeling. "Tomi is boarding. Everyone in place?"

In his earphones, three voices responded from different dock locations. All were ready. The ship had arrived from North Korea several days ago. It would leave tomorrow for Hong Kong. A sister ship in Hong Kong would depart for this port. They would pass on the way. Few people knew that these North Korean ships were the main link between North Koreans living in Japan and their homeland. No formal telephone or mail systems had as yet been established by Japan with the last of the Stalinist communist states.

While members of the North Korean ship could travel only as far as the custom shed to deliver and receive bags of mail or merchandise and parts, a resident of Japan could request permission to board the ship to meet with its North Korean personnel and deliver parcels. It had taken Tomi Chang years to reach a level in the North Korean Association that won her an invitation aboard each month to meet with compatriots from the homeland. Mori had considered the risks before he'd asked her to take on the assignment. However, it was clear that this case could have huge implications for his own government and the North Koreans as well. He was quite sure now that the deaths of North Korean pachinko owners were linked somehow to a rift in Pyongyang over the issue of democratization of North Korea.

DeCovasi had provided a valuable clue. A North Korean pro-democracy group funded by the U.S. government was backing some Korean pachinko owners—those who were trying to boycott an extortion racket run by Pyongyang. The murders were Pyongyang's attempt to stop the boycott. With fear.

"They are on the ship," a voice in Mori's ear said. "Security check passed."

Mori breathed in relief. Had the wire on Tomi been found at the North Korean security check, he couldn't have saved her. Foreign ships, like foreign-flag airliners, were considered foreign soil even while in Japanese territory.

"We're going live with simultaneous translation," a voice said in Mori's earphone.

There was the sound of chairs scraping.

Korean voices greeted one another. One of the voices said, "Alpha will be here in a moment."

"Alpha?" Mori turned quickly to Ayumi, his assistant.

"Code name for the head of North Korean intelligence," she replied.

There was the noise of a door opening. "Good evening. Good evening. I am sorry to keep you waiting." Alpha's voice was deep, commanding.

The meeting lasted two hours. All of it was recorded. There was no reference to the killings, no information of value. Mori was left wondering if he had endangered Tomi, a major field operative, for no reason. Or if perhaps she'd tipped off her North Korean friends about the operation. In either case it looked like the Public Security Bureau had wasted its money.

At ten-fifteen a team of six Korean crewmen suddenly hurried off the ship toward its bow. A port door on the North Korean vessel swung open and a ramp slid across the narrow gap to the dock. The crewmen made it fast. Police at the surveillance points were preparing to leave but remained hidden with no lights showing. The dock appeared deserted. Six new Mercedes sedans emerged one after another from the bowels of the ship. Mori could barely believe his eyes.

"Chikisho," Homma, the Niigata police chief, cursed as what was happening became clear. The customs shed had closed at seven, and all officials had departed. No night security was maintained in the dock area unless there was a special request.

Mori and Homma watched as the lead car drove up to the gate and stopped. The driver got out, unlocked the gate, and waved the other cars through. Then he drove through, carefully relocked the gate, and headed off into the city. Homma cursed again, but Mori held up his hand. "If you arrest them, it jeopardizes my mole and the entire boarding operation. We'll get them later."

On the bullet train back to Tokyo, Ayumi again listened to the meeting tapes. Finally she put them away and stared out the window. Mori had finished two bottles of the local sakè, a parting gift from Homma. He was dozing when Ayumi nudged his arm.

"We almost there?" he asked, rubbing his eyes.

"Another hour. I wanted to ask you what those cars that came off the ship were all about."

"Stolen cars," Mori grunted, not a little annoyed for being awakened. "Please don't mention them to anyone."

"But why would the North Korean government deal in stolen cars?"

"Not the North Korean government, Ayumi. Probably an enterprising branch of their military. Cars from Hong Kong mostly. One hears stories. . . ."

"What stories, sir?"

"That they take some cars back to North Korea for their own VIPs and sell the rest at other Southeast Asian ports they visit. Hard up for foreign currency, the North Koreans."

"Mmm." Ayumi squinted in thought. "This ship is run by North Korean intelligence. We know it has sensitive electronics and serves as a spy ship part of the time. Intelligence is in the army chain of command. Their chief was on the ship tonight. Maybe they're the ones who run this car business."

Mori blew his nose. "Could be, but I don't want to get involved. Let's leave that to Homma. Okay? Our problem is the murder of North Koreans. As far as the meeting goes, I didn't learn a thing. Never should have gone ahead with it." Mori yawned. "Next time we'll know better. Now if you don't mind, please don't disturb me until Tokyo."

Ayumi took a tape recorder from her bag. "First maybe you should listen to this." She handed Mori a set of earphones, then turned up the sound. Alpha was speaking.

"The KMB proposal—do you have it?"

"Here, sir." There was the sound of paper rustling.

"This is unacceptable," Alpha said finally. "Tell them the procedure is too slow and get back to us next trip."

Ayumi turned off the tape.

"That's it?" Mori asked.

"Yes."

"No wonder I missed it."

"It refers to the KMB, you see."

"Whoever they are." Mori yawned again.

"It could be a lead," Ayumi persisted.

"Okay," Mori said, to humor her. "Tomorrow try and figure out what the KMB stands for."

"But I know that already," Ayumi said. "The Korean Merchant Bank."

Mori was suddenly wide awake. Of course! A money-laundering operation required a bank. Hadn't FBI agent DeCovasi told him this morning the girl's father managed a bank branch in L.A.? Same name! Did it operate in Japan? Would it lead to those behind the pachinko deaths? He'd have Ayumi check the KMB out first thing tomorrow.

14: **KOREATOWN** Los Angeles: Tuesday, 7:00 P.M.

THE FAST-FOOD RESTAURANT was close to Koreatown's statue of the first Korean immigrant to Los Angeles. Steig couldn't help feeling as if he were in Asia. Perhaps it was because he had just stepped off a flight from Tokyo and come directly here. Everything was in Korean, even the newspapers.

Several tables were occupied by families out for an early dinner. At the counter, a wavy-haired Caucasian with large luminous eyes was eating the Special, rice noodles with slices of chicken. Steig slid into the seat beside him, checking the distant expression on the man's face.

Late thirties and too soft. Not enough size for a street man, with that double chin and the hint of a potbelly. In his former life he'd no doubt been a handler, Steig thought. He'd heard the quality had deteriorated recently, and here was proof.

Until he began to speak, the man had given no sign of recognition. "Snow White's got a boyfriend who stays over some nights. Caucasian and looks like he can handle himself. Lawyer. Triathlon type."

The accent and voice surprised Steig. Firm, deep, and no-nonsense. A distinct Slavic trill. "Thursday she's going to San Jose. That looks suspicious—maybe she knows something. You'd best get it done soon."

"Let me worry about that," Steig said. "What name shall I call you by?"

The man turned to study Steig a moment. "Aleksei. We're counting on you, Steig. No room for mistakes, intentional or otherwise."

"What is that supposed to mean?"

"She's exceptionally pretty."

Steig grunted. "Don't worry about that. I just follow orders."

"I'd suggest the garage, then. Usually takes her car to the airport. Her return flight from San Jose brings her back Thursday night. Late. I'd do her then if it was me."

"I'll take care of it in my own way."

The handler took out a pack of cigarettes without offering Steig one. Apparently they knew Steig did not smoke. "Your work in Japan was excellent. Lots of green pee on the Korean Pachinko Association office carpets these days. I believe you'll get it right."

"Thanks," Steig said calmly. Aleksei intrigued him. The man was dressed curiously for an American if he was that, as if he'd come off some college campus. Harris tweed jacket, rep tie, button-down blue Oxford shirt, cordovan shoes. "Did you bring the weapon?" Steig asked. "I don't have time for polite conversation."

The man's foot moved a sports bag on the floor. "I hope you're careful with it."

"Sights checked?"

"Yes."

"My ticket out?"

"Tokyo. Open."

"Tokyo?"

"We have more work in Asia. Possibly a big job. Something political that would look good on your résumé." The man threw some bills on the counter. "Get this one right and you can retire, eh?"

15: **THE ULTIMATUM** Los Angeles: Tuesday, 8:00 P.M.

HELIM'S APARTMENT IN Westwood was in a high-security condo with a flower garden in front and a single elevator for all the floors. The dining-living room was just large enough for a white couch with chairs to match and a black dining set that filled one corner. A window looked out over trees, but tonight the curtains were closed. On one wall was a reproduction of a Gauguin painting—a copper-skinned woman lounging naked against a tropical tree on the edge of a lake. On the other walls were unsigned watercolors of the sea Helim had painted.

Steve had gulped a microwave dinner at the office, so while Helim made cappuccino, Steve was reintroduced to her Egyptian cat, Pusan.

Helim placed the tray on the coffee table in front of the couch and served them both, then glanced at him sideways. "You're curious, right?"

"You mentioned another trip. What was so urgent you had to see me tonight?"

"I wanted you to be with me. Alone." She smoothed a pillow absently.

"That's it? No problems with the Japan trip you want me to solve?"

She ran her tongue over her lips. "I'm always traveling and you're always tied up at your damn office. This trip might take two weeks. I was just being selfish. Mad?"

"Not really. Relieved, I guess. I've got a backlog at the office that'll explode if it takes on anything more. I get caught up in the work sometimes."

"Understatement of the year. Actually, I did have a reason I wanted to see you. But do I always need one?"

"Of course not." She looked tired and strung-out tonight, he thought.

She'd been traveling too much and working too hard. He wondered if he should make some excuse and let her get some rest.

"I wanted to tell you some things about my past. Why I make all these trips and never talk about them. You've also probably wondered why I've never said much about my time in Japan. Maybe it would help if you knew more about me."

"Yeah," he said, but help what? he wondered. Hadn't she told him she didn't want commitments? To him that meant an open relationship with no questions, no strings. Women were hard to figure, but he had to admit it—he was starting to want more from her.

"Let's start with why I don't talk about Japan, then. It's very simple. I wasn't happy there. I lost my mother. My father and I lived apart, then moved to the United States. The Japanese were hostile. My grandmother was busy with her pachinko parlors, though she did her best. I never knew what would happen next. The childhood memories aren't good. Except for my mother. My memories of her I keep always."

"You lost her when you were a child, right?"

"She went away on a trip and never came back. My mother was special. I remember her smell, her hair, her eyes. I never saw eyes like hers. Soft and gentle and beautiful."

There were lots of other things she remembered too, and she told Steve about them. Best of all, she remembered how her mother would take her on walks to Ueno Park Zoo. They'd sit on a wooden bench near the Museum of History at the park and eat lunch. Monkeys were their favorite animals; neither liked bears. Bears you couldn't trust.

One day during a visit to the zoo a man joined them for lunch. He was very tall, and dark-skinned from the sun. His teeth shone white in his face when he laughed. He wore his hair in a pigtail and had on a bright sports shirt. Helim liked him.

"This is Uncle Alpha, Helim."

She bowed politely as her mother had taught her to do, and the man laughed and bowed in return.

"Where are you from?" Helim asked, because he didn't seem to be Japanese.

"He is from Pyongyang," her mother said, and the man suddenly looked at her sternly.

"She's just a child," her mother replied to his stare.

After that Uncle Alpha joined them often. Her mother told her that he lived in a country far away. He even came back to the house sometimes when no one else was there. Helim would have to go to her room, and she'd listen to the laughter and low voices and sometimes an occasional cry from another part of the house. Her mother and Uncle Alpha enjoyed each other's company—of that she was sure.

"It wasn't until later that I figured it all out," Helim told Steve. "And my grandmother told me, just before I left for the United States. I mean, I suspected something, but you know how it is—you never want to believe. It turns out my father was a real ladies' man. In Japan that wasn't so unusual then. And my mother was strong-minded. Her father was an American, did I tell you that already? She wasn't going to behave like the Japanese or Korean wives who pretended nothing was going on. Not my mother. She got even. She took her own lover."

"Reminds me of someone I know," Steve teased.

She blushed and touched her neck as if she'd suddenly found an ache there. "My father and I didn't get along. He always tried to control me, but never took responsibility. My grandmother raised me. When I was a teenager, he left to set up the bank branch in L.A. I felt abandoned. He was selfish, I thought, only lived for his work. But my mother was different. I never could measure up to what my mother was. Maybe I've grown stronger now, I don't know. But as a Korean child growing up in the sea of Japanese, I had no real friends. Just pachinko. Particularly after my mother was gone."

Steve paused to think. "You know, it's possible that your mother might have taken off. She and your father weren't getting along. She had a boyfriend who lived abroad."

Helim stared at him, her face frozen with shock. "Don't ever say that again," she ordered. She stood suddenly. "Not if you want to see me . . . ever!" She went into the kitchenette.

"Jesus, sorry, Helim," Steve said, confused by her sudden change. He hadn't meant anything. It just seemed like a logical possibility.

She put rice cakes in the microwave to give herself time to think. She'd been afraid their relationship wouldn't work from the beginning, hadn't she? The distance between them wasn't just because of his workaholic ways and her trips. She had too many secrets. Her life, her soul, could never be shared. Things she'd done were inexplicable to a Western mind. Unacceptable in a Western culture. Some considered her mother a traitor. She did not. Her mother's soul was divided East and West. Sometimes she wondered if her own wasn't.

"Oh shit." She pulled the singed rice cakes from the microwave.

"You okay?" Steve called.

"No," she said. "I mean, yes. Look, I'm sorry. I shouldn't have gotten angry. My mother's special to me. I forgot—you're always so . . . logical."

"Let's just forget it happened."

"I will if you'll stop being so analytical. Now I'm afraid to tell you anything."

He was standing in the kitchenette doorway, his eyes puzzled. "What d'you mean?"

"Shamanism teaches there are six types of men. I've figured out which you are. Intelligence—someone dominated by intellect."

"Should I be flattered?"

"Be my guest. If you like the fact your mind dominates. And you hate any show of emotion because your mind is in total control, not your heart."

"Now you're being judgmental."

"Sometimes that's good. If it's the only way to cause change. You've never done anything illogical in your life, I'd bet. Just for the emotion of it. Everything's had a sensible reason. Even your first wife. It wasn't really for love, was it? The first marriage?"

"That's not very nice."

"Maybe. But I ask you to see me and you tell me you have work."

"I came over, didn't I?"

"Yes. But I know what's most important in your life. You come over and your mind's somewhere else, reviewing a contract or considering tomorrow's schedule. I'd like to have all of you just for once. Maybe you'd enjoy it."

"I thought you didn't want any commitments."

"Then you didn't get the point. I want someone who's there for me when I need him. I know you *can* feel. But right now, instead of being angry at what I've said like any normal human, you're weighing both sides of our argument as a good legal mind is trained to do. Right?"

"This isn't an argument," Steve replied. "It's what my mother used to call a frank discussion."

She turned abruptly away from him so he wouldn't see her face. He hadn't gotten angry as she'd wanted. Instead, she felt herself weakening. "Oh hell, I don't know why I brought this up."

"I used to box."

"What?"

"I was pretty good. Golden Gloves. Collegiate champion. Offers to go pro."

Helim took a deep breath. "I'm not following this."

"Know what my coaches taught me?"

"I can't wait."

"Mental toughness. That's what it takes to win. To knock the other guy out when you're behind on points. To keep your cool when all hell breaks out around you."

"Am I missing something here?" She cocked an eye at him.

"It's very simple. See, mental toughness is about controlling emotion. You were pulling my chain, but I didn't react. I don't get angry—gave it up long ago. Required software for winners in any sport. Any profession. Particularly law."

"And?"

"Maybe I learned to control myself too well. Maybe I wiped out the good emotions with the bad. They don't tell you about side effects when you buy the product. Control anger, fear, anxiety, loneliness, but lose the fuzzy warm feelings too. Trained it all out of me in sports and law school."

She leaned over, lifted her face to his, and kissed him on the cheek. "Or maybe you're making excuses for the fact you're scared to death of letting go. As I am."

He kissed her back.

She pulled away. "It's not just you. I'm exhausted from all the traveling."

"Why?"

"Simple. I miss you. These trips I take for the UN are classified. I'm not supposed to talk about them. But I go to North Korea. I work on nuclear reactor projects. As translator. Okay? It's no big deal."

"Sure. I can handle that."

"I'm beginning to wonder if I can." She found a bottle of wine, removed the cork, and poured two glasses full. "Let's get drunk."

"I have a better idea. Let's make love."

"Maybe." She handed him a glass, and he followed her back to the sofa. She sat in his lap. "Drink some wine and I'll see how I like you."

"You want a massage?"

"Last time you kept massaging the wrong places." She drank some wine and moved her legs against his. "Anything wrong, Steve? Another woman?"

He tasted his wine. "Why don't you quit this international stuff?"

"Business. You used to travel a lot, didn't you? When you were married?"

"That was different."

"Because you were leaving her each time. The leaver never feels sad. The leavee suffers."

"You should have been an analyst." Steve massaged her leg.

"You're afraid of loving someone more than yourself. Just as I am."

"Oh, shut up." He kissed her on the neck.

"Don't ever leave me, Steve. Warn me you're going to, so I can leave first. Deal?"

"You never tell me where you've been, what you've done."

"I just did. You know all about this next trip. Japan this weekend. TV interview. Pachinko."

"How about your last trip?"

"That was UN nuclear work. Secret."

"See what I mean?"

"You're not drinking," she said.

He lifted his glass and chugged the wine down. "How'm I doing now?"

"How would that overworked brain of yours mind staying the night?" she said.

IN THE EARLY morning Steve lay beside her. He turned on his side and marveled at the serenity of her sleeping face, her flawless skin, the tiny mole that accentuated her full lips. She had a privacy about her, rooms he could never enter. Ever. But the sex was great. The taste of the night came back to him, and he wondered if she really did love him.

That made him chuckle. Hadn't he decided to have no more serious affairs? One divorce was enough, right? No more building his own ego through others. After his divorce, he'd shifted attention to inanimate objects. Mountains filled with Himalayan pine, whitewater chutes he kayaked, the surging feel of swimming in open sea. Maybe he didn't believe in real love anymore. He looked over at her again. Or did he?

He lay thinking and staring at the ceiling. Was he afraid of loving someone else more than himself? Maybe. Had he lost the ability to show his real feelings? Probably. Long ago in the success maze where men didn't cry or show emotion over winning and losing. Took the hits and moved on. That was the macho process. Mental toughness. You controlled everything. Key to success in sports, the coaches advised you. Also business, women, life. And he'd gotten so good at the control, so good at controlling his fear of failing, that he'd lost the joy of winning. Lost the capacity for feeling anything—love included. Maybe Helim could show him the way back.

He dozed for a while, then looked at his watch. Time to get up. Today he had a lunch with Helim's father, he remembered. Chul Kim's bank had put Steve's firm on a retainer to handle all its overseas ventures. Two hundred thousand dollars a year. Cheap by L.A. standards, but it would cover overhead. And he should return Ron Uemura's call. For the moment, his personal problems seemed unimportant as the reality of making money and finding out what his FBI friend wanted invaded his thoughts. He rose without waking Helim and began to dress.

CHUL PICKED STEVE up at his office, and they drove over to the Korean Club for lunch. They discussed a few business matters during the meal, but Kim was unusually quiet. Steve understood there was something on his mind. Over dessert, Kim said he had a favor to ask. They could discuss it on the way back to Steve's office.

As the driver eased the car out into traffic, Kim turned to Steve in the backseat.

"Helim is planning a trip to Japan. I'd like you to stop her from going."

Steve's mouth opened as if to answer the totally unexpected request. Then he closed it. "She has a very independent mind," he said at last.

Kim ignored his remark. "She has some damn foolish idea in her mind about helping my mother-in-law get her pachinko company listed on a Japanese stock exchange. It's not only foolish but dangerous."

Steve felt a flush creep up his neck. "Dangerous?"

"Yes." Kim nodded abruptly. "In Tokyo and Osaka, seven Koreans have been murdered in the past month. The Korean community in Japan is divided, like the one here—divided in its loyalty. Only deeper. What's more, in Japan there are Korean yakuza. Some are controlled by the North, others by the South. A war is going on in Japan for the soul of the Korean peninsula, and Helim is putting herself in the middle of it."

"A war?" That was hard to believe, Steve thought. Japanese cities were the safest in the world, weren't they?

"Dammit, Steve, do you have to repeat everything I say? *Yes!* A war." Kim composed himself. "Sorry. Helim is all I have left. Her grandmother and I don't get along. Not since I lost my wife. For some reason my mother-in-law blames me."

"I understand," Steve said coolly. "Who's this war between?"

"Why," said Kim, as if it were obvious to anyone, "between those who want to see liberalization and a peaceful reunion of the two Koreas and those who want domination of the other at any cost. That's why the Korean peninsula is a dangerous flashpoint."

Steve wondered if Chul Kim wasn't being melodramatic. "I thought her pachinko firm was just some sort of amusement company."

"So, you do know about it, do you? Good. Allied International's not some 'amusement company,' Steve. Not at all! Once, perhaps, but not now. It's very profitable, a very large cooperative in which Helim and her grandmother own shares. It's owned by a group that has a strong influence on the entire pachinko industry. And the Japanese government refuses to control it."

"Why not?"

"Because certain Japanese politicians have a stake in pachinko. That's why I need your help to keep Helim from meddling. It's too big. Way too big for her. The Japanese will destroy her without a second thought."

"But all she wants to do is get the company listed." Her father must be exaggerating, but how could he check it out? Ron Uemura would know about any pachinko war in Japan, he decided. Steve planned to meet the FBI man this afternoon.

Chul Kim sighed. "Look at it this way then. Pachinko is owned privately. It throws off incredible profits, profits that are used to benefit both Korean sides, but mainly the North. If a company is listed, then strict auditing rules suddenly apply. Financial statements become transparent. Published. Helim has no idea what she's getting into, although God knows I've tried to warn her. She could also cause severe embarrassment to me, my bank, my career . . ."

"But how can I . . ." At a loss for words, Steve hesitated. Kim would have made a good prosecuting attorney, he thought.

Chul held up his hand. "Let's talk man to man. No more bullshit, okay? I know when my daughter is sleeping with someone, yes?" His piercing eyes stared at Steve. "We have a Korean proverb, 'The only one who can control a Korean woman is her lover.' Helim listens to no one except her current boyfriend. I know that she's very attracted to you. And you've accepted her love by sleeping with her. In our Korean society we take such things seriously. Under our system, you are responsible for her. We consider her your mistress until you are married. If marriage doesn't take place, then a compensation is involved. You are the only one she will listen to. You know it and I know it. To her, I'm just a worthless old man."

"She respects you a great deal. Doesn't she?" He couldn't tell Chul Kim how his daughter truly felt about him.

"Not really. She didn't listen to my advice to settle down and marry a Korean from the community, did she? No."

"She told me her grandfather—"

"Her grandmother married an American officer in Tokyo during the Occupation," Chul interrupted as if correcting a mistake. "At least that is the story my mother-in-law tells. The papers were somehow lost. They had a child, Helim's mother. Then the American disappeared. Killed in the Korean War. I've seen nothing in writing. No marriage documents, no death certificate, you understand. This I am willing to live with. Such is the hidden cost of wars."

"So Helim is one-quarter Caucasian."

"Maybe." Chul Kim grew solemn. "I can understand why you're interested in her—why any man is. I think you'll agree I have been very fair with you."

Steve flushed. "You've helped my business a great deal."

Chul Kim smiled ironically. "For some reason she's never dated Korean men. Before you, it was a Costa Rican fellow. Tomás. He worked with the UN. Still loves her, he says, when he calls me trying to find her. He wanted to set up a company in Asia with her one day. I know she respected him, but then you came along. I just follow along behind her, picking up the debris of her flings." Kim offered his most servile grin. "I've been offered unheard-of amounts to arrange her marriage, but I've chosen to set her free. Why? Maybe it's because I've never known that feeling myself. Still, there's a limit to what even I can let her do."

"I understand," Steve said, not sure that he did. Not sure he was being told the whole truth. "I'll see what I can do about her trip."

"I am afraid 'see what I can do' is not good enough. It was you that gave her this fool idea about appearing on Japanese TV, or that's what she said."

Steve thought a moment. "I didn't take her pachinko business very seriously."

"Well then," Kim declared through compressed lips, "now you must! You are a very fine lawyer. Better than you think. I can help you immensely if I choose, and I can destroy you. Just what I'll do depends on just how seriously you take Helim's problem."

Steve turned toward Kim, barely containing his anger. Kim had failed Helim as a father, she said, by never taking responsibility. Now he was blaming Steve for his own inadequacy. Threatening him, in fact. "What the hell does that mean?"

Kim looked at him unflinchingly. "I want her trip canceled, or else you will get nothing from me. Your retainer will be terminated. And no more business from our community!" Chul Kim smiled at Steve warmly, though his expression remained hard. "I'm doing this for both your sakes, Steve. Please understand."

16: **PRICE OF ADMISSION** Vienna: Wednesday, 10:00 A.M.

"YOU SEE WHAT the problem is, Mr. Velaquez." Carswell was Tomás Velaquez's immediate superior in Vienna. "This is an attack on the integrity of the very IAEA investigation system itself. On the whole United Nations concept of controlling nuclear proliferation by rogue nations. I mean, it was *your* personal initiative, after all."

"Of course," Tomás said softly. He stared out the window. From their perch high in UN City, they could see the graceful curve of the Danube weaving through the clutter of Vienna. "What's going on, Carswell? Just spell it out."

"Dear God, it's nothing personal. But the British intelligence service is one of the best in the world, if I may say so." Carswell pulled out a handkerchief as if considering a good cry. "Besides, the British consul wouldn't have revealed this much unless they were damn worried. I mean, I have a few contacts inside, and I know how these people work. If this was from a less credible source, our director might not have gone through the roof this morning."

"Certainly," Tomás said, beginning to get the drift. There'd been some shouting earlier from the direction of the director's door. Tom had been called into Carswell's office suddenly on an entirely different matter and the door shut. All calls held. A letter signed by the local British consular head had been silently passed to him. It made the problem horrifically clear. There was serious doubt about procedures to maintain integrity of the North Korean plutonium sample once it arrived in Hong Kong.

"Ample and adequate opportunity existed for a switch in the sample to have occurred," the letter complained. Several scenarios had been suggested by British intelligence. Finally, the most telling blow: one staff member of the hotel where Tom had registered and kept the sample overnight (before he had turned it over to proper authorities) admitted being approached with a bribe for a master key to the safe in Tom's room. The employee had been taken into custody by the Hong Kong police and was still being questioned.

"So far," Carswell went on, "the entire affair is being kept confidential—only a few governments are being advised. But once the media get hold of it . . . well, I wish I could put it more gently, but I'm afraid this is beginning to look like a huge fuckup."

"Certainly it looks that way." Tomás kept his temper. No need to waste his emotion here. Later maybe, when he found out who the executioner would be.

"Anyway, *I'm sorry*." Pause. "I know you were following procedure in keeping the sample personally until you could organize valid security— the U.S. embassy wasn't open at that hour. You'd arrived at night from Pyongyang and so you just marched through customs checks in Hong Kong with the stuff, waving your UN credentials. Cheeky, Tom, but I suppose that's why we hired you. You called the U.S. embassy first thing next morning and by noon had the plutonium safely inside the compound, where it remained until cleared. It was only an envelope's worth, after all. And we know for that amount, the radiation level wouldn't dent tissue paper. But I am afraid the one night and morning is the problem."

Tomás sighed. "When we got the Iraqi sample, military flights from Kuwait took us directly to London for the tests."

"Right. The real problem is we didn't get your fax from Pyongyang, if you ever sent one, advising you'd gotten the sample. Otherwise you'd have been met in Hong Kong with full orchestra. However, no sense crying over spilt milk. Right now I have to deal with the present."

"I understand entirely," Tomás said, his temper beginning to tug at his words. He wondered what his liability would be, if any. Civil? Criminal? He thought of his bank account, which was virtually nonexistent. Pay wasn't at the top of perks for UN personnel. And Vienna was an expensive city. Not to panic, he told himself. Just be cool. He'd figure a way.

Carswell had selected a green pencil and was rolling it between his thumb and forefinger. "I have to tell you that there are some people who would like to talk with you. The *boss*"—here Carswell's voice paused with a tremble—"agreed that *they* could see you this afternoon and that *you* should be entirely frank."

"Yes, certainly I will." An intelligence service was already in the act, then. He could see a British government man tapping his molars with the plutonium report and smiling straight into his eyes. *We understand that a woman played a key role.* Christ, not Helim. That would really put him in a fix.

"Our damage control team has recommended you go on leave as of . . ." Carswell managed to look at Tomás's left ear as he handed him an envelope. "Well, immediately. As soon as this clears up, naturally you will be reinstated. No change. Back pay. Everything just as before."

"Sure, that's just fine." Tomás took the envelope, put it in his pocket without looking inside.

"There are certainly rumors flying around," Carswell said. "One is about how you had a tryst with some translator on your team in a Hong Kong hotel, which I just don't believe for a minute." A glance at the Costa Rican for some reply. Tomás looked at his hands, not willing to honor him with an answer. "It would be a breach of IAEA code, now wouldn't it? The director felt he had no choice, until the air is cleared. About your leave of absence, I mean. I really don't know where people get these things."

THEY LED HIM to a clean, brightly lit, windowless room with a table and three chairs. The American embassy has a clean smell, he thought, as though they scrub the floors with disinfectant every day to rid it of "contamination" by foreigners. The room itself made him apprehensive, but he told himself there was no reason to be nervous. After all, he had done nothing wrong. He was being "played." His job was sensitive, and someone had seen the chance to discredit him and his agency—in fact, the entire inspection system, as Carswell said. So far they had done a damn fine job.

"Good afternoon, Mr. Velaquez. Thank you for stopping by." The American was in his thirties, with a clean smile. He didn't offer his hand. "My name is DeCovasi, and this is Mr. Pipe." Another American suddenly appeared behind DeCovasi. Older. Taller. Wider.

The man called Pipe also wore a clean smile. Tomás handed the first man his card.

"Not necessary." DeCovasi waved it off. "The marine guard gave us your name, and you know who we are now. Just think of us as . . . family. So. Please have a seat."

Tomás sat in one of the straight-backed chairs, feeling the sweat on the palms of his hands. "Could you tell me which branch of the embassy you represent, Mr. DeCovasi?"

"We work for the intelligence section, Mr. Velaquez," Pipe said, folding his hands in a cat's cradle.

DeCovasi leaned forward, "Now, Mr. Velaquez, Tom—may we call you that?"

"Certainly."

"We're going to make this as easy as possible. As you no doubt have heard, some questions have arisen regarding your procedures after you left North Korea. The findings of that visit were very sensitive. Tests show the sample indicates cheating by the North Koreans. The North has not been made aware of these results as yet. Before anything is said to them, our job is to decide whether the sample was or was not tampered with. 'Contaminated' is the technical word. If there's any reasonable doubt, we scratch the sample, the North is told nothing, and everything goes on as before. Maybe we try to get another one." He paused.

Lots of luck with that, Velaquez thought.

"Of course, if the sample holds," DeCovasi continued, "the White House may decide to unravel all the financial relationships and business deals that have been initiated by ourselves and our allies with North Korea over the past three years. Four billion dollars in loans. Nuclear reactors. Oil. Peace and reunion talks. The works. Get it?"

"I understand the importance." He understood as well that the appearance of peace meant more to some than facing hard realities. Let the shit hit the fan on the next watch—not theirs. Had these two been ordered to disprove the plutonium findings, whatever the cost?

DeCovasi closed his eyes. "Joe has a few simple questions he wanted to ask you, Tom. Piece of cake."

Pipe took it from here. "We understand the plutonium was passed to you by the North Koreans because you charmed them off their feet and they thought a pinch or two was too little to test. I'd like to state at the outset that you did a great job to get it."

"Thank you."

"And, may I say at the outset that questioning an IAEA officer is distasteful to us. However, North Korea has never provided a sample before, so we're being extra-careful."

"I understand," Tomás said and wondered if they were going to claim he'd conjured up the sample himself. Good God!

"It's what happened in Hong Kong that concerns us mainly. That in contravention of current IAEA procedure, you maintained possession of the plutonium overnight in Hong Kong when you arrived from North Korea. That you stored it with the U.S. embassy only the next day. We first want to confirm this is what you actually did, by the way. And that you later took repossession for the flight to Heathrow and went directly to the Uranium Institute in London, where you turned it over to a Dr. Jordan."

"I kept the sample overnight in Hong Kong, yes. The contravention part I frankly don't get." Tomás folded his arms across his chest. "I was following procedure."

DeCovasi was in total agreement. "Your office here tells us the fax you claim to have sent from Pyongyang never arrived. Can you give us a time-stamped copy for our record of the investigation?"

"No. The North Koreans said they sent it. I believed them. I can give you a copy they returned to me, but it has nothing on it. They returned it after they said it was sent. Stamps are put on faxes there after the event anyway, by a clerk. Sometimes there's this little red dot. I didn't check it at the time."

"Anything in your defense would help." DeCovasi referred to a transcript. "The IAEA procedure, as I understand it, would normally be to turn the sample over to a UN officer in Hong Kong immediately upon arrival there. He would then deposit it with one of the local embassies—the British or American—for safekeeping. Isn't this so?"

"Right. No one met me. Maybe because they didn't get my fax." No one figured he would come out with any plutonium. No one else ever had, and a plutonium sample wasn't on his wish list from headquarters. He'd played a long shot and scored. Maybe they'd received the fax but ignored it or not believed it. Maybe someone had lost it. Maybe the North Koreans hadn't sent it. He didn't remember any instructions about how the sample was to be handled during the Hong Kong overnight, and none had reached him during his trip. Hell, it was just a pinch of what looked like dirt in a damn envelope. It sounded like everyone was covering his ass.

"I didn't tell anyone else I was keeping it locked in a safe in my room," he said. "I didn't tell hotel management. No staff surprised me while I put it in the safe. It was in exactly the same spot when I took it out."

With his eyes, DeCovasi handed him over to Pipe. "Did you leave the room while the sample was in the safe, Tom?"

"Of course I did. I shaved, I took a shit. The next morning I had breakfast in the dining room. Before I came back to the room I made a phone call to the U.S. ambassador and explained my situation. He said he'd take care of it right away, and he did. A team came over from the embassy within an hour, and I signed the sample over to them. It was returned to me at the hotel with all documentation for hand-carry to Heathrow, which was negotiated by the embassy with the Hong Kong government and London. It took them two days."

"So you made a telephone call from your hotel to explain to the ambassador."

"Yes. I called from a public phone in the rear of the lobby near the coffee shop. I felt the room phone might not be safe."

"Yes. Good thinking. How long were you out of your room with the plutonium unguarded?"

"I bought a paper, so it was fifty minutes for breakfast at the coffee shop and then the phone call on the way back to my room. After my call I went immediately to my room."

Pipe spoke with admiration. "Not bad, Tom. Not bad. Okay, you sure you didn't tell anyone you had the plutonium?"

"Of course not. Nor anyone on the plane."

Here DeCovasi and Pipe exchanged a quick glance. "How about the negotiation?" DeCovasi suggested. "It took how long, altogether?"

"One week. I went in to talk about storing rods. Not to get plutonium. To talk with the American team there checking the Koreans' in-place reactors. The North Koreans decided only at the last minute to give me a small sample."

"You must have been brilliant to convince them. You speak Korean?" Another shrewd glance from DeCovasi to Pipe.

"No. I had a translator." Here it comes, Tomás thought, and he took a deep breath. Without Helim's flattering words in the introductions, her eloquent translation of his thoughts, her advice on who was who, where the pressure should be applied, the charm turned on—no, without her, the plutonium would not have been possible.

"So, she knew you got the plutonium out too." DeCovasi was referring to notes.

Tomás realized they were way ahead of him. DeCovasi had said "she," so they must know about Helim. He wondered how much else they knew. His stomach began to tighten. "She was the only one," Tomás agreed.

Pipe leaned back. "Attractive woman, from what we hear." He stared at a page in front of him. "Name Helim Kim—that sound like her?"

"Yes."

It was DeCovasi's turn. "You take any precautions to determine if someone opened the safe while you were out? Hairs across the door? Some lineup of the sample that couldn't be duplicated exactly if it was moved? See what I mean?"

"I'm afraid I'm not up on all that spy stuff," Tomás said. "I assumed it would be secure. It was only overnight, for Christ's sake."

"You assumed." Pipe scratched a note on a pad in front of him. "Yet you did take the precaution to call the ambassador from a public phone because you worried the room phone was insecure. Your inconsistency bothers me."

"Don't mind him," DeCovasi interrupted. "I would have played it the same way, frankly. Now, let's go back to the beginning, after you were given the sample. Could you tell us everything you can recall about the way in which the plutonium was secured? Who had possession, how it was handled, what procedures you took—ah, just a moment." Here DeCovasi lifted a phone and said to the operator, "Could we get some coffee?" He cocked an eye at Velaquez. "With or without?"

"No cream." Tomás was beginning to wonder where this was leading. His mind was racing. What should he do when he got out of here? He'd been effectively released from his job. He'd been thinking of heading back home for a vacation. Now that didn't look like a good idea. If he was going to extricate himself from this mess, he would need some help.

"Two blacks and one white." DeCovasi put the phone down. "Where was I? Oh yes. Unload everything you recall after you picked up the plutonium. All the dull detail."

Doggedly, Tomás went through the key points of his schedule from the moment the plutonium was handed to him on the way to the airport in Pyongyang.

"Be more of a virtuoso here," Pipe complained. "What was the lay of the land? See troop movement? Tanks? Lots of birds at the airport? Anything spicy?"

Tomás had forgotten about it with his preoccupation for the plutonium, but in fact he had seen lots the last day. "Like Tiananmen during the revolt," he said.

"More," Pipe urged cheerfully.

"There were thousands of troops being transported in columns," he recalled. And twice they'd had to wait for tank battalions to cross inter-sections. He'd nearly missed the flight. "I was getting nervous," he con-cluded.

"If it was my call, sounds like someone preparing for a coup," DeCovasi said with the earnestness of a priest.

"Okay." Pipe stuck a finger in his ear and twisted. He grimaced as if in pain, although those close to him knew it was a sign he liked the conclusion. "You're in the plane and heading for Beijing now. We won't interrupt any more. Promise."

Tomás reviewed his flight to Beijing, then a plane change to Hong Kong, his departure from Hong Kong, and arrival in London.

"So." DeCovasi picked up the thread when Tomás finally ran dry. "You were actually two days in Hong Kong, just clearing the plutonium shipment with customs?"

"Two nights. Two days, yes. Well, it wasn't quite that simple. I had to wait for the U.S. embassy to clear the plutonium out of Hong Kong under their Hazardous Materials Act, and then I had to get British gov-ernment clearance to bring the material in through Heathrow. It went smoothly enough, but with one thing and another, two days spent, yes."

"No time for anything else, then?" DeCovasi led him through the recitation, an insidious grin on his face, like a kindergartner hearing "Peter Rabbit" for the first time.

Tomás felt his neck heat a degree or two. "I spent the first afternoon with forms and whatnot."

Pipe perked up. "The second afternoon free, was it then, Mr. Vela-quez?"

"Yes."

"And how was that afternoon spent? Enjoyably, I'd hope."

Tomás plunged in. It seemed like they already knew. "Spent it with my translator as a way of thanking her for the superb job she did in North Korea."

Pipe glanced at DeCovasi. Just a peek, but it was enough. Tomás saw the way things were going to be.

"Well, that does sound enjoyable," DeCovasi said.

"So what did we do?" Pipe gave his voice a "just us boys" roll. "You had her for the afternoon, so to speak. Why don't you take us through the menu? Where we went, what we did."

Tomás visited Victoria Peak and Stanley, took the boat ride out of Queen's Pier. At each stop DeCovasi interrupted and asked how you spelled the name of a shop, where the table was at the Victoria Peak restaurant, near the window so you could see arriving flights into the new airport or the other side with the delightful trees. Finally he asked for the name of the boat they'd hired. Tomás had difficulty remembering that but finally came up with *Asian Queen.* The only part he left out was the stopover in Discovery Bay on the way back. It wasn't important, really.

"What time you get back to Queen's Pier, then? Dark, so you could see all those wonderful lights coming up Victoria Harbor, or still afternoon, through all the ships moored up tight like a parking lot?"

"It was dark."

"Say six?" Pipe urged him on like a croupier at the crap tables of Macau. "It gets dark about six this time of year in Hong Kong, doesn't it?" He looked up at the ceiling as if expecting to hear an answer from God.

"No. Dark around eight, actually."

"Dark at eight, then." Pipe's eyes went to his notes. "So you left the pier about three-thirty. Boat you hired, takes a half hour to Lamma, as I recall. You ate some fish, you said. Another hour. We're at five and a full stomach. Back on the boat, you are easily at Queen's Pier by six, I would make it. Wouldn't you say we have about two hours and change there to deal with? If it was dark. Like to tell us about that?"

"We stopped on the way back at Discovery Bay." He could read the smugness in Pipe's face. DeCovasi appeared disappointed they'd destroyed his story so easily. It didn't matter, Tomás thought. He'd just tell the truth. He felt his heart pounding in his chest.

Pipe was scribbling furiously in some sort of shorthand. DeCovasi's eyes did an inventory of Tomás's features as if he'd found something missing. "Now I'm a bit confused. This is the first you've mentioned Discovery Bay. Nice resort as I recall, about a half hour by jetfoil out of Hong Kong Central. Lantau Island, yes? Let me see. Great marina, a Robert Trent championship golf course with spectacular views of the South China Sea. But too late for a round of golf, wasn't it? Or were the lights on? Friends there, Tom? That what you didn't want to tell us?"

"They were her friends."

"Helim's?" Pipe's voice was at the top of the hill preparing for the charge down. "So you had your *Asian Queen* stop for a visit. They met you at the pier, Tom? Her friends?"

Tomás negated that. "No cellular phone on the boat, so we just went on up."

Pipe now grinning like a cat. "Up, Tom?"

"Yes. The condo was on the side of the foothills there. Up toward the reservoir. Great seaview when you open the door."

"Ah." Pipe was off in a frenzy of shorthand again while DeCovasi gathered up the puzzle pieces and began to put them in place.

"Her friends, Tom. What kind of people were they?"

"They were out. She had a key, so we just went on in."

"You hurried the Lamma Island stop a bit then, eh? Wanted to get to Discovery Bay, for the main course? Had some business there, then."

Tomás felt the heat growing inside him. These people were monstrously rude. Insulting not only to him, but to his entire relationship with Helim. He stared silently from one to the other of his tormenters.

Pipe's lips had puckered as if lining up a ball on a difficult putt. "Let's cut to the chase. You're in this elevated room overlooking the ocean with her. A great bod. A real looker. You poke her, Tom? Nobody'd blame you in the least. Hell, young DeCovasi here would be disappointed if you hadn't at least given it a shot. Start asking questions about your mother, wouldn't you, Thumper?"

He didn't get a reply from Tomás.

DeCovasi suggested, "She made a deal with you? I mean, her family background is North Korean, isn't it? Just a bit confused in her loyalties, isn't she? Switch the plutonium, she says, and you say what the hell, no one will ever know. She proposed it on the boat out to Lamma or in the room after you'd tossed her, where she could call her people and tell them you've agreed. Frankly, I don't give a shit if you laid her. Pipe here's the romantic. I'm more a pragmatist, if you really want to know. Just tell us what happened with that fairy dust you were carrying."

Again, there was no reply from the Costa Rican.

Pipe spoke. "They offered you money, right? What? A quarter of a million? A half? Very tempting for someone with your kind of debts. That bank account of yours at the Deutsche Bundesbank is beginning to echo when you look in these days, right? So what was it—a million? Did they go that far? Some of the fanatics would, I'm sure."

Tomás stood suddenly and walked deliberately toward the door.

DeCovasi's voice stopped him. "It's locked. Sorry. No offense, but we wanted the meeting kept private. Shall I let you out? You're free to go whenever you like. We live in a democracy, after all."

Tomás turned and looked at them both. He wanted to laugh. They were determined to twist the facts to prove their theory, whatever the cost. He wasn't going to let them, no matter how bad it looked. Fuck them.

"All we're doing here is trying to get at the truth," Pipe said. "I think now is probably as good as any a time to tell you why we're taking this all rather seriously, don't you, Mr. DeCovasi?"

DeCovasi was in total agreement. "Should have brought it up earlier, really. My fault."

"There is a whisper that you have a contract with the Russians. Absurd, I'm sure, but you see the dilemma it places us in. They're friends now after all, the KGB. And we have no clue why they'd want the plutonium switched. Ever meet a gentleman by the name of Romanov? Aleksei Romanov. Short. Wavy hair. Quite a dresser."

Tomás circled back behind his chair and grasped it until his knuckles went white. Son of a bitch, these people were confusing. A Russian? They were making that up too. He'd done his job and they were trying to destroy him.

"Nothing subtle about you two, is there?" he said. "Made up your minds already, you and your government. Know what I think? The plutonium sample findings put the U.S. nuclear reactor deal with the North Koreans in jeopardy. The Geneva Accord with all its trappings goes down the drain with my little sample, right? Don't want it to happen, do you? Those are your orders. Everything has been figured out. To answer your question. No. I don't know any fucking Russians."

Pipe clucked his tongue. "I'm detecting self-pity, Tom. Not a satisfactory ingredient in the mature and universal man your superiors consider you. They give you very high marks, so we're trying to bend over backwards. But there are some little pieces of your character that concern us. You do have some debt, we understand. Not much of a salary and very little in your bank account. That's a profile that makes us wonder just a bit. We're all human. We all get tempted. No one's going to blame you, even if you sat down right now and said yes, you switched the damn stuff. We're not going to tie you up and throw you away in some dark hole. There'd be a perfectly legal trial. You'd have every advantage to defend yourself. Where it would be held is still being discussed. The Hague, perhaps. The Dutch courts are very honest, I'm told. We'll do everything we can to see you get an honest hearing. Or if you decide to cooperate, then we'd be willing to consider canceling all charges. You'll find us very fair."

"You have nothing," he roared suddenly. "No case." His ears

pounded like a seismic drum. Everything was agonizingly clear. Make it appear that he's hiding something, they'd been ordered. Send the bastard away forever. Any charge will do. In Costa Rica, at the time of the generals, it had been the same. When his father had disappeared. Justice had meant nothing. "You both can go to hell," he exploded.

"Try and do a little better than that."

"It's a setup, that's all I can tell you. Why? Who? How? I haven't a clue. But one thing I have to tell you. You jump on my head, I'll take you all the way to the goddamn Supreme Court in any country you choose."

"All bluff, Tom. Nothing in your hand, I'm afraid."

"I am telling you the truth about the girl. I'd hoped you'd have figured that out by now."

Pipe sighed. "It's just not your day, is it?"

DeCovasi cut in quickly. "Tell you what. Those are all the questions we have for now. We'd like to ask you to stop by again for a visit tomorrow. Give us some time to regroup. We'd hoped this might be a bit more cut and dried, but you've offered up some pieces we didn't glean from our other interviews. Please understand we're on your side, believe it or not. The Brits, love them, have quite a bit of wind in their sails on this one, however, so we've got to think everything through." He chuckled as if this was the best he could do.

"You believe someone is out to get you, then?" Pipe summarized.

"I don't know."

"But Tom, my friend." Pipe leaned forward, elbows on the table. "Why should the North Koreans bother? I mean, why give you illegal plutonium in the first place? Everything's going their way so nicely. Lots of Western investments being discussed. Someone even said Disney is thinking about a theme park for Panmunjom. What's the point?"

Tomás pounded his fists against the table. "Damn you people! Don't you understand? I don't know." He paused, suddenly out of breath. "Maybe they don't like the idea of inspections. Maybe they want to destroy the IAEA system itself. So I'm the fall guy. I haven't really figured that out yet, sir."

Pipe stretched. "Well, when you do, be sure and let us know." He leaned back in his chair. "One last thing that bothers us. Our records show you dialed a Los Angles number last night. A number registered to the name Helim Kim. Then you called a Mr. Chul Kim. Spoke for seven minutes. What was the call about? Why did you call them? We'll want to hear your answer to that tomorrow as well."

• • •

BACK IN HIS apartment, Tomás threw a change of underwear, a sport jacket, and slacks into a hand-carry bag and checked his window. It was late afternoon, the sun slanting through the trees in the small park across the street.

He pulled the shade, removed a floorboard in the small closet, and retrieved a shoe box, which he stuffed in his bag with his clothes. He knew there was great evil out there watching and waiting. He would have to be clever.

There was nobody suspicious on the street below, but no doubt orders had already been cut. His only chance was that their surveillance wasn't tight. That they assumed he wouldn't bolt. But if he didn't escape, to-morrow or soon his freedom would end, and with it any chance of suc-ceeding. Of fighting back. Of seeing Helim. Christ, they already had his phone tapped.

He headed downstairs, checked the back alley, and, seeing it clear, raced out the door and up the pavement until he reached a main street. Here he took a bus to the State Opera House. Then he changed to a tram heading out of the city on Kärntner Ring past Schubertring Park, crossed the Danube at Reichsbrücke, glimpsed the towers of UN City where the IAEA offices were, and finally, satisfied no one was following, stopped at a post office. He took a large Priority Mail envelope and put the box in it. As to contents, he wrote "Printed Matter." For address he printed a PO box at the Tokyo international post office in Marunouchi, with a "Please Hold" followed by his name. He could purchase a new identity in Hong Kong if need be. For now, time was on his side. He knew a Chinese travel agent in Kowloon who specialized in any nationality for a price.

Outside again, he headed back. It was now the beginning of rush hour, and he used the crowds. He bused to several sections of the city, then back again. Finally satisfied no one could have followed him, he headed for the central train station and purchased two tickets, one to Paris, the other to Stuttgart.

17: THE COUP Washington: Wednesday, 5:15 P.M.

A DEEP VOICE answered the secure phone: "John DeCovasi speaking."

"You wanted me to call," said Park.

"Yes. Thank you. We have a problem you might want to help us with."

"What is it?"

"Remember the plutonium sample we discussed?"

"From the North Koreans. Yes."

"The sample was illegal. Not from their reactors."

"Really!"

"The IAEA man's disappeared. Tomás Velaquez."

Park's voice was confident. "Helim's not involved, I'm sure of that. As I told you."

"We'll have to talk with her."

"Why?"

"Someone tried to tamper with that plutonium sample in Hong Kong. We don't think they succeeded. Just routine. Could have been her."

"Delay bringing her in for now."

"Why?"

"Remember that operation of hers you approved? A Tokyo TV station's invited her to Japan this weekend. Let that happen first."

"I'll need some answers to do that."

"Like what?"

"We don't think the plutonium was switched. At least not by Velaquez. He was telling us the truth. What we can't figure is, why would North Korea give him the plutonium? And why would he run?"

"I know how Alpha thinks. This is his work, no mistake."

"What are you saying? North Korean intelligence passed an illegal sample deliberately?"

"All ties in with the series of murders of Koreans in Japan."

"Now I'm confused."

"Both the murders and the plutonium are part of an endgame. To irreparably damage the image of Park Tai Jin. The current leader's out of favor with the hard-liners in Pyongyang. They think he's about to open up to the West, that they've lost his support."

"The North Korean leader?" DeCovasi sounded incredulous.

"The murders make it look like he's reverted to the old Stalinist ways. The plutonium makes it appear that he's building atomic bombs with smuggled plutonium. North Korea's allies are pissed off because the West will blame Russia or China. The West is angry at him because he's talked peace while deceiving them. That's what the hard-liner endgame makes it looks like. Isolates the leader, doesn't it? Exactly what the hard-liners want for the next step."

"Next step?"

"A coup."

DeCovasi was silent a moment. "I'll need specifics on that."

"Look at the facts. Rising power of the liberal technocrats. Hard-liners losing power. Shake well in the tribunal that runs North Korea. Stir in economic crisis. Bring to a boil."

"You sound like Chang Can Cook."

Park could tell DeCovasi was beginning to like it. He thrust the dagger home. "Two in particular—Alpha, head of intelligence, and General Myun Chun Kuk—want Park Tai Jin gone. He's listening to the technocrats. This week he met the Chinese. They tell him to open his markets as they have. He's thinking why not. Next, he visits Hong Kong and boards a North Korean ship to return to Pyongyang. Becoming clear?"

"He's vulnerable. Yes."

"Tribunal knows he hates to fly. On the way he'll stop in Niigata. Meet an American VIP. Talk about reunion. An opening to the West. Hard-liners in Pyongyang are getting nervous."

"How did you know about that VIP meeting?"

"Read the papers. Top U.S. official to meet North Korean leader. We figure the coup'll take place after Niigata, before the ship reaches North Korea."

"Why didn't you warn us about this earlier?"

"Just came in. Wanted to check it out. Now I'm sure." And because,

Park thought, you wouldn't have bought it. The second dagger was in. Helim, his queen, had been put into play. Her final moves. The rest was up to the Americans.

DeCovasi was mulling over the information. "The plutonium was part of a plot to discredit the North Korean leader, then."

"Exactly. The murders too."

"How about this fellow Tomás Velaquez?"

"Merely a pawn. They used him to convince the world the sample was his brilliant work. He'd pulled plutonium from Iraq, had a strong reputation. They didn't want anyone to suspect the truth."

"Any hard proof?"

"A large-scale military exercise. An excuse for troops to deploy on alert in Pyongyang and the DMZ. The hard-liners don't want other states to take advantage of turmoil. Read coup."

DeCovasi knew Park was right about that. Velaquez had mentioned troop movement, and satellites had confirmed it. "Do you know how the coup attempt will be made? Precisely where and when?"

"We're working on it. One thing I am sure of. That two hard-line members of the tribunal are behind it: Alpha and General Kuk."

"Yeah. Beginning to make sense."

"I'm heading for Niigata next week to keep in touch with events. Meet Helim tomorrow in San Jose about her TV operation. Got that information on her boyfriend, Juric. Thanks."

"Okay. Keep my office advised. We'll hold off on pulling Helim Kim in."

"I've given you an explanation for the plutonium."

"So you have."

"Don't tell me you won't consider stopping the coup."

"We'll consider all possibilities."

"All you need to do is stop Alpha and General Kuk."

"Intriguing idea, but not easily done."

"They'll both be on Dear Leader's ship when it reaches Niigata. It's an opportunity you'll never have again."

18: JAY'S Los Angeles: Wednesday, 3:00 P.M.

STEVE LEFT A message for Ron Uemura at the FBI office. He'd be at Jay's for the afternoon. Then Steve called his secretary to announce he wouldn't be back today. Urgent business.

Jay's was the kind of place where you could sit back and try to sort things out, just what Steve needed to do. It was located in Burbank next to the Hilton, the bar was large and comfortable, the barmen and waiters left you alone if that was what you wanted.

Damn that man. And he knew Chul Kim was serious. His luck had been too good to last. This whole Korean thing was turning into a disaster, unless he could get Helim to cancel her trip, which he really didn't want to do. It looked like he had no other choice. Or maybe he should just forget the whole thing. Start over. Move to Asia. Yeah, on what, he wondered to himself.

He stared at the dark drink in front of him, watching beads of perspiration slide down the outside of the glass.

"Hey man, what's that frown for?" Ron Uemura slipped onto the stool next to Steve. Ron was a head shorter than Steve but had a strong stocky build. His smooth skin and jet-black hair gleamed with health. He was wearing a dark suit and a conservative tie.

"If it isn't J. Edgar himself. You guys all look alike."

"I know, I know. You're just jealous because I have a steady job."

"How'd you guess?"

"So what's up?" Uemura asked.

"Just wanted to talk. Bummer."

"Let me guess. That Korean angle you've been playing? Last I heard it was going gangbusters."

"Tell me about it. Just exploded in my face."

"How come?"

"My patron is refusing to pay . . . unless I do him a favor regarding his daughter."

"So sue him. You're a lawyer, right?"

"Not that simple."

Uemura cocked an eye. "Nothing to do with this Korean chick you've been thumping?"

"Careful. I'm in love."

"Yeah. Right."

"Her old man."

"What's this tic you've got for hanging out with chicks and ending up working for their old men? First it was Edie. I mean, you married her, right? Worked at the old man's law firm? Now your Korean princess. What's her old man do?"

"Banker."

"Wouldn't be Korean Merchant Bank, would it?"

"Gold star, but stop trying to impress me. There're only three Korean banks in town."

Uemura grimaced. "He wants you to lay off? Leave her alone?"

"No. Why'd you figure that?"

"Well, he's a Korean. Don't get me wrong—there's a lot of Koreans who are my friends. But they usually don't like intermarriage."

"No. It isn't that. Something else."

"I told you before, going with that woman could get you some trouble."

"You know, Uemura," Steve laughed, "sometimes I think you're prejudiced."

"Not at all. But Koreans are a funny race. They don't like Japanese. Chip on their shoulder. Inferiority complex may be the cause. Japanese army occupied their peninsula. Then they got to stay permanently. It was a perfect little arrangement: Japan agreed they wouldn't interfere with the U.S.A.'s takeover of the Philippines if the U.S.A. didn't interfere with Japan's occupation of Korea. Teddy Roosevelt was awarded a Nobel Peace Prize for that little piece of imperialism. The irony was that the U.S.A. eventually kicked Japan out of Korea."

"You talk like you're still Japanese sometimes."

"You know what I mean. I'm trying to educate you. Give perspective. You don't know squat about us Asians, you just think you do. We're a lot more complicated than you give us credit for. So what's the problem?"

"He wants me to talk her out of a trip to Japan."

"What's the big deal?"

"There's more to it. She's involved in a pachinko deal. A company listing. The old man's afraid she's in over her head. He says there are yakuza involved. Danger for her. Seven Koreans murdered this past month. You hear anything?"

"Naw. Not my area. I could check it out, though. But first, why don't you go talk with her? You know. See if she'll back off—think about what she's doing."

Steve reflected. "Yeah. Suppose it wouldn't hurt."

Uemura lifted his glass and pointed it at Steve. "You know what, I don't like this noise I'm hearing. So let me say it again. I wouldn't get too deep with the Korean crowd."

"There you go again."

"Okay, Steve, I'm going to break the rules, because you and I go way back. There's an investigation going on locally. My group's involved. Foreign money. Foreign banks. Illegal election fund contributions to local and national politicians. Beginning to look nasty."

"Koreans?"

"All I can tell you is, be careful."

"I thought we were all through that."

"Yeah, well, think again. It started in '96 with the Chinese guy from Macau. Now it's spread to the Korean peninsula. Like the flu."

Steve thumped a fist on the bar. "Okay. I'll see her tonight."

If Koreans were playing illegal games, maybe Helim was in danger. Anything that happened to her would be his fault. He'd brought up the TV idea, hadn't he? Now he wished he'd never given her advice.

"I mean, find out where her head's at," Uemura said. "Is this other shit more important than your relationship or what? Maybe you don't want to invest any more of your time. See what I mean?"

"Yeah." Steve lifted his drink. He felt anxious, morose, frustrated all at once.

"There's one more thing. This I could get canned for. But there was a work order out on you. A request to investigate your background."

Steve felt everything stop for a moment. "Stop bullshitting me."

"I'm serious. Usually I refuse to get involved in a friend's personal problems. Today I make an exception."

"What's the reason? Why are they investigating me?"

"Take it easy. No reason given. Paper came in from Washington head office. Highest priority. Confidential. Everyone stood to attention. I was asked to contribute. Not every day your best friend is investigated by the brass in D.C."

"Damn." Steve shuddered as thoughts collided in his brain. The FBI kept files on everyone, didn't they? Not really. Only those suspected of wrongdoing. He felt a pinch of fear. His career, his plans, his law firm, his future—calamitous possibilities pulsed through his mind. He took a deep breath.

"Got to be your Korean buddies, that's the way I see it," Uemura said.

"Yeah." Steve tried to sort it out, but nothing made sense. He'd done nothing wrong. Maybe Uemura was right. Maybe Helim's father was passing out illegal funds to American politicians. That would make the FBI interested in him. "Appreciate it, Ron. Really do. Man oh man. This is getting crazy."

"Well, I'm not going to be around to save your ass for a while. So all I can say is, be careful. Big wave coming in."

"What's happening?"

"Leave tomorrow. Special assignment."

"Where?"

"Can't tell anyone. Not even my wife. Involves protection of a VIP is all I know."

Steve grunted. "And they need some Japanese language."

"Okay, smart guy—it is Japan. Buzz is, a former president."

"Call me when you get back. We'll have a drink and I'll let you know how everything turned out."

"Just make sure you're still around."

PERHAPS PARK'S COMMITMENT to a solitary life was the cause. Or the fact that his wife had left him years ago. Or that he demanded perfection of everyone else because he had not yet found it in himself. Whatever the reason, he had constructed his own internal universe, one that did not admit the futility of his plans for return to glory in North Korea. Or the fact that his goals would have been declared insane by any honest court, including the one that Alpha had engineered to exile him from his homeland. For hope was Park's survival mechanism, and it worked in the prison that his life had become.

For that reason he did not size up events properly. He captured them in his verbal and written memos to the FBI's DeCovasi on a canvas that glorified or downgraded depending on whether they enhanced or threatened his personal paradise. In a weak moment he had admitted to Helim his personal spin. For what, he complained, was intelligence if it was not airbrushed to remove the scrotal hairs?

And Park had become good at that. Staying ahead of the tide that he knew was sweeping toward him.

His impending trip to Japan was a current case in point. What could he accomplish there besides getting himself killed? He considered this as he constructed his latest invoice for services and expenses guaranteed by the United States government.

Attention John DeCovasi. "Strictly Confidential." Park knew De-Covasi needed him as much as the moon needed the sun. Didn't like to admit that to anyone else. And that in a computerized war-plans room at the Hoover Building, options to stop the coup were already being analyzed and considered. John didn't fool him with that pretense of disinterest. DeCovasi had taken the bait.

There was a long list of services and costs this time. The list had grown since Park had invented the coup scenario. Bit of genius, he congratulated himself. John had needed something to explain events to his superiors, and Park had delivered. It would accomplish Park's own goal in the bargain.

To remove Alpha and General Kuk for the good of all mankind.

Which left Helim's little end run in Tokyo to bag the killer as well. It would be out of Park's hands, really. The only question was how many would be left standing at the end.

The Americans were paying for his lodging at the Executive Suites in preparation for his meeting with Helim tomorrow. He sealed the letter and invoice with a flourish. Yes. Paid for by the U.S. government. Billed monthly.

The money was remitted to a private account Park maintained at a Swiss institution on an interesting island off the coast of Malaysia that seemed to have only banks as inhabitants. Occasionally he reviewed his monthly statements to determine how high the pile had grown. There was a drop-dead number at which he could pack his bags a final time. Six months, he told himself. Less if he hurried. And if this didn't work, maybe it was time to quit anyway.

He had to see Helim one more time tomorrow. Then he'd book to Japan. Couldn't miss Niigata during the American operation, he decided. Dance on Alpha's bier. No matter the risks. There was a chance to get it right this time. Might be his final one.

19: THE DINNER Los Angeles: Wednesday, 6:30 P.M.

AFTER UEMURA LEFT, Steve invited Helim out to dinner. As he expected, she'd insisted on her turf—a Korean restaurant in West Hollywood. She knew her father didn't want her to go, he'd decided. Maybe she also knew why Steve was being investigated by the FBI's D.C. headquarters.

Evening rush hour was reaching its peak as he headed for the downtown area. Around him, foothills were covered by tracts of silent homes. The crawl of traffic was slowly accelerating as every ramp digested more homeward-bound vehicles.

The first question was how to get Helim to cancel a trip she was so committed to. He could force her to make a choice—the trip or him. But he couldn't take Uemura's advice and simply dump her. She understood him as no one else ever had. He wanted to save their relationship, not destroy it, so forcing her to choose wouldn't work. He'd come up with no other ideas, and tonight might be his last chance to change her mind. She was flying to San Jose tomorrow on business, she said. Soon after to Tokyo.

HELIM WAS DRESSED in a beige Armani suit with a beige Hermès scarf tied over her shoulder. They were seated at a small table in a private room with an inset grill. The air was smoky and smelled of garlic and roast meat. "They have good soju here."

Steve wasn't hungry. "Sounds fine."

A waiter brought wine, and Helim filled both their tiny cups. She had a favor to ask, she told him. He wondered if she knew he had a favor to ask too. A two-hundred-thousand-dollar one.

She lifted her cup, and he did the same. As they drank, their eyes met briefly over the rims. His shifted away first.

"Good," he said. She poured him another. "What's the favor you want?"

"Not now. Later. First drink, but more slowly. Enjoy its flavor and the feel in your throat. Be more gentle. Perhaps," she teased him, "you have only been drinking with kisaeng girls on your Korean trips."

"Maybe I've got a problem tonight. That's why I'm drinking fast." But he drank the soju wine more slowly this time.

"What is it? Your problem."

"Friend of mine tells me I'm being investigated by one of our government's federal agencies. Kind of pisses me off."

"Why on earth would they do that?"

"I was hoping you could tell me."

Helim sipped her wine. "I have no idea."

"It's okay," Steve said, sorry he'd brought it up. "Forget it. Probably just some routine thing."

"We could help each other more if we knew each other better. I started to work on that last time at my apartment. Tonight I want to tell you something more about myself. It may surprise you."

"Not sure I want surprises." Last time it had been secret trips to nuclear reactors in Korea. Every time they met lately, it was like a strip show. She took off a little more of her past.

"If I make you uncomfortable, then let's make it mutual, like playing doctor." She grinned. "You show me and I'll show you. Tell me a little more about yourself first."

"But I already have."

"Not everything. No one tells anybody everything."

Steve wondered if that was some kind of warning, but he shook off the thought. Couldn't be. Not Helim. She was his best chance to escape his emotional wilderness. So he talked about growing up and how hard a time his mother had had when his father lost his job and started drinking and began to disintegrate. How they hadn't had decent food most of the time until his father left and they moved to Fullerton. How his mother had been a shrewd but spiritual Irish woman who worked in a drugstore chain.

People would come to her with prescriptions that had run out or reasons for requiring certain medicines that had not been confirmed by doctors. Fortunately, she had a flexible soul. In return, she would suggest that her son was entering the Golden Gloves and was badly in need of shoes, or that her family liked watermelon, or that there was a certain brand of food she had difficulty finding in the stores of her neighborhood.

She always got what she wanted. When Steve would ask how she had managed his new boxing shoes, she would answer with a mysterious smile. Like Helim's.

Over the meal, he shared with her in detail what he had only mentioned in passing before: how he'd decided on a law degree, worked his way through school lifeguarding and teaching water sports. A few semipro bouts. Then he'd married the boss's daughter, joined his father-in-law's international law firm, become an Asian specialist, and for five years traveled the Orient on one contract after another. She knew the rest.

"That's so interesting," she said. "I love it when you open up to me like this. Now it's my turn. Can I tell you a story? It's quite different from yours, but it'll explain the favor I need to ask you."

"Sure."

"Involves an ancient shaman princess named Jingu. She's my childhood idol."

"Okay."

"Then close your eyes and think of a beautiful woman."

"Right." Helim's face filled his internal vision.

"This is Jingu," Helim began, "a Korean princess who conquered Japan in the fourth century. She and her son introduced Confucianism and changed Japan forever. Afterward, when her son became emperor of all Japan, she passed away. Her son was the first Korean emperor of Japan. Japanese deny this happened, of course, but Jingu really lived, the son really ruled Japan. Confucianism took root. This all happened because of Jingu and is history written in the *Nihongi*, the ancient Japanese chronicles, over a thousand years ago. There are even royal burial mounds near Osaka the Japanese government will not allow anyone near."

Then she told him the rest of the story.

In the fourth century, Jingu was commanded to conquer the Land of Across by King Chuai, leader of the Paekche. Even then, Japan was a land of many riches. So with fierce cavalry troops from Paekche led by Old Bear, Jingu's lover, and money from Silla, she built a fine fleet of ships, which were loaded with cavalry and landed in Kyushu, the southernmost island of Japan.

They won victory after victory, moving steadily up the main Japan island as far as what is today known as Osaka. But Jingu had become pregnant by her lover. In order to delay the birth until she had won a total victory over the Japanese, she inserted egg-shaped rocks in her loins. Thus, her pregnancy lasted over eleven months, enough time to gain control over most of Japan and ensure that her son would be ruler. According to the *Nihongi*, Ojin, her son, was born on the fourteenth day of the twelfth month. After she took the rocks from her loins.

Old Bear died, but she carried on alone. After reigning for many years, she had her son enthroned as emperor. When she saw her son was a good leader over Japan, she knew her work was done. One evening, after she had bathed and prayed to her forefathers, she found a high place by the great ocean which was father and mother to us all. There she took out a jeweled knife that had been handed down from her ancestors. This she set by her side. Two snow-white gulls appeared in the rocks near her. She thought of her life and was satisfied. When she saw the gulls fly together out toward the setting sun, she knew it was time.

She clasped the knife between her teeth and threw off her robe so that her still-beautiful body was nude. Then she dove into the ocean and swam toward the setting sun to return the sacred knife to her ancestors.

"She ended her life?"

"She flowed into another life in the never-ending stream of energy where the sun meets the horizon. To live again, she died, yes." Helim sat back and peered at him through latticed fingers. "You see, she was a shaman."

For a moment, Steve felt closer to Helim than he'd ever been. He believed he understood. She was Jingu. He wondered what her mission was.

Helim gazed with half-closed lids at distant destinations. "There's a war being fought for the future of the Korean peninsula. I'm interested in the future of Korean women. The listing of pachinko firms has far-reaching implications for them. More than I can say."

"Your father told me it's very dangerous."

"That's not the reason he tries to keep me here. My father didn't tell you the whole truth. He and my grandmother hate each other. If Allied International gets its listing, my grandmother will be much richer than she is now, and richer than my father. I too will become rich. My father will no longer have control over either of us. That's why."

Steve took a deep breath. "Helim, your father . . . suggested that I try to stop you from going to Japan, from getting entangled in this whole pachinko listing business. I'm starting to agree with him it sounds risky. Besides—"

"Besides what?" Helim said quickly. "Are you afraid you'll lose his approval? I thought you were stronger than that." She looked at him with a hint of disgust.

"Don't be ridiculous," he said, offended, although a part of him wondered if it was true. He sensed her determination, which caused a fear to rise inside him. He could lose more than her love. He didn't want anything to happen to her. "I don't want you to go either."

"Many people are counting on me," she countered abruptly, wishing Steve could understand that she was bound in irrevocable ways to a homeland she'd never known.

"Something terrible's going to happen, I feel it in my bones. Look, why don't you just delay your trip to Japan? Your father and I are both worried. You don't know what you're getting into. He is exerting a lot of pressure."

She glanced up at him quietly. "He knows your business has been slow, Steve. Perhaps that's why he picked on you to help him. He always does that. Tries to control people. What did he do, threaten to cancel your contract?"

"Look, it's not the money!" He was trying to keep her from getting hurt, he told himself. Worse.

"He'll back down in the end. Don't worry." She was gathering her things, her voice tight with emotion.

Like hell he will, Steve thought. Chul Kim was as stubborn as his daughter. "What are you doing?"

"I have an early flight tomorrow. The Japanese TV station will release the story I've given them in a few hours."

"Please understand, Helim, I'm very happy for you. But this stunt you're pulling in Japan could be very dangerous. Your father said Koreans *are being murdered*. I really don't want you to go. Maybe you and your father and this trip are why I'm being investigated by my own government."

"No. You're wrong. I'm dealing with Japanese who want to control the Korean peninsula. Who look down on Koreans as their former slaves. As inferior beings. It's my duty—as it was Jingu's—to show the Japanese we Koreans are equals. That's the reason I am going to Japan."

Damn, she was obstinate. She saw herself as another Jingu. A gallant, brave, capable leader. Even if that was true, she was taking on the Japanese government. "But you're an American. Why get involved in all this foreign stuff?" It didn't make sense to him. Why was she so obsessed with her past?

Helim sat up straight, her eyes flashing. "Is that what you think?"

"My father's Yugoslavian, my mother's Irish, but I didn't rush over to get involved in either of their wars. You're not North Korean, your ancestors were. You're American! Meddling in others' affairs is dangerous. It could get you in trouble with our government."

"Everything's so logical for you, isn't it, Steve? So simple. One day maybe you'll understand what I've been trying to tell you. For some things, you have to follow your heart, not your mind. Then you'll know what true love is. I'm sorry I couldn't teach you that. I tried." She stood.

"Let's not fight, okay?"

"You think danger is only for men. Do you know what a comfort woman is?"

"Yes."

"My grandmother was one. Does that shock you?"

Steve blinked. "Jesus, Helim. No. I . . ." He couldn't find the right words. Something was pounding in his brain.

"You want to know danger? She was kept near the front lines. To service the troops. She nearly died many times. Horrible things happened to her."

"Look, I'm sorry." His mind was in tumult. My lover's grandmother was a sex slave? Tabloid fare! He waited for his logic to kick in. Just say it's cool and go on to the next surprise. But wait. How many more did Helim have? His emotions were churning.

"I work with an association," Helim was saying, "that started out as a society of comfort women. The pachinko listing will raise funds to help our causes. Many have joined our work. Including men. That's another reason I travel often to Asia. I work with an Asian pro-democracy group. Because the members, both men and women, understand the soul of Asian women. We don't want to be used. To be looked down on. To be raped, burned, circumcised, bought and sold. To have no self-esteem."

"But that is all changing."

"Because Asian women are fighting for their rights. And the rights of their children!"

"I can understand that. But I still want you to stay."

"No way." Her eyes smoldered as she picked up her pocketbook, adjusted the strap over her shoulder. Steve was siding with her father for money. For concern over his own career. For fear of being investigated. For all the logical reasons. She tried to hide her disappointment. She took a step back from the table. "This isn't going to work, Steve. It's my fault. I travel too much. And now you know the real me. My Asian side wants to be a crusader. My American side is trying to organize the crusade. One foot in the clouds, the other in . . . oh hell, it's just better if we don't see each other for a while."

"I love you." It was the first time he had uttered those words to her, and he realized that he meant them . . . completely.

"Too late, Steve. Much too late."

"Please let me help you."

"No! I have baggage. Family. Money. Politics. You don't want this. Believe me."

As she walked out of the room, a final urge to turn and throw herself into his arms surged through her body. She lengthened her stride, furious with herself. She was trapped. And the cage was stronger than her will or power to love.

20: ATTEMPT Los Angeles: Wednesday, 8:00 P.M.

STEIG HAD FOLLOWED Helim to the Korean restaurant, watched her meet a good-looking fellow and take one of the private rooms containing a table with barbecue grill. He could see them through the open door. Her body language told him she liked this man. This was the boyfriend Aleksei had warned him about. The American was nearly his own size and looked fit. Still, there would be no problem taking him if he had to.

He sipped a Bushmills and water. Not too much drink tonight, he warned himself. Only arrived yesterday. Want to keep the edge. He was looking for a chance. It depended on what she did. And what this American did. Although they could not know it, their lives depended on each other now.

Not that he liked this contract. The girl was too good to die. Too young, with looks that one did not see often enough. He liked efficiency, not waste. Still, clients like his were increasingly hard to come by. She had done something that angered them. Whoever the clients were. Not Asian, he'd decided. One of the majors. Using Asians and the Slav, Aleksei, to contact him and front the operation.

Steig paid his bill as Helim and her escort were finishing their meal. Then he went outside to wait. The parking attendant came up to him. "Your number, sir?"

Steig gave it to him with a tip, knowing he'd be recognized here. He never took chances. That was his rule. He'd have to do it wherever they went next.

He was about to pull away when Helim stormed out. He stared at her. She looked even more ravishing when she was angry. She thrust her ticket at the attendant.

Shame, Steig thought. He waited near the entrance until she left. Alone.

Staying several cars behind, he followed her white Audi into the foothills. East. Here the road began to wind tortuously. She was driving very fast. Love quarrel, Steig figured. Happens to the best of us.

They flew by homes arrogantly perched on precarious hillsides. Lit by floodlights, for security as well as ostentation, he told himself. Key characteristics of the best democracies. Then they were through the residential area and into the hinterlands. She drove even faster now, and for a moment Steig worried that his rented car might not keep up. He floored it. His bigger car gradually gained momentum and began to close on the Audi until he eased off again several hundred yards back.

Finally they were in higher canyons. He turned off his headlights, narrowing his eyes. His target's decision to speed furiously through the Hollywood Hills was going to have disastrous consequences. He focused on the road and began to overtake her.

TWICE BEFORE WHEN she'd wanted to vent her anger, Helim had done it up here on Canyon Drive. On Park's advice last year she'd taken a race driver's certificate at a two-week course in Sacramento. "You never know," he'd said.

She dared herself not to brake, downshifting on the hairpin turns, the tires squealing their own anger. She was going to forget all about Steve. Damn him. She couldn't believe he could be such a coward. She should have known better than to trust him. Any man, for that matter.

She noticed the car without lights trying to pass on a section clearly marked for no passing.

"Idiot," she shouted. She wrenched the gearshift into high and floored the gas pedal. The Audi took off, leaving the other car in its wake. She did not let up on the next turn, nor the next. Not until the other car had disappeared completely did she swing suddenly into a turnoff, douse her lights, and wait. The other car came screaming past. Still on the hunt.

There'd been times she'd been followed from restaurants before. Some Casanova who thought he was a hot shot. Unless it was . . .

No. So far, no one knew about what she planned to reveal on Japanese TV. Except Park and the Japanese TV station. Just to be sure, she pulled out of the turnoff and, heading in the opposite direction, drove back to her apartment. Not until she was safely in her garage did she relax.

Could someone at the Japanese TV station have leaked her plans? Very possible. A clever intelligence service could easily have found out. Helim was sure it wasn't Park. An attack on her wouldn't serve his cause. If it did, however, she had no illusions about what he'd do. She recalled a Korean proverb: "Nothing is certain if you are." She wouldn't trust him again. Or Katano. She wouldn't trust anyone.

PART THREE

Long live the snake that doesn't bite me.

Korean aphorism

21 ⁝ THE POL Saitama: Thursday, 6:30 A.M.

"EAT YOUR FISH," Mitsuko ordered.

"I don't feel like fish this morning." Mori prodded the saba with his chopsticks. A saba was full of bones; eating it took concentration.

They were sitting on cushions at a low lacquer table in the tatami room of their new apartment in Saitama. Mori had grown up in two tiny rooms less than one-fifth the size. It was six-thirty in the morning. His wife usually left by seven for the ninety-minute trip to Tokyo—an average commute, with flat prices so high close to the city. His wife worked at a government think tank charged with developing new-generation computers. A perfectionist, or at least so it seemed to him. She thrived on technology, which Mori understood little about. And she drove him crazy with rules that kept their new apartment spotless. Otherwise, they got along fine.

The demands of his job didn't destroy their marriage, but simply created a traditional Japanese one. The husband and wife went their own ways, expecting only their due. Mitsuko controlled all money; Mori was away from home frequently. She had insisted on one safety valve: when she considered any of his bad habits slipping into excess, she was free to say so. That had led to several fights, which his mother, who lived with them, had arbitrated by taking his side.

"You were late again," Mitsuko sighed. "I thought you were going to cut back on your drinking. How many times have I told you it's bad for your heart? And you're going to lose your hair too. Then the bar girls will ignore you."

"I was working until late last night."

"You were drinking again, weren't you?" She turned to face him.

"You wouldn't drink so much if you really loved me. You promised you'd ease up last time we discussed it."

"I wasn't drinking much. Just a few with the boys." Mori shifted uncomfortably. Even the appearance of a marriage had its cost. "If I didn't love you, I would drink more," he said. "This case is driving me crazy. We're chasing a killer who specializes in Korean pachinko hall owners. No one can figure out why." Mori leaned across to kiss her, but she turned her cheek.

"So don't worry so much about each assignment they give you."

"This case is my responsibility. I don't want to lose face."

"You always have some excuse, don't you? How come you're not eating the fish? You don't like it?" She eyed him suspiciously. "I can't cook fish like your mother can. That's it, isn't it?"

"You cook it fine," he said. "I'm sick of this business, that's all. Lost my appetite." He reminded himself that he had an eight-thirty at Jiro's for breakfast with Ayumi. All day yesterday she'd been doing research based on the trip to Niigata Tuesday. He'd asked her to see what she could develop on the Korean Merchant Bank. Probably stayed up most of the night. "Why pachinko hall owners should be singled out is hard to fathom. Except that they have a lot of money that somehow gets sent back to the Korean peninsula. All North Koreans, too."

"Maybe it's political," Mitsuko said. "North Korean groups are demonstrating in front of the Diet with bullhorns for and against reunion. Causing disturbance. Asking for money."

Mori stared at her. She'd gotten part of it right, anyway. Sometimes her insights frightened him. Ever since his trip to Kobe, he'd been mulling how to locate a foreigner hired by hard-liners in Pyongyang. Couldn't arrest the entire North Korean government, could he? Mitsuko had an uncanny instinct. Did she know he played around occasionally? She'd never mentioned it. "Good thinking," Mori said.

"I can tell you one thing—people here are beginning to worry what will happen if the North liberalizes and sets up joint ventures with the South. Maybe one day reunites. Companies like Samsung would have access to cheap North Korean labor. Many Japanese in the electronics field fear a North Korean liberalization. The Korean semiconductor industry is already overtaking Japan. They've won thirty percent of the chip market away from us in three years. And all this recent economic turmoil in Asia hasn't helped."

"Reunion isn't feasible. Both countries are nearly broke. Liberalization's another matter." It bothered Mori that she could put her finger on something right away that had taken him weeks or months to figure out. That was why he found it best to agree with her no matter what his private opinion. Today as at other times, he'd decided the best policy was just to listen.

She said, "There are some who argue the Koreans are going to pass us in the future. If there is a liberalization."

Mori started to read the morning paper. The headlines this morning were about another scandal in the Diet.

"Kenzo Tanemura gave a talk to us several weeks ago, and he thinks so. As head of the semiconductor cartel, he must be well informed, don't you think?"

Mori looked up. Tanemura was a high-ranking member of the Diet and sat on the Intelligence Committee, although he rarely attended the meetings. Some said he was next in line for the prime minister's job. His daughter, Yuka, was a public prosecutor, the only one of them Mori could stand working with. Sometimes they had lunch.

"Tanemura-san is promoting closer relations with North Korea to prevent a disaster from happening," Mitsuko went on.

"Well, I hope we don't have to depend on our politicians to save us," Mori said.

"You don't have to be sarcastic, anata. Some of them are clever. And don't spill that soup on the tatami."

22: THE KMB Tokyo: Thursday, 8:30 A.M.

AYUMI WAS WAITING for him when he arrived at Jiro's. As always, he felt rejuvenated when he saw her eager face. It was a marvel how she looked bright and fresh every morning while Mori felt wrung out.

Formally, she handed him the report on the Korean Merchant Bank.

Mori read the summary over the special advertised on the front window: one poached egg, toast, coffee, and two pieces of lettuce that passed as a salad.

There were few surprises in it. The bank was owned by local Koreans; most of the money deposited there was Korean. The objective of the bank as stated in its incorporation papers was to foster Korean-owned business in Japan. Looked perfectly routine to him. Except for one thing: ten years ago, it had opened a branch in Los Angeles.

"How are the Korean directors chosen in the Tokyo head office?"

"We don't know."

"Okay. Then what do we know about its political connections?"

"Apparently it's close to the North Korean Association. The Chosen Soren."

" 'Apparently' bothers me."

Ayumi explained that all executives of the bank were of North Korean heritage, but it was not known if they were North Korean Association members. The lists were kept secret. Most of the bank's major depositors in Japan were also known North Koreans. Both personal and business accounts. But again there was no proof they were association members.

"Can we assume that if this KMB is owned by North Koreans in Japan and is close to the North Korean Association, it essentially acts as an arm of the North Korean government too? A foreign exchange bank here for North Korea?"

"That's what the Bank of Japan privately believes," Ayumi agreed.

"Nice work." Mori put the report down. He'd bet anything the damn bank was virtually an arm of the North Korean government. "How about the bank's Los Angeles branch? Could it be involved?"

"In laundering, sir? Not directly, I wouldn't think."

"Just a minute. Something's been bothering me about that L.A. office. How did a North Korean–controlled bank get a license to operate inside the U.S.A.?"

"The bank's headquartered in Japan, isn't it? Therefore the California banking license was applied for and obtained in the name of a Japanese banking entity. California authorities probably didn't check very carefully. Many Japanese banks were applying for licenses ten years ago at the same time the KMB did. The California Bank Board just considered it another application from Japan. There was no way of uncovering the North Korean connection. Even we can't say it exists for sure."

It all made sense. Ayumi had done a thorough job. "Why would the North Koreans want a bank branch in the United States, their sworn enemy? Think about that while I get more coffee."

"I'll have a Pepsi."

Mori went to the counter. When he returned, Ayumi said, "There's a huge immigrant Korean population in the United States. Many are naturalized Americans. However, their roots are still in North or South Korea."

"So they send money home, like all other expats in the U.S.A.?"

"Sure. The KMB could easily route money to North Korea through Hong Kong. But there are ways they could use money in the U.S.A, as we know."

Mori had lifted his coffee cup and now paused it in midair. "Like?"

"Paying lobbyists in Washington to influence the U.S. government's policies toward North Korea. Paying others to collect information. The KMB could be an intelligence clearinghouse."

Mori understood the FBI interest now. DeCovasi had paid him a visit to find out more about a Helim Kim. He'd have to get that done soon. Could be a connection. "Okay. I get the point. Who's in charge of this Los Angeles banking operation the North Koreans are running? Any background?"

"Yes." Ayumi checked her documentation. "It's run by a former executive of their head office operation in Tokyo. Nothing about North Korea in his background, though."

"What is the director's name?"

"Perhaps you know him. Mr. Chul Kim?"

Kim? Many Koreans were named Kim. Probably a coincidence. "Local Korean, born in Japan?"

"Yes. I pulled a background on him. Born in Japan, graduated from the local Korean university. Joined the Korean Merchant Bank in 1975 and rose to a vice presidency. Ten years ago he was sent to the United States to negotiate the opening of the branch. Since then he's directed its operations. He's a widower with one daughter born in Japan. A Helim Kim, who is a naturalized U.S. citizen now. Her father never applied."

Helim Kim! So there *was* a connection. Mori made a note and underlined it. "How about Kim's political activities in Japan? I'm sure he was watched. Any connections to Pyongyang?"

"None I could find. Lots of connections in the Japanese business and banking community. A very astute and successful executive. Comments about him are that he's just like a Japanese. You can't tell the difference. That is the supreme compliment for a Korean, right?"

"What are his business connections?"

"The Sakura Bank Group, Mitsui, and Fuji Securities. And he's close to some Social Democratic Party pols."

"Which pol in particular?"

"Mr. Kenzo Tanemura. A Diet member some people say is in line for the prime minister's job. He helped Kim get his visas for overseas travel when he first went to the U.S.A."

Tanemura again! Mitsuko had said this morning that Tanemura was concerned about North Korean liberalization and reunion. He wondered if there was any connection to Pyongyang here. Perhaps a Korean banker would know. "Why was Kim's visa a problem?"

"Because most Koreans here are stateless. Every time they go abroad, they have to apply for Red Cross passports. That's time-consuming and complicated. Mr. Tanemura helped Kim get one right away with no waiting."

"How come you have so much on him?"

"Computers are wonderful animals. Besides, there's a punch line."

"Tell me."

"He's a widower, as I said, sees a local girl when he's in town. Took her on a trip to Phuket last year. A Korean girl who works at a cabaret and feeds us information. There's a cross-reference to your name in the file, so I assume she is one of your field. Tomi Chang. Club Reo." A keenness entered Ayumi's eyes as she watched Mori's face. To her great disappointment, there wasn't the slightest glimmer of surprise.

"One last thing," Mori said after a long pause. "Do me a favor and see what you can find out about this Helim Kim. No one else—absolutely no one else—is to know. I understand from what you've said that she used to be a resident of Japan. There should be a file on her."

23: **COMPUTER CHECK** Tokyo: Thursday, 9:30 A.M.

AYUMI SAT DOWN at her computer and started her search.

An hour later the name Helim Kim had been checked thoroughly, using Japanese tax, resident, and police record files. She had been born in Japan in 1970, had lived in Tokyo and attended a Korean school through twelfth grade before immigrating to the United States ten years earlier. She was registered on tax office files as co-owner of an apartment in Asakusa, Tokyo, with her grandmother, Jonquil Kim. Land tax payments for the apartment had been received annually from a Miss Helim Kim, present address Kim Associates Inc., La Vista Condominiums, Westwood, Los Angeles, California. Her grandmother's name was listed on the board of directors of one Japanese company, Allied International Ltd.

Ayumi checked Jonquil Kim, and found she had entered Japan in 1945 as an alien and, like most Koreans, had never been granted Japanese citizenship. She had never traveled abroad. Until a merger in 1996 with Allied International, Jonquil Kim had been owner of a chain of twenty pachinko halls located mainly in the Asakusa district of downtown Tokyo. So the grandmother had a connection with pachinko!

The Allied International computer printout was completed thirty minutes later.

It had been formed three years earlier. One hundred pachinko hall owners, representing over three thousand pachinko halls, or 20 percent of all halls in Japan, had incorporated. In 1998, it accounted for an estimated 15 percent of the pachinko industry's annual revenue. The company was privately controlled by the original owners, who were of Korean descent. Detailed financial information was not available. The report concluded with a list of Allied's banks, which included the Korean Merchant

Bank, Tokyo head office. A footnote added that Allied International Ltd. had recently filed for listing on the Tokyo Stock Exchange. The application had been turned down.

"YOU SAID IT was quite important. And off the record. I am always pleased to help the Japanese police when I can." Sugiura was a director of the Korean Merchant Bank and in charge of public relations. Mori had called after his meeting with Ayumi.

"Thank you," Mori said. "We need some background on your bank, that's all."

"No problem."

"Excuse me, I notice that your name is Japanese. But you are Korean?"

"Many Koreans change their names to Japanese," Sugiura said petulantly. "It makes things a little easier here. Actually, I have a Korean name as well."

"The Korean Merchant Bank has its head office in Tokyo, I understand."

"Yes. Incorporated in Japan and therefore a Japanese bank."

"I've heard it's owned by Koreans. Mainly Koreans of Northern ancestry who reside in Japan."

"I haven't studied our shareholder list recently, but that could be true."

"Investments are made in North Korea from time to time, then?"

"With approval from the Bank of Japan, of course."

"Of course. And you have a Los Angeles office, headed by a Mr. Kim?"

"Yes, we do."

"What is its main purpose?"

"To support Korean business in the United States."

"Import, then?"

"A variety of business. We've helped the Korean community in Los Angeles become autonomous."

"Admirable, Sugiura-san. So U.S. business is good?"

"You could say so. Many Koreans live there now who escaped from the North during and immediately after the Korean War. They are upstanding members of the U.S. community."

"Marvelous, yes. And Mr. Chul Kim, he's an American?"

"No. Stateless, like most Koreans who were born in Japan. Our bank branch acts as his guarantor, and every three years he renews his U.S. residence. One day he'll return to the Tokyo head office."

"Married, then?"

"Widowed. His wife died some years ago."

"And I understand he has a daughter?"

"Yes. Lovely girl. I should say woman."

"You know her?"

"Oh no, not well. Just seen her a few times when she's stopped by the office on business."

"What kind of business?"

"Well, as I recall it was for her grandmother. She has a chain of pachinko parlors."

"Done well?"

"Yes. The daughter handles her investments. Bright girl. I've heard she has a photographic memory."

Mori thought about that a moment. Good memories made good spies. "We believe her father knows a Diet member, Mr. Tanemura."

"I can't help you there."

"We believe that the Diet member's office helped him to obtain travel documents when he first went to the United States."

"Tanemura knows several of our board members and helps out with problems like that. I frankly doubt that Mr. Kim knows him personally. He is a friend of all North Koreans living in Japan."

"An outstanding human being," Mori agreed. "Does Mr. Tanemura visit your bank occasionally? Or does a member of his office?"

"Only on business related to developing relations with North Korea and other sister Asian nations."

"Do you know the purpose of these visits lately?"

"Of course. He's promoting a huge free trade zone adjacent to North Korea where the borders of China, North Korea, and Russia meet. The Asia Tomorrow Project. It will be for the good of all Asians."

"Is that all?"

"Yes."

"Thank you for speaking with me on the phone this morning, Sugiura-san," Mori said. "And you needn't worry about anything. Your secrets are safe with me."

A few moments after he'd hung up, Mori had a call from Ayumi. She told him what she'd found out. He decided it was time to visit the Kims' apartment. He put his burglar kit together and headed out.

24: TRIP Los Angeles: Thursday, 10:30 A.M.

ON THE PLANE to San Jose, Helim considered the nightmare last night. The fight with Steve. That wild ride. She'd nearly killed herself up on Canyon Drive purging Steven from her thoughts. Absolutely insane.

When she returned to her apartment, she'd yanked the phone jack out of the wall. Eaten all the chocolate she could find and levered a chair against the bedroom door handle, left the lights on, and, just in case, placed the lady's-weight Makarov pistol on her bedstand. Russian-made. Silver. Present from a friend. Maybe that crazy driver, who nearly ran her off the road, hadn't been just some Romeo. She needed time to think.

She had nightmares when she tried to sleep. The strange car on Canyon Drive returned. She dreamed someone was chasing her. When she awakened this morning, she'd felt drained. Steve was gone, she told herself. Erase him from your thoughts. But she couldn't. She was just upset; no one was trying to kill her.

Helim's appointment in San Jose was not, strictly speaking, a business engagement. She'd rented a car at the San Jose airport, then driven to a small Italian restaurant located in the Stanford Mall.

"Good morning, Park Chung Il," she said in North Korean dialect.

"You are looking well, as always." Park handed her a package that was surprisingly light.

"What is it?"

"That lacquer box you admired at my flat last time you visited Helsinki. I found a duplicate in an antique shop. An exquisite piece from one of our northern provinces."

"I'll open it when I get home. How very thoughtful." She took the package, wondering what had caused this sudden act of kindness. She thought of their last meeting at LAX. That wild drive on Canyon Road last night. Did he expect a gift to replace a loss of trust? She'd nearly decided to cancel her trip. But the TV exposure might get pachinko firms listed. If it did and she sold her shares, it would make her rich. Free. Money that also could be used in good causes for Asian women and children.

"So, I understand you got the trade you wanted."

"Yes," she said nonchalantly. "KSB-TV bought my deal."

Park congratulated himself, since this would really upset Pyongyang. "Who agreed?"

"Hideo Katano. The news celebrity who takes up people's causes. In return for the diary, he agreed to give me airtime to talk about pachinko extortion and laundering problems."

"That should scare the shit out of anyone behind the killings. Be careful. You told this boyfriend of yours nothing?"

"Nothing of importance. It was his idea, of course, so I had to say something. But when I mentioned it to him he seemed to have forgotten entirely about it."

"Bless you, Helim. Part brilliance and part charlatan—what power you wield. I have to, ah, make an admission."

"About what?"

"I took the liberty of doing a little background research on your good friend Steven."

"I could have saved you the time. He has nothing to hide."

"Not quite true. But then none of us are faultless, are we?"

"Stop it, Park."

"His former employers were scathing. Apparently he negotiated several contracts in Asia that embarrassed them."

"He divorced the boss's daughter, Park. You can't expect them to exactly cover him with praise."

"I'll accept that. But there was the matter of a South Korean venture he negotiated—the brother of a government official who approved the venture sold the American client a factory site in Taegu at twice the going price. And also a production facility in Taiwan—the nephew of the prime minister was given a lucrative outside directorship."

"I'm sure it's all explainable." She remembered Steve's telling her how his father-in-law had taught him how to cheat. How he'd put that all behind him. The father-in-law was cynically blaming everything on Steve.

Park said, "He sails rather close to the wind. Bit of the clipper captain in him, I'd say. Just a touch of rogue. One of his best friends is with the local FBI. They're investigating a series of improper election fund contributions by Koreans and other Asians in the Los Angeles area. This friend and Juric meet frequently. Your name has come up. Your father's. That's all I can tell you."

"You're being really unfair." Park was paranoid, that was the problem. Particularly when it came to men who were close to her. Whatever else Steve was, she couldn't imagine he'd do anything to hurt her. Or her father.

"I'm being careful. I wish you'd be the same."

"If it makes you feel any better, last night, Steve and I split."

"Thank you, Helim."

"It wasn't for you. I'm not making any guarantees."

"When will you go to Japan?"

"In a few days." She had booked two flights, one for this weekend and one for next week. Katano had said to come as soon as she could, to fax him when she departed and he'd meet her at Narita. Tonight, she'd fly back to Los Angeles and decide.

"They may not live up to your conditions."

"They will. Particularly Katano. He believes he is the conscience of all Japan."

LATER THAT NIGHT, Park called a Finnish contact in Helsinki, a man with connections to the KGB. He was brief. He was trying to learn the whereabouts of an American woman who had been working for the Red Cross circa July 1941 when she was taken prisoner by Japanese soldiers and forced to work in a military brothel in Harbin. Harbin had been repatriated by Soviet Red Army troops. There was a possibility she was still alive and in Russia. Perhaps some information about this woman could be obtained. First name Elizabeth, with a Z. Efforts appreciated.

25: **THE FIND** Tokyo: Thursday, 11:15 A.M.

MORI WALKED INTO the pachinko hall and looked around.

A morning crowd played with the intensity of the unemployed needing luck. The seats were half full. It was a relatively small pachinko hall, maybe two hundred machines, he estimated. A tough hall. Maybe business was too good.

This was the first pachinko parlor owned by Jonquil Kim, according to Ayumi's report. Mori had the urge to try a game or two, but resisted. The owner's office was in back near the gift counter. He peeked in. An elderly lady was working at a desk. Mori thought about paying Jonquil Kim a visit, then decided against that too. His training warned him off.

Don't touch the pachinko hall, he told himself. That's tax office domain. Just check out the apartment.

Local Koreans could be trouble: emotional as children, not given to telling the truth, and their history in Japan was at best unfortunate.

Mori left the hall and walked across the street to a gray concrete derelict of an apartment building. Unwashed glass doors slid open, then closed behind him, cutting off the shriek of pachinko music. In the lobby, a store selling shrine ornaments reeked of incense, as did the single creaky elevator that served all eight floors; the Kims' apartment was on the seventh.

With all the money this old lady must have, why did she still live here? He remembered his Oyabun telling him once that the really smart rich were those who didn't show it. Particularly the pachinko Koreans in Japan who don't like to pay taxes, Mori thought.

Mori stood in the dim hall, getting his bearings and taking out his lock picks. Behind a nearby door, Korean music blared. He found the

Kims' door and worked the lock expertly. The door opened. Minute and a half. Getting rusty, he told himself.

Most apartments in Japan were built according to code. A kitchen and hall as you entered, with a living room and bedroom in the rear. Everything was predictable and interchangeable. No surprises, the way Japanese like things. He closed the door carefully. No noise.

In the bedroom he went through three chests of drawers, locating the secret compartment in back of the jewelry cubbyhole that was common to such chests. He found a photocopy of a book of lined paper and flipped open the yellowed pages. The photocopy had been made many years ago. He wondered where the original was. Written in Japanese, it was apparently a diary kept by the grandmother. Her name was carefully printed on the first page, Jonquil Kim, with the date, 1941, and the place, Harbin, China.

The first words described a woman in great distress and mental torment.

He stopped reading after a few pages. Kamisama, god, it was not what he'd expected at all. Jonquil Kim had served the Japanese Imperial Army as a comfort woman, sent to Harbin from Pyongyang. She had been only eighteen, a senior in high school.

"This is shameful," he murmured to himself. It was a common enough story, though. And now he knew why Jonquil Kim had chosen not to return to Korea.

Mori closed the book and replaced it. At least in this case the tragedy had had a happy ending, it seemed. There was nothing in the apartment that would interest his FBI friend DeCovasi. Or that was related to the pachinko murder case. Nothing at all.

WHEN HE GOT back to his office there was a note from his boss, Aoyama: "See me immediately." As Mori headed down the hall, he had a sense of foreboding. Yesterday, Aoyama had threatened to take him off this case if he didn't see results soon. "Why should we be spending good Japanese tax money on Koreans?" Aoyama had inquired. "My friends at the Diet will have me replaced for seditious behavior, won't they? And you'd laugh all the way to my hanging."

"Not at all," Mori had said. He and Aoyama rarely agreed on anything. "We're training people here for other divisions, are we not? One must light fires before making swords."

Mori stepped into Aoyama's office without knocking.

Aoyama looked up and frowned. "Intelligence Committee meeting this afternoon at four P.M. Usual place. Tanemura-san will attend today, so be on your best behavior."

"Certainly, Aoyama-san." Mori waved with mock cordiality.

"What is this I hear about a North Korean boat operation Tuesday? You put one of your field agents aboard a North Korean ship wearing a wire?"

"The boat left today. For Hong Kong."

"You jeopardized one of our best Korean—"

"Moles," Mori said. "And Tomi *is* our best."

"Tomi Chang? Our best and brightest, and you jeopardized her without an authorization from the Intelligence Committee!" A cloud passed behind his eyes, and Mori knew then that there was something more coming. Something to Aoyama's benefit. "I assume she was working on one of your cases?"

"The pachinko murders."

Aoyama pretended to be surprised. "Really? You jeopardized her over a couple of Koreans? And after I told you we're thinking of discontinuing the case? Handing it back to the police?"

Mori's dislike for Aoyama went back to the days when they were both in the National Police. "I asked her to explore something."

"Explore something? She was unauthorized, Mori. You didn't run your 'explore something' by me or the Intelligence Committee. This could be very serious."

Mori swallowed his anger. "The operation came up with valuable yield."

"I heard there wasn't any value whatsoever! What did you get?"

"A possible laundering operation to the North Koreans. Involving Japanese government officials."

"Don't be ridiculous. I hate to say this, Mori-san, but I may have to bring up the entire mess to the Intelligence Committee this afternoon."

"Please do." Mori understood Aoyama was bluffing. "It's volatile, Aoyama. And the PM can't risk another scandal."

Aoyama hesitated. "You made an independent decision to insert a valuable field agent aboard a North Korean ship. Foreign territory, which requires the highest level of approval. That you didn't get! And now you're also setting Japanese government policy?" His voice rose. "If the PM's office gets hold of this, they'll blame me. You knew that, didn't you!"

Mori tried unsuccessfully to swallow his smile.

"Don't laugh! This is going to be your ass, not mine. I guarantee you that. And from today on, I want you to stop wasting our assets and time on this Korean case. Today I'm going to suggest this at the Intelligence Committee meeting. Let them decide. We're going to turn it over to the Tokyo police and the prosecutor's office. Let them deal with those deaths. Clear?"

Mori bit his lip, then turned suddenly and strode out of the room.

26: **THE COMPROMISE** Tokyo: Thursday, 1:45 P.M.

BACK IN HIS office, Mori sat for several minutes deliberating. He didn't feel like lunch. He needed results. His team wasn't getting them. Aoyama was going to cut off his nuts if he could. He swung around to stare out the window.

Like his forebears, Mori possessed sensitivity of character combined with a warrior's spirit. He could applaud or commiserate with his team's tiniest triumphs and most serious failures; perceive the honest reasons for their inadequacies, and, when the time came, take responsibility for every failed case and distraught superior.

"We're just beginners," he liked to say. "We must accept failure if we are to grow." Or, "There's a bit of the thief in all good law enforcers—we just don't have enough thieves around here yet." In fact, he decided, there was only one thief. Himself.

That's it, he thought. He picked up the phone and asked Ayumi to come in.

"I understand you write renku?" Mori said softly as she stood before his desk.

A schoolgirl bob of her head caused her hair to swirl around her face. "I'm in a group that meets once a month to compose renku, yes sir. Thirty-six lines, using Basho's rules."

Infinitely more complex poetry than haiku, Mori thought. Renku required extraordinary discipline and intellectual skill. "Like solving an equation, I imagine."

"I enjoy figuring things out, yes sir."

"That's why I called you in. It's time to give you more responsibility. As of today, I'm taking others on the team off the pachinko murder case and assigning you full-time. You'll work with me, of course."

His assistant stared down at her shoes. "I am very honored."

"Don't be. Our budget's going to be very restricted. You might say nonexistent. Any questions?"

"No sir."

"The first thing I need is all data we have about the pachinko case. This afternoon I have to present our progress to the Intelligence Committee. So get that file right now. And please tell no one in the department you're working on this case. Understood? For now I want to keep this between just you and me. Our secret."

THE MEDIA HAD once unkindly remarked of the Intelligence Committee that it was a consortium of old men with no experience in the art of penetration except with their wives. Mori's case was last on the agenda, and the discussion lasted over an hour. A compromise was finally reached. A public prosecutor would be assigned to oversee the case. Mori was to obtain prior approval from the PP for all future plans and actions. Mori was given two weeks to solve the case. After that it would revert to the National Police. Mori agreed, with one condition—that he choose the public prosecutor.

Although Aoyama opposed any concession, the committee saw no harm in allowing Mori's request. When Mori selected Yuka Tanemura, the committee was greatly pleased. Not only was she the daughter of Kenzo Tanemura, who was expected to become the next prime minister, she also had the highest conviction rate at Justice.

MORI DIDN'T HEAD home right away that evening. He needed a drink after dealing with Aoyama and the Intelligence Committee. It hadn't been a defeat, but neither had it been a victory. He decided to hit a few bars in the vicinity of the last pachinko murder. That way he could charge the drinks to his expense account.

The Telephone Karaoke Club was located on a street directly behind the pachinko hall. "Looking for a foreigner," Mori said to a man behind the bar. "He was in the area last Sunday evening."

The rooms were down a hall separated by a beaded curtain. Men and women came in and paid for videos of available girls and boys. The girls were usually high school age. He'd never looked at any of the boys. Each room had video equipment. You played the video and called the number at the end if you liked what you saw. Invited the girl or boy to come over or set up a date. It was very democratic and technically legal; the girls or boys decided if they wanted to go with you for sex. If money changed hands, no one ever admitted it.

"Two girls came in about seven-thirty. A foreigner joined them later."

"You sure?" Surprised, Mori took out his notebook.

"The thirteenth. Yes. Seen the girls before. They came in occasionally to giggle over the videos and knock a few back. Not regulars. Never seen the foreigner, though. First time for him. I remember because I was going to leave here early that night and let my staff run things. Then this big foreigner came in, so I decided to stay. Sometimes foreigners cause trouble—they're not like us. Seems like the girls had been waiting for him."

"What time did the foreigner show up?"

"Say a half hour after the girls, nearly eight. Not an American. The girls were keeping a bag for him while he did an errand. Winnings from playing pachinko, he said, and rather proud of it too."

"What kind of errand?"

The owner couldn't recall. Just remembered that in the bag was a bottle of Rémy Martin and cigarettes. "I offered to buy the cognac, but he gave it to the girls. Generous gaijin, that one. During the time they were here he took a room and looked at some videos and made a few calls. Pretty decent he was, as foreigners go. Didn't make any fuss about costs. Not loud like Americans and Aussies can be. Steady drinker, and didn't push the girls, from what I saw. Maybe they fooled around a little, but nothing serious, know what I mean? Ran up quite a bill too—didn't complain."

"The girls go with him?"

"The tall one did. Think she fancied him. They headed somewhere else. Maybe a love hotel."

"He use a card to pay?"

"No, cash."

"You hear any name?"

"The girls called him Helmut Stern-san. Something like that."

"So what did he look like?"

"Never seen any eyes like his," the owner said. "Light blue, and kind of scary until you got to know him. Tall fellow. Hundred and ninety centimeters at least. Looked like a big cat. Lot of tawny hair. Late thirties maybe. Dressed modestly. Mind if I ask what he's done?"

"Nothing, probably," Mori said, "but we're checking every lead on this pachinko murder." The inspector laid a card on the counter. "Give this number a call if either of the girls come in again. Need their names and contact numbers. Like to follow this up, if you don't mind."

MITSUKO HAD LEFT food for him, and he ate it when he got home.

She came in, fixing her hair. "Sorry, we didn't hear you come in. What did you do, sneak in? Have you been drinking again?"

"You were watching your *Naruhodo the World* quiz show again and wouldn't have heard the god of thunder."

"No we weren't, but you're nearly right! Actually, tonight Katano has a special on about an American comfort woman. You know, during the war the women who—"

"I know all about it."

"Some Korean woman who also was in the brothel wrote everything down. They've found the record."

"Really? What was it all about?"

"Katano says he has proof that during the Great War our military held an American woman at some military brothel in Harbin. Just for the officers, of course. She'd been drugged. Oh, it's perfectly awful."

"Another scandal. Just what the government needs."

"It looks like it. Katano interviewed several people in the Diet today. Some members of the opposition called for the prime minister's resignation. He's claiming it wasn't Japan's responsibility. Awful what we did to these women, just awful. They should publish this Korean woman's diary for all to read."

"Diary?" Mori stared at her. It had all suddenly hit him.

"Where are you going?"

"I'll be back in an hour or so."

"But you just came home. You haven't digested your food."

"I just thought of something that can't wait."

HE RACED BACK to Jonquil Kim's apartment and was able to retrieve the diary, duplicate it at a nearby 7-Eleven's copy machine, and return it to her apartment. On his way home he felt elated. Now he had the leverage he needed to make some moves.

27: **NEWS BREAK** Tokyo: Late Thursday

Kanto Shimbun, Tokyo:

News of an American comfort woman was aired on KSB-TV's *World News Show* Thursday night, shocking viewers. Show host Hideo Katano initiated the telecast by reminding viewers that comfort women were conscripted by the Japanese Imperial Army during World War II to provide sex for military personnel. Three years ago, the government officially admitted this policy did exist, but only after a group of Korean women produced irrefutable evidence that, as teenagers and young women, they had been kidnapped, drugged, raped, and forced to become sex slaves for the Japanese army.

"We knew there'd been Asian comfort women, but the idea of an American comfort woman was at first unthinkable," Katano stated during his show. "When this information first came to my attention, I thought it must be a sick joke. That is why we have authenticated the paper on which the diary was written. I am now convinced that beyond any doubt this information is true."

Kansai News Bureau, Osaka:

Charges of a cover-up by Japanese government authorities since World War II are being levied by Hideo Katano, who Thursday night revealed a diary from 1941 written by a Korean that described an American comfort woman at a Japanese Imperial Army brothel in Harbin. "There is no doubt that it has been carefully covered up by those in control of our country," he charged at the conclusion of his bombshell telecast. But who was this American woman? What became of her? Where is she now? These are the questions being asked in the coffee shops of the Ginza today. Katano claimed that no one really knows. Interviewed after his show, Katano explained that his staff was attempting to trace the American and would keep viewers informed on a nightly basis. In addition, a reward of one million U.S. dollars is being offered to anyone who can supply information leading to the location and identity of the mysterious American comfort woman.

Tokyo Evening Shimbun, Tokyo:

Using blowups of diary pages and maps of the street where the alleged military brothel stood in Harbin, hard-hitting news commentator Hideo Katano made an attack tonight on Japanese officials for covering up the existence of an American comfort woman. Videotapes showing a Chinese communist government building on the site where the brothel once stood and interviews with Chinese in Harbin who remembered the brothel were vivid reminders of a part of Japan's past that most would rather forget.

Nationnews, U.S.A.

Angry comment from a cross section of Americans poured in just hours after news of an American sex slave or "comfort woman" during World War II was announced on Japanese TV. The source of the story is a diary written by a Korean woman describing the horrors of a Japanese army brothel. The American woman's name and whereabouts are unknown. Experts speculate she may have been executed by the Japanese as the Allies swept to victory in Asia, in order to keep her tragic experience from ever becoming public. However, a $1 million offer by the Tokyo TV station that broke the news has already resulted in a deluge of sightings.

28: LA VISTA Los Angeles: Thursday, 8:30 P.M.

STEIG WAITED OUTSIDE La Vista Condominiums in Westwood, a hat pulled over his face in the parked van as if he were asleep. In fact his mind was working overtime. Considering angles, the approach. In the German's pocket were the tickets. Afterward he would catch the last flight out to Tokyo.

His hand rested on the silenced Beretta M93R. He could fire one-handed in three-shot bursts if he chose.

His preparation had been meticulous. No mistakes this time, he told himself. The unsuccessful attempt on Canyon Road still rankled. He knew she had flown to San Jose this morning, leaving her Audi at LAX. He'd been able to determine the arrival time of her flight home. Indeed, she should have landed a half hour ago. Soon she would be turning into this street.

His van was parked with the lights out in the shadow between the streetlamps, facing both the front door to her condo and the underground garage entrance. She'd arrive a little tired, glad to be home after the flight. Piece of cake.

Again, he considered the sequence. The garage door was triggered electronically by a device attached to the resident's car. She would open the door, drive in, get out, open the rear trunk to take out her luggage, and . . .

His mind played the picture of the girl. That kind of a face walks into a room, you know it's trouble. She was a real looker. He wondered what she'd done. Something to do with pachinko like the others, he decided.

A car came up the street. White. Audi. Steig opened the door noiselessly and got out. A man was walking a dog, opposite side. He turned on the van engine and listened to it idle. Then he closed and locked the door, took off his jacket, and slung it over the snub-nosed weapon. The Audi turned into the underground garage entrance of La Vista Condominiums. A woman was driving.

He considered a kill shot from here, but knew angles on car metal or glass could deflect even the most accurate bullets. Earlier he'd scoped the garage. He'd do it inside.

The car braked in front of the garage door and triggered the electronic door mechanism. Steig crossed the street. The Audi pulled into the garage. The door began to close. Steig ducked under the door, confirming his escape exits. Stairs on the left behind concrete pillars. Elevators opposite. Goodbye Pachinko Woman.

The Audi was backing into its parking space. Steig's mind calculated angles. He would not have a clear shot when she opened her door. She would be between cars. Difficult target. After she got her luggage out, then. Or . . . do her as she waited for the elevator. Good angle from here.

Women were lousy backers normally. She braked and he could see the flare of red light against the white concrete wall, like a danger signal. The light went off, and she unhooked her safety belt and sat a moment as people do after a long trip. Great to be home, she was thinking. Only, Steig thought, she didn't know . . .

Damn. She'd lifted a cellular phone, one of the folding kind. What was she doing? She snapped the phone shut, hit a button that opened her trunk. Steig breathed a relieved sigh as she got out of the car. He put his finger on the trigger of the weapon, flicked the safety off, raised it to a forty-five-degree angle.

She raised the lid of the trunk, disappearing from his sight line. He listened. No sound, except the noise of the elevator. What was she doing now? Waiting? For what?

The elevator stopped, the doors opened. Someone came into the garage. Shit. Steig ducked again, barely in time. A man in a uniform. Middle-aged. What the hell was this? Looked like a superintendent or night manager. Had she seen Steig? Was that why she'd phoned? But the man's actions indicated he was not responding to a call for help.

Steig sized the man up. About his own height. But over the hill. Paunch. Weak back. No problem taking him out too. He'd see what this was all about first.

"John." Helim came out from behind her car. Clear target now, but Steig waited. "Thanks for helping me. It's in the trunk. Not heavy, but awkward to carry, a present."

So that was it. The guy was going to take her stuff upstairs. Damn her, Steig thought. She was the type who could get any man to jump. He thought again about taking them both.

"No problem, Helim. Good trip today?"

"Yeah. Just great." They walked together behind the car, and John took out the package while Helim secured her briefcase and pocketbook. They walked together toward the elevators. The doors opened.

Now, he decided. It had to be now. Steig rose slightly, lined up the weapon, and slowly squeezed the trigger. Easy targets.

An explosion of gunfire swept through the garage. The force of the bullets threw them together inside the elevator. The door closed, shutting out the carnage. Steig walked calmly up the stairs and out the front door.

29: **EMERGENCY** Los Angeles: Friday, 8:30 A.M.

THE NOISE WAS insistent. In his dream it was a drum being played by a beautiful woman in traditional Korean dress. Steve woke from sleep. Damn, he was tired. Someone was pounding on his door.

"Mr. Juric, open up!"

A warning sounded in his brain. He staggered to his feet and opened the door.

An L.A. cop was standing in front of him with a clipboard in his hands. "You Steven Juric?"

"Yeah."

"I'm Officer Barret. Can I come in?"

"What? Sure."

Barret stepped into Steve's studio. "Do you know a Miss Helim Kim?"

"Yes." A high-pitched scream was sounding in his ears. He closed the door and turned to face the officer. "What's going on?"

"Is Miss Kim here?"

"Helim? No."

"Do you know where Miss Kim is?"

"At her apartment, I would think. Look, what is going on?"

"Is her address . . . La Vista Condominiums, 225 Haymen in Westwood?"

"Yes. Right." Steve felt an ache in his back; his body was beginning to tense.

The cop lifted a radio off his belt. "Officer Barret here, Captain. I have Mr. Juric regarding the killing."

Killing! The word pounded into his brain. A welter of thoughts confused his eyes. "She's dead?" He felt dizzy.

The big cop held up the palm of his hand. "You want to talk to him, sir?" A pause. "Yeah. Just a second."

He handed over the device.

"This is Captain Tagget, Mr. Juric. Do you know Miss Kim?" A Western accent.

Steve tried to focus. "Yes."

"What is your relationship with Miss Kim, sir?"

"I'm a close friend. Look, what's going on?"

"You know if she has any enemies?"

Steve calmed the manic throb of his pulse, remembered the opposing views of the Korean community, the danger her father had warned about. "No," he replied. A sinking sensation in his stomach became a fevered rush. "None that I know of."

"Give me back to Officer Barret."

"What happened? Where's Helim?"

"Just give me Officer Barret. He'll explain in a moment."

Barret took the speaker and listened, then cut off his radio.

"I'm going to have to search your apartment."

"What the hell is going on?" What were they after? Did they think he . . . Jesus, he loved her. Please, God, let her be alive.

"I can get a formal search warrant if you wish."

"No. Search away. For what?"

"We'll see."

"How did you get my name?"

"Her address book. We talked to her neighbors. You stayed with her a couple of nights ago, right?"

"So?"

"You two ever argue?"

"We did Wednesday."

"About what?"

"Look, where is this going? What happened to Helim?"

"Tonight she nearly got herself killed. We're just trying to figure out why."

"She got hurt?" Steve felt his knees go weak with relief. She wasn't dead!

Barret started to check the room. "That's the strange part. Perp sprayed over twenty rounds. Super got killed. She wasn't even scratched. Calm lady. Very cool."

"The superintendent?" Steve remembered him. Nice man.

"Yeah. The night super was helping her unload her luggage. About eight-thirty P.M. She'd just come back from a trip to San Jose. They'd gotten as far as the elevator when the perp opened fire. Super died instantly. Didn't have a chance. She got lucky." Barret stepped back. "Okay, your room is clean."

"What were you looking for?"

"A weapon. Just routine."

"Why me?"

"One of the descriptions we got was of a tall dirty-blond fellow about your height and age. Man walking his dog caught a glimpse as the perp left the garage. Neighbors gave us your description."

"So, I look like the suspect?"

"Yeah. And you had an argument with her, you admitted. Can you tell me where you were yesterday evening?"

"At my office working late."

"Anyone with you?"

"No."

"Can I have your office address, please."

"Sure." Steve found a card. "I hope you guys don't—"

"We have to check everything out, sir." Barret studied the card a moment. "We've already checked your sheet at the station. Clean as a whistle. Bet you eat oatmeal every morning, right?" Barret jotted notes on his clipboard and started for the door.

"So where is Helim?"

"Last night they interviewed her at the scene. *She'd caught a glimpse of the perp. Saw a flash of blue eyes. Ice blue.* Said it wasn't you, by the way. The super had a minor drug record. He made somebody's short list. She agreed to come down the station after she showered and changed. Figured she could help us. Didn't show. So we're looking for her."

"She's disappeared?"

"Guess so, Mr. Juric. Not in her apartment. Some of her things were gone. Looks like she left in a hurry. Any idea where she'd go?"

Steve thought about Tokyo. "No," he said.

IT WAS JUST after nine when Steve called Chul Kim's number at the Korean Merchant Bank.

"Kim here, Steve. What can I do for you?"

"Is Helim staying with you?"

"No." Kim's voice rose a notch. "Why? Where is she? Has she agreed not to make that stupid Tokyo trip yet?"

"No, sir. The police just came by. There was a shooting at her apartment last night. They think it was a drug hit on the superintendent. He was helping Helim unload her car when the hit took place, but she escaped unharmed. However, she's disappeared."

"Disappeared?"

"Do you have any idea where she might have gone?"

Kim was silent a moment. "Maybe I have an idea. Her old boyfriend called last night. Tomás. He was trying to reach her at the apartment in Westwood and couldn't get through. Busy signal. Then when he called a while later there was no answer, so he called me."

She'd mentioned her former boyfriend only once to Steve. He was a Latin, she'd said. Too much emotion. She laughed and said the opposite of Steve. "At what time did he call you?"

"About ten. He said he'd phoned her two days ago and she said she was going to Japan, possibly today, and that she'd call him. He wanted to find out if she'd be staying at her grandmother's."

Steve felt his face flush. "Why would Helim call him?"

"You tell me," Kim replied acidly. "You didn't know she was flying to Tokyo today?"

"Of course not."

"I was counting on you to prevent this."

"Look, neither you nor Helim has been honest with me. Something's going on here I don't like at all."

"Oh, for God's sake." Chul Kim took a deep breath. "Just find her and bring her back. For a number of reasons, I can't. You have to find her!"

"This former boyfriend—do you know where he called from?"

"No. He travels a great deal for an international atomic energy group with the UN. Helim translates for them occasionally. She got back from a job several weeks ago. In Pyongyang. That's all I know. Look, I'm in a meeting."

"Okay, I'm going to find her. Whatever it takes, I'm going to find her and bring her back here."

30: ESCAPE Stuttgart: Friday, 12:30 P.M.

THE LANDSCAPE OF the Austrian mountainside gradually changed into the dense forests of southern Germany. Tomás Velaquez saw little of it from his train window. He was thinking about Helim Kim. Trying to decide what to do. Where to go. Mainly it depended on her, he thought. Whether he trusted her or not. She could help him, he thought. Or she could destroy him.

He arrived at the Stuttgart terminal at dusk and took a cab to the airport, watching the lights of the city flash past and considering his options.

There was a clerk in Hong Kong that he had to find. Carswell had said that the man had been offered a bribe. The police were holding him. Others were involved. British intelligence had initiated the complaint. American intelligence had agreed to cooperate. What were they doing? he wondered. Why didn't they want the world to know the North Koreans had nuclear weapons?

At the airport he went straight to the Lufthansa counter and booked a flight to Hong Kong. There was barely enough time to clear immigration and customs.

Tomás wondered if he would ever see Germany again. His doubts about Helim Kim wouldn't go away. Could she have been involved somehow? Switched the plutonium? She couldn't have. Not Helim. For it would mean Helim was working for . . . who? The Russians? The South Koreans? North Korea? Now it really made no sense. None of it. All he knew was that in twelve hours he would be in Hong Kong. And that the dangers there might cost him more than his job.

31: **THE CONVOCATION** Sierra Golf Club: Friday, 2:30 P.M.

THREE MEN RODE the specially constructed golf cart, hunched over their seats. They crested a hill and were silhouetted briefly against the Sierra Madre mountains. They plunged down the other side toward a green where a white flag fluttered like a butterfly in a puff of wind.

The driver, Jefferson Archer, former president of the United States, pulled up short of the green, where the second shots of the threesome had landed. "Damn, it's hot. Sorry about that, folks. Ordered a nice cool day for our convocation, but you can't have everything."

"Beautiful course. More than makes up for the heat." The speaker, Sherman Whitlow, was also a former president, but the strong chin and clear blue eyes were still the same. He took a pitching wedge from his bag and made a practice swing. "So, what's this all about?"

"Want you to think back, Sherm." Archer selected a nine iron and took a practice swing. "Our current president is no longer in control— he can't get elected again. The wannabes are scrambling for position, and the country is on hold." Archer hushed his voice so it would not carry. Only his golf partners could hear his words. "There's rancor between the White House and Congress, vindictiveness and hate. The United States is wavering as a nation. There's talk of isolation. We're not as strong as we once were. Hell, if we're not careful we'll become a second-rate nation. And the last thing we can afford is another war."

"The public won't let the isolationists win. We'll come back. We always have." Cole Todman, third man in their group of former U.S. presidents, had held office before either of the other two. Todman had gained too much weight since the days of his presidency, and had recently gone through heart bypass surgery.

Todman would not ordinarily have flown in for the weekend, but Archer had called personally, said there was a matter of utmost national urgency he wished to discuss.

Archer leaned on his club. "Gentlemen, we've been asked to provide advice on an issue neither the president nor the Congress can touch. Call us an informal channel. The purpose of this meeting is to consider what should be done about the North Koreans. We all know the North Koreans leader, Park Tai Jin, has recently made a sudden trip to Beijing. Most people don't know why."

Todman turned to him. "And you do?"

"Several weeks ago, a member of the UN's IAEA team obtained a plutonium sample from North Korean engineers at Yongbin. The first time a sample has ever been handed over to us."

"I see." Todman frowned.

"Sounds like they goofed," Whitlow said.

"They didn't know a test could be conducted on a very small amount. The Chinese did. Now the Koreans know too. That sample has been found to be contaminated. In other words, it did not come from North Korean reactors but was illegally purchased through the black market."

Sherman Whitlow whistled.

"Which means, gentlemen, the North Koreans have been cheating on their nuclear program. Which means—"

"They may be churning out atomic bombs," Todman interrupted.

"Right."

"So how come we haven't brought it up in the UN?"

"One minor problem." Archer looked at both men. "It seems the IAEA man who obtained the sample left it in a hotel room in Hong Kong overnight on his way to London. So now we have questions about whether it could have been switched. To make matters worse, after questioning by two of our best people, the IAEA man disappeared."

"Great," Todman grumbled. "An American?"

"No, but a girl who worked as his translator is. North Korean descent, too. Our people intend to call her in for questioning."

"So where do we come in?"

"Our intelligence people have a theory that this is all part of a larger operation. The tainted plutonium was passed to embarrass the current leader. The Chinese were furious that any plutonium was handed over and demanded a meeting in Beijing. So the North Korean leader had no choice but to fly there and calm them down. He hates trips."

"What were the Chinese so upset about?"

"You probably guessed it, Sherman. Our people think it's a sign of a guilty conscience."

"You mean they supplied the plutonium?" Todman demanded.

"A possibility. Could be Beijing wants to make sure the North Koreans don't talk and spoil China's chances for a favored nation treaty."

"So what's the larger operation? What's this all supposed to be part of?" Whitlow asked. "Why would someone want Park Tai Jin to take a trip to China? As you say, he hates to travel."

"So they could stage a coup."

"They?" Todman squeaked.

"Hard-liners in the military tribunal that runs North Korea."

"Oh, great."

"Doesn't really surprise me," Whitlow said. "He's opened up talks with South Korea and us on reunion. He's establishing a free trade zone on their northern border. And he's talking about an oil deal with one of our multinationals. Pissed a lot of the old guard off in Pyongyang, I imagine."

"Apparently," Archer agreed. "Several different sources are providing consistent information about a coup attempt. We've had the same rumor from Japan. It looks real."

"You mean they're going to assassinate the North Korean leader?" Todman said, as if suddenly comprehending the enormity of it all. "Have they all gone crazy over there?"

"Now let's just take it easy." Archer understood that while Todman's health might have affected his emotions, his agreement was essential. He had already been sent on missions to several smaller foreign nations to clean up minor messes. Jefferson Archer needed Todman to lend his credibility to their decision. "At issue is a covert action."

"Is it constitutional?" Todman asked. "Doesn't Congress—"

"Hell, Cole," Sherman Whitlow interrupted, "since when is any covert action constitutional? C'mon. Let's hit first, then hear what Jeff has to say."

"Who's up?" Archer asked.

Todman's ball was farthest away. He hit first, putting his ball into a sand bunker. "Shit. We going to play golf or talk politics? I can't do both."

Archer studied his ball. It was in the first cut of rough but stood up well enough for a clean hit. The ball flew toward the flag and dropped a par chance away. "Lucky shot."

"Like hell," Whitlow corrected. "You've been doing that all day."

"My course," Archer said, shrugging, then his face turned serious again. "There's an interesting operation proposal on the table regarding the North Koreans."

"From whom?" Todman asked.

Archer walked toward them. "The concept comes from one of our own intelligence services," Archer said. "A way to clean house in North Korea." Archer stared from one face to the other. "The president won't be shown the details, just summaries. He can't touch it."

"Clean house," Cole said petulantly. "What the hell's that supposed to mean?"

Whitlow chuckled. "From my days on the Senate Intelligence Committee, it means only one thing, Tod. We stop them before they stage a coup. Right, Jefferson?"

"About right. Our intelligence boys just got wind of it. So I don't have all the details. Park Tai Jin was in Beijing last week for urgent meetings, as you know. He's taking a boat from Hong Kong for the return trip, with a three-day stop in Japan on the way back. That's when the coup is supposed to happen. Or soon after. Someone—it may be one of us—will be asked to meet him in Japan on his way back. Our operation will be under cover of that meeting."

"Well, it won't be me. They're all a pain in the ass if you want my opinion," Todman said.

"Two hard-liners have been identified as behind the coup," Archer went on. "One of them is a general, the other is the head of their intelligence."

"Lord's sake, Jeff." Todman's jowl was shaking. "You mean the hard-liners are going to try and destroy our agreements? The nuclear-freeze deal? Geneva?"

"That's what we hear."

"What the hell's the hard-liner's opinion?" Sherman Whitlow demanded. "Not . . . ?"

Archer sighed. "Could be. Another Korean war." He squinted at both men. "We're told the hard-liners figure the only way to fix their economy is to take over South Korea's."

"Well, I'll be damned." Sherman Whitlow's drawl showed no emotion. He'd been close to the CIA during his years in the Senate. Knew that crises required a calm head.

"It's our call, gentlemen," Archer said. He held up three fingers. "Discussion time is over. They want our opinion in Washington. The

Intelligence Oversight Committee is convening tomorrow. They'll pass it along. Three alternatives to consider. First, if there is an attempt on Park Tai Jin's life, we try to protect him. Try to keep anyone from getting hurt. Second, we take out the two hard-liners behind the coup: the head of intelligence, who goes by the code name Alpha, and General Myun Chun Kuk. If we take them out, we've cut off the head of the snake. Third, we let the act succeed. Then take out the two hard-liners afterward."

Cole Todman drew a sharp breath. "If the present leader is assassinated, that would leave a power vacuum, wouldn't it? And the remaining hard-liners would rush into it."

"Hard to say, Cole. We have someone in mind who could replace the leader. Fellow who has pro-democratic leanings, for which he was exiled to their Finnish embassy as a consul two years ago. Name's Park Chung Il. Travels abroad freely but isn't allowed back inside North Korea. Cousin of the current leader, so he has special status. The military clique wanted his head but were afraid to touch him. Park still has a lot of support among the younger technocrats. At least he could return to Pyongyang and try. Key is getting rid of the two hard-line leaders, in my opinion."

"If we take out the two key hard-liners after they kill the current leader, then do you really believe there is a chance for a liberal like this Park fellow to regain control of North Korea?" Cole asked.

"Good point," Archer agreed. "So you'd take them out before they strike to prevent anyone from getting hurt."

Whitlow grimaced. "I think we have to take them out. The North Korean military could still believe they could overrun South Korea in a couple of days. All the financial troubles the South has had have weakened them. Some of our people agree it's possible."

"It sounds like a real crapshoot, gentlemen." Todman pulled out a large handkerchief and toweled his face.

Archer's jaw firmed. "We have to make a choice, Cole. North Korea is moving toward liberalization. The hard-liners will do their best to regain power. It could get bloody."

"Bloody!" Sherman Whitlow whispered. "It could go fucking atomic. How much time is there left?"

"Not a whole lot. That North Korean boat docks in Japan in four days. Our people believe it will happen any day after that and before the boat reaches North Korea—another reason why the Intelligence Oversight

Committee called us in; they can't fart around. The president doesn't have time to take this to the Senate and roll around in the mud for a month or more."

"How about leaking it to the world press?" Whitlow asked. "Wouldn't that put the brakes on?"

"We've thought about it, but that might not work and we're out of time. This is supposed to happen very soon. We need to decide today. Our intelligence people have to move immediately. They're waiting right now for our answer."

"What the hell can they do, Jeff?" Cole demanded. "We've never been able to get much human intelligence on the North. Just satellite reconnaissance data. Something changed?"

"Yes. They have an asset inside who's getting the place, the time, the way they're going to do it."

"Who is running this?"

"The FBI."

Cole made a face. "What're they doing meddling overseas? How come the CIA isn't involved?"

"FBI has been chosen because the CIA and State can't agree—they've become polarized. So the FBI is responsible. It's been building its assets overseas."

"What does Langley say?" Todman asked nervously.

"They want to let the hards take out the North Korean leader. Then act. Cut off the hard-liners' nuts. They think that this is the one window for us, the only chance to influence the North Korean leadership we may ever get for the next thirty years."

Whitlow turned to Archer. "What does the State Department think?"

"They don't want anyone hurt. If we stop the coup, we can have a media show and get brownie points with the world press and the South Korean leadership. Maybe the current leader of the North too. Since State and the CIA disagree about what should be done, we're being called on to umpire, make the final call. The FBI team will carry it out. We're not involving the president. Everything is deniable. But, as I said, one of us may be asked to help out, travel to Japan to meet the North Korean leader one on one. Only way to warn him."

Whitlow shook his head. "Park Tai Jin is a fucking flake. They call him 'the kid' at Langley. He's an unknown factor at best. Womanizer, alcoholic—"

Cole Todman butted in, "Now, now, Sherman, that's hearsay.

There's another view, not shared by Langley, I admit. Some say that he's just a shy, awkward technocrat who'd love to be recognized as a statesman and is trying to be a responsible leader."

"I guess we have a split opinion here, too," Archer said. "Only problem is the stakes are very high. Further, we get this one free shot—if it is a shot. One in a billion."

Whitlow said, "He serves wine with live snakes in it, kidnapped a South Korean director to make movies for him, enjoys racing battery-operated toy cars, summons people to middle-of-the-night parties where the local circus performs just for the hell of it. At last roll call our intelligence had him down for three live atomic bombs. You want someone like that rolling the dice in Asia?"

Archer glanced ahead at the green. The Secret Service vehicles had drawn up around the apron, and walkers were coming back up the hill toward them. "A lot of that's just rumor. Couple of European machinery salesmen who get invited to his place for dinner say he loves Al Pacino movies. We can't decide policy on that basis either. Okay, let's vote before the baby-sitters are in our laps. The Intelligence Oversight Committee wants me to call them tonight. Cole?"

Todman licked his lips. "I don't believe force is the way to settle it. I say our role is referee. Not participant. Therefore, we don't land punches. Just see the fight is clean. Let 'em sort their own laundry. I say be the Good Samaritan. Stop anyone from getting hurt."

Archer turned. "Okay. Sherman, what about you?"

"The current son of a bitch deserves whatever he gets—I'll vote for letting the coup succeed. Terminate the two key hard-liners afterward. We're talking hundreds of thousands of lives if any idiot punches a missile button with an atomic warhead. There's no doubt in my mind the hard-liners will do that if we let them take full control of the government there. Take out the leader and the assassins!"

"Okay." Archer's voice was husky. "Guess I have to cast the deciding vote. And I'll need a little more time before I make up my mind. Thank you for helping your country once again. You are both true patriots. Now, let me show you how to par this hole."

PART FOUR

One who would go a hundred miles
should consider ninety-nine as halfway.

Korean proverb

32: THE GOAT Tokyo: Saturday, 4:40 P.M.

HELIM'S FLIGHT ARRIVED at Terminal One, Narita Airport, thirty minutes early. Before leaving LAX she had faxed KSB-TV her arrival time.

She wondered if there would be anyone there to meet her. She'd caught the first flight out Friday morning, the horror of the night before still clear in her mind. She'd managed to draw a rough sketch of her attacker and fax it to Park's pro-democracy office in Tokyo. Park said he wanted to catch the killer; she'd given him the chance. But Park had disappeared, as he usually did in any crisis.

Deep down she'd always known North Korean intelligence would eventually find her out and she'd have to run. She wanted four more days. Not until she finished the business ahead—the comfort woman diary and the pachinko company listing—she told herself.

During the flight she had reviewed her store of information about comfort women, or "ianfu" as Japanese called them. Usually, they were known by the letter P coupled with nationality. Chan-P for Chinese, Chom-P for Koreans. The P came from the Chinese "p'i," meaning vagina.

The weather was gray and cloudy. Humid with impending storm. A representative of the TV station held up a sign as she came through immigration into the public area. Thank you, God, she told herself. Now just give me the four days.

As she followed him, two silent young Japanese closed in behind her like sheepdogs herding a valuable flock. Both were perspiring. Maybe it was the leaden humidity. Or perhaps they already knew of the attempt on her life in Los Angeles. Whatever the cause, she was impressed by their intensity. Things were suddenly better.

She told them she needed a phone and stopped at a telephone booth. She inserted a card and dialed a Tokyo number.

"Koreans for Democratic Action. Who's calling?"

"Helim Kim. Did you get my fax?"

"Yes. We were waiting for your call. Are you all right?"

"Thanks. I'm okay." At least the pro-democracy group was functioning, she thought. It had a small office in Marunouchi.

"Where are you?"

"I just arrived at Narita. Where's Park?"

"Still in the United States. Arriving tomorrow."

"He didn't tell me he was coming here."

"Perhaps because it was not for your project. Something in Niigata City. How can we contact you?"

"I'll call again as soon as I know where I'm staying."

"We set watches on Narita and Osaka arrival terminals, using your sketch. He was spotted eight hours ago at Narita arriving on a flight from Los Angeles."

"He's here?" Helim tried unsuccessfully to keep a quiver from her voice.

"Yes. But don't worry. We have several of our best people watching him, and we know his hotel. An operation to take him into custody is imminent."

"Good." She took a deep breath. "May the KDA succeed. I'll call soon again." She hung up the phone and made another call. "It's me," she said.

"Helim! Jesus, I've been worried about you." Steve's voice was hoarse.

She calculated the time, approximately twelve o'clock in L.A. Yesterday. "Sorry to call so late. You know about the attack, then?"

"Yes, I know. I know. The police came here looking for you. This morning. Been going nuts trying to locate you since. Are you okay?"

"Sure. But my attacker's now in Tokyo."

"Your attacker? The police said he was after the super. The guy had a drug record."

"He was after me."

"I knew it! I had a feeling something terrible would happen. Your father said there were bad people involved in this pachinko business. Powerful people."

"I couldn't tell you more then. I'll explain everything next time I see you." She wondered when that would be. If she would ever see him again.

"Okay." He paused for a moment. "Where are you now?"

"Tokyo, Narita Airport. I arrived a few minutes ago. To be honest, I'm scared."

"I would be too. Why didn't you call me after it happened?"

"Pride, I guess. I was mad at you, remember? Oh, I don't know. I'm mixed up. Someone checked out your background. Said you were involved in a couple of illegal Asian deals. That too."

"Who said that?"

"A person with connections to the U.S. government."

"Just what was this illegal business I was supposed to be involved in?"

"One was a Korean venture where the land price was sold at double the going price to a U.S. company. A kind of kickback."

"Great! That was in Taegu, a deal I negotiated at my old law firm. It was the first U.S. majority ownership in the electronics field approved by the Korean government. It was applauded in the financial media. The land had recently been rezoned and was valued by our local lawyers—I wasn't involved. Somebody's been bad-mouthing me, and it sounds like my former wife's dad."

"I figured there was an explanation. Sorry I doubted you."

"Please get the first plane back here today!"

"I can't. I've already been met by the TV people. KSB-TV."

"Then I'm flying over."

"I don't want you to come, Steve." I can't let him, she thought. It would be insane.

"Helim. I love you. Your father told me something might happen, and it has. I'm coming over there to take care of you. Understand?"

Helim held her breath for a moment. This was the voice she'd wanted to hear since they'd met. She could feel his arms holding her, safe. But still she hesitated. If she involved him, it would change his life forever. "No, Steve. These people are . . . professionals."

"I can deal with it. Anyway, I'm coming. Tell me where I should contact you after I arrive."

His certainty eroded her fears. She knew she wanted him to come. "You sure?"

"Yes."

"Hideo Katano. KSB-TV. I'll tell him to expect your call. He'll tell you where I'll be."

• • •

THREE MORE YOUNG Japanese fell in behind Helim when they reached the outer airport doors. My God, she thought, perhaps they too knew her assailant was in Tokyo. But she was less worried now. Steve was on the way. She could trust him after all. She felt strangely calm. Finally, a man she could rely on.

They hurried out onto a wide sidewalk into the late-afternoon gloom. She saw a luxury Japanese car waiting, the motor running. It had begun to rain. The Japanese believed rain on a journey was good luck, she recalled. It washed away ill winds and bad air. But she did not believe in Japanese superstitions.

Katano was waiting for her in the backseat.

The protection closed the door, and she sat there in the sudden air-conditioned silence pretending to feel at ease while she tried to make out the man next to her. She could smell his aftershave, detect he had a curly black hairdo and expensive clothes. He was wearing a yellow silk sport shirt and tan Italian slacks. White wing-tip shoes. A manicured hand lifted away his sunglasses. She saw deeply intelligent eyes, carefully attended skin. In Japanese, he said, "I hope our precautions do not alarm you. Welcome home."

Maybe this was stupid, she told herself. Maybe she should reconsider. She had been occasionally reckless when she was younger. Usually, however, it had been for a weekend with some muscular blond she'd met at a party. Not to cut a deal with a Japanese TV station that she knew practically nothing about.

"Did you tell anyone of our agreement?" she asked.

"None. The American comfort woman has created a sensation. It's the talk of Tokyo. And I'm delighted you could come so quickly. The timing is perfect. We have many things to discuss."

"I was attacked as I was getting out of my car last night. Someone tried to kill me."

"You're joking!"

"No."

"So you have enemies, Miss Kim?" He glanced at her for the first time. "You needn't worry here. Japan is the safest country in the world. We've arranged for your full protection." As if to conclude the subject, Katano spoke to the driver. The car spurted off at reckless pace and soon settled into the Tokyo-bound traffic flow.

"About my conditions," she said. "You are prepared to meet them?"

"Yes!" Katano grimaced as if he'd momentarily forgotten and was angry with himself. "Your interview taping will begin tomorrow, Sunday. The first day will be devoted to pachinko—that's what you wanted, right? A juicy esposé, we're hoping. Monday we'll cover the treatment of Koreans in Japan. Possibly some background on the American comfort woman issue. Tuesday we will be finished, if all goes well. Ever done this before?"

"No."

"Don't worry, it'll be fine. You have a good TV face. We're already taping interviews with government officials related to the pachinko industry. Of course, they think it's routine; they have no idea what is in store for them. The third day, Tuesday, we'll do background shots, some special lighting effects for your close-ups, although I see we won't have any problem making you look gorgeous."

How insincere some men were and how openly they showed it, Helim thought. Katano disappointed her. His celebrity didn't overwhelm her, she could see his obvious intentions. He underestimated her. And that would be his loss.

"Originally, I had not planned to show my face at all."

"A waste. Your looks will sell your story. Viewers connect beauty with honesty."

She digested his compliment, knowing he would want something in return. All men did. "Your insight is encouraging. And since my enemies obviously are out in the open, perhaps there is no reason to hide from them. They know who I am."

"Wonderful!" Katano took her hand and patted it. "It's settled, then. No need to worry. Our protection will stay with you until we're sure there's no risk."

AT TOKYO STATION, Katano waved Helim aboard a train bound for Atami. A pleasant resort town, he explained. A seaside hamlet with few roads, and little congestion on the off-season weekdays. They'd booked her at a Japanese inn; the security men would have adjacent rooms. Helim could enjoy views of the ocean, and a garden where the poet Basho wrote several of his haiku. Helim told him that a friend named Steven Juric would call him. Katano should give him—and only him—her phone number and address in Atami.

33: **THE ATTACK** Tokyo: Saturday, 6:30 P.M.

NOT A SPRING chicken, but nice. Gunther Steig sipped his beer and glanced again. Good. An earnest, scared, pretty Asian girl. He had arrived in Tokyo early this morning, was well rested and in the mood to celebrate. Perhaps she was behind with the rent.

The bar was one he had frequented before his U.S. trip. There'd been a congratulatory note awaiting him at the small hotel he'd booked into. Helim Kim had disappeared. The newspapers had reported nothing, but with ten or more L.A. murders per week, that wasn't unusual. The client would be in touch shortly.

She made the first move. Took out a pack of Seven Stars. "Do you have a light?" Steig noted that her hand was shaking.

He took matches from an ashtray on the bar and lit her up. "I am a businessman from Geneva," he said by way of introduction. "My name is Helmut Stern. Plastics."

"Tomi," she said. "I'm a Korean." They began to talk in the casual way of strangers who have decided on a relationship. She spoke without evasiveness; looked at him as if she had nothing to hide. He enjoyed staring back into those dark eyes. Imagining. Otherwise, he might not have seen the signs. Not have bothered. Otherwise he would have gone back to his rented room, packed his bags, and thought about the things he had to do.

They went to a hotel nearby. In the room, she took off her earrings first.

"Nice," he said, staring at their glitter.

"Solid gold," she said proudly and put them carefully on the dresser.

"Reindeer," he said. "What for?"

"No reason. I just collect animals." She lifted the phone and ordered cold drinks and a bucket of ice from room service.

"I'll use the bath first," she said. "But I'll be quick. When I call, you can come in."

Steig knew that in Asia, bathing was a ritual. A kind of erotic foreplay. She undressed in the bathroom, and he watched her shape through the translucent glass. She had not talked of money yet. But he knew from experience it would come eventually. Before they left, she would ask to borrow a little. Say thirty thousand yen. He would negotiate, perhaps. It would depend on the experience and his mood.

Steam from the ofuro began to lick her figure, obscure it until finally there was only a moving shadow. She had fine legs, he decided. And large breasts for an Asian. A splendid way to return to Japan. He watched her hesitatingly get into the hot bath, like a wild animal at a new watering hole.

He went over to her pocket book and quickly checked the contents. Never hurt to be careful. No weapons. A wallet. He opened that and took out an identification card. Tomi Chang. Club Reo. Shinjuku. So. She worked in the mizu-shobai trade. That explained things. Now he knew where he stood.

Tomi had been in the bath five minutes when she called to him, "You can come in now."

He undressed quickly, taking a knife from its sheath and placing it under his clothes, which he put in a wicker basket and carried into the ofuro. She was in the tub facing away from him, splashing water over her shoulders and face. He put the basket behind the door where it would not be noticed. Then he stepped upright near the bath so that she could see his body. She did not avert her eyes, yet neither did she seem to look at him. She rose to get out of the bath as if oblivious to the fact that she was also naked. A Japanese woman under these circumstances, Steig had discovered, would normally cover her breasts.

Tomi pushed him gently onto a tiny wooden stool. Then she dipped a wooden bucket in the bath and poured searing water over his back. After three buckets, the water began to feel pleasant. His body relaxed.

She soaped him while he sat on the tiny stool. Massaged his back and admired his shoulders. Working from his toes, her strong fingers worked up the muscles of his calves to his thighs. She talked to him while she worked. Did he hate the Japanese?

"Of course," he said, understanding her mood.

"Do you speak Japanese?"

Steig laughed. "Oh no. Too difficult."

She washed his genitals, which gave him an erection and made her giggle. Then she put him in the tub to soak. She noticed the basket filled with his clothes. "I'll put these outside."

"Leave them there," he ordered.

"But they will become damp from the steam."

"Just do as I say."

She left the clothes where they were. There was a knock on the door. "Room service," she said. She slipped into a robe and went to open the door.

Steig could hear a Japanese voice say, "Your order."

"Please come in," Steig heard her reply. "He doesn't speak Japanese."

"Where is he?" the male voice said.

Steig was out of the bath, moving for the knife under his clothes. He heard the outside door close and someone come toward the bath. The knob on the door turned slowly. He readied the knife.

The door burst open. A squat Japanese with tattoos on both bare muscular arms fired two shots into the steaming bath before he realized there was no one in it. Steig leaped from behind the door, grabbed his assailant's neck, snapped it sideways until it cracked, then thrust the knife under his shoulder blade and into the heart. The man died so quickly that no scream could be uttered. Steig jumped away to avoid the blood and dashed into the other room. Tomi Chang was gone.

34: **AFTERMATH** Tokyo: Saturday, 9:05 P.M.

MORI HAD MOST pieces of the puzzle. His yakuza contact at the Ichiwa-kai in Kobe had told him the killer was a hired foreign professional. A sex club owner in Shibuya had put a name and description to the man. Helmut Stern. Tall, blond, blue eyes. But anyone could be behind him. The West, the Russians, China, the North Koreans, even South Korea.

The FBI had given him another piece. Told him that they were promoting listing of pachinko firms. That it was to stop an extortion racket that laundered money to North Korea. What were their motives? His Oyabun said the Americans had their own agenda, were involved in a power fight for the soul of the Korean peninsula.

So maybe the killer had been hired to stop the listing and maybe not. Which left Mori with a rift inside North Korea. Liberals opposing hard-liners. Tensions high. A division that was echoed inside the Japanese government. A person or people high in the government protecting the laundering of funds to North Korea, according to his Oyabun.

Then there were the Kims. He had Jonquil Kim's diary, which had created a sensation. Knew she'd been a comfort woman and probably hated Japan. Knew she was owner of a pachinko chain, and pachinko was linked to the murders. Knew the FBI suspected the grandaughter, Helim Kim, of working for both the West and North Korea. What were her motives? And did he trust what the FBI told him? And finally he had the father, managing a Korean bank in L.A. that had connections to the North Korean government. But which side?

Mori had the pieces, but how did he put them together?

Tonight he was reading the diary again, hoping something in it could provide a clue. So far it had not. As he turned the pages, he began to relate the horror of the comfort woman's story with the tragedy in his own life. His father had been a general whose honorable suicide he had witnessed at the war's conclusion. Atonement for Japan's loss in the war, or so he'd been told at the time.

There were questions that he'd never been able to answer. They became connected to ingredients of this pachinko murder case in his mind. His father had been a decent man, but he had sacrificed his life as atonement for defeat. Westerners might have cheered at the time. His father was an enemy, after all. He must have known about the comfort women program. Approved of it. To Japanese military minds, comfort women were a necessary part of the logistics of war. Yet his father was honorable. The comfort women might have been honorable too, although the older Japanese shrugged them off as prostitutes in the stories they told. What did the sons and daughters do about it? How did one atone for his nation's past?

Were these murders, the money laundering, the pachinko mess some kind of retribution being visited on Japan for its past sins? Must we all symbolically commit suicide—chosen death? he wondered. Was money necessary, as the British prisoners of war thought? So much per destroyed life. How long did one have to pay, according to rules laid down by the winners?

As he read the diary tonight, the horror that had been inflicted on these poor women became real. And a motive the Kims might have became clear. Any of them could be in pursuit of the Japanese pol involved in the pachinko racket. The three Kims could be central to a solution of the case. But Helim Kim, he decided, was the most likely pursuer.

Mitsuko called from the other room. "Phone call, anata."

It was the PSB duty officer from Mori's office. "Sorry to disturb you, sir. There's been another killing."

"Shit! Where?"

"A love hotel in Shibuya. The victim is a Korean yakuza."

"Connected to pachinko?"

"Same knife."

"Be right over."

"The prosecutor's office said they would handle it, sir. With the police. Their case."

Mori controlled his anger. Yuka Tanemura might be his favorite public prosecutor, but she wouldn't let their friendship get in the way of her controlling this case. "Log everything, then. Put a copy of their report on my desk. I'll check it out Monday."

Mori had just hung up when the phone rang again. Tomi was calling. She wanted him to meet her at a Kirin beer pub in Takadanobaba. He could tell from her voice something was wrong.

"What's happened?"

"I need a favor . . ." Tomi began as her voice choked.

"The reunion business?"

"Not on the phone," she said shortly. "In an hour. At the Kirin pub."

MORI GLANCED THROUGH a *Yomiuri* evening newspaper as he waited for Tomi. A lead article described rumors that the current prime minister, Ohno, might resign. The American comfort woman scandal had been badly handled, most agreed. There were other, larger economic problems.

If Ohno resigned, the article continued, election of the next prime minister might be uncontested. For the first time in the history of the Diet, one person only could be nominated for the post of prime minister, Kenzo Tanemura.

Mori folded the paper in disgust and stared out the window. Tanemura was Yuka's father, but Mori did not agree with his nationalistic policies. What was Japan coming to? That was Katano's nightly closing question, wasn't it?

THE PUB WAS frequented by college kids, and was across the square from the station. Mori had a window seat and could see the brightly lit square where a statue of a nude girl held doves in both hands. A memorial to the local war dead, civilian and military. He ordered a lemon juice for Tomi and an Asahi Super Dry for himself.

Tomi burst through the pub door, and he waved. "All hell's broken loose," she blurted.

"Take it easy. What happened?"

"Listen, will you do me two favors?"

"Certainly."

"I have to go away for a week, maybe longer. Could you arrange for my boy to be taken care of?"

"Yes. In fact, he could stay at my place. What's going on?"

Tomi took a gulp of air. "It's about those Korean murders. Some of my friends took matters into their own hands. One got killed for his troubles. And now I'm being followed."

"What are you talking about?" Couldn't be! Mori thought. Her friends knew where the killer was? *Who* he was?

"We narrowed the murder suspect down to a foreigner."

"How did you do that?"

She hesitated. "Promise me that you'll kill him. This is my second favor. A demon like this should not live. He killed one of my friends."

"I'll get him. Trust me."

Tomi took a deep breath. "In bed you used to tell me how beautiful I was and how our love was endless. Trust me, you said."

"How did you find out who he was? Just tell me that."

"A North Korean woman in Los Angeles was attacked but escaped. She faxed a drawing of his face to the KDA."

"What is the KDA?"

"Koreans for Democratic Action. A worldwide pro-democracy group. It was started by an exiled North Korean and spread from there to all the ex-pat Korean communities. The North Korean authorities consider it a dissident group. Terrorists. All Koreans murdered were members. So is this woman. A leading member."

"A faxed picture, is that all? How did they confirm who the killer was?"

"By persuading some witnesses to talk. Several mentioned a foreigner in the hall before the killings. The descriptions were all the same. The picture sent from Los Angeles was confirmed by all those who had seen him. So we're sure it's him. A watch on all the airports spotted him returning to Tokyo. He checked into a hotel in Shibuya. Face matched the drawing perfectly."

"But he got away."

"Yes," Tomi said. "Killed one of our best people. I was involved. He saw me. You see . . . I set him up."

Mori stared at her, aghast. No wonder she was scared. "Do your friends know who's behind him?"

"No. We had hoped to capture him alive and find out."

"Did he tell you his name?"

"Yes. Helmut Stern. A Swiss businessman. Plastics import-export. That's all I know."

Mori scribbled the name on a napkin. "Thanks, Tomi. Appreciate it. Let me give you protection for a couple of days. Till we get him."

"No . . . I'm okay. Just scared."

"Maybe this will make you feel better." Mori passed her an envelope full of ten-thousand-yen notes, payment for the Korean ship operation. She slipped it into her pocket unopened.

"This woman," Mori said. "The one who was attacked in Los Angeles. You know her name?"

"I can't give you that information."

"Why not?"

"Her grandmother's influential in the Pachinko Association. She's part owner of a large pachinko group."

Grandmother! Mori thought. "Listen, I won't tell anyone. Not a soul."

"Sure," Tomi said sarcastically.

"Really. I mean it." In normal circumstances, Mori would not have begged. But an idea was forming, a way to get at this killer. "No one will contact her. Anyway, I may know who this woman is already. I just want you to confirm it."

"How could you know that? It's impossible."

"Helim Kim?"

She stared at him.

"I'm right, eh?"

"Where did you get that name?"

"Long story. Listen, do you know why someone would try to kill Helim Kim?"

"No. Except that she's active in the KDA and her grandmother's pachinko firm. She was working on some special project to get pachinko companies listed. I'm not that important. I don't know details."

"What are the KDA's goals?"

"It's for freedom, justice, liberalization. That's all I can say."

"In North Korea?"

"Right."

"And all those killed were members. You told me there was a conflict inside North Korea between liberals and hard-liners."

"Yes."

"Wouldn't pachinko companies applying for listing on stock exchanges here favor the liberals?"

"I don't have a business mind, Mori. I don't know about such things."

Mori thought about that for a moment. "He's failed for the first time, hasn't he, our killer?"

"Yes. He'll try again until someone stops him."

"Of course!" And there it was. In every case there was an opportunity for closure. A gamble. A significant trifle that provided a glimpse of the assassin that could lead to his downfall. The killer was a professional. He had been hired to take out Helim Kim and failed. He would try again.

Tomi gathered up her pocketbook. "I have to be going."

"No. Wait. Just one more question. Only take a minute."

"I'm tired, Inspector. Really, really tired."

"Who is Alpha? The one who ran the meeting on the Korean ship? We know he's with North Korean intelligence, but that's all."

Tomi looked suddenly old. Her eyes were fixed on the door, which had just opened. "He's the leader of the hard-liners inside North Korea. Those who do not want change. Ever. Behind them—who knows?"

Mori turned to see what she was staring at. Two heavyset men had come in and taken seats. Not the usual lecherous salaryman types that came here to stare at the college girls. He lowered his voice. "Did you take evasive procedures on your way here?"

"Yes. Of course."

"Good. Anything else about Alpha? What's his background?"

Tomi paused before answering. "Some years ago there was an attempt on the life of the South Korean prime minister at a temple in Burma. They missed him but killed twenty of his cabinet ministers. The North Korean para-squad that did it was wiped out, all but one. A bastard with a pitted face known by the code name Alpha got away. Then just before the Korean Olympics, a transistor radio bomb blew up a South Korean airliner over Thailand. A Korean girl and an old man were caught. The man committed suicide, but the girl told all on South Korean TV. Turned out her North Korean handler was the same pit-faced bastard who escaped from the Burmese temple. No one knows his real name. Alpha is now head of North Korean intelligence. That's all I know about him." Tomi checked the two heavyset men, who were ordering drinks at the bar. Her eyes were suddenly afraid. "I think I'd better leave now."

Mori took her hand. "Let me give you protection."

"No." She reached into her purse and pulled out a piece of paper. "That would only make matters worse. Whatever happens, I can tell you this. A foreigner has been hired to kill North Koreans. Very big, very tall, with blue eyes. Light blue. Like this picture Helim Kim drew of him." She handed Mori the paper. "He's also very well trained, very clever. Perhaps Alpha is behind the killings, I don't know. You have the killer's description. It's all I can give you. The rest is up to you." She eased out of the narrow booth and stood exposed and alone.

Mori bowed his head in gratitude. "If he's in Tokyo, I'll find this foreigner. Where shall I pick up your son?" He could see that the two men at the bar were watching her.

"I'll contact you tomorrow or the next day about the arrangements. I'm sorry to trouble you tonight."

"No trouble, Tomi, we're friends . . . aren't we?"

For a moment she regained her composure. "No, you've used me, and I've used you." She said this without rancor. "I'm sorry. I know when something is over. Believe me, I'll never bother you again after this."

"Tomi, wait!"

But she had headed for the door, hurrying through it as if late to an appointment. Several moments later, the two men paid at the bar and followed her, their drinks left untouched. Mori moved quickly, planting himself between the men and the door.

"Excuse me," Mori said, grinning with embarrassment as Japanese do in addressing strangers. "I believe you forgot something." He could smell the kimchi on their breath. See up close from their hard faces and permed hair they were Korean yakuza.

"No," one replied mildly. "We forgot nothing." The other was looking at the door through which Tomi had disappeared.

Mori hit the first one in the throat, a karate chop that could have been better timed. He was out of practice. But the big Korean went down. The second reached inside a coat pocket and drew a handgun. Mori was already moving as it came up. He kicked straight for the groin and, as the Korean started to buckle, hit the bridge of his nose with two lightning fists. The gun fired, the bullet grazing Mori's leg. He heard screams, then kicked again and the man went down for good. Mori picked up the gun and waved it at the first thug, who was gasping for air. A Chinese Black Star pistol.

It was not a reportable action, Mori decided. He dropped the revolver in the first container he came to. A cop from the kiosk near the station was hurrying toward the entrance when Mori reached the street. Mori hailed a cab. "Waseda Station."

In the cab, he checked his leg. The bullet had torn his trouser leg but fortunately only scratched the skin. It looked like something he might have sustained in the nightly subway rush hour.

Mori bought a ticket for Iidabashi and an evening newspaper. The American comfort woman issue was again on front pages. A lady in New York had come forward claiming to be the woman but that had turned out to be a hoax. When he reached the station he found a public phone and placed a call. It was time, he decided.

MORI'S UNCLE ANSWERED his call.

"Yes?"

"I need an introduction."

"For God's sake, Mori, it's Saturday night."

"Sorry. I'm running out of time."

"Good, then maybe you will use it more wisely in future. Who is it this time?"

"Katano of KSB-TV. I need to meet him tomorrow."

"It's a Sunday."

"I know. As I said, I have no time."

"But why Katano? What on earth for?"

"He knows someone I want to meet. Someone whose life is in danger."

The tone of the Oyabun's voice changed. "Someone's life?"

"Yes."

The Oyabun thought a moment. "I'll do what I can. I know you wouldn't say that unless you meant it. Katano was in trouble several years ago, wasn't he? That's usually a good place to start. Let me see . . ."

"An army colonel, as I recall," Mori prompted.

"Yes. Right. An army colonel. Katano had him on the show without approval of his superiors. Preaching a coup by the sword to cleanse our corrupt government. Offended some sensibilities, the colonel did. Although a large number of people privately agreed with him. And still do."

"I'd like to meet him soon," Mori said. "Tomorrow at the latest."

"Why the hurry?"

"I've been assigned a public prosecutor for the case. Her approval's required even when I pee."

"Her?"

"Yuka Tanemura."

"Daughter of the next prime minister?"

"She's not like her father. I've worked with her before. She's flexible, the only prosecutor I can stand. If I meet Katano on the weekend, I can report it Monday or later. After the fact."

"Always the impatient one, aren't we?" The Oyabun's voice was gradually coming awake. "I hope you know what you're doing. My main complaint about you even when your father was alive was you couldn't wait to do this or that. A friend of mine, former president at Dentsu, can help us, I think. The defense minister wanted Katano's head. Gave an interview saying advertisers should boycott Katano's show. Dentsu pulled Katano's chestnuts out of the fire. I'll have my friend give Katano a ring. He hangs out at some club in the Ginza. Has a woman there."

35: THE QUEST Hong Kong: Sunday, 8:30 A.M.

TOMÁS VELAQUEZ AWOKE with a sense of urgency. Through the window, rust-colored sails of a junk prodded the wind. A Star ferry roved Victoria Harbor looking for Kowloon. The white wishbone wake of a red Macao jetfoil scarred the metallic ripples.

I'm in Hong Kong, he thought. How did I get here? And then the nightmare returned. The long flight came back to him. The Chinese couple next to him who tittered at everything he said. A Lufthansa 747 one-stop, and he'd thankfully slept most of the way. But then he'd wasted the first two days getting acclimated and figuring out what he should do.

Tomás had been sweating in the humidity, so the sheets were damp, the pillow too. He'd turned the air-conditioning off during the night because it blew right on his head. It would take several days to adjust to the heat.

He'd call Helim again. Last time they'd talked seemed ages ago; she'd suggested they meet in Hong Kong. They really needed to meet, but would she agree? Being on the run only increased his doubts. Now he was doubting her.

He decided to pay a visit to the hotel where he'd kept the plutonium overnight coming through from North Korea. Triumphant then. Cocky. A beautiful girl on his arm. While he shaved, his thoughts went back to Helim. The more he thought about her, the more he wondered. She'd been in his room. Knew where the plutonium was. If it had been switched, she could have done it easily. You're tired, he told himself. You've flown too far too fast and shouldn't make any serious decisions until the jet lag wears off. A month at least. Piss off, he told himself. Early mornings were his most vulnerable time.

It was like being unfaithful, Tomás realized after he'd dressed. When

186

you distrust someone once, the next time is easier. You begin to hear things inside your head. Something in the relationship begins to tear apart. Since their breakup, he'd trusted her as a friend. Hoped they'd get back together one day. Now, he wasn't sure.

Before he'd left Germany, Tomás had called the IAEA. Carswell had been upset because Tomás would only talk for a minute thirty seconds and wouldn't tell them where he was. The Americans had made up their minds, Tomás explained. So if anyone was going to clear his name, he had to do it himself. He would find out first if the claims made by American intelligence were true. Who at the Mannix Hotel had been approached and in exactly what way. The story had been fabricated, he was sure of that. Once he confirmed that his interrogators in Vienna had lied, the rest would be easy. Grudgingly, Carswell agreed he was doing the right thing. But he pointed out that as far as the IAEA was concerned, Tomás had violated no rules. "So don't do anything rash," Carswell pleaded.

FORMER PRESIDENT OF the United States Sherman Whitlow took the call at his lodge in the Colorado Rockies. He was spending the weekend there prior to his hastily arranged trip to Japan to meet Park Tai Jin, the North Korean leader. With him for briefing purposes were several Asian experts from the U.S. Trade Commission as well as a key negotiator for ConnOil, which was fronting the proposal to the North Koreans. The concept, most everyone agreed, was brilliant.

"Mr. President, how are you?"

"Fine, very well. Who is this calling, please?" The familiarity with which the caller spoke had made him hesitate, and he wondered if he knew the woman behind the voice. A cultured, educated, husky voice. Not young. A desirable mature woman, although he rarely thought about such things.

"Consider me an old friend, though you wouldn't recognize my name now."

"Perhaps you should try me." While there was no coquettishness in her voice, there was an appealing note of urgency. His hand reached for a red button that would connect the call to an FBI intercept, then hesitated.

"One day, I'll tell you. I'd like to meet you in Niigata. That's why I called."

"I'm sorry—perhaps you have confused me with someone else?" He had been assured that the meeting with Park Tai Jin had been organized under tightest security.

"Let's just say I have inside connections. I know about your earlier career in China."

The former president flushed. "I don't know what you're talking about." His hand moved away from the red button.

"Oh, I think you do, Mr. President."

"Who's this? What do you want?"

"I'd only like to suggest a meeting once you're in Japan. I have interesting information for you. Information related to your past that is timely, sir. I regretted to learn last year that your lovely wife had died."

"I can hardly understand why this is related to my—"

"Trust me. I'll contact you again about a meeting. Niigata is where you'll be spending most of your time, correct? Won't interfere with your duties as a statesman. We would hate to hinder the culmination of your career with a crowning diplomatic success."

"I really don't know what you are talking about."

"Does the city Harbin do anything for you, sir?" The phone went dead.

Sherman Whitlow stared at the phone for a long moment, feeling the beads of perspiration forming on his forehead. Then, unbidden, a groan escaped from his lips.

36: TRIP Tokyo: Sunday, 2:45 P.M.

THE FIRST FLIGHT to Tokyo Saturday was on United and arrived the following day in the early afternoon Tokyo time. Steve checked the arrival message board as he went through immigration formalities at Narita. Nothing from Helim. He took the express train into Ueno Station. On the plane he hadn't slept. His brain ached for rest.

When he reached Ueno his first call was to the number Helim had given him for the famous newscaster. A girl answered in Japanese, and he said, "Katano-san, kudasai."

"Dare?" Who?

"Katano-san."

"Iya. Chigaimasu." The line went dead. Wrong number. He must have copied it down incorrectly. No problem, he thought. I'll just go over to the TV station. They should know where to find him.

KSB-TV headquarters was located on a small hill in Akasaka. The building had been renovated many times and was now a labyrinth of studios and floors, one of the largest TV complexes in Japan.

Steve arrived just as the evening shift was taking over. The highest-priced talent were arriving for their Golden Hour shows. Groups of young girls and boys jostled for space on the crowded pavement in front of the studio doors waiting for their idols to appear. The crowd held out paper and pens for autographs and shouted their idols' names.

Steve struggled through the crowd in front of the studio doors. His shirt and trousers were wrinkled from sleeping on the plane, and the sour taste of stale air still fouled his mouth. God, I need a shower, he thought.

The receptionist in the lobby pretended not to be horrified by the bad-smelling foreigner who asked for Mr. Katano.

"Holiday," she replied politely in English, even though Steve had spoken to her in Japanese. "Maybe you call his agent tomorrow." She wrote down a number on a piece of paper.

Steve thanked her and found a public phone. He dialed the agency but got a tape announcing working hours Monday to Saturday.

It was after six-thirty. He gave up and headed for a nearby hotel.

A receptionist bowed when he asked for a room, noted his clothes, then looked around for help.

A manager hurried over and asked politely if Steve had a reservation.

"I've just arrived," Steve replied briskly.

"And where are your bags?"

"At Ueno Station. I'll pick them up after I sign in and shower."

The manager sucked air between his teeth. "All right. We have several rooms left. Three hundred dollars per night. Do you have a credit card?"

Steve hesitated. Three hundred dollars a night? Robbery. Prices in Tokyo were soaring. He took out his wallet; his card was missing. He searched his pockets. His mind raced back over the past twenty-four hours. The last time he'd used the card was when? He fought back tiredness and forced his mind to think. He hadn't brought much cash with him.

The United Airlines counter in L.A.! He hurriedly paid for his ticket there. Rushed off to catch the flight. But wouldn't they have noticed if he'd forgotten the card there? Notified him once he'd boarded? Perhaps the ground staff hadn't found the card until later or not at all. Maybe he'd left it on the counter and someone else had picked it up.

"Is something wrong, sir?" the manager asked impatiently.

"I must've lost my card, and I didn't bring extra cash," he said, more angry at himself than anything else. Usually he was totally organized. Yet here he was rushing around the world chasing a woman without any rational plan or preparation. He had no idea what would happen next. That wasn't like him. He suddenly felt jet-lagged and bone-weary.

"Very sorry, sir." The manager motioned toward a security man. Steve stalked out of the hotel feeling in his pocket for the few hundred dollars in yen he had left. He'd phone his bank in the morning. Everything would be okay. Tonight he'd just have to rough it.

Heading for a subway, he recalled that the benevolent Japanese police allowed down-and-outers to sleep in Yoyogi Park. Nothing like a little fresh air, he told himself cheerily.

From Harajuku Station he walked across the stone bridge in front of the emperor's Meiji Park. The iron gates were closed, and behind them a huge wooden torii stood somberly like a sentinel guarding a tomb. Behind the emperor's park was another park. A sign on the open gates read "Closed," but Steve ignored it and followed the paths. Many of the benches were already occupied by sleepers. He finally found an empty one and sat down.

How was he going to find Helim now? He'd wasted a day.

He should have called the FBI before he left Los Angeles, he told himself. Ron Uemura was in Japan on some operation. No, Ron had more important matters than to help find his girlfriend. He'd use Ron only if he had to, he decided. He had to get Helim out of Japan. Away from whoever was stalking her.

THE TWO FOREIGNERS walked silently together until they reached Kabuki-cho, where the porno bars were. Here the girls would do anything. "You ever try the action, Steig?" Aleksei asked.

"Occasionally. The saunas are relaxing. The love hotels are the best in Tokyo. I was in one the other night over in Shibuya. Someone tried to take me out."

"We know all about that. It was in the morning papers."

"I have her name. Where she works. I'm going to find her."

Aleksei sighed. "No, no, Steig. My connections with the local yakuza will do that. She'll be taken care of—their way. We have more important matters for you."

"Someone knows I'm here."

"You botched Helim Kim in L.A. Now the police have your face."

Startled for a moment, Steig quickly recovered. "It's like she's being magically protected," he muttered.

"She arrived in Tokyo yesterday. Some of us cynics think you've grown fond of her. We're going to give you a second chance to prove we're wrong." The mouth grinned lewdly.

"I was unlucky, that's all." But Steig knew it wasn't only that. He wondered what it was that had prevented him from finishing her off. Was it her physical beauty, something he had always valued to the point of obsession? He knew he had been less focused, more haphazard, with his aim in the garage—he never missed. It was, of course, impossible that he could be "fond" of her—it was all just a job. He had built defenses of character against all possibilities. No, he was not fond of her. But somehow she bothered him.

"We've decided on a change in strategy." The man walking beside the German was shorter than Steig remembered him in Los Angeles. "This time you're to take her alive. We'll do the rest."

"Alive?" Steig stopped on the sidewalk in the middle of the crowds. "Why?"

"It's been discovered she's a double. Our friends want to assess the damage she's caused. She's to be delivered to a city on the west coast of Japan. A slightly higher risk operation."

"Slightly?"

The shorter man ignored his displeasure. "If you feel the risks are too great, you may withdraw. However, your fee will be doubled if you succeed. Nothing will be paid if you don't. It'll be your last chance."

Steig thought a moment. Double was not enough. A kidnapping created huge complexities. "I'll need asylum as well."

"It can be arranged."

"Where?"

"In Russia, of course."

So! Steig nearly exploded. It *was* one of the big powers behind his work! He'd thought so. And that explained how they'd found him. His old boss had put his client onto him, he was sure now. Markus Wolf, who had run East Germany's Central Intelligence Administration in the Ministry for State Security and had close connections to the KGB. Well, that changed things, didn't it! Most certainly, he couldn't let word get back to Markus that Gunther Steig had been unable to complete an assignment. Markus was the best spymaster ever to roam Europe. He, Gunther Steig, would not be the one to let him down. "I will deliver the girl if you agree to provide asylum and the money."

"It will be arranged, then."

"Where is she?"

Aleksei told him the name of the inn. There would be heavy security, and she would be leaving Atami on Wednesday. That day was his window of opportunity; security would be relaxed the day she departed. "But minimize your risks," Aleksei repeated. "They know what you look like. You'll need a disguise."

"I'll handle it."

"Whether you like it or not, I'm going to assist you this time. First, with a suggestion."

"I'll listen, but I do things my own way."

"On the outskirts of Atami is the fastest-growing religious sect in

Japan. The sect preaches healing by spiritual and physical contact. Each week a flood of sick converts detrain at Atami Station, visit their hotel, and pray for health. Amazingly, some are cured. Beside the hotel is a temple, museum, shops. One of our contacts has booked you for Tuesday night under the name Stein. Police will not look for you there."

"How do you know?"

"The wife of the chief of police is a strong supporter of the sect. They pay a certain amount of money annually to ensure there is no police interference in their activity."

"I follow you."

"Good. The amount of money is substantial."

"So I pose as a sick convert who wants to pray for his health?"

"You are ill and wish a conversion, yes. A donation is possible. You're from a wealthy family. There are two days to prepare if you choose this venue. Remember also—Helim Kim's more important alive to us now than dead." He handed Steig a book.

"What's this?"

"Teachings of the Master. The Kami-Hai bible. Might come in useful."

Steig glowered. "I prefer weapons. I'll need a small automatic weapon that can be broken down, Uzi preferably. And a handgun."

"We have North Korean copies. Quite good actually."

"Ten clips for it. And the handgun a Luger."

"Optimistic, aren't we? That arsenal has to get through Atami Station security. Or roadblocks on the coastal access roads if you choose that way. They'll be searching cars. And watching all trains too."

"Just leave the rest to me."

37: THE FAVOR Tokyo: Sunday, 9:30 P.M.

THE OHASHI CLUB was in a second basement off Ginza-dori near Shimbashi, two buildings past Takashimaya Department Store.

An outer room harbored a solid walnut bar, a tinted mirror ceiling, and paintings carefully copied from originals at the Louvre. Inside, the appointments resembled the first-class lounges at Japan Airline terminals. There were ankle-deep burgundy carpets, glass partitions with etched grape arbors, and easy chairs with TVs, phones, and faxes for those who wanted privacy.

The room was lit by gold tiers of crystal chandeliers. Japanese businessmen from elite corporations pursued conversations that a female pianist on a rotating elevated platform tried not to interrupt with a Schubert repertoire.

Katano was sitting alone in a far corner drinking a Courvoisier. He stood as Mori approached. His face held the arrogance of one who had considered the meaning of life and decided there was none. A hedonist if Mori had ever seen one. That simplified matters a great deal. Mori introduced himself, ordered a Hiroshima sakè.

"I have some questions about your famous diary."

"That's privileged information, Inspector. I'm afraid I am not at liberty to discuss it."

"Were you given the entire diary or just several pages?"

"About five pages altogether. Covering the American comfort woman. That was all we were interested in, really. Why?"

Mori tried not to show his relief. "We know who gave you the diary, Katano-san."

Katano shifted in his seat. "Can't say anything about it, Inspector. Lawyers."

"Right. Well, it certainly made the impact you hoped."

"Is that what you came for? To commend me on the job I'm doing? I hardly think so."

Arrogant bastard, Mori thought. Very well, I can play your game. "We understand the only politician you admire is Kenzo Tanemura. You've taken some trips together; your show provides favorable support. You've spoken at his rallies."

"We know each other."

"This diary didn't help the prime minister, did it? And it could be coincidence, but Tanemura is next in line—a shoo-in for the job when this prime minister falls."

"I am simply reporting the news, Mori-san."

"How about helping me then? I need a little information about Helim Kim."

That stopped him. Katano could not suppress a gasp. "Who is Helim Kim?"

"You'll have to do better than that."

"Perhaps you could give me some hint."

"Perhaps I could find some reason to detain you for a few days."

"I'm sure you could." Katano shrugged. "So I'll do the show from Funabashi Prison. Might add a few points to the nightly ratings."

"You're a cocky son of a bitch."

Katano didn't say anything more, just sat nursing his drink.

A waiter brought Mori's sake. "Kampai." The inspector lifted his cup.

Katano beamed at him, as if considering a change of heart. "I believe in give and take, Inspector. Little things sometimes have great cost. Diamonds, for example."

"I'm pleased you are willing to consider an offer." Mori swallowed some sake. He hadn't expected the TV personality to be a pushover.

"Always willing to listen." Katano leaned forward.

"I'm working on a case that's much larger than this pissant American comfort woman thing. Eight North Koreans have been murdered."

"Go on."

Mori watched his face. "It has to do with pachinko. A killer is at large. Miss Kim can help me to catch him. I need to know when she's scheduled to visit Japan next. You know."

He could see the flicker of curiosity light Katano's eyes, and he threw another log on the fire. "I'm willing to make a deal. Help me on this and you get the exclusive story. Everything."

Katano finished off his Courvoisier and raised his hand. A waiter understood immediately. "I happen to be planning a story on the pachinko industry. What a coincidence, eh?"

Mori talked into his drink, as if lifting his eyes would break some spell. "As I said, if you help, you get the story."

Katano sat back in his chair. "Sorry I can't help you, Inspector, much as I'd like to. I've promised her confidentiality."

Katano wanted more, Mori thought. Good. He knew how to deal with greed. "The president of Dentsu will be disappointed in your answer." Mori knew Dentsu controlled some 60 percent of all KSB-TV prime-time advertising. Booked it well in advance, then sold it piecemeal to privileged clients.

Katano remained impassive. "The president of Dentsu can screw himself."

"Times that good, are they? So then we talk to the president of your network. About that fourteen-year-old girl in Thailand. And I believe we could persuade a ten-year-old boy to testify too."

Katano's face reddened. "That's totally untrue."

"I have no doubt. But many people want your ass. We'll wreck your career. If not today, tomorrow. I'm a patient man." Mori downed his drink and rose to leave. "Pity."

Katano belched. "Helim Kim arrived in Japan yesterday afternoon."

Mori sat back down. "You're doing fine. Keep talking."

"She'll be here for four days at least. Five maybe. That's all I know. We're doing an interview tomorrow and the next day. You're a real bastard, Inspector."

"That's what all my friends say. Where in Japan is she?"

"You must guarantee one thing. You do not contact her until our interview session is completed."

"Agreed. Where, Katano?"

"An inn near Atami." Katano scribbled a number and address on Mori's napkin.

"Very generous of you, Katano."

"Remember, you don't contact her until after Wednesday."

"Since she's in Japan already, we might not need to contact her at all."

38: A CHOSEN DEATH Tokyo: Monday, 6:45 A.M.

MORI'S PHONE RANG at his home. The captain of the Homicide Division, Jiro Mizuno, was calling in an emergency—Mori was required on the scene. Public prosecutor's orders. Mizuno delivered an address. A detective would brief him there.

After nearly an hour and a half in the morning traffic, Mori arrived at a temple in a quiet upscale Tokyo neighborhood, an island of ancient cedars in a sea of glazed tile roofs. Huge trees towered into the humid sky above somber stone deities and ancient wooden temple buildings.

The dignity of the temple was not disrupted by the police or the early crowd that, barred from the stone-inlaid courtyard by control tapes, pushed and shoved to see. The temple remained a place of solitude and introspection. Not to know is Buddha. Not to see is Paradise.

As Mori stepped from the cab, the gallery was ten deep. A zaru-soba peddler had set up his cart, and business was brisk.

The officer at the crowd control tape saluted when he saw who it was. Mori ducked under the tape and went up the chiseled stone steps that led to the courtyard and main buildings. Uniformed police and plain-clothesmen crowded the area. Chosen deaths—suicides—were still assigned to the Homicide Division for authentication.

"Inspector Mori!" A veteran police detective whose name Mori couldn't remember came up to him. "Sorry to disrupt your schedule, sir. Hasegawa of the Third Detective Division. We were occasional kendo partners in the old days. Complicated situation here, I'm afraid." He waved a woman's pocketbook at the organized confusion. A still photography team was taking photos. A sweating video unit was filming the body, an ominous lump under a white sheet, and panning the blood-soaked stones, the location of exits. A DNA team was busy collecting samples of blood smears near the victim. Other detectives, in suits and incongruous Japanese army field caps, were scouring the courtyard.

The sun came out. Mori squinted against the light as if unused to it. "Was the victim a woman, Hasegawa?"

"Woman, sir." Hasegawa pulled off the sheet.

Mori's eyes found the body.

In his days with the Homicide Division, Mori had seen every kind of death. He had viewed bodies chopped to mincemeat, sword-hacked torsos, rape victims rotted after months spent under dank forest floors, the blackened faces of the gassed. Still, this death jolted him.

The beheading had been clean, from the left. The pavement surrounding the headless trunk now yielded thousands of congealing islands where blood had flown like seaspray in a storm. The head, several feet from the sprawled body, was covered with a second white cloth.

Hasegawa offered Mori a cigarette.

"The kaishaku was a right-hander," Mori offered.

Hasegawa grunted without emotion, as if discussing a golf shot. "There obviously was a kaishaku who was right-handed, yes, but the deceased made the first cut. We called you because you may have known the deceased. We need some corroboration."

"That so." Mori looked at the headless body again. A woman's. Then at the pocketbook Hasegawa held. Identification in that, he assumed. So what was their problem? Why the urgency?

He recalled that the swordsman could not technically be charged with murder in Japan. Only as an accessory. In chosen death, the kaishaku performed the beheading if the self-inflicted cut was not fatal. He was usually a friend of the subject's. For a moment, pictures from Mori's childhood flickered through his brain.

The palace grounds. A child, he watched his father, the general, kneel and make his final preparations on the incendiary-scarred grounds before the palace. His father had requested the honor of seppuku from the emperor. His wish had been granted. When the general had completed his preparation, he had carefully taken the wakizashi, the short sword, and held it with both hands extended in front of his abdomen.

Hasegawa's voice interrupted his thoughts. "There are several curiosities to this death. First, why a Bushido ritual was used. Second, the deceased is Korean."

Hasegawa was preparing him for something, Mori realized. Little steps to soften the blow that was to follow. "A Korean." Mori forced his mind from the past to the present. "The kaishaku has disappeared. And it is a Korean woman who performed this ritual?"

A curious shadow crossed the detective's face. Expectant.

"Could we kindly take a look at the head, then," Mori said as nonchalantly as possible.

Hasegawa walked over and pulled the white cloth off.

Mori tried to stifle the gasp that escaped him. Felt his stomach turn, his breath catch in his throat. The once pretty mouth frozen with anticipation. The eyes wide with final horror. Eye shadow flecked with her blood. He swallowed lest he retch.

Tomi-san, what have I done to you?

The detective was reviewing the scene like a well-rehearsed tour guide. The sword had cut her cleanly, yes? Surgically. The hand of an expert. She'd felt little pain, no doubt. The mouth would have moved for several seconds. The tongue always protruded like that when final death came. "The gray color is displeasing, no? Her file was cross-referenced to your name. We understood that you met her frequently. Just a week ago, in fact."

"She was one of my field agents." He forced himself to concentrate. "What about the kaishaku? No clues?"

"Evaporated," the detective said. "The death occurred approximately four to eight hours ago. The temple was closed this morning, and the temple keeper was asleep. It's a small local temple, not busy. Religion has gone out of favor, he told us. People are too rich. There are no clues so far."

Mori made some notes. But his mind wasn't focusing. Trivia drifted through his turbulent thoughts. He remembered Tomi the last time he'd seen her, looking so worried. And her boy—what would become of him?

"How are you treating this?"

"A suicide. According to an ID found in her pocketbook, this woman worked in mizu-shobai. We believe the kaishaku was yakuza, which explains the use of the ritual. He would have been charged as an accessory under current law; and no doubt he knew this. That explains why he disappeared. The missing short sword can be explained. It might have implicated him also. We can't treat it as murder even under such circumstances."

"Was there any note?"

"Just this." The detective handed him a trinket. "We found it in her hand."

Mori stared at the earring. A golden reindeer. Her pro-democracy group had tried to take out the foreign killer and had failed. So she'd come to him. "Trust me," he'd said.

The detective asked, "It tell you anything?"

Mori blinked several times. "This is a symbol of Korean reunion and democracy." He paused. "Not even murder as an option, then?"

"There are no witnesses. Nothing indicating murder. Was she involved in any cases we should know about?"

Mori stared at his cigarette. "No." A suicide would be a nice whitewash. Mori could feel the quicksand beginning to tug at his feet. She was trying to tell him something. The earring. Liberalization. Reunion. Alpha? Who could be behind him? This was the work of ruthless people who sought power for their own careers and fortunes. For their own countries. Mori's anger had given way to icy calm.

"You bastards," he said softly to himself. The golden reindeer. He would find the killer and those behind him if it took the rest of his life.

39: PROSECUTOR Tokyo: Monday, 12:00 noon

PUBLIC PROSECUTORS IN Japan were considered to be as powerful as Shinto gods. For that reason, Mori didn't like them meddling in his business. However, Yuka Tanemura was the exception—the one public prosecutor in whom he confided his lesser secrets, even though he didn't share her famous politician father's convictions.

One needed to keep an arrow in the quiver for those special occasions, his archery friends liked to tell him. So he did. And if he had ever needed her, it was right now. The fact that she readily agreed to lunch when he phoned did not surprise him. Bad news traveled fast.

He arrived at an Indian restaurant in Hibiya exactly at noon and was led to a reserved table. It was less than two hours after his visit to the scene of Tomi's death.

Yuka would be late, as usual. He used the time to consider what must be accomplished. If Tomi was to be avenged, he needed Yuka to agree to his plan, and the way to do that was to convince her he knew who the murderer was. However, that wouldn't be easy. She was the best of the prosecutor's team. Prepared by the finest schools in Japan. She would question every weak link in his hypothesis.

"MORI-SAN." YUKA TANEMURA sat down opposite him. "I was sorry to hear about your Korean friend."

"Then you know already. Thanks for coming."

Her eyes were alert and intelligent. "Shall we order first?"

"Yes."

"Your turn to pay or mine?"

"Depends on how much help you plan to give me." Mori pretended it was a joke.

Yuka understood. "I'll help you, Mori-san. Don't I always?"

"In that case, it's on me."

She closed the menu. "Then I'll take the full Indian lunch."

Mori explained that the body had been set up to look like a chosen death. "The coroner's verdict will be suicide," Mori said matter-of-factly. "I just came from the scene. It wasn't pretty."

"She was North Korean, right?"

"Yes."

"Beginning to look like an epidemic. You quite sure it wasn't suicide?"

"The suicide verdict will be a cover-up. Whitewash. This was murder. Same people behind it as the other Koreans." He spoke calmly, although his anger was dangerously close to the surface.

"Number eight, then?"

"Nine, if we count a Korean man found in a love hotel Saturday night."

"I've been reading the file. Do you have any ideas?" The tone of her voice was not hopeful.

"I think it was the same killer as the others, even though it was a different MO. No long narrow knife this time." He forced his mind away from the scene at the temple. "The coroner's office will claim it was suicide, because it makes everything easier. There are no witnesses. No murder weapon. The detective squad on the scene had reached that conclusion by the time I arrived."

"Nothing you can prove, then? You just have a hunch?"

Mori knew this was the crux. "I have a foreigner named Helmut Stern. The day before she died, Tomi—the deceased—gave me his name. Said Korean friends had traced this guy, thought he was the killer."

"Thought? Nothing more substantive?"

"A pro-democracy society she belongs to was investigating the murders. They came up with a sketch of the suspect that several witnesses confirmed, found out where he was staying, and set him up. He escaped. Tomi fronted the operation to take him. He must have found out where she worked. She was scared yesterday when we met. Two heavies were following her. I offered her protection, but she refused. She asked me to take care of her boy. I think she knew . . ." Mori put his hand over his eyes.

"It's okay, Inspector. I understand."

Mori cleared his throat. "I also have the owner of a bar near the pachinko hall who saw a foreigner meet two girls at his place. Just after the seventh murder took place. Same night. Same name. Stern."

"How about motive for the pachinko hits?"

"Someone wants us to think it's for money. Not true. Political's my guess."

Yuka shifted in her seat. "According to my father, there was an Intelligence Committee meeting about your putting this same girl on some North Korean ship with a wire. The operation wasn't authorized."

Mori massaged his eyelids with a thumb and forefinger. "Yuka, you know the system. These authorizations take a month or more. And then everyone and his brother knows about it. We've had leaks, you name it. This couldn't wait. It had to be secure."

Her look was sympathetic. "Aoyama?"

Mori grimaced. "Doing everything he can to ensure I don't succeed. Koreans aren't going to make him points with his political friends. And he's afraid I'll take his job."

She smiled. At least they agreed on one thing. Aoyama had invited her out several times and come on very strong. "Perhaps she was killed because someone found out about that wire job. Why do you think the killings are political?"

"Because the dead pachinko parlor owners were Northerners, members of a pro-democracy society strongly pushing for liberalization in North Korea. There's a lot of money in pachinko. Money being sent to North Korea one way or the other."

"Didn't Justice do a confidential review of that issue last year? As I recall, the National Police told us only a small amount leaked annually."

"That was another whitewash. When Tomi died, she was holding a gold earring in her hand. A tiny reindeer. This was a symbol of Korean reunion and liberalization. She was trying to give me a motive and clue."

"What you have so far is pure conjecture." Yuka broke off a piece of nan and chewed on it thoughtfully.

"We have a prime suspect. We place him near the last of the pachinko murders. We have two girls that can ID him whenever they phone in. I have a picture drawn by someone he assaulted in L.A. Tomi's murder is the only one that doesn't fit his MO. But she set this killer up. One of her group tried to take him, and it got him killed. This foreigner's the killer. I have a way to take him. We'll know who's behind this and why when we catch him, but I can't move without your okay. The Intelligence Committee tied my hands."

"How are you going to do it?"

"We're going to make him come to us. It's already being organized. I've been putting a team together. We're meeting this afternoon, if you give me a go-ahead."

Their orders came, and they both sat silently until the waiter left. Tanemura lifted a fork and studied it. Like most Japanese she didn't really like to eat with metal reusable utensils. Knives and forks and spoons were unclean. "My father would like to invite you for an evening soon. He suggested next week."

"Your dad?" That was strange. No. Incomprehensible.

"Yes. Dinner."

Mori flushed. "What's this about, Yuka?" Her father, the most famous politician in Japan, was inviting a humble investigator for dinner? Kenzo Tanemura? Idol of his wife.

"He knew your father. They were friends. It bothers him that you don't share his position on North Korea. Or Japan's destiny." She turned to face him. "Look at it this way. Japan has never been allowed a position of parity with the white power elite in the U.S. government. Nor will we ever be. We are always the servant. They are the master."

"Yes. I have heard this before."

"My father envisions an economic alliance with China, Russia, and the two Koreas. The first step is a free trade zone in which all will join. The key is North Korea, since their borders access the raw material wealth of Siberia and the most weakly defended area of China. Our main interest, however, must be the Russian Republic. Asian Russia."

"Siberia?" Mori had always considered Siberian Russia a useless waste. "What on earth for?"

"One day, Russia will become a close trading partner. Our ally. Closer even than the U.S.A. has been in the past. At first it will be mainly a huge source of raw material; eventually, a consumer market surpassing the United States."

"Really?"

"It's inevitable. Our trade relation with the U.S.A. isn't inviolate. It has to be reconsidered. Before the Asian economic crisis, our exports to Asia exceeded those to North America. The Americans now accuse us of targeting their market, exporting our way out of the crisis. My father heads up a committee that's negotiating with various former Soviet republics for investment and technical aid. Aleksei Romanov, a Russian commercial director at the embassy here, has been very supportive. He's a friend. We would hate for anything to disrupt our negotiations. I think you can see what I'm driving at."

To his horror, Mori did. "You're suggesting a trade? My operation for your—"

"You misunderstand. Let me put it this way. If we're to become the world leader, we can't be dependent on the U.S.A. It's a very simple equation. The Russia of today may not realize it needs our help, but the Russia of the future will become our supplier and subordinate. We'll turn the Soviet Far East into a modern high-tech industrial complex connected to us by MagLev trains and ships. North Korea's location is critical to this strategy.

"Already the first project is under way—a multilateral development of the river delta at the junction of the Russian, Chinese, and North Korean borders. The area will become known as the Asia Tomorrow Project. The Chinese will join as well. They've never declared war on anyone, have they? All thunder and no lightning. China is too busy managing Hong Kong and its other vast provinces to do more than go along with our leadership. Think of it: we'll control the two giants. But first we must control North Korea."

"How will you do that?"

"We already do—indirectly." Yuka brought the glass up to cool her cheek. "That must not be disrupted by you or anyone else. It will confirm Japan's world leadership position. Have I confused you?"

"Economics was never my best subject, I'm afraid," Mori said quietly. "So if I promise my cooperation, you will let me go ahead?"

"I'll authorize you to go ahead immediately."

"Good. I agree to cooperate."

"Fine. Now why don't you tell me what you plan to do."

"Make him talk," Mori said. "Tell us who's behind him."

"But first you must catch him."

"We set a little trap, using a girl." Mori began to describe in detail his plan.

THE FINEST WEAVE of a spider's web is made closest to the center. In the same way, the trap for the foreigner had been quickly woven by Mori's team that afternoon and by evening was complete.

By late in the day as well, the leaks about Helim's visit and hotel accommodation were already out. The oversights that allowed others to learn her arrangements were nothing flagrant. They could not be traced to Mori's office, nor, for that matter, to the police. There is an old adage among the politicians that information in Japan is always available to those who are diligent and connected.

Organization by Mori's team to capture the foreigner had begun with a meeting. Shortly after his lunch with the public prosecutor, Mori had summoned Ayumi to his office.

"We'll need eight people. Our best team. The foreigner is a hardened professional."

"Watanabe then, Oishi . . ." Ayumi looked even younger than usual.

"And yourself too," Mori continued. "Watanabe will be team leader. Oishi, yes. Sato. Couple of our black belts. The hard-asses. Have them here for a briefing in half an hour. After that I want you to run over to Forensics and see what their result is on the Tomi Chang autopsy. We may not have much time later."

Mori then called Ohashi, the telephone sex club bar owner who had met the foreigner, and asked for his help. The owner showed up at the computer technical lab a short time later, understanding that obligation incurred between the mizu-shobai trade and the police was like gold. You never knew when you might need a favor returned. With the sketch from Tomi and Ohashi's refinements, it was only a short while after the team briefing that Mori was able to hand his men a computerized three-dimensional color mockup of the foreigner's face.

Now it was up to the foreigner. If they captured him, he would lead them to those behind the killings of Tomi and the others. If they didn't, he'd face that when he had to. Mori prayed to all the gods that this would go right, that Tomi would be quickly avenged.

Ayumi called in an hour later from Forensics.

"They haven't prepared the paperwork yet," she said. "I just finished grilling one of the assistants."

"I'm sure he enjoyed it immensely," Mori said. "How will they say she died?"

"A chosen death. She made the first cut. The final cut, the beheading, was requested. Not murder. Best we could get is manslaughter, if that."

"Why would a Korean bar girl . . ." Mori groaned. Hadn't he expected this would be their conclusion? "How about drugs?"

"A relaxant, yes. Big dose."

"Good. What else?"

"Traces of ejaculate in her vagina and abrasion on the external labia, indicating a forced sexual episode."

Mori's body ran hot with a molten tide of rage. He tried to control his voice. "Rape, then?"

"Yes."

His voice was succinct, freezing out Tomi's high-pitched scream that pierced his soul. "I need confirmatory notes from your assistant friend. Promise him anything."

"I tried, sir. But they said . . ."

"Yes. I know I'm not very popular with Homicide these days. What did they say, Ayumi?"

"They said it was their case. They said that you were . . ."

"Washed up?" Mori chuckled. "Don't take that stuff too seriously. Part of the politics of this job. If we don't solve the case, I very well may be."

"I'm sorry, sir. I'm trying to help you solve it the best I can."

"I know." She would never guess his gratitude. "She wasn't hit?"

"Except there appears to be ligature on what's left of her neck. Unexplained. Pathology can't or won't confirm."

"That sounds like she was strangled," Mori suggested, feeling life return to his body.

"Exactly. Which might have been proved, if the neck hadn't been bruised and collapsed from the sword cut. In strangulation, the blood tends to burst vessels in the neck area where circulation is cut off. There is limited trauma from this, but the beheading erased documentable proof. Path's verdict is suicide." Tomi hesitated. "Why are they trying to hide the truth?"

It hurt Mori that Ayumi was finding out police life was dirty. Life in this work, life in any work. Politics everywhere. "I know this is hard for you," he said. "We're all supposed to be the law. But sometimes political interest intervenes. People do things because they're afraid for their jobs, their careers. How are they explaining the semen?"

"They insisted the kaishaku who wielded the sword was an old friend. One last fling, they claim. It doesn't make sense."

"How about the DNA analysis?"

"They've only had time for the PCR, but it was definitive."

"What?"

"A foreigner."

Mori began to pace as he talked now. PCR was a quick DNA check that was directionally accurate. "Can we get nationality from that DNA stuff?"

"No. A scrotal hair was found, and it's being checked."

"So we're sure the kaishaku was a foreigner?"

"Yes, sir. The PCR-DNA check. Some Asian and Caucasian chromosome characteristics differ slightly."

"Thanks, Ayumi. You've done well."

She lowered her voice. "Someone said your old friend Komatsu is on the desk here this afternoon from four-thirty. Perhaps you should stop by—he might tell you more."

40: A FIGURE OF SPEECH Tokyo: Monday, 5:20 P.M.

THE POLICE FORENSIC lab was immaculate and smelled of varied anti-septics like a perfumery gone mad.

Komatsu grunted when he saw Mori come in. The forensic specialist's face was gaunt, the skin taut and sallow. "Haven't seen you for a while, tomodachi." Mori knew what he meant. He and Komatsu had worked on numerous cases together when Mori was with the Tokyo Metropolitan Police. The politics were getting worse.

"No bodies until recently," Mori said by way of apology. "They give us the worst internationals to do. Iranians selling bogus telephone cards in Yoyogi Park. Thais selling underage girls in Shibuya. Times have changed, Komatsu. We're rich. Everyone wants us."

"I know what you mean."

Mori took a deep breath. The worst Forensics could do was tell him to bug off. "Came about the Korean girl."

"Figured. Nasty business, that."

"Wanted to check out a couple of things that don't add up."

"Keep it simple. You're not exactly popular here right now."

"I know. I know. What's going down as the cause of death?"

"The woman lost her head, Mori. That's all it takes."

"You can do better than that. You guys checked body fluids. Bruises."

Komatsu pulled a file from the front of his desk. "You're way off limits, you know. Nobody's supposed to talk to you. Homicide wants an exclusive on the girl's case. You piss somebody off at National Police headquarters?"

"Just being my usual charming self."

"Sure. They get under my collar sometimes too." Komatsu flipped through the file. "No drugs, if that's what you wanted. Did find some barbiturate. Body was relatively free of bruises. If it was murder, there should have been some evidence of a struggle. Chosen death. Open and shut." He closed the file.

"Not if she'd been drugged."

"No proof of that."

"How about that barbiturate you danced by?"

"Over-the-counter stuff. Lots of women take relaxants."

Mori let that go for now. "How about the wrists? Had she been tied?"

"Negative. No signs of binding. Hands or feet. It was chosen death, pure and simple. Assist to the kaishaku."

"How about the semen?"

"The beheader was an old boyfriend, we figure. Bar girl, right? Lots of male friends. Foreigners. Before she did it, they had one last go for old times' sake. Nice bod she had. I would have done the same."

"You're being grotesque."

"Age, Mori. I'm getting too old for this shit."

"What about the cut? She suffer?" He tried not to show that this mattered to him.

"It was somebody knew swords, I can tell you. Had tremendous power. Did it in one cut. Severed the sternocleidomastoid, sternohyoid, upper intercostal nerve, external jugular anterior and internal jugular, carotids, and neck above the cervical in one sweep. Home run. No, she didn't suffer. Like a blink."

Perspiration soaked the back of Mori's shirt. "From the cut, would you say the victim was sitting at the time of the sword stroke?"

"Of course, we assumed so."

"Assumed. You have pictures of the death site in your file?"

Komatsu opened a drawer. "Yes. Polaroids and a videotape noted. Which is your pleasure?"

"Both. At the scene, I recall that blood had flown quite far from the body. Three, maybe four feet. The pictures confirm that?"

Komatsu looked at the Polaroids. "Quite far. Right. Looks like it sprayed."

"Anything strange in that? If someone is beheaded, would the blood fly around like that?"

"Never seen one of these before, old friend. It would be best to talk to an expert." He lifted the phone. "Could Dr. Sugamo step over for a minute?" He hung up. "Sugamo served in the war. Saw a lot of beheadings. So, what are you after? A second opinion? This isn't sounding like a social visit."

"Just being careful. What are the mechanics of a beheading?"

Komatsu steepled his fingers. "It works like this. The carotids would pump blood for a second or two. The jugulars would spurt blood from the face and brain. But to say it would spray as the pictures show, we didn't consider that. I really can't say."

Mori wondered what else they hadn't considered. Dr. Sugamo showed up several minutes later. He was an elderly, brisk man with humorous eyes, as if death somehow amused him.

"The inspector has a question I can't answer," Komatsu said, then handed Sugamo the pictures.

Sugamo studied them, then looked up. "Normally a beheading scene wouldn't look like this. The blood is usually centered and rivered. Not fragmented as if it was thrown."

"Thrown?" Mori repeated. The beheading must have occurred after death.

"A figure of speech," the doctor said.

MORI ARRIVED HOME early after a final briefing of his team.

Mitsuko looked up from her cooking. "You're home?"

Mori hung his jacket on the back of a chair. "There was a murder earlier today."

"Yes? You went rushing out of here like your pants were on fire."

"A Korean girl, one of my field agents."

"I'm sorry. Do you know who did it?"

"Same killer who did the others. I have a plan to catch him. A team has been briefed. Everything's ready. All I can do is wait."

The kitchen smelled of misoshiru and ayu fish frying. His wife said, "Taking an awful long time, isn't this case?"

"Soon, anata, and we'll have him. Any whiskey left? I feel like a drink."

Mitsuko went to the liquor cabinet. "Only one you get. No more. You look tired. You should relax more."

Mori settled into his chair and thought for a moment in silence.

"How about adopting a child?" he asked, feeling his way. Tomi must've been taken before she could call him about her boy as she'd promised.

"I've never heard you talk this way." Mitsuko's tone was flat.

"Is that your answer?"

"Why has this come up so suddenly?"

"The boy is bright. Handsome."

"Who are the parents?"

"The father they don't know. The mother was murdered by people she fought against. This morning. She was very brave. . . . Otherwise, the boy will end up in an orphanage."

"Korean, wasn't she?"

"So what?"

"What will the neighbors say?"

Mori stretched. He suddenly felt restless. "You need anything at the store? I'm going to get some cigarettes." He headed toward the door. A thin feathery mist was falling. The humidity crawled inside the collar of his shirt.

Mitsuko followed him. "I don't know where you get your ideas!"

"Her death is on my hands."

"Well, I just wish you had said something before."

"I didn't know she was going to die. Anyway, I need some cigarettes: I'll be right back."

His mother came out of her room, waving her hands. "You two are always arguing. Listen, I just heard on the TV. The prime minister has resigned!"

41: SEARCH Hong Kong: Monday, 4:40 P.M.

TOMÁS VELAQUEZ STRODE into the lobby of the Mannix Hotel and headed for the information desk, where he'd recognized the foreign girl behind the desk from his previous trips.

"Hello, Mr. Velaquez, welcome back." Her accent was Australian.

"Hi, Miss Larsen," he said, reading her nametag. "Need a favor."

"Sure."

"I'm after some information about a member of your hotel staff who was detained by the police after my last trip. I'm afraid it was partially my fault."

Her eyes went blank a moment. "Oh, that! Tempest in a teapot, wasn't it?"

"I'm sorry?"

"Well, they let him go with apologies several days ago, didn't they? All about something taken from your room, wasn't it?"

"Yes. Nothing really. I felt I should apologize. Is he on today?"

"Yes, Winston's on duty."

"Winston?"

"Winston Yip." She pointed toward the bell desk. "He's the bell captain. That's him. There."

Tomás saw a slight, neat Chinese giving directions to a party of Germans. He walked over to the bell desk and waited until the captain was done with his guests.

"Can I help you, sir?" Winston asked.

"There'll be a thousand Hong Kong in it for you if we can talk for a couple of minutes."

The bell captain studied Tomás to see if he was serious. "You need a woman?"

"Just some information."

"So what is this about?"

"About you and the police. Why you were called in." Tomás pulled out a Hong Kong thousand-dollar bill and handed it to him.

Winston pocketed the money. "Nothing much really happened. I told them about the person who contacted me."

"Someone did contact you?" Finally, Tomás thought. Now he could prove he hadn't been involved.

"Yes. One of my friends owns a gym in Kowloon. The Stanley Gym. An ex–kung fu actor named Jimmy Lee Wong."

"What happened?"

"Wong called me and asked if I wanted to make some extra money. So I says, does a hobbyhorse have a wooden dick? Anyway, I went to the gym that night and there was this guy."

"Chinese?"

"No. Maybe Korean, because he spoke Mandarin with a guttural accent the way Koreans do. Well-dressed. Rich. Anyway, guy made me an offer. Told me I would be paid one hundred thousand Hong Kong dollars for a favor. I nearly crapped my pants. 'Who do I have to kill?' I asked. But this guy was a real sour-face. Never cracked a smile. He gave me a room number here. That was when I told him, 'Impossible. Can't help you.' He wanted me to steal a package from a hotel guest. Can you imagine?"

"What was the room number?"

Winston told him. It was Tomás's room.

"Need a description," Tomás said.

"I was scared, so I can't give you much. When you're scared you don't remember things. You forget, you know."

Tomás pulled out a Hong Kong five-hundred-dollar bill. "Try not to be too scared. Let's start with the hair. Black, right? How about age?"

"Yes. Black. Graying at the temples. Rich-looking guy, like I said. Bit soft. Not a thug. Say mid or late forties."

"Height?"

"About one hundred eighty centimeters." Winston held his hand a foot over his head.

"Great, Winston," Tomás said. "You're doing fine. How about a mustache? Beard?"

"No. Clean-shaven. Wore some expensive aftershave. Jules, I think. Reason I know is I use the same sometimes." He straightened his tie as though he had another life.

"Clothes. He wore a jacket and tie? Flashy?"

"Not flashy, no. Suit, yes. Dark. Nice clothes. Real expensive. And a gold watch and ring."

"So what did you tell this guy?"

"I told him I couldn't help him. So he threatened me. That was why I went to the police."

"The police ask you the same questions?"

"Goddamn police arrested me. I mean, I'm reporting a serious crime going to happen, right? They arrest the messenger. You go figure."

"They detained you?"

"Two days. They asked a lot of questions about the Stanley Gym. One of the officers said they didn't have a case but they had orders to hold me. Then suddenly they released me. Just like that. Two days." He snapped his fingers. "You need anything more?"

"If I do, I'll contact you," Tomás replied. "Thanks."

TOMÁS WALKED ALL the way to Causeway Bay feeling good. Now he knew someone had tried to steal the plutonium. Yip's story proved Tomás's innocence. He could return to Vienna with that alone, or pursue it further. After all, the information Yip had given him wouldn't mean anything in court. A rich Korean. It could be someone Helim knew.

Tomás finally decided to visit the Stanley Gym. He stopped at a pay phone, dialed the number, and asked for Jimmy Lee Wong. A rough voice said Wong wasn't there and hung up. He thought about going to the gym. But why was he checking up on Winston Yip? Tomás asked himself. He already had an idea who it was, right?

A good newspaperman always uses two sources, he told himself. That was the rule. Was Yip a bit too smooth, or was it just that Tomás wanted to believe someone was playing games within games? And that it was not Helim Kim.

Tomás was heading back to the hotel when someone stopped him.

"Excuse me, sir." A Chinese in a suit and tie. "Could you tell me where Alexandra House is?"

The next moment, he felt something hard in his back. Another voice. "No sudden moves. Just do as we tell you."

Tomás didn't feel anything. No shock. Or surprise. Or fear. The bellhop had been a ruse, he thought, used to identify him to these people. They had found him finally. Either the British or the Americans.

But the car he was pushed into didn't head for either the British or the U.S. embassy. Instead, he was driven through the tunnel to Kowloon, toward the harbor. They blindfolded him there and led him onto a small boat, where they pushed him down hard onto a bench. He was in the cabin, and there were guards on both sides of him. There was a discussion in Cantonese, and then the engine started, the boat moved. He tried to get a sense of distance.

Fifteen minutes later by his calculation, the boat bumped into something, and he could hear other voices high up over him shouting harshly. Not Cantonese now. Korean. Rough arms lifted him to his feet, then pushed him onto the deck. He heard the movement of well-oiled chains, water slapping against a hull, winches grinding. A fresh salty wind whipped his face. He was out a half mile or so from shore, he guessed. On the outskirts of the harbor. They had pulled alongside a much larger vessel. Korean. But why?

Two men, one on either side, led him up stairs fastened against the side of the larger vessel. Thirty steps he counted before he reached a deck. Big oceangoing ship. They went through a door and then another. He was guided along a grilled metal catwalk, pushed through other doors. At various times he could smell machinery oil, food. The flagrant odor of kimchi dominated. He was certain now this was a Korean ship. A very large one.

Finally, they stopped him and made him turn. He heard a metal door open in front of him. They pressed him through it roughly, and he tripped over the bulkhead and fell onto the steel floor. They removed the blindfold and a door slammed shut behind him. All was quiet except for the distant throb of the ship's engine.

He surveyed the small room. Wheeled tables holding surgical instruments. Metal arms holding tubes fastened to plastic bottles. The truth gradually came to him. The room smelled of sweat and urine and fear.

The door opened. A Korean woman in a white coat entered and turned on a glaring overhead light. She was tall and high-cheekboned, with an expressionless face. In her hand was a small pistol that was pointed at his genitals. "Please take off all your clothes," she said in perfect English.

PARK PURCHASED A clone cellular phone from a street dealer to prevent anyone from finding out what numbers he called. The first call was to a number in Japan. Then a number in Washington, D.C.

"John, we secure?"

"Just a minute," DeCovasi said. "Yeah, okay, go ahead. What have you got?"

"Definitely during or after Niigata City. Figure day after."

"How?"

"Plutonium. Don't know how yet. Somebody'd have to inject it."

"Jesus Christ."

"Good luck."

"Thanks, Park."

"One last piece of information. Don't think it's related but it could be."

"Shoot."

"Helim's diary operation has created a media sensation in Japan. Looks like she might get those pachinko listings after all."

"Yeah, the American comfort woman. Congratulations. I've seen articles in the U.S. media too. Pissed people off."

"I've been checking out the whereabouts of the American woman through friends. Came up with a couple of female MIAs from the China theater in the approximate time frame. One in particular looks interesting."

"Really?"

"Yes. Want them?"

"Better than nothing."

"Red Cross nurses, all of them. Carol Schattuck, Ruth Grissard, and Elizabeth Stronsen. Elizabeth Stronsen might be her." Park pulled out a paper and read: " 'Born in Redwood City, California, March 3, 1921. Assigned to Harbin District Chinese Red Cross Relief, 1940. Believed taken by Japanese forces, 1941. Protest lodged. Japanese denied all knowledge. Believed repatriated by Russian Red Army, 1945. No further information.' You want the others?"

"No. Russian Red Army?"

"They were allowed to occupy and loot northern China as their reward for declaring war on Japan that year."

"She could still be alive, then?"

"Could be. Have you decided on an operation in Niigata City? As I recommended?"

"You know I can't answer that question. One way or the other."

"Good luck, then. As the pope said in his farewell speech to the Cubans, 'An irreligious country will die because it has nothing to nourish its virtues.' I'll keep in touch."

•   •   •

DeCovasi HUNG UP and considered Park Chung Il's call. Park would love to see the leader of North Korea burn. DeCovasi could hear it in his voice. And what was the innuendo on that American comfort woman information? Trying to involve the Russians, was he?

DeCovasi pressed a scramble button and picked up his red phone. It would be his ass if anything went wrong. Park was his man. He'd brought him in, sold him to Pipe and the director, and was his sole controller. God help me get this right, he thought. Then he dialed the number of the highest-ranking naval officer he knew at the Pentagon.

42: REVELATIONS South China Sea: Monday, 6:20 P.M.

ALPHA STOOD BESIDE the hospital gurney staring down at Tomás Velaquez. The Costa Rican lay naked, secured to the table by gray straps fastened around his legs and chest. An incandescent light bathed the room, reflecting off the polished surfaces of instruments on the table beside the gurney. A sole porthole had been covered over.

Besides a number of scalpels and probes, there was an electric console, which the tall Korean woman monitored. Tubes and wires ran from Tomás's body.

Alpha put on a pair of surgical gloves. "Can you hear me, Mr. Tomás Velaquez?"

Velaquez tried to see through the glaring light. His drug-saturated mind was trying to remember what had happened. He saw an imposing man with pigtail. His eyes blinked.

"Excellent," Alpha said.

Alpha's leering face blocked out the glare temporarily. Tomás was able to focus for the first time since the drug injection. He glared at the face floating over him, trying to recall the name of the element that had been central to what was happening to him. "Plutonium. You're the ones who switched the plutonium."

Alpha laughed. "I wasn't involved in that. Concerned, but not involved. It is like bacon and eggs, you see. The chicken is concerned. The pig is involved. Your girlfriend, Helim Kim, was involved. We believe she has been consorting with a traitor to our country. My interest is simply to find out the truth."

"Helim?" He felt pain from her name. What lies had she told him?

"Yes. She may be here soon. Aleksei will meet her, bring her to us. Then you can sing together. Aren't you pleased?"

Alpha moved out of range, and the sudden glare of lights sent arrows of pain shooting through Tomás's brain. Or perhaps it was the thought that Helim had betrayed him.

Alpha said, "How are his organs functioning, Miss Suk?"

"Pulse, blood pressure normal. Lungs clear." She looked at a chart. "No solid waste for the past hour. His urine is clean. He is only receiving intravenous supplements now: sugar, protein, vitamins. And I have begun the thiopental."

"Then I think we're ready." He nodded to the woman, who fastened two wires to Velaquez's testicles. She stared at the foreigner, her expression a strange combination of lust and amusement. She had not done a foreigner for several years. Such hairy creatures. Alpha honored her by allowing her to assist in this interrogation. Afterward, she would favor him in any way he wished.

Alpha sat by the gurney. "You are an amateur, Mr. Velaquez. Forgive me for saying so. A meddler. You're at my mercy. When we're through with you, you'll be begging for us to kill you. However, if you cooperate, there's some hope. Think about it and make a choice. I've found our interrogators often are unable to suppress their patriotic tendencies. So I've decided to handle your case personally. You'll be given a balanced diet. Proteins, minerals, vitamins. We've found that starvation causes memory loss. And we're using some experimental drugs to ensure you try hard to tell the truth. But since there hasn't been sufficient time for your body to become totally conditioned, and our time is limited, we've decided on a stronger dose of drugs. Not as efficient. But faster." Alpha smiled mischievously.

"Now for the ground rules. You won't receive any electric shocks unless you lie." He waved his hand at what looked like an open laptop computer next to the monitor. "Voice analyzer, Mr. Velaquez. Let me demonstrate what happens when you disappoint us."

He moved a dial on a black transformer.

"Ieeeeah . . . ahhhh!" Velaquez's teeth chattered and his eyes rolled back in his head. The pain was agonizing, shooting through his groin with a piercing intensity.

"Enjoy it, did you?" Alpha said calmly. "Good. That was only a sample. It gets much worse, I can guarantee. Now what we are after is quite simple. Think back to your last trip to Pyongyang. We don't worry about her sleeping with you. Those were her orders. She helped you to obtain a plutonium sample, yes? The plutonium sample you were given was pure. Not reprocessed, we're certain of it. Our people in London tell us the sample you tested had different characteristics. Correct?"

Tomás glared at him.

Alpha flicked his hand over the transformer.

"Aghhhhhh . . ."

"Let me suggest that this could become very unpleasant if you try to play the hero. I asked a very simple question. Please try harder to co-operate."

Velaquez opened his mouth. Saliva ran down his chin. His face was bathed in sweat. "Yes. It showed two reprocessing dates."

"There, you see? Not so difficult, was it?"

"Helim switched it then? Why?" His brain staggered with the truth. She had deceived him with her love then too. Everything. Or was this man playing some vicious mind game? He couldn't think straight.

"I'm the one asking questions. Perhaps she had a change of heart. After all, it embarrassed our leader, didn't it? He's been getting cozy with Chinese and Western leaders. Perhaps she felt Park Tai Jin has certain shortcomings, don't you think? Well, in time they'll be corrected. Helim should never have tampered with the sample. That was naughty of her. She is the root of the trouble. So we are beginning to worry about Helim's loyalty. You were raised in Costa Rica, yes?"

"Y-yes. Costa Rica."

"The government during your childhood—run by generals, wasn't it?"

Velaquez nodded.

"Good. Financed by the CIA, who were worried about the resurgence of democratic movements. You joined such a movement, I believe. Russian money behind your group. People simply disappeared, didn't they, during those terrible times? Your father, for example. No trace?"

"My father . . . yes. Under the generals, it was a military dictatorship."

"So you were a communist?"

"No, I supported the people."

"Ever run across Aleksei Romanov?

"No."

"He did some good work in Central America and hopes to return Russia to the good old days. Like North Korea."

"North Korea is a dictatorship."

Alpha's hand flicked angrily.

"No! No! . . . Ahhh!" Velaquez's body arched off the gurney.

"I forgot to tell you one of our other rules. I can't allow anyone to slander my homeland. So your father was taken. Pity. No great love for the U.S.A. then, is there? They the ones who interrogated you in Vienna? Before you bolted?"

"Yes."

"They set you up. We think they're setting us up too."

"Bastards."

"Agree, Tomás. How do you feel about the new Russians?"

"They've become politicians."

"Good answer! We may let you live after all. I have an extensive dossier on you. You took a degree in physics at the national university while you supported the insurgency, which eventually succeeded in overthrowing the generals. You're a revolutionary who became a member of the new government, which eventually led to your position with the International Atomic Energy Agency. At heart, you'll always be the revolutionary. But you couldn't take the politics and infighting. So you quit for a gypsy's life with the IAEA. Now I am going to tell you something pleasant: Suk finds you attractive. So you will get a reward for telling the truth. Which is more fair, isn't it? If you only receive pain, it could lead to resentment. A lack of cooperation. Sex later," he whispered in the Costa Rican's ear, "if I feel the session has been worthwhile."

On cue, Miss Suk approached the table and ran a hand across the prisoner's penis.

"Feels good, does it? Okay, that's enough. Did you know there's someone trying to gain control of the Korean government by taking over pachinko companies in Japan?"

"No."

Suk looked at the screen and nodded.

"Good. Did you know there is an opposition group in North Korea, Japan, and North America dedicated to reunion and the overthrow of our government by terrorist acts?"

"No."

"Lie," Suk said.

Alpha's hand moved, Velaquez screamed. His body shuddered against the belts that held him. Suk reached for a bottle of liquid, which she passed under Tomás's nose.

Alpha spoke softly into a phone. "Tell the general we are almost ready for him." He turned back to the table, where Velaquez had begun to moan, and repeated the question.

"Yes . . . I knew . . . there was an opposition group."

General Myun Chun Kuk entered. He was barrel-chested and squat, with a strong cleft chin and wide-set eyes that stared intently at the figure on the table.

"What has he told you?"

Alpha spoke casually. "That he knew about the opposition to us. We're just warming up." Alpha scratched his chin and stared at Velaquez for a moment. "Do you know someone named Park Chung Il, Tomás?"

"No . . ."

"Lie," Suk nearly shouted.

Alpha's hand began to move.

"Don't," Velaquez bellowed. "Y-yes. I know him."

Alpha winked at the general. "Did you ever meet Park Chung Il, Mr. Velaquez?"

"Yes . . . possibly."

Alpha glanced at the LCD screen. "That's a clever answer, Mr. Velaquez. Don't get too clever."

The general picked up a knife from the table. "Perhaps I should cut off his testicles. Then we will get the truth."

"Why are you not sure, Mr. Velaquez?" Alpha asked.

"He was . . . introduced only as Mr. Park."

"Where did you meet him?"

"In California."

"More specific."

"In Westwood. Los Angeles."

"You can do better than that!"

"Helim Kim's apartment," Tomás whispered with a sob.

Anger showed in Alpha's eyes. "How many times did you meet this person with Helim Kim?"

"Twice. Maybe three times."

"What did you discuss?"

"I don't know. It was in Korean."

"Lie," the woman said woodenly.

Alpha twisted the dial viciously.

Velaquez's body bounced so violently against the straps that the gurney danced. His bladder released.

"Heart rate," the woman warned.

Alpha cursed. He picked up a hypodermic from the instrument table and sank it into the Costa Rican's arm. "Watch the heart monitor," he ordered Suk. "He should come around in a minute or two. The general and I will be outside."

THE TWO MEN approached the railing of a catwalk high above the forward hold of the ship. Alpha took out a pack of North Korean cigarettes and offered one to the general. "It's as we suspected. Helim is working for Park."

The general frowned. "I suspected her all along. You may as well know, I contracted with an East German to terminate her one week ago. Hard data about her activities for the dissidents came to my attention."

"Where is she now?"

"Atami. Two days ago the dissidents tried to assassinate my East German and failed. So I've decided to give him one more chance at her. You might say he's pissed off."

"You didn't inform me of this. Why?"

"Come, Alpha. Since when do I have to explain every minor operation of my military intelligence unit to you? She was not considered important enough to bother you with."

"This was not a 'minor operation.' You apparently didn't know she was working directly for me. I want her alive, at least for a while. I am astounded that you didn't tell me!" Alpha bristled with impatience.

"Perhaps you have grown too fond of her. Perhaps that is why you were not told. There are rumors, you understand."

"No, General. You *don't* understand."

The general smiled cruelly. "There is a rumor that it was your intelligence group that switched the plutonium our engineers provided the IAEA. That Helim Kim did it for you."

"A rumor only. A lie. The point is, she can help us to succeed in our plans! And perhaps to counteract American intelligence."

"Counteract?"

"Fool! I know she's been working for both Park Chung Il and for us. A double. But she can still be useful. Remember, Park once worked for us too, so he knows how we think. Now he's reported to be in the pay of American intelligence. They have a larger objective in mind, I'm sure. Niigata City has been flooded with American agents, and not just Secret Service to protect the former president. Something's going on, be sure of that!"

"What are you saying?"

"Why so many agents, General, unless . . . ?"

"An operation against us?"

"They know our leader, Park Tai Jin, is weak. That in fact we of the tribunal run North Korea."

"And what if they do?"

"They have dossiers on every member of the tribunal. Just as we have on their leaders. Our strengths and weaknesses. Which members of the tribunal favor rapprochement with the West. That you and I don't. That the Chinese are pressuring us to open our markets to the West. Embrace capitalism as they have. That on this trip Park Tai Jin has indicated that he might. Now he's inviting the chaos of an oil deal with the Americans on a ConnOil project. Americans will infiltrate this ship for the first time at our next port in Japan when they will be allowed aboard to discuss their capitalistic enterprises. Something we must not allow to proceed. Our leader is also meeting this former U.S. president in Niigata. None of it will come to any good."

"So what? Nothing comes of these high-level meetings. Unless we let it."

"Of course. Of course. But think, General. Their plan could be brilliant. Their strategy to get plutonium from us using the IAEA was the trigger—the reason Park Tai Jin's trip took place, after all. The Americans, or someone, wanted our leader out of the country, don't you see? Where he would be vulnerable. Exposed." Alpha raised his finger. "So they can claim a coup attempt is about to take place, and move to foil it!"

"That's playing with fire."

"It would be set up so they couldn't get burned."

"How?"

"Their intelligence people look only to create the illusion of reality—in this case to convince their leadership of a coup attempt against our leader so they can justify an action to prevent it."

"But why would American intelligence—"

"One reason only," Alpha interrupted. "To get rid of us."

The general looked shaken. "They've not run a wet affair for years."

"It will be made to appear as an accident."

"We are to be their targets?" Alpha could see the fear in the old soldier's eyes.

"If I'm right, the target is you and me. Yes. Us!"

"The Americans aren't that clever!"

"No. Perhaps not. And the fact that the Americans interrogated Tomás is hard to explain, I admit. Unless one American intelligence agency isn't telling the other what it's doing. Or, it could be the genius of Park Chung Il that's behind this deception. If that's what it is."

"Yes. If there is an operation at all! Perhaps this is a figment of your imagination, Alpha."

"I agree. But are you willing to assume that? Our lives are at stake. Not to mention the future of North Korea."

"All right, then," the general said. "Assume one of their services or Park has convinced the Americans that a coup will take place. Convinced them to act. It's feasible, I admit. They rely on Park heavily for all information about North Korea, since they have no one on the ground. Only their silly spy satellites."

"In any case, we have to find out if there's such a plan."

"What do you suggest?"

"First, let me tell you what I have done. I've taken the liberty of contacting Aleksei Romanov. You were using him as an interface to the East German. As soon as I learned of your intentions, I persuaded Romanov to take Helim Kim alive, not dead. And bring her to Niigata City as a first step. I want you to stay out of it. Leave the rest to me."

"You interfered with my orders? How did you get Romanov to disobey me?"

"By explaining my plan to give the Americans their coup. But in such a way that it will appear the Americans are behind it! We won't need the approval of the rest of the tribunal. Niigata is crawling with American agents. Embarrassing to explain to the world press. Once we carry it out, we move to consolidate our position inside the tribunal."

The general stared incredulously at Alpha. "Terminate Park Tai Jin? What a devious mind you have, Alpha."

"I see you understand."

"I didn't say that I agree, but it is enticing. Yes. Our reserves of fuel and food are dwindling. In another six months we won't be able to launch an offensive that could win, wrest the peninsula from the Southern bandits, even if we wished to. However, the South's financial problems have weakened them."

Alpha waved at the door. "Exactly. We must act now instead of waiting. Otherwise, it may be only a matter of time before we lose power. Or die mysteriously."

The general exhaled cigarette smoke. "You have a plan?"

"It will take place in Niigata City. When Park Tai Jin meets the former U.S. president. However, I'll need your help to make arrangements for our leader's termination."

"How will it be done?"

"Plutonium."

The general's mouth twitched. "Plutonium?"

"Yes. I like the irony. Plutonium is one of the most toxic substances on earth. A tenth of one millionth of an ounce is lethal to the human body."

"By whom?"

"Not by a Korean."

"What nationality?"

"American."

"Helim Kim?"

"As I said, I need her alive."

"How? An explosive device?"

"No. My idea is to become a thorn in his side, so to speak."

The general chuckled. "I believe I underestimated you. It seems to me this plan of yours is not a sudden inspiration. Could it be your group have been working on it for some time? Were you preparing to go it alone no matter what my opinion was?"

"It's our job to be prepared for every alternative." Alpha gestured at the gleaming machinery below. "Have you picked out a car? The two of us will be in complete control soon."

"A new Mercedes for my second wife, I think. What are you going to do with your prisoner?"

Alpha spat over the edge of the catwalk. "He'll become my unimpeachable witness. Proof the Americans engineered the coup."

43: COMMITMENT Tokyo: Monday, 7:30 P.M.

STEIG'S FIRST VISIT that morning had been to a twenty-four-hour printshop to order business cards under the name Hendrik Stein, Manager, Stein Agency K.K., with a Kanda address. Next he stopped at a nearby Japan Travel Bureau office to seek advice about a trip.

"I'm planning a visit to Atami," Steig explained at the JTB counter. "I need information on the places of interest and the best way to get there."

The girl selected several brochures. "There's lots to see. I'd recommend the bullet train. One every twenty minutes. When will you be going?"

"Tomorrow. Say the five-o'clock."

"How about your return? Trains are crowded, so you'd better book early."

"I'll decide that after I reach Atami."

She punched a keyboard, and the ticket printed. "Anything else?"

"I'm looking for a quiet place to spend the first day. I'll be tired from travel."

"Atami has many. Near the beach, tropical gardens, in a castle?"

"I hear there's a religious sect with a hotel that's very quiet."

"Quite. Yes."

"Do you have a map of the layout, brochures?"

She handed him several folders. "My disabled aunt visited there once, and they picked her up at the train. Special van for the handicapped. She came back raving about how gorgeous the complex was. The museum, private hotel, prayer halls, restaurants, healing shops. And a Peace Arch."

"A Peace Arch," Steig marveled. "I believe you've cured my worries."

After leaving JTB, he'd made several long-distance calls to Atami. The rest of the day was taken up with purchases, the major one being at the medical equipment section of a major downtown department store.

The largest item was delivered to a pipe-fitting and welding shop near Shimbashi he'd scouted. Rush job, and he'd pay double. Needed tonight for a disabled friend. Steig explained specs: how he wanted frame ends fitted with removable covers, a false bottom to the seat with a fifteen-centimeter clearance, and removal of outer trimmings to narrow width so it cleared the aisles of bullet trains.

"Sounds like he's trying to hide valuables," the shop owner suggested. "Worried about theft, is he?"

"Sickness makes one paranoid," Steig replied sadly. "Everyone knows Japan's the safest country in the world."

Thus reassured, the shop owner did a splendid job. Steig was able to pick up his order before 8:00 P.M. The rest of the evening he spent stowing his equipment for the next day.

44: THE TRAP Tokyo: Tuesday, 8:30 A.M.

SHORTLY AFTER MORI arrived at his office Tuesday morning, Aoyama stormed in. "Who approved all these preparations in Atami?"

"The public prosecutor." Mori calmly waved a fax at him. "Read this."

The fax was signed by Yuka Tanemura. Aoyama read it quickly, then threw the paper on Mori's desk. "Very clever. But this is an American life you are risking."

Mori knew Aoyama didn't really care whose life was being risked. He was concerned that Mori might actually succeed and upstage him.

"What if it goes wrong?" Aoyama continued more mildly. "Aren't there enough problems with the Americans over this comfort woman issue already?"

"She's under investigation by the FBI as a double agent working for the government of North Korea, Aoyama. She gets killed, we're doing them a favor. Anyway, it won't go wrong."

"Says who?"

"Me. A team of our security is all over the train station. The local police are guarding the inn. Roadblocks cordon off all the access roads. Once he's inside the trap he can't possibly get out."

"Won't work, Mori. The Americans are behind this killer, believe me."

"Better not make up your mind before we take him, hey?"

STEVE'S ATTEMPTS TO connect with Katano had been fruitless. The TV personality was out of town, and his office wasn't willing to help. He had an assistant who handled such matters, Steve was told, but she was out of town too. Katano would be back Wednesday. Please call then.

His money problem forced Steve to spend two nights in the park. He'd called United, which was holding his lost credit card at LAX. Since his own bank didn't have a branch here, Steve tried to reach Chul Kim for a loan through his Tokyo branch. The banker was away, back Monday night (Tuesday midday here). This left Steve with little cash until then.

The sky was a white haze. The humidity was agonizing. He had to keep moving. To do something to find Helim. Although he knew it was useless, Steve tried to reach Katano again.

"Katano is out of town today," the receptionist said.

"Everyone is out of town," Steve barked as he slammed the phone on its hook.

He went to the TV station for one last try. Carefully, he explained his predicament to two uniformed girls at the information desk. "Katano's not here," one said. "But his assistant just arrived." After several phone calls they finally reached her and handed the phone to Steve.

"Hello," Steve said. "I'm trying to reach Helim Kim."

"She's not in Tokyo. Who's this, please?"

"Steve Juric. She told me to contact Katano to find out where she is."

"I'm afraid he's not coming back until tomorrow."

"I'm Helim's boyfriend, and I've spent two days trying to reach Katano."

"He's very busy. He left strict orders not to be disturbed."

"I have to reach Helim. It's urgent."

"Katano has to approve that. I'm sorry."

"She told him I'd call. Why the secrecy?" Steve doubted they knew of the attack on Helim in L.A. That her life was in danger.

"I don't ask questions, Mr. Juric. I follow orders."

"How soon can you contact him?"

"They're taping this morning and he can't be disturbed. Sometime today."

"Sometime today!"

"Look, Mr. Juric, I'm very busy."

"Wait! How will you reach me?"

"Give me your number. I'll call."

"No. It's complicated. How about here?"

"Okay. I'll leave a message at the reception desk. As soon as I can."

45: **INTERVIEW** Atami: Tuesday, 3:30 P.M.

SUNDAY AND MONDAY had gone off perfectly, except that Steve hadn't called as he'd promised. She had spent Sunday with Katano taping her review of the pachinko industry. All its flaws. On Monday, they reviewed the condition of Koreans in Japan and the comfort woman issue. That night, Katano televised his nightly show from a local TV affiliate's studio, inviting her to watch. Today, they had done another half-hour segment on the pachinko industry. Katano was thinking of making the pachinko story an hour long rather than a half hour. It had been much easier than she'd imagined.

In between taping sessions, Helim thought of Steve and wondered what had happened to him. Why hadn't he contacted her? Had he decided not to come without even telling her? She couldn't stand that thought, so she forced it out of her mind.

Last night, after she had returned from Katano's news show and a drink with him afterward, she had called Steve's office. He wasn't there, and she left an angry message on his machine. Then she called her father. He demanded she return home immediately, as she thought he would. He didn't have any idea where Steven was. "I'm disappointed in that young man. I hope you don't plan to see him again."

Despondent now, Helim called her grandmother and invited her to Atami tomorrow. After their conversation, her spirits lifted. She would stay an extra day and spend it with her grandmother, then leave Thursday for Tokyo. Her grandmother was arriving at noon tomorrow, and Helim occupied her mind considering what they would do. She would try to forget about Steve and enjoy herself in Atami. Forget all about him. They would take a tour, see the sights, and discuss shaman techniques. She had learned to summon her power animal, the snow-white tiger, with spirit energy, mental imagery, and strength. The dance her grandmother had taught her was no longer necessary. Nor drums. Her grandmother wanted to renew a "kut" she had performed last time to keep Helim from harm. "No one can hurt you," she had promised. "Only you can destroy yourself."

She hadn't decided what to do after Thursday. Since Steve had abandoned her, she had considered meeting Tomás. But what had become of him? The last time he called, he'd sounded troubled. He couldn't talk over the phone. Something at the office had gone wrong. And don't try to call him, he had said. He was traveling. Poor Tomás, she thought. He tried so hard.

She had left the Shimizu Inn number with the KDA, warning them to ask for Katano, since she wasn't allowed to take any calls directly as a security measure. Earlier today, Park had called her to say he was on an assignment in another part of Japan. He didn't say where. He never trusted her. Never trusted anyone. He was pleased the taping had gone well and was nearly completed. After all this was over she would have to think seriously about her future with Mr. Park Chung Il. Right now she just wanted to relax.

Katano had promised to take her for a drive this afternoon, after the taping was finished. She suspected he had taken a fancy to her. Her boyfriend had disappeared and she couldn't bear to think about it. What she needed most now was distraction. Katano could provide just that.

SHERMAN WHITLOW TOOK the call in his bedroom a few minutes before he was about to turn in for an afternoon nap.

"Sorry to bother you, Mr. President."

"It's you again, is it?" The pleasant voice he had initially found intriguing now annoyed him, and he wondered how she had obtained his direct number. Only a handful of advisers were supposed to have it. He pressed a red button, which triggered a taping machine at Secret Service monitors downstairs in the Japanese hotel.

"I've been busy, as you can imagine. In my last call I told you Park Tai Jin is visiting Japan after China. We now know he has boarded a North Korean ship in Hong Kong for the return journey. The ship will stop briefly in Niigata, on its way to Pyongyang. Arriving tomorrow, I believe. And you are scheduled to attend a ceremony the day after at dockside to greet him at noon."

"Look, who is this?"

"A person with modest desires. Our name is not important. I'm running out of time, however. I'd like to meet you during your Niigata stay. At a time that will not interfere with your schedule. A few minutes is all."

Curiosity won. "A brief meeting, fine. But nothing more! You mentioned Harbin last time."

"Yes. We can talk about it. Shall we say early Thursday morning, when you're fresh? It's rumored that Kenzo Tanemura, who everyone believes will become the next prime minister of Japan, will be there. So shall we say nine o'clock? Fifteen minutes will do. I'll come alone and unarmed, so to speak." She chuckled. "Agreed?"

"Yes. Now I really am intrigued. What is your name? We'll need one so that you will be let through security."

"Elizabeth. Tell them to let Elizabeth through."

46: **TRIUMPH** Yokohama: Tuesday, 5:25 P.M.

GUNTHER STEIG, FORMERLY of the East German Stasi, graduate of the infamous Soviet Spetsnaz and professional killer, was enjoying the scenery. The 5:00 P.M. train from Tokyo to Osaka had stopped at Yokohama first, then Atami. He felt his adrenaline begin to pump. He would get through police surveillance at the station, then head for the religious sect's hotel. Tomorrow he would take care of the Pachinko Woman.

Sunday night, after leaving Aleksei, he'd walked aimlessly for an hour thinking about the Russian's religious retreat idea. He wondered how he could make it work. The last thing he looked like was a religious convert.

He found himself in Harajuku, a place of fashionable stores, bars, and restaurants that tourists frequented. He studied the older foreigners. Several were being wheeled around. These he studied most carefully.

On the way back to his hotel that night, he considered getting to Atami.

Trains were crowded and hard to watch—no matter how expert the surveillance. Road access was limited and easy to roadblock. A boat made no sense, since hirings were monitored by marine police and the trip from Tokyo would take six hours. Storms could disrupt plans. He considered wilder ideas, like parachuting in, but no parachuting was allowed in the crowded coastal area, he learned. Train it would be, he finally concluded.

Last night he had studied material about the Kami-Hai given him by the Japan Travel Bureau. Thousands of religious sects had sprung up since the property bubble burst. Media called it "the Rush Hour of the Gods." The Kami-Hai had grown fastest. It had a documented history of healing that earned the facility worldwide media attention. Over one billion dollars in contributions had funded growth of the lavish religious complex. Tourists were welcome.

When he'd phoned Monday, the Kami-Hai confirmed that a seaview suite had been booked for Mr. Stein. They welcomed converts and agreed that someone with his disabilities should be met at the train.

On Tuesday morning, Steig had visited several clothing stores, a contact lens retailer, and a pharmaceutical outlet. When everything was complete, he'd stopped at a barber shop and told them what he wanted. Then he'd ordered his eyebrows dyed black. Black? they asked.

Do it, he said.

Now, the bald, dark-eyed foreigner who sat hunched in his wheelchair in the dining car of the bullet train did not look at all like a cold-blooded killer.

THE NAME, PHONE number, and address of the inn were neatly printed on the card left for Steve at the TV station's reception desk. However, when he called, he was told Helim Kim was not registered. He tried the number several times. Same answer. Finally, he asked for Katano. Katano was registered but was not in his room.

The Shimizu Inn was in the foothills above the city. As Steve walked through Atami Station, a policeman stopped him and asked for his passport. The officer looked at it, then pulled out a piece of paper with a face printed on it. Steve wondered what this was about as the policeman motioned him on. A sudden wave of dread washed over him, but he quickly chided himself for being paranoid.

The trip to the inn was only a short cab ride, or twenty minutes by foot, he was told at an information booth.

Since the sky was clear, and the train ride had consumed nearly half his remaining cash even though he'd taken a local line from Shinagawa, Steve walked. He hadn't shaved, and his clothes were soiled from sleeping in the park again. People stared at him, but his spirits were high. Everything would turn out fine.

He reached the inn in less than half an hour. Over the entrance was a sloping thatched roof around which great hedges grew. He could hear the sound of a waterfall as he entered, and the walk was of round black stones. Shoes were left at the entrance; from here an immaculately polished wood floor led inside the inn. He rang a bell. Shortly, an elderly woman in a kimono appeared and, looking at him with distaste, asked what he wanted. He asked for Mr. Katano.

She said he was out, then turned. When she saw he was not leaving, she came back to him and repeated, "No Mr. Katano. Go out. Very sorry."

Steve held his ground. "Then Miss Helim Kim."

"Eh?"

"Kim. Miss Kim."

"One moment, please." This time she hurried away.

Steve suddenly realized that two men had closed in behind him. Two more men in black uniforms approached from the halls on each side. Before he could resist, his arms were pinned behind him tightly and he was forced to kneel on the round black stones like a prisoner awaiting execution.

THE PLAN HAD been carefully conceived. All possible avenues to reach Atami had been considered and surveillance teams assigned. Most likely, the killer would attempt to reach the resort by train, Mori reasoned, although roads were a possibility, and roadblocks had been set up. As further precaution, the Coast Guard had been notified, and all unscheduled craft in the area would be checked. But the trains were the killer's best hope of escaping undetected. Bullet trains stopping in Atami left Tokyo Station three times an hour and were extremely crowded, while local trains from Shinagawa were only one every two hours, took twice as long, and were rarely used by foreigners. The killer would ride the crowded bullet, Mori decided. He'd be too easy to spot on the local line.

Since late Sunday, teams had been assigned to all entrances and ticket windows in Tokyo and Atami stations. In addition, every bullet train leaving Tokyo was boarded by a member of Mori's team for the hour-long trip to Atami. During this time, he or she checked every car and washroom. If the foreigner was spotted, a boarding team in Atami would be notified and would go into action when the train arrived. The main goal was to avoid injury to other passengers and make the arrest on the train before the suspect could disembark at Atami Station and disappear in the crowds.

A backup team would take the suspect to Atami police headquarters for interrogation. Public Security Bureau teams would coordinate with local police directed by their chief, Captain Kurai. Mori would arrive by helicopter at the police headquarters rooftop landing pad once a suspect had been taken. Captain Kurai would meet Mori at station headquarters and assist the operation from that point, but Mori and the PSB would be in control, and Mori would have final say on all matters, including the interrogation procedure. All these details had been agreed upon in a series of phone calls between Mori and Kurai on Monday.

On Tuesday, at three o'clock, the hot line had buzzed. A Tokyo Station team at the rear-exit location had spotted the foreigner. The operation was going red.

"Confirm it," Mori barked.

Five minutes later, his operation line had buzzed again. Suspect was a tourist who claimed he was going to Atami on a model agency contract. Nothing in his luggage. Passport was in order. On closer inspection, his features didn't match the computer composite. "Hold him anyway," Mori said. "Find out the name of the model agency, check it out." He didn't want any mistakes.

At four-forty-five, Mori's hot line had buzzed again.

"We have him!" It was the excited voice of Captain Kurai.

"The gaijin?"

"Yes. The fool asked for Helim Kim at the entrance to the Asako Inn. Our SWAT team overpowered him."

"You're sure?"

"Yes, of course. It's the man you want, Inspector. The resemblance to the computer composite is striking. Same color hair, eyes."

"Where's he now?"

"Atami police headquarters under heavy guard."

"Hold him as he is. I'll be there within forty minutes."

47: THE KEY WEAKNESS Atami: Tuesday, 5:35 P.M.

FOR OVER TWO hours they had driven the winding coast road with its panoramic views of the Pacific. Tonight Katano was hosting a farewell dinner for Helim at a restaurant that had once been a daimyo's castle. Tomorrow morning, they would part company.

Halfway to Shimoda, Katano had ordered the driver to turn and head back up the coast. The setting sun was hidden by thick fog. A storm front of billowing clouds was rolling in from the south. As they neared Atami, Katano had raised the subject of comfort women.

"No TV documentary has ever been aired on one," he said. "Maybe we should try. The diary has renewed public interest."

She was prepared. "Comfort women are a symptom of a deeper malaise that sickens Japanese society—and other Asian cultures as well. Women are sex objects. Trophies. At first you denied comfort women existed, then you refused them compensation. In a way, all Asian women are comfort women."

Katano had merely smiled. "Then you agree?"

"Why not?" She told him about the comfort woman association her grandmother had founded, sponsored by prominent expatriate Korean women who, among other things, sought to raise the position of all women in Asia. It supported Nobel Prize winner Aung San Suu Kyi in her brave fight and favored reunification of the two Koreas. It helped former comfort women who were suing for damages. At first, the association had been groups of Korean comfort women organized by shamanists in Tokyo and Osaka; now many housewives throughout the world had joined. Men were joining too. However, Asian governments were reluctant to recognize the society.

"Why is that the case?"

"Because Confucian, Buddhist, and Islamic societies in Asia are male-dominated. Few women gain positions of power. A TV documentary would help our cause if it's done right."

"Yes! Good! We could start with the comfort woman problem, then move to the broader issue. But I'll need your help. And of course we'd have to present both sides of the issue."

"Both sides?"

"Certainly. There are still some of us who feel it was a perfectly legal thing to do."

"You're offering excuses, that's all. I can't be involved in anything that tries to whitewash what the Japanese military did."

Katano was silent a moment. "Yet I feel your grandmother and you harbor no grudge."

"Only against the Japanese officer who tricked her into thinking she was going to be a nurse and then raped her. His name was Sakamoto. Perhaps he was killed in the war. Nowadays, we resent only those men who try to use us."

"Anyone in particular?" Katano had taken the bait.

Helim hesitated as if reluctant to reveal more. "There's one politician who still uses us Koreans for his own gain."

Katano's eyes came alive. "A Japanese politician?"

"Yes. A politician with close connections to pachinko. I know things about him that could destroy his career. But I'm reluctant to do this." She spoke in an offhand manner, in the way of one who might be inclined to handle such secrets casually.

"Have you ever told anyone?"

"No. Not yet. Perhaps one day."

"Can you tell me who he is? This politician. Consider it part of our interview?"

"No. I'm sorry. That's my secret."

The TV newsman tried several other approaches, but finally fell silent.

Helim knew it was only a matter of time now.

THE GIRL HAD entered the dining car earlier, stood near the cashier, and checked passengers as if looking for a friend. Her eyes lingered on Steig.

She left, then returned twenty minutes later, after they pulled out of

Yokohama Station. Time enough to check each car for blond foreigners, Steig decided. Could police be screening every train leaving Tokyo? She'd ordered tea. The diners in the car were rapidly thinning. She was seated near the door.

Too well dressed for police, he told himself. Nice face. Wearing one of those high-fashion scarves the Japanese girls commonly wore around their neck and shoulders. She'd become deeply engrossed in her magazine. Fashion, of course. Other Japanese who came in ordered, gulped their food or coffee, and left. It was ingrained in their work ethic to eat fast, he supposed. But not Miss Clean. She was nursing her cup of tea.

An office lady on a business trip, no doubt. Normally, he'd try to pick her up.

THE THRUM OF the helicopter engine massaged Mori's brain; he felt the tension of the wait leaving him. Relief. The foreigner had been taken. It had all been so easy. Maybe too easy.

"Weather coming," the pilot had warned as he boarded.

"Just get me there." Suddenly, he felt drowsy. He willed himself awake. Not yet. They still had to interrogate the killer.

He flicked on his radio and punched in Watanabe's code, and his friend's voice boomed in his ear.

"Watanabe here, sir. Just going to call you."

"There's been a development in Atami," Mori said. "A foreigner who matches the killer's description had been captured there. Your team will continue the operation until I confirm it's the killer. I'm on my way to Atami to interrogate the prisoner."

"Right. I have a situation here too. We're following another foreigner who was on an earlier train. Blond. Tall."

"Where are you?" The possibility of decoys stung his mind. Or maybe the killer had disguised himself somehow. Mori doubted that even he could blend in very easily, no matter what identity he had assumed. He hoped he wasn't falling prey to wishful thinking.

"On the station platform at Atami Station, sir, following instructions."

"You are in Atami and you have a second foreigner under surveillance," Mori mused. He didn't like what he was sensing.

"Yes. And Ayumi has called in a third possibility. She's on the five-o'clock."

"That makes three. Have Ayumi give you the car number where her suspect is. Send a boarding team in to detain him." No matter how many decoys they threw at him, he'd take them all, Mori thought. One was the killer.

"Right. I'll check with Ayumi now. Should we detain the blond we're following?"

"Yes! Bring him in too. With Ayumi's. No formal arrest procedure. Take both suspects to the Atami Station police kiosk for screening. Use force only if necessary. You have that?"

"Yes sir."

Mori's mind was churning furiously. This could turn into a public relations disaster if he wasn't careful. One of the three was surely the killer. Only a matter of time before he knew which one.

48: THE FATE Atami: Tuesday, 5:43 P.M.

IT WAS BEGINNING to darken outside Steig's window. Something—the angle of the earth, perhaps—brought twilight earlier to Japan than to Europe. The dining car was empty of patrons, except for himself and the girl with the scarf. Miss Clean. Steig wheeled over to the cashier and paid his bill.

"That's a beautiful wheelchair," the cashier said, eyeing it as she handed him change.

"Designed by two Americans," Steig said proudly. He'd taken some time in selecting it. "The frame's aircraft aluminum tubing. Light."

"How do you get on and off trains?"

"See the tires? They're nobbed like those of mountain bikes."

"Yes."

"Also has disk brakes, not rim ones. Some people race these things. Stable as a goat on hills. Very manageable."

"Unusual."

"They go down stairs, or get off trains if no one's there to help." Steig glanced to see if Miss Clean was listening. She was looking at him with an expression that he had become used to. A mixture of pity and relief that it wasn't her in the chair.

"It's very nice. Thank you for your patronage."

The loudspeaker announced that they would be arriving at Atami Station in twelve minutes.

Steig looked at Miss Clean again. She was putting her magazine into a Gucci bag. Brand-new. Then he saw the clear plastic wire running from inside her blouse to her earpiece. Nearly invisible, but not quite. Police.

Instinct took over. Wheeling toward her, he placed himself between the woman and the door. Did she suspect him?

"Hello," he said in Japanese. "I'm stopping in Atami. How about yourself?" His eyes studied her blouse, shoes, skirt.

"Yes. Me too. I'm sorry, I have to leave." She stood. Her manner was neither curious nor frightened. She had something on her mind other than Steig.

"Have a nice stay."

He wheeled to the exit doors. The policewoman hadn't recognized him, he was sure. She'd hurried off through the next car and disappeared. Now he must get through the station. He wondered if the Kami-Hai had sent a van as promised. That would be critical. He would succeed this time, he told himself. He felt confident now.

THE HELICOPTER DROPPED Mori off at five-forty-five on the roof of the Atami police barracks. Captain Kurai was waiting for him on the perimeter.

"We have the gaijin downstairs," the captain said.

"You're sure it's him?"

"Yes, yes. Striking similarity to that computer sketch you faxed. Most important, he knew her name. Asked for Helim Kim right at the inn. Our men took him into custody without much of a fight."

"Let me talk with him then."

"You'll have to hold your nose. He smells like a rotten egg."

Three officers stood to attention as Mori entered the downstairs interrogation room. Amid the three burly police officers stood a tall foreigner. Mori stared at the foreigner. The captain was right. He smelled terrible. His clothes were a mess. And he looked confused. Not a professional, Mori thought with disappointment. No professional would walk up to the front door of the inn and ask for her by her name. Perhaps he was a decoy contracted by whatever intelligence service the killer belonged to.

The foreigner said in English, "What the fuck is going on?"

Mori nodded. "Please be silent." He turned to Kurai. "Bring a copy of the computer sketch. There's some resemblance, I admit. The coloring in particular. In other respects, I'm not so sure. He doesn't have the same eyes."

"But they both have blue eyes."

"Yes, I can see that," Mori said testily. He glanced at his watch. Perspiration crawled down the small of his back. "Please get the sketch quickly."

The captain gave the order, and one of the men hurried from the room and returned with the computer composite. Mori stared at it, then at the foreigner. Why was it that foreigners looked so alike? He turned to Kurai. "You said he has identification?"

"Yes. An American passport. Probably forged. However, the entry permit is in order. He has the automatic ninety-day visa all Americans are given. A wallet with driver's license, credit cards. The name he uses is Steven Juric. He also had a paper with the inn's name in kanji."

"Any weapon?"

"No."

Mori turned to stare at the foreigner again. They were all like zebras. In English, he asked Juric, "Where did you get the paper with the name of Helim Kim's inn written in Japanese?"

Steve was surprised to hear fluent English from a policeman. "In Tokyo. The KSB-TV receptionist gave it to me," he replied. "Helim Kim's a friend. She's meeting a Mr. Katano for an interview at the Shimizu Inn. Katano works for KSB-TV. His assistant left the number at the reception desk for me."

"A receptionist at the TV station gave you this?"

"Yes."

Mori continued to stare at him. "I wonder."

"That's why I'm here, dammit!" Steve said loudly. "Now what's going on? I want to see her. She'll tell you!"

Mori turned to Kurai. In Japanese, he said, "Call KSB-TV. Ask reception there if they gave this gaijin the inn's name and phone number. Call Helim Kim at her inn. Did anyone think of that?"

Captain Kurai waved his hand dismissively. "The foreigner told our interrogator the same thing. It was a patent lie. We called the inn, but Helim Kim was out. We called KSB-TV reception and they said they had never heard of the foreigner. Anyway, our interrogator could tell it was all a lie."

Mori hit his radio button and heard Watanabe's strained voice. "Yes, sir."

"What's your situation?"

"Man we were following was detained and is now at the Atami Station police kiosk. Ayumi's train is pulling into the station now. Our boarding team is ready to go. I haven't been able to raise Ayumi. She's probably gone to powder her nose."

"Keep trying. The one you were following—did he resist?"

"No. Seemed surprised."

"What have you found out about him?"

"He's Dutch. Amsterdam. No knives or other weapons. Looks like an illegal substance in his luggage. Need a narc expert to check it."

"Anything else?"

"He claims he's on a modeling assignment. Some agency in Tokyo contracted him for two days. Gave him a ticket and expense money. Supposed to meet people here, but they haven't showed. We're checking the company now. Storm Model Group, Harajuku. He's with a Dutch woman. She's been complaining. Making noise."

The decoy possibility became a reality in Mori's brain. "Didn't we get the same story from a blond gaijin we detained at Tokyo Station an hour ago?"

"I'll have to check that, sir."

"Hold the man. I want to question him. We'll be right over."

49: ATAMI Niigata City: Tuesday, 6:08 P.M.

JOE PIPE HAD arrived at the compound on the outskirts of Niigata City that afternoon to review preparations with DeCovasi, who had been in Niigata since the beginning of the week. The ship would arrive tomorrow and remain in port until Friday evening. The press had been given the wrong dates as a security measure. The North Koreans would be ferried by a captain's launch to and from the ship. Tight harbor security would be in force during the North Korean leader's short stay.

The secret meeting between former president Sherman Whitlow and Park Tai Jin would take place on Thursday in the presidential suite of the Niigata Prince Hotel. No press releases would be issued. However, the local media had sensed that something important was about to occur. The sudden influx of Americans in Ray-Ban sunglasses meant one thing; a visit from an American VIP was imminent. The guessing game of who it would be had been going on for several days.

One of the American specialists who had flown in to secure the hotel introduced DeCovasi to Haruko's, a place where he and Pipe could relax for dinner.

"You handled the logistics very well," Pipe told DeCovasi. "The hotel looks good." He had decided to begin with the easier issues.

"The Japanese fussed at the beginning as they usually do, but no real problems." DeCovasi sat back and smiled, enjoying the relaxed atmosphere of an outlying Japanese city.

"The canisters?"

"Got fifty."

"So who's going to plant them?"

"One of the Jap Public Security boys, I think. Stolen car operation is the excuse."

"Stolen cars on the Korean ship?"

"Yup. Seems the North Korean military are great entrepreneurs."

"How about our diver?"

"He arrived yesterday. The best. Navy SEAL. Absolutely reliable. Tomorrow I'm introducing him to Homma who heads up the local police."

"That brings us to Tomás Velaquez. Any word?"

"Not since he met people in Hong Kong and gave our boys the slip. We know he caught a flight to Hong Kong from Stuttgart before that. And in Hong Kong, two Asian characters met him just before he disappeared."

"He'd better show up on that ship," Pipe said pleasantly to no one in particular. "And so had Alpha and General Kuk."

As they finished their meal and summoned the bill, DeCovasi said casually, "By the way, had a call from our good friend at the KGB in Tokyo. You remember Aleksei Romanov?"

"Sure. How is that devious son of a bitch?"

"Courtesy call. Just to let us know he was in town."

Pipe squinted at his junior. "Something's up, then." He let DeCovasi pay.

"WE'LL PUT MR. JURIC in a car with us," Mori said as he and Captain Kurai left the interrogation center. "I want to talk with him on the way to Atami Station. Later we'll take him to our safe house."

"He could be dangerous."

Mori smiled. "I admit he could be working with our killer, Captain. If he tries anything, however, I'll defend you."

As they drove to the station, Mori considered what he should do with this foreigner who sat beside him in the backseat. The captain sat in front and turned to face them both as the car made its way through crowded streets, its siren wailing. "We'll be there in seven minutes."

"Call the Shimizu Inn again," Mori snapped. "Find out where Helim Kim is."

The driver made the call.

"Miss Kim left this afternoon and is not expected back until after dinner," the driver said over his shoulder. "They don't know how to reach her."

"You hear that?" Mori said. "Your friend's disappeared. We're going to hold you until we reach her. She'll tell us if you're her friend or enemy."

THE BULLET TRAIN slowed for Atami Station. Waiting by the door in his wheelchair, Steig considered everything that could go wrong. The next few minutes would be his most vulnerable. Hidden in the wheelchair's tubular frame and in the compartment rigged under his seat were equipment, ammunition, and the dismantled Korean Uzi. The Gerber knife was in his leg sheath, the Luger in his belt. The only thing he feared was capture. If necessary, the Luger was for himself.

Drops of rain were falling as the bullet train's doors hissed open. Down the train in the direction Miss Clean had taken, Steig noted a commotion as men bustled onto the train before passengers could debark. Apprehension cleared his mind. Move, he commanded. He eased off the train.

Three men in black suits approached as he wheeled onto the platform. "Mr. Stein?" they asked.

Steig felt his nerves tense. "Yes."

"Our van is outside. May we help you?"

The station opened onto a disconsolate square. Police were everywhere, but they ignored Steig except for a young by-the-book officer who stopped the lead Kami-Hai member. The man showed his card and explained that Steig was a disabled guest being escorted to their complex. The officer waved them through.

Two of the black-suited men cleared a path, while the other pushed Steig through the crowds. Steig didn't allow himself a sensation of victory. He conserved his energy, remained calm and focused. There would be more challenging decisions ahead. Life or death depended on wits, not prayer, he told himself.

He smelled the salt air, sensed a decadence, and liked the place immediately. Black Sea resorts of his youth came to mind: sulfur springs that cured anything contractible, consorts that made every evening an exotic festival of the flesh.

As they stopped at the curb in front of the station, a police car raced into the square and pulled up near the quartet. People craned their necks. Steig felt his heartbeat quicken. One hand crept toward his Luger. The other reached for the straps that held his legs. The doors of the police car swung open.

A small Japanese man with calm eyes stepped out and surveyed the scene. A police officer in a captain's uniform was next. Behind them came a disheveled foreigner flanked by two uniformed police. Steig gripped the Luger in his hand under his jacket. Then he froze.

The Japanese man glanced at Steig's party and asked something. The captain pointed to a white van, with "Kami-Hai" inscribed in Japanese and English, that had pulled up. The Japanese man nodded and moved on toward the police kiosk. Steig let out his breath. Team leader, he thought. Mark him.

The driver slid open a door. It took all four of them to lift Steig in.

One handed Steig a book. "Have you read the teachings of the Master? This is our English edition."

"Of course. Thank you," Steig said feeling generous with relief. "Beautifully written book, isn't it?"

Outside, a fountain struggled to spout while hawkers offered special prices for the rooms, girls, hot baths. Whatever the tourist wanted. Steig opened the book and pretended to read. His mind raced ahead, reviewing his next moves.

50: **THE DESPERADO** Atami: Tuesday, 6:33 P.M.

NOTHING MADE SENSE. When Steve asked for Katano at the inn, they had told him the TV personality wasn't there. When he asked for Helim, the police had swarmed all over him. What was going on? Was Helim Kim involved in a police operation?

From snatches of police conversation, he could understand there had been eight or nine murders of North Koreans. But why would Helim be connected to that? And why would they suspect him?

Whatever Helim's involvement, he was now in very deep. Eight murders! Helim, what are you doing to me? he thought.

The arrival of the new officer they called Inspector Mori had eased the situation. At least the man seemed reasonable. But still, his situation did not look good. Steve's exasperation at being arrested gradually turned to thoughts about what he should do.

Now, as he sat downstairs in the police kiosk in front of Atami Station, he considered his options. Inspector Mori had gone upstairs with the captain. What were they doing? he wondered. Why didn't they release him? He looked around the small police station wondering what would happen next.

Two policemen sat at a counter in front of him. One was working on a printout from a desktop. The other was on the phone. He was innocent, he told himself. And he liked the one called Mori who was upstairs. He'd have to trust these people.

A team of three men burst into the station leading a tall blond foreigner. They bustled him upstairs. Behind them came a petite Japanese woman. She was dressed immaculately and hurried up the stairs after the blond. What in hell was going on?

• • •

MORI SLAMMED HIS fist on the desk in the upstairs police observation room, causing Ayumi to jump. "None of them is the killer!"

"Sumimasen. I'm sorry," said Ayumi, who was standing beside him. Watanabe studied his fingernails. Captain Kurai paced the tiny room looking upset. Through a one-way window, two angry blond foreigners could be observed.

The blond from Ayumi's train and the one Watanabe had followed and detained both told the same story. So had the man detained at Tokyo Station. They'd all been approached on the street and offered a job in Atami. Needed foreign models, they had been told. Urgent. Client wanted blond men. For a fee they'd be crazy to turn down. Working visas not necessary, and he would take care of taxes. The man who had approached them was a short, dark, wavy-haired Caucasian. Not the blond killer.

Which meant that the intelligence agency behind the killer was not Asian, Mori reasoned. The Dutch were clearly decoys, innocent but part of the operation nonetheless. They would be held overnight. Longer if necessary. He then considered the American, Juric, downstairs.

Juric was not a decoy and obviously was not the killer. Mori believed he'd told the truth, that he was Helim's boyfriend. If so, he could be useful. Juric would be held until they located Helim and questioned her. He might help them to get her cooperation. His FBI friend, DeCovasi, believed Helim Kim was a double, working for North Korea. If that was true, the killer could be from either side, American or North Korean. But right now he needed answers. Not questions. "Why all the decoys?" he asked the room.

"A decoy," Ayumi said, "is to attract attention away from something."

"Right," Watanabe agreed. "How about the other avenues of approach? Roads? Sea? Air?"

"All covered." Captain Kurai stopped pacing. "No decoys or detainees at the roadblocks. Coast Guard reports no unusual unscheduled activity. No helicopters or other nonscheduled aircraft in the area. We've drawn a blank."

"Then he still hasn't made his move," Watanabe suggested. "Maybe our people scared him off."

"But if he wasn't, how could he have done it?" Mori murmured. "Decoys are used to lure wild birds and animals into traps. So what's the trap we've been lured into? Eh?"

"Maybe our killer knew we had a likeness," Ayumi suggested. "Maybe he changed himself somehow."

"Then used the decoys," Mori mused. "Knowing we'd chase blond and tall."

"You know," Ayumi said suddenly, "I was just wondering why a crippled person would wear worn shoes."

"What are you talking about?" Mori said.

Ayumi shrugged apologetically. "Maybe it's a crazy idea, but there was this guy in the dining car of the train. In a wheelchair. He was bragging to the cashier that it was custom-made and that he could get on and off trains without assistance. I noticed as he wheeled by me that his shoes were worn. If he can't use his legs, why?"

"Wait a minute!" Mori said. "What did he look like?"

"The wheelchair took away his height, so I have no idea about that, but he had big shoulders. Yeah. And he was bald. Black eyebrows. A little mustache."

"His eyes," Mori prompted.

"Dark. Black, I think. He wore spectacles. He looked older."

"Couldn't be him," Captain Kurai said.

Mori picked up the phone and dialed the computer center in Tokyo that had done the composite sketch. He told them what changes he wanted. Within five minutes, the computers downstairs transmitted the revised features. A copy was handed to each person in the room.

"It's him." Ayumi stood, gesturing. "The guy in the dining car."

Mori's eyes jolted as the thought hit him. "Kurai, that foreigner when we arrived! Wheelchair and bald! You remember?"

"No, I really don't think so. Couldn't be him. That fellow was heading for a local religious sect. They're very strict about guests."

"Don't you see? It's perfect. A place the police won't bother him!"

"Sir?"

"The decoys were lures," Mori shouted. "To attract our attention, while the real killer slipped through. You mentioned the sect's name. What was their name again, dammit? Kami . . ."

Kurai said, "The Kami-Hai. They have a large facility overlooking the ocean. But I really think this is all wrong."

"Watanabe, get our team together." Mori stood. "Kurai, how long to organize enough men to surround that facility if we have to?"

"I couldn't do that."

"Why not?"

"I can't authorize that massive an operation until there is proof."

Mori was already heading out the door. "You'll have your proof, Kurai, trust me. And he'll raise hell in that sacred place of yours if we don't stop him."

THEY WERE ON a moving sidewalk in a long glass-covered tunnel heading from the parking area to the hotel entrance. Drops of rain began to splatter against the glass. How much did the police know about him? Steig wondered. Did they know his forged passport name was Stern? Aleksei had booked him under the name Stein. If the hotel required a passport, he'd have to explain that the clerk had got the name wrong. Not that it mattered. Whatever happened, he couldn't linger. They'd eventually figure it out. He'd check in and bail out. Within an hour. Find a safe hole to hide in overnight.

"Here we are." The wide curve of the lobby was in white marble. They rolled him to the check-in counter.

"Mr. Stein," one of his tenders announced to the girl at the desk. "We'll take him up. VIP suite, I believe."

The clerk consulted her computer, then passed keys to the man. "A lower floor, as Mr. Stein requested. Please enjoy your stay." She bowed.

"Registration forms can be signed after you settle in," the man said as they wheeled him to the elevators. "A service for all our disabled guests."

Once they'd stowed his bags, Steig turned down offers to assist him further. He wanted to rest. "Give me an hour. Have them bring the registration forms then, if you don't mind."

"In an hour? Certainly."

After the door closed, Steig removed the Luger from his belt, then used an electronic device to sweep the room for listening devices and hidden TV cameras. None detected. From the wheelchair tubing he removed needles and plastic vials, lock picks, plastic twine, and surgical gloves, among other items. From the compartment under his seat, ten ammo clips and metal stock, barrel, and muzzle-flash shield for the Korean Uzi. From his luggage, he retrieved a waterproof backpack and adhesive bandage.

After he had assembled the Uzi and slapped a clip into the magazine, he packed everything in his backpack. Then he changed into black waterproof jogging pants, T-shirt, and running shoes, removed his contact lenses, and flushed them down the toilet. Forty-five minutes gone. Can't linger, he reminded himself. Opening the curtains, he reviewed his mental map of the facility. Head for the underground garage. Steal a car. It wouldn't be missed until morning, if then. Light rain was slanting against the window. The ocean was a sliver of aluminum less than a mile away. Light was fading and it would be dark soon. The sky ominous. Excellent. He slipped into the jacket and tried the hood, which could be tied low over his forehead once outside. Changed his profile. Slipping into the surgical gloves, he wiped down all surfaces touched and shrugged on the backpack. Opening the door, he looked out to the right. A covey of guests was waiting by the elevator. To the left over a door at the end of the hall was a red emergency exit sign. He waited until the elevator arrived, then strode to the exit door and tried the knob. It opened.

The stairs led to the underground garage for staff cars, which had an exit that opened onto the main parking lot for visitors. One main gate. Once through that, he'd head up the coast and sleep in the car overnight. Tomorrow morning he'd take the Pachinko Woman. This time do it right. He heard a noise. A security guard. He slipped back into shadows and waited.

"ASAKO! THERE. THAT'S the Arch of Peace." Captain Kurai, in the front seat, pointed. Inspector Mori and Watanabe stared. On a hill above them, lights had suddenly flooded a huge glittering complex. They played on a white dome, a soaring arch.

Mori didn't like it. He'd hoped for something smaller. "How many exits, Captain?"

"One from the parking lot, that's all. Once he's in, he can't get out."

"We'll bottle him up in the complex until your team arrives, then." But Mori knew that wouldn't be easy. He was dealing not only with one man, but with another intelligence agency. Possibly one of the big powers.

"Juric's in the last car," Watanabe reminded them.

"I want him with us until we find Helim Kim," Mori said. "Keep him out of the way. We don't want him hurt."

"We should have a search warrant," Kurai complained.

"You know these people?"

"My wife's a member. She's here now. There's a prayer meeting tonight."

"How soon can your backup team arrive?"

Kurai squinted at his watch. "After I call them, fifteen minutes."

They stopped under the curved glass canopy that led down into the Kami-Hai hotel. The three other squad cars carrying Watanabe's team pulled up behind them.

Mori ordered the two rear cars to block the main gate and control traffic. Watanabe assigned two men from his team to the cars, leaving six men for the main buildings. Mori then gave Kurai the deployment he wanted for reinforcements if they were needed. Hardly enough, it seemed, from the size of this place. The two cars pulled out and headed for the gate, with Steve Juric in one.

Mori signaled his team. "Let's go."

They raced down the moving sidewalk and into the dazzling lobby. Mori headed straight to the front desk and held up his National Police card. "A foreigner checked in a few minutes ago. In a wheelchair. Named Stern."

The clerk bowed, looking flustered. "No one by that name."

"All right. What name did he use?"

A manager strode over, frowning. "Can I help you?"

Mori turned impatiently. "Guest safety your responsibility, sir?"

"Of course."

"We're looking for a man who has killed eight people."

"Not here, I'm sure."

"Fellow in the wheelchair who just checked in."

Kurai came puffing up. "Why hello, Mr. Hongo."

"Captain Kurai! What's this about?"

"I'm terribly sorry to disturb you. Inspector Mori is with the National Police Public Security Bureau. I'd appreciate it very much if you'd cooperate with him." Kurai bowed, clearly embarrassed.

"We certainly want to cooperate. However, I can't believe one of our guests is—"

"Then you won't mind if we just check his room," Mori said impatiently.

"Are you sure this is necessary?" Hongo said to Captain Kurai in a voice tinged with hidden meaning.

"The Public Security Bureau reports to the prime minister," Kurai said unhappily. "An exceptional situation, Mr. Hongo. National emergency."

"No more time," Mori muttered.

"This is most unusual," Hongo said. "But all right. Quietly, please." He glanced at the clerk. "Whom do they want?"

"Mr. Stein, sir. Room 203."

"Watanabe, take two men upstairs to secure that room," Mori barked. "I'll be right up." He turned back to Hongo as Watanabe's team headed for the elevators. "What time did Stein check in?" At least Kurai was good for something, Mori thought.

The clerk stared at her computer. "Forty-five minutes ago, sir."

"How many guests on the second floor?"

"I'd have to check."

"You do that, please," Mori said. "And call each one. Tell them all to stay in their rooms, doors locked, until you call again with an all clear. Explain it's a test."

"Is this absolutely necessary?" the manager asked.

"Yes sir, it is. And keep the second floor clear. No guests off that floor may return to their rooms. Same drill. There's one more thing you can help us with, Mr. Hongo." Mori turned and pointed at Kurai. "The manager will provide you with a map of this place and advise you about all escape routes from the building. Assign a man to each. If there are too many to cover, concentrate on the most likely. If anyone spots the killer, don't try to take him alone. Call in. Wait for my orders. A backup team will be called in. We'll take him when they're in place." Mori noted the concerned look on Hongo's face. "*If* Mr. Stein turns out to be our man."

STEVE'S DRIVER POSITIONED their car sideways across the main gate entrance so that only five feet of pavement was exposed. He lit up a cigarette. On either side were eight-foot walls.

"What's going on?" Steve asked.

"We wait here. Don't worry." The driver turned on a police radio. A second car pulled up alongside theirs.

The two drivers talked briefly, and two men got out of the other car. They were armed with repeating shotguns and wore armored vests. They occupied positions along the wall. The two vehicles blocked the road, so no cars could get in or out.

Over the police radio, Steve could hear the crackle of terse conversation. He tried to decipher what they were saying.

The captain's voice: "Six escape routes detected and covered. Where are you?"

"In the suspect's room." Mori's voice. "He's gone. Left a wheelchair. The frame's made from hollow tubing. Looks like something was concealed inside. A compartment under the seat could have held weapons. Assume he's armed. One overnight bag contains clothing. Kurai, order that backup team. No question about it—this is our man!"

"Yes sir. Backup team will be here in fifteen minutes."

"Good. Our people are deployed on all escape routes?"

"In place. There's an evening prayer service in progress, as mentioned. It'll finish in another few minutes. You can't block the entrance when all those people—"

"We'll do what we have to!" Mori interrupted. "Each man call in his status. Immediately!"

No CARS HAD tried to enter or leave since they'd arrived. The driver put out his cigarette, unbuckled his seat belt, and sat up straighter. His eyes scanned the parking lot. It was half full of cars and surrounded by stucco wall. The road to the Kami-Hai entrance wound up a hill above them lined with plane trees. Dominating the scene, the brilliantly lit dome of the main auditorium and Peace Arch filled the parking area with shadows. It seemed as if everything was in motion.

Helim's attacker was here, Steve thought. Somewhere inside this place. His mind was suddenly focused and clear. He'd known fear before, but he had never felt it so acutely.

The radio broke into his thoughts.

"Oishi here. Underground garage. Someone's starting a car."

"Get a look at the driver. Okay. Who's next?" The call-ins continued. Each post reported no activity.

A terse voice suddenly broke into the chatter. "I've got him, sir."

"Where? Who's this, dammit?" Mori's urgent voice.

"Oishi. Underground garage."

"Describe him."

"Big foreigner for sure. Bald. Shit, he's looking this way. He heard me."

"We're on our way," Mori said. "Get out of there, Oishi. Take cover!"

"Yes, sir—"

To Steve, it sounded like
a string of firecrackers exploding. Distant and harmless. Kids having fun.

"Oishi, come in," Mori's voice demanded.

No answer.

Mori's voice was shrill. "All team members converge on parking lot immediately. Killer's making a break."

The driver suddenly stiffened, pulled his revolver, and flicked off the safety. He got out of the car and stared up the hill.

Then Steve heard it too. A car engine somewhere, gaining speed. Then he saw it.

A large black shadow, no lights, speeding through the parking lot like a cougar. Coming toward them.

A spotlight on the other police car flicked on, pinned the oncoming grille in its beam. Steve's driver fired.

A silver car, shining, hurtling though the light rain. Engine whining like a banshee. Other guns opened up. Fascinated, Steve watched the car careening toward them, saw its door swing open, a shadowy figure drop and roll. Reflexively, Steve flung open his door and dove.

The sound of firing was extinguished by an explosion of metal and shattering glass, followed by screams of pain. Steve kept rolling on damp pavement until he reached grass, then crawled under a shrub. He remained very still.

He waited. He was outside the gate, in wet deep grass that had soaked his clothing. He could hear the staccato shriek of an automatic weapon on the other side of the wall and the responding blasts of a shotgun. The entrance was blocked by mangled steel hulks. They were beginning to smolder. A figure in one was slumped over the wheel. The vehicle was rocking under repeated hits from an automatic weapon. The other policeman was nowhere in sight. The screaming had stopped. All firing suddenly ceased.

A shadow leaped effortlessly over the wall twenty yards away. Dropped silently and disappeared. Steve could hear shouts from team members racing through the parking lot, converging on the slaughter.

Up the hill, a stream of worshipers emerged from massive temple doors, heading into the parking lot. The wreckage blocking the entrance started to burn.

"Shit," Steve screamed at the brilliant white complex. "Oh, shit." But his voice was lost in the crackling flames that rose into the darkening sky.

Rain started to fall again. He strained his eyes in the gathering gloom. Something moved downhill in fields bathed in fading light, far away from the road. Heading for the rocky coast. On the other side of the wall, he could hear radios, people shouting excitedly.

In the distance, a long string of tiny police cars, blue lights flashing, was winding up the coast road. Too late, he thought. Never catch him. Bastard's getting away, going to kill Helim.

Several forms catapulted over the wall and headed in the wrong direction.

"Here!" he shouted. He stood.

The two weapons fired at once, their muzzleblast igniting the gloom. Something seared Steve's forehead, knocking him to the ground. He sat for a moment stunned, then touched his skin where a bullet had creased his forehead. The fingers came away dark and sticky with blood. "Damn you," he hissed and lurched to his knees. The bastards thought he was the killer. The police hadn't moved; they were shouting for backup. The rain was heavier now.

Steve's numbed mind was astonished to realize he was moving, crawling into shrubs, hugging the growing darkness, away from the police, willing himself forward as if compelled by some primal instinct. Then he was running—downhill through the brush and grass—stumbling over rocks and sudden depressions toward the place where the killer had disappeared.

51 ⦂ THE DEBACLE Atami: Tuesday, 8:00 P.M.

THE REMNANTS OF Mori's team had combed every inch of ground to the seacoast. The killer had disappeared—he had either risked the sea or slipped through their cordon.

The police radio buzzed with haphazard reports of sightings, which turned out to be false leads. It was gradually dawning on Mori. Becoming fact. The killer had escaped. From the elite of the Japanese police system.

Mori raised his head. "Ja shoganai," he grunted. A Japanese expression that covered all defeats. It meant acceptance of what the gods had wanted. For now, he must put on his best face. That was what the Japanese were good at, wasn't it? Putting on an appearance that concealed their true emotions.

"Shoganai," Captain Kurai concurred.

Order had been restored in the parking lot. Fire trucks had extinguished the blaze. A tow truck had cleared away wreckage. Ambulances had delivered the four wounded and two dead to hospitals and morgues. Mori was directing the search from a police car parked on a rise near the seacoast.

"The sea," Kurai said. "It's the only explanation."

"Perhaps," Mori replied, his voice dulled by shock. His team would never catch the killer in that case. "The Coast Guard—do they have patrol boats in the area?"

"Yes. The local commander is a friend."

"Contact him immediately."

Anger flooded Mori's thoughts. The only way to live this down was to finish the killer tonight. His death was the only possible resolution.

Two police officers dead. Oishi critical. Others wounded. He'd call on anyone who could help. Freshening winds were whipping huge waves onto the rocky coastline. Staring through the darkness at the worsening weather, Mori had another thought. The killer would be lucky to survive this sea. Maybe the sea gods would help. "What's the forecast for tonight?"

"Severe storms."

"Pray the gods will finish what we have been unable to," Mori said.

"The commander will send two cutters with skilled captains," Kurai responded. "The currents here are very dangerous, especially tonight."

"Excellent."

"What about Juric's escape?"

"I don't understand it at all," Mori said.

"I told you he was with them. You wouldn't listen. He's in the ocean with the killer. Bet you anything."

Mori said nothing. He'd always considered himself a good judge of men. Now Juric was a fugitive.

"I've invited the Coast Guard commander for dinner tonight. I hope you can join us. Not much more we can do here, is there?"

Mori wondered what his Oyabun would say to that. No doubt he would quote Mencius.

Words of the philosopher came to him. "Nothing happens which is not one's destiny, but one should accept willingly only what is one's proper destiny."

On the way back to Atami, they reviewed details for the continuing search operation. Kurai's backup team would continue to guard the seacoast while the cutters roamed offshore. The killer wouldn't escape alive, one way or the other. No one would survive the seas tonight, Captain Kurai promised. Juric and the killer were doomed.

STEVE HAD ONLY glimpsed the dim figure running steadily ahead of him. When Steve reached the edge of the ocean, the killer had disappeared. Waves crashed on rocks nearby. The air was dank and the sky had darkened ominously. As he scanned the beach, Steve could hear shouts of police searching the fields behind him. Coming ever closer. Wait until they get here, he told himself. It was useless.

He waited, barely breathing. There was no way the killer could get back into the city and escape now. The police were spread out in a long picket line combing the countryside. He stared out over the sea. Menacing clouds were gathering. Fierce waves were building. A storm was imminent. He put himself in the killer's place. Gradually, his predicament became clear—the sea was his only chance.

Searching the waters, he found a black speck out in the waves. The speck surfaced then disappeared behind growing swells. A swimmer in the darkening water, or just debris? He watched for several moments. It was heading for a far spit of land barely discernible in the fading light, the outermost point of the bay.

Without thinking, Steve raced to the water's edge and dove into the waves. He used a dolphin stroke to stay underwater until he was well out beyond the breakers, then turned toward the bobbing head, now several hundred yards offshore.

Ahead of him the ocean had become the color of steel. The waves began to lift into endless lines of foam. The bobbing head was closer. Good, he thought. The ocean squares our strength.

Against the darkening sky, the rolling waves became grim claws. Large raindrops spattered around him like bullets. The wind quickened, lifting water in huge mountains, spray flying from the peaks in devil's tails. Steve rode them as he had learned to ride the California surf, relaxed, letting them take him farther and farther out. Each time he was lifted high on the back of the foaming sea, he saw the killer's head bobbing closer before him. The man must have great courage and strength, he thought, deciding he would have to come in from behind. To surprise him.

But the gale was almost upon them, and he could feel its strength in the shuddering sea. Waves fought one another for supremacy. For the first time he wondered if he could survive. But the winds massaged a rhythm of waves that he could tame with his body. A final wave lifted him into the air, then released him, brought him power-diving down on the thrashing figure below him.

The first blow was glancing, and the cold, shallow blue eyes turned on him, rheumy with the sea but still violent and confident. Steve struck out smashing into the nose. The face suddenly dove to come up behind him. Before Steve could turn, he felt the tear of his flesh as a knife ripped him open. He heard a high-pitched scream, remote and surreal. His own.

The killer raised the knife again, but Steve twisted away, driving a foot into the man's chest, then diving deep and surfacing as yet another wave bore down on them.

He felt his strength draining into the sea with his blood. Desperately, he struck again at the killer, but the thrashing sea muted his blows. Gasping and struggling, he caught the man in a headlock, trying to hold him under, but the man slipped away, cutting into Steve again.

Treading water out of reach, the killer watched Steve with serene blue shark eyes. Waiting for Steve's strength to ebb completely before closing in for the final kill. Steve cursed him, taunted him to fight, but his words were lost in the sea and wind. He must save his strength, he thought. Otherwise, it was hopeless.

Suddenly, fierce waves came roaring between them. The sea bore them both now on its path, and they were helpless against its strength. Above the tumult, Steve heard the man cry out in terror. Then he too saw the reef. Huge and black, covered with barnacles that would cut like razors. The killer fought to avoid it with a madman's strength.

Steve body-surfed toward the reef, praying for a gap. Rain slashing against his face, he turned to see a giant wave throw his opponent high above the reef, hold him there flailing in the air, then dash him downward.

Ahead, a gap widened for an instant, then narrowed. Steve flung himself forward. Rocks slammed into his sides. He cursed the sea and the storm. His vision blurred, and he fought with the final fury of the doomed before the darkness overwhelmed him.

PART FIVE

When Heaven sends down calamities,
There is hope of weathering them.
When man brings them upon himself,
There is no hope of escape.

T'ai Chia

52: **THE DINNERS** Izu Peninsula: Tuesday, 7:45 P.M.

KATANO AND HELIM pulled up before the restaurant. Tanabe, Katano's agent, greeted them both at the car with an umbrella. Rain fell relentlessly, and the wind gusted.

Helim experienced a foreboding she could not define. As the restaurant's thick, scarred wooden doors opened, she tried to shake her premonition. After all, she told herself, looking around, Katano had believed her story about the Japanese politician. In reality she didn't know who was protecting the pachinko laundering racket. No one did. But if Katano believed she knew, then her plan might work.

The other members of the crew were waiting for them. Helim chatted with the team, trying to pull herself out of her melancholy state, while Katano talked alone with his agent. An urgent business matter had come up, he explained to her. Helim knew better.

She wondered if there would be enough time for Katano to react to the seed she had planted. Wait and see, she told herself. Japan was a big factory constantly producing and refining people. The already refined ones were not involved in the process. They were out in the showcase for others to see. That would be her man. A politician.

She thought of the risks she was taking. Maybe her grandmother's visit tomorrow wasn't a good idea after all. No. They were alike, she and her grandmother. And her grandmother knew all about risk. Even now, there were secrets of her past the old woman still kept, dark rooms of her mind that Helim had never been allowed to enter. Perhaps they were too alike, Helim decided. They both had their secrets.

• • •

ANOTHER DINNER THAT night was being hosted by Captain Kurai, chief of the Atami police. Mori was guest of honor. Also present was the commander of the local Coast Guard, Masami Murata. Earlier, a policeman had spotted two swimmers heading out of Atami Bay. The Coast Guard cutters had scoured the seas. No swimmers had been found. That had been over two hours ago, just before the full fury of the storm hit.

After dessert, Murata made a final telephone call to search headquarters, then returned to announce his simple conclusion. It would have been impossible for anyone to survive. Already, one of his cutters had been overwhelmed by ferocious riptides. Whoever the swimmers were, they definitely had perished.

"We know who the swimmers were," Kurai said. "I'll release the news to the press tomorrow morning."

After dinner, Mori went straight to the hospital. A doctor was waiting for him outside his subordinate's room, hands clasped behind his back, looking grave. Oishi had died fifteen minutes earlier of complications.

IT WAS PAST ten o'clock when an old Japanese lady heard a knock on the door. She was mending a fishing net and did not want to move. She nudged her husband, who was dozing in front of the TV.

"Someone's at the door," she said. Outside, the wind was beating against the shutters and the rain had started up again.

"It's just the wind. Don't bother me."

"No. It's someone. Perhaps he's lost."

The old man got up, grumbling, and went down a hall, opened the door, and peered out. For a moment, he could see no one. A voice from the shadows made him start.

"Excuse me for bothering you." The voice spoke in grossly accented Japanese. "I've fallen on rocks night-fishing. Could I use your phone to make a call?"

"In this weather?" the old man said. Night-fishing? But all tourists were insane. "Come in then. The house is damp enough without more wet and draft."

He led the gaijin to the main room, where he swept twine and rusted hooks off a chair. "Sit there if you will."

The gaijin sat down gratefully. His clothes shed pools of water onto the wooden floor.

"What does he want, the foreigner?" the woman said, looking up for the first time.

"He's had an accident, Baa-san," the man said. "Fell on the rocks night-fishing."

The woman cocked her head at the gaijin.

"The angler—
His dreadful intensity,
In the evening rain!"

"What?" the foreigner asked.

"Don't mind her sense of humor," the fisherman said. "It's just a haiku by Buson she likes to quote."

The old lady turned back to her fishing net. "Doesn't he listen to the TV? We're having a major storm. He's a damn fool hopping around in the dark in weather like this."

"I was careless," the foreigner said.

"Tell him if he waits awhile, I'll boil water and make seaweed tea."

The shadows cut into the stranger's face, although he tried his best to keep out of the light. The fisherman was studying him thoughtfully. "I once had something like that happen to my eye, gaijin. None of my business, of course. Didn't do it on a rock. Fight. Rocks make a different kind of bruise."

"Could I use your phone?" the foreigner asked.

The fisherman burrowed under the net his wife was mending until he produced a battered telephone, which he set by the foreigner's chair. "Help yourself."

"Where's the call to?" the old lady asked. "You can dial foreign countries just as easy as next door."

"Doesn't matter. He's in trouble, Baa-san." The old man's voice was as steady as a sailing ship.

"I know he's in trouble. But I never did like people who hide the truth."

When the foreigner dialed eight digits, the old man knew that it was a Tokyo number.

On the fourth ring a voice answered in guttural Japanese.

"I'm badly in need of a shoe," Steig said in Korean.

"A passport cannot be arranged."

"I must leave the country immediately."

The voice was muffled for a moment, as if a hand had been placed over the receiver. Then it said, "Go to Niigata City as you were told. There will be a ship. Call the number given you when you arrive. That is all we have been advised to tell you."

"How far is Niigata City?"

"Three hours from Tokyo Station by bullet train."

"How about by car?"

"Twice that time, maybe more. I will tell them to expect you. Do you have the woman?"

"I'm working on it."

"Call the number when you arrive with the woman. I cannot say more." There was a cough, followed by the piercing dial tone.

Steig stood and replaced the phone on the receiver, then held out a thousand-yen note. He knew what he needed to know. That he could not escape this country without Helim Kim now. "Thank you. I'd better be going."

But he did not turn to leave.

54: REVENGE The Japan Sea: Wednesday, 9:15 A.M.

THE EFFECTS OF the drugs had worn off. Tomás Velaquez lay strapped to the gurney. He had lost track of time. Days had passed, he was sure. The room stank from his sweat and urine. His tongue had swollen so much that he found it hard to speak. The skin all over his body had become hypersensitive, and his back was a mass of sores. So far, his mind had overcome everything. He had achieved a hypnotic state. But he did not know how much longer he could hold out.

It wasn't the first time in his life that he recognized the taste of raw hate. His tormentors understood just how much pain they could inflict without killing. And there were those moments when Tomás wished they would just end it all. Finish him off.

Thoughts of Helim tormented him. He had learned that she was working for Park Chung Il, as well as for these people who were torturing him. At Helim's apartment once, when Park Chung Il was visiting, the Korean dissident had spoken of his enemies as hard-liners. Horrible men who thought nothing of killing. That described this monster perfectly, Tomás thought. But why had Helim chosen to become a double agent? He had seen the anger in Alpha's eyes when Tomás revealed Helim's duplicity. That had been real. And the rest too? Had she slept with him under their orders, then? Had she never loved him? That had hurt him more than the torture. Or the fact that she had switched the plutonium. But for whom did she deceive him?

While Park claimed to be a champion of democracy in North Korea, Tomás saw him as an opportunist, as bad as his enemies. It made no sense to Tomás that Helim had chosen to become a double agent for two such opponents. Whatever her reasons, Tomás had compromised her. Revealed that she knew Park and met him often. These people would torture and kill her too, he was sure. And it would be his fault. They would kill him soon, he knew. Perhaps that was justice.

Strapped to the table, he could feel the throb of giant engines and the slight sway as the ship sliced through the waves. He wondered what the ship's destination was. How soon would they get there? How long had they been under way?

Suk entered the room. He had caught her staring at him sometimes when they were alone, as if he were some ensnared creature that fascinated her. Several times she had run her hand through the hair on his chest or touched his genitals speculatively.

He moaned. "Could I have some water?"

"Do you have a family?" she asked.

"What does it matter?"

"Because you will be imprisoned in North Korea. You will never see them again."

"No, I have no family."

She brought him a paper cup filled with water, and he drank it greedily. They had taken the tubes from his body and deprived him of nourishment for a long time. His stomach felt hollow. What remained of his strength was slipping away. The woman was lying about his pending imprisonment in North Korea, he knew. They were preparing to kill him.

"There is something wrong with my skin," he said. "Can you loosen these straps? It feels like it's on fire one minute, the next minute it itches. I can't move."

"Where is it that you itch?"

"My back."

"No," she said. "Later, maybe. If you are good."

"Please let me sit up. Just for a few seconds. I can't stand this."

"Only the chest and hand straps then." She unbuckled them.

Tomás couldn't gather enough strength to sit up. He rocked the gurney with his effort. It moved slightly each time he tried, inching closer to the table on which the console and transformer lay.

"Great. That is wonderful." He stretched and scratched his back. His hand brushed the table.

"Move away from there," Suk ordered. "You're too close."

"I can't move," Tomás protested and fell back against the table. She moved toward him.

When Suk leaned over him menacingly, Tomás grabbed a clamp,

pressing it to her neck. His free hand found the transformer and twisted the dial.

Her scream was like a whistle. A bolt of electricity surged through her body, which erupted in spasms and contorted grotesquely. She collapsed to the floor, twitching and convulsing. The smell of burned hair and flesh filled the air. Tomás released the wires and fell back against the gurney. His hand where he had held the clamp was a violent red.

A voice inside his head screamed for him to get up. By sheer force of will, Tomás made his muscles respond. Barely able to control his shaking hands, he fumbled with the strap buckles on his legs. His heart rate had slowed from the shocks, and he seemed to be in semidarkness, for the shock had affected his optic nerves too. When he finally removed the straps from his legs, he slipped off the side of the gurney, nearly falling before he pulled himself erect. Suk was moaning unintelligibly on the floor. Using the gurney for support, he moved toward her.

Suk's eyes opened. Her trembling hand pulled up her dress and reached down to her thigh. She pointed a pistol at him, a stream of Korean invective pouring from her lips. She tried to get up but fell back. The gun wavered. Tomás saw her finger tighten on the trigger. He summoned all his strength and heaved the gurney on top of her. She collapsed under the weight of the table, and the gun spun across the floor. Tomás fell to his knees, searching frantically until he found the weapon.

The door opened.

Tomás turned. A figure clad in olive gray stood in the doorway, a gun gripped tightly in one hand. Tomás raised his own weapon with both hands, eyes focused on the target, and squeezed the trigger. The weapon shuddered in his hands, and all strength left his body.

TOMÁS SAT UP slowly and stared at the empty door where, just a moment ago, the threatening figure had stood. A thin curl of smoke snaked from the muzzle of his weapon. Gradually, his eyes focused. Images sharpened. In the doorway lay a moaning figure dressed in fatigues. Tomás took several steps without any support. His body was beginning to function. The pistol still in his hand, he stepped closer to the man. Blood on his pant leg. He'd hit the man in the thigh. Immobilized him. Tomás felt relieved. Carefully, he looked outside.

The room in which he had been imprisoned could be reached only by a metal catwalk high above the ship's hold. One way the catwalk led toward stairs and a closed bulkhead door. The other way it led to steps descending into the hold toward the bow.

He wondered what time it was. Voices from somewhere down below called to one another in Korean. He stepped next to a railing and hung on to it for support with his free hand. Then he looked down.

There must have been a hundred of them. Cars. He stepped back to the railing and recognized the familiar makes—of Mercedes, Rolls-Royce, BMW, Lincoln, Cadillac. His eyes swung to the port side of the hold, where a large door had been opened. Tomás could see water flowing past the open door. *What on earth?* He felt cold, and he shivered. Then he remembered he was naked.

He dragged the soldier into the room, stripped him, and slipped into his uniform. Suk was in a sitting position, her legs pinned under the gurney. He pointed the gun at her, watching her mouth contort with fear.

"You don't deserve to live," he said bitterly, but he bound her arms behind her with wires from the transformer. Taking the soldier's weapon with him, he went out the door. Sensation was gradually returning to his legs as he headed toward the stairs that led down into the hold.

He made it down unnoticed. He hoped that he looked like a Korean. Mechanics were busy working on several of the cars, their heads under open hoods. A few glanced in his direction but otherwise ignored him.

The cars were neatly parked in squares of six with open lanes on either side so they could be moved. All were polished and looked to be in perfect condition. They had Hong Kong license plates. Strange, he thought. These weren't new cars then. They must be stolen.

He reached the open door. This was how they were driven on and off the boat, he decided. The door was large enough. As far as he could see from the door, there was open water. He was hurrying back among the parked cars when suddenly, from somewhere above him, he heard a shrill military whistle. Then shouts. The sound of feet running. They had discovered his escape!

He scrambled in among the cars as a group of six soldiers clambered down the stairs and fanned out. He picked a car nearby, a Mercedes. Clambering into the backseat, he huddled as low as possible. Inside the car it was very quiet; it must be soundproof. All he could hear was the incessant pounding of his own heart.

Tomás lay hidden in the car for what seemed like hours. The North Koreans had taken his watch in Hong Kong, and he had lost his ability to estimate time passing.

The search party had swept through the area with only cursory checks inside random cars. The vibration of the ship's engine had stopped—the ship was not moving. Tomás slipped over to the bow door and saw a coastline of green trees and mountains. In the distance he could make out white buildings. A city. He wondered if this was North Korea.

"Hands in the air!" said a harsh voice behind him in Korean. Tomás whirled to see a soldier with a rifle pointed directly at his heart. A blow in the chest knocked him backward out into space. He was falling. Falling. His body hit the water, and he sank into a welcome unconsciousness.

55: THE VISITOR Atami: Wednesday, 11:15 A.M.

STEIG PARKED ON the side of the road near the Shimizu Inn. It was a small, traditional inn, perhaps fifteen or twenty rooms, Steig guessed. Such places were common in Japan. He knew that traditional inns prided themselves on their gardens. If this inn had one, he could gain entrance through it. The rest would be easy. If she was still here. Aleksei had told him she would leave today.

He circled behind the two-story buildings on a narrow path. The inn was surrounded by high hedges, sparse enough in patches to enable him to glimpse a green lawn and, finally, the glimmer of a carp pool in the center of a garden. He burrowed his way through the hedge and stepped into the garden, grateful that, since there was little theft in Japan, people did not worry about security as they did in other countries.

He found himself by the pool, which was crossed by stepping-stones. As he strode from one stone to the next, large calico carp surfaced, at-tracted by his shadow and expecting food. He remembered that some of these carp cost as much as fifty thousand dollars. Looking up, he noticed a maid watching him from a second-floor window. He waved, and she turned away. No sign of Helim's security people so far. Maybe they felt she was safely hidden in the inn.

On the lawn, Steig adopted a meditative stride as he imagined a guest would, and studied all the rooms and windows that bordered the garden.

Several seemed occupied, but for the most part he could not tell for sure, because the inner shoji doors were shut. He caught the glimpse of a female shape in a corner room where the shoji doors were partly open. Like the others, occupants could directly enter the garden through sliding glass doors. Helim Kim's tall figure appeared, crossed the room, and disappeared. A door closed. Steig heard a car stop at the front of the inn. A door slammed. He walked swiftly through the garden until he was close enough to hear, and heard the driver say, "The car for Miss Kim is here."

"Just a moment," a girl at the front door replied.

He wondered if she was leaving but there was nothing he could do. Damn. Steig waited until Helim got into the car. Then, moving quickly, he reached the sliding doors to her room and tried them. They were locked, but succumbed easily to his expertise. He stepped inside.

IT WAS A small village with fixed rituals. Each morning the wives visited the market stalls in the center of the town to purchase what they needed for the day. Shopping only once a week was considered a barbarous practice of city-dwellers and Westerners. So when the old lady did not appear, as she did every morning, there was some comment.

The shopkeepers mentioned it to other regulars, and the network gradually passed it along. Perhaps she was ill. By eleven o'clock, one of the neighbors had been nominated to check to see if anything was wrong.

When there was no answer to the old lady's phone, the neighbor decided to visit the house. Perhaps she had fallen. Although the old woman was not a close friend, she was kind and respected.

The neighbor reached the fisherman's place by bicycle and knocked. She'd noticed that the car was gone. Had the husband stayed home and taken his wife on a trip today? The old lady didn't drive, the neighbor was quite sure. She looked down onto the beach. The boat was missing also. That was certainly strange.

When no one answered her knock, the neighbor pushed the door and found it open. This was not unusual; there had been no theft in this neighborhood for as long as she could remember. Doors often were left unlocked.

She called the old lady's name, but the house was quiet. No one was moving; the air was still. She began to check the rooms. All were empty. She was about to leave when she noticed a piece of fishing net protruding from a large cupboard. She opened the door and peered into the darkness. The old lady was wrapped in a fishnet. She looked as if she had just gotten entangled by accident. But then the neighbor saw blood and, staring out at her, the lifeless eyes.

She let out a piercing scream and kept screaming until, frantically pedaling her bicycle, she reached the Manazuru police station nearly two miles away.

56: THE DUPLICITY Atami: Wednesday, 12:05 P.M.

ON THE WAY to Atami Station, Helim considered how much she should tell her grandmother about what was going on. Katano had returned to Tokyo this morning, taking his security with him.

She needn't reveal anything about what she'd been doing, she decided. On the phone, she'd mentioned only vaguely that the purpose of her trip to Atami was to settle the pachinko company listing issue. That was all. Perhaps she'd better say nothing more to Jonquil Kim.

Too much excitement would upset her grandmother. Besides, there were still mysteries about her grandmother's past that Helim didn't fully understand. Particularly what had happened at the end of the war. Jonquil Kim was a traditional person, and her ideas were sometimes puzzling. Helim had never revealed her connections to Pyongyang, of course. She couldn't. No, she concluded, it was better to say nothing.

Jonquil Kim did not look like the other tourists at Atami Station this morning. She walked proudly erect with a dignified air, wearing a simple dark travel suit. She walked faster than the porter who was carrying her bag and seemed to know where Helim was in the crowd without even looking for her.

"You are elegant and beautiful as always, Grandmother." They did not kiss, since this act was considered too personal to perform in public.

"And you, child." Jonquil gave Helim a formal hug.

There was always that little wall, Helim thought. The formality the old lady kept between herself and the rest of humanity. Perhaps because of what had happened in her youth.

She did not seem to be in her seventies. Her skin was still smooth, her bearing regal, and her eyes clear. "So what have you been up to?"

Her grandmother's eyes seemed to stare into Helim's soul. Maybe that was what scared Helim most. Why she decided she must not lie.

"I've had a lovely interview with a TV producer who is going to do a show about the pachinko industry."

"A man or woman?"

"A man, of course. The one I told you was interested in your diary."

"Don't trust him. Why on earth was he interested?"

"Remember, I explained about that American woman you met. They're interested in her."

"Well, I can't understand that. Do you know what you're doing?"

"Yes. I thought you wouldn't mind. It'll help us get the pachinko company listing." Her grandmother still considered her a child, Helim thought. She would avoid all further discussion of Japanese TV.

"Of course I mind. However, if it helps the listing, I suppose I shouldn't complain. The less Japanese men know about us the better."

"But they've been very kind to me. And I only gave them a few diary pages. They don't know who it belongs to. I've been very careful."

"They are very kind to anyone they think they can use."

Helim had her answer to one question at least. "Here," she said. "I have a cab waiting for us."

When they returned to the inn, they found a phone message in an envelope on the floor against Helim's door. A Mr. Saito requested a return call. Urgently.

Jonquil Kim insisted she needed a bath to wash away the dirt from the train. Helim nodded agreement. It provided a convenient excuse for her to find out who had called and how he had found her here. She ushered Jonquil to her room and then, feeling a tingle of anticipation, returned to her own quarters.

She settled on cushions at the low Japanese table by her phone. She didn't know any Saito. Perhaps it was a mistake. Or perhaps it had something to do with Katano. He was the only one who knew that she was here. That must be it, she thought. She dialed Tokyo.

"The honorable Tanemura's office."

Helim nearly put the phone down. She had reached the office of the most famous politician in Japan! "Mr. Saito, please," she said.

"Who is calling?" the voice asked querulously.

"Helim Kim, returning his call."

"Oh yes. Thank you. I shall put you right through."

A deep authoritative voice came on the line. "Miss Kim, thank you for returning my call so soon. I'm Diet member Tanemura's assistant. His private secretary."

"Your call honors me." She tried to keep the excitement from her voice. A private secretary was a very important person, she knew.

"Mr. Tanemura is concerned about your listing problem."

Helim tried to conceal her surprise. It was Katano who had done this. He was the only one who knew; her trick had worked. "How kind of him to worry about a lowly pachinko company."

"We believe your pachinko company can be satisfactorily listed on the Second Section of the Tokyo Stock Exchange. Not the First, however."

"That is extremely generous." She was pleased at how calm her voice sounded.

"In fact, Mr. Tanemura has authorized me to give you his guarantee that your company will be listed in the near future."

"That is very kind of him." She had won, she thought. Won!

"However, there is a condition."

"And what is that?" Her euphoria faded. Perhaps it was a trick.

"Tanemura-san or companies he designates will have the right of first refusal for all shares offered for sale by your company after they go public."

Helim's hand shook. That was tricky, she thought. It would place the Japanese politician and his business associates in a position of control over the company. What if Tanemura was close to the North Korean government? Or even working with the pachinko industry? Or protecting it!

Her mind was working furiously now. "Tell me, Saito-san, why would Tanemura-san be interested in controlling our company?"

"I'm afraid I don't know the answer to that. But why should you care? You and other owners will make a large amount of money."

"Does Mr. Tanemura have close friends in Pyongyang?"

Saito's voice was clearly puzzled. "I don't understand."

"Mr. Saito, please explain to Mr. Tanemura and his keiretsu friends that I cannot agree to your conditions. I cannot be bought." She hung up. She had lost her temper. Had she done the right thing?

She was so distracted she did not hear the bathroom door slide quietly open or see the tall figure enter.

57: **LAST CHANCE** Manazuru: Wednesday, 12:30 P.M.

STEVE SPENT THE morning hidden in the woods off the beach near the tidepool that had saved him. The rain had ceased. It was quiet except for the sound of surf and the murmur of the wind in small pines that clung like bonsai to outcroppings of rock along the shore. Using salt water, Steve washed the burning cuts along his side where the killer's knife had torn into his skin and then massaged the stiffness where rocks had slammed into his body.

He could see the reef that had nearly claimed his life last night. It appeared harmless today; the sea was calm. He looked for the killer's body, calculating where it should have washed ashore. There was nothing. The high waves had erased all tracks from the beach. Could the foreigner have survived? Perhaps the body had been trapped beyond the reef. Washed out to sea.

He walked several hundred meters down the coast searching in vain, then turned inland and headed through woods to a road. Set back from the road were small rice fields and the occasional tile-roofed farmhouse. He should call Helim, he thought. Then he remembered how the inn had denied her presence on all his earlier calls. Still, he must at least try to reach her before she left.

There should be a town nearby from where he could phone her. He'd call the police only if he couldn't reach her. After a half hour of walking, he began to pass more houses and farmers working in the fields. Two policemen were riding white bicycles along the road. Seeing Steve, they slowed. Instinctively, Steve turned off the road and hurried into the woods toward the safety of the beach. One of the officers shouted at him to stop.

Steve's legs were weak from exhaustion. Before he could reach the water, arms grabbed him and tried to wrestle him to the ground. Something heavy hit him in the back of his head and drove him to his knees. Then another blunt object struck his shoulders and head until he sank into blackness.

STEIG DROVE CAREFULLY, well within the speed limit. By late evening, he was in the mountains of Niigata Prefecture. The new expressway was straight and well marked, in both Japanese and English. He was now less than 150 kilometers from Niigata City.

Twice he had stopped at fast-food restaurants by the side of the road and bought hamburgers and packages of french fries. He removed the gag from Helim's mouth only to feed her. He wanted her to feel dependent on him. That was the first step.

Helim tried in vain to free the rope that tightly bound her hands and feet, but not only was she tied, she was also wrapped tightly in a sheet from the hotel. It was difficult even to sit up. Her mind tried to piece together what had happened. Her assailant was the same man who had attacked her in Los Angeles, of that she was sure. He had tracked her to the inn, broken into her room, and waited for her return. Why had he not killed her instantly.

She tried desperately to remember what had happened before. She had phoned Saito, Tanemura's assistant. He had offered to get her pachinko company listed, but in a way that would have turned Allied International, the largest pachinko organization in Japan, over to the group that would shortly run the Japanese government. A group who, according to rumors, led a supremacist movement that supported the military tribunal in North Korea. This meant Tanemura could be involved with the pachinko industry in some deeper way. He could be the one who protected it. Yes! He could be her politician!

She had just hung up the phone when the man attacked her. She thought of her grandmother. Was she all right? Possibly. But why had this man kidnapped her? The same man who had tried to kill her in Los Angeles. Only now they wanted her alive.

"Where are you taking me?" she asked when he had removed her gag to offer her food.

"To Niigata City. Isn't that exciting? There will be a ship. You and me together. It will be like a honeymoon, Helim. Just you and me sharing a room." He must have seen her shudder. "Relax. I am only joking. They want to talk with you. That's the truth. About what, I can't tell you."

"Who?" She felt her voice tremble, although she tried her best to control it. Had Alpha discovered her treachery? If so, he would torture and kill her. She'd known this might happen. But how could he have found out? She had been careful. Tomás, she thought suddenly. If they had captured Tomás . . . A chill swept through her body.

"I really don't know who," Steig said. "But I'd be honest with them if I were you. Tell them whatever it is they want to know. If necessary, they have certain drugs." He leered. "So sleep on that, my beautiful puzzle."

THE POLICE STATION was small and cramped. A front office where the public was allowed boasted a large map of the area, useful when tourists asked directions. In the back was an office with three metal desks where duty officers filled out reports. In a narrow kitchen behind the office was a hot plate for making tea and a tiny fridge.

A crowd of angry citizens gathered in front of the station, spurred on by the ominous warnings of the mayor, who had run on a protectionist platform. News had quickly spread that one of their neighbors, the elderly lady, had been brutally murdered. Her husband had been found dead on the beach. An autopsy had determined that it was death by strangulation.

Steve Juric was kept out of sight in an upstairs room until the crowd began to disperse. The handcuffs they had put on him looked brand-new. When one of the younger officers suggested they try out the ankle chains as well, the captain on duty told him that they were waiting for someone from Atami.

News of the murders and the fact that a foreigner was being held in the next town reached the Atami police chief, Captain Kurai, at two o'clock. Mori had been urgently summoned to Tokyo to explain what had happened the previous night, and the morning's papers had been filled with news of the massacre, reporting four officers injured, three dead. Kurai had held a news conference in which he stated confidently that the two escaped killers were presumed drowned in the sea during last night's storm. He promised to release names of the men as soon as the investigation was completed.

Thus, when Steve Juric's description was handed to him along with charges in the Manazuru case—two murders, a stolen white Toyota owned by the victims, and resisting arrest—Kurai sent one of his men over immediately. By three o'clock, the officer had contacted headquarters, confirming the gaijin as the one apprehended at Helim Kim's inn yesterday.

Another hour was occupied with the local prosecutor's office. At four-fifteen, Manazuru agreed to release Juric for arraignment in Atami as an accomplice in the three police deaths, the wounding of four officers, and the murder of the fisherman and his wife. Under heavy guard, he was taken to Atami police headquarters to face the charges.

58: RESOLUTION Tokyo: Wednesday, 5:06 P.M.

THE CALL FROM Atami reached Mori after he returned from his briefing at National Police headquarters. He had taken several hours to explain the operation all the way to its conclusion: both suspects had tried to escape amid treacherous waves but drowned at sea. So far their bodies had not been found. He added that Oishi and two other police officers had died of wounds inflicted by the killer. He had a splitting headache.

When Mori took the phone, his host from last night's dinner was on the line. Kurai's voice was a shriveled imitation of the Atami police captain's normally haughty bark. Mori soon learned why.

Two officers from the village of Manazuru had spotted a foreigner on a road near the ocean about noon today. They had given chase and overpowered him. It turned out to be Steven Juric—the same man who had been taken into police custody at the Shimizu Inn yesterday.

"I thought he drowned in that ocean storm," Mori said, astounded.

There was a silence on the other end. "My hat's off to him. He must be a fantastic swimmer."

"What else?"

"An old woman and her husband were killed early this morning. Their car stolen."

"Mother of hell. Go to the Shimizu Inn immediately. See if Helim Kim's still there. Put a security team around her if she is. I'm leaving immediately."

"Ah, just one moment, Inspector. We already tried to do that." There was a long silence.

"What? *What?*" Mori shouted.

"Helim Kim has . . . somehow disappeared."

"You're joking. Tell me this is a joke," Mori bellowed. The disaster hammered at his brain, pounding like a manic drummer. The killer had escaped. Helim Kim had been kidnapped.

"I'm sure it can all be explained," the captain protested.

"What time was Juric arrested?"

"Twelve-fifty."

"What time did Helim Kim disappear?" Mori felt his stomach tightening, then ripping apart as he heard the answer.

"About one-fifteen."

"So it couldn't have been Juric. The killer is alive too!"

"Perhaps she's just gone off shopping. But her grandmother's upset. She hasn't seen her since morning. My apologies—"

"Apologies! Fax me the license number of the fisherman's car. Now! You hear me?"

"Yes sir."

"Release nothing to the news media. A complete blackout on this! And the gaijin, Steven Juric. Hold him until I arrive. You think you can handle that, goddammit?"

Mori reached Atami by seven-thirty that evening and took a cab to the Shimizu Inn. A policeman was guarding the entrance. "I want to talk to the owner of the inn," the inspector said.

"He saw nothing, sir," the officer said. "We've already spoken to him."

"Get him out here. Right now!" The officer hurried inside and soon emerged with a thin, elderly man dressed in a dark blue kimono. The inn owner spoke in a voice hoarse with fear.

"T-this has never happened in the two hundred years of our inn's history. I can assure you. Even in the old days of the samurai, there was more respect. What's Japan coming to?"

"You tell me." Mori questioned the owner without further satisfaction. He interviewed each of the maids, but, no one had seen anyone except Helim, her grandmother, and other guests enter the inn that morning. Nor had there been any sound of a struggle or argument. Nothing out of the ordinary that morning. It was very, very strange.

"Where's the grandmother?" Mori asked at last.

She had insisted on staying until her granddaughter was found, the officer advised. At government expense.

Mori knocked on her door. He heard a firm voice say, "It's open."

Jonquil Kim was sitting in front of the TV wearing a blue floral yukata. Her black-dyed hair was freshly combed. Mori was surprised at how young she looked.

"You are police?" She made no move to get up or see his face.

"Yes."

"Where is my granddaughter? Did you people take her?"

Mori seated himself cross-legged on the floor to one side of the TV. The tatami had a nice grassy smell, and the room was in simple Japanese style, with no Western furniture to clutter it. Sliding glass doors opened onto a lush garden. Through the screen, a wind bell chimed. "I'm sorry to tell you we don't know," he said.

"I hope you're smarter than the other people who were here. They acted as though my granddaughter had something to hide. I'm outraged."

"My apologies. They were only trying to do their job. Could you please go through what happened this morning, Mrs. Kim?"

"I already told the others. Why don't you ask them?"

Mori gently explained how miscommunication could occur when information got passed around. Occasionally, important pieces were left out.

This seemed to please Jonquil Kim. She gave him a brief summary of what had happened. After taking a bath, she had briefly fallen asleep. It was one-thirty when she awoke, surprised it was so late. Her granddaughter was supposed to call her. She phoned her granddaughter's room, but no one answered. She thought perhaps Helim had peeked into her room, had seen she was asleep, and hadn't wanted to bother her. Perhaps she had gone out. To be sure, she went to Helim's room and knocked. Again there was no answer. The door was open and she went inside. No one was there. All Helim's clothes were in the closet.

"Did you hear anything at all?"

"Nothing." Mrs. Kim had checked with the hotel staff, asking if they'd seen her granddaughter. After about an hour, when she still had no clue to Helim's whereabouts, she decided to tell the manager. He suggested they wait awhile longer. After another half hour, she insisted he call the police. "The police didn't take it very seriously at first. Perhaps because I'm an old lady and she's a young girl. They told me not to worry, she'd probably decided to go shopping. I think they still expect her to return. But I stayed here all day waiting and she still is not back, is she? It isn't like Helim to just go off like that."

"Anything you left out?"

"She had a phone call while she was picking me up at the station. A message was under her door when she returned."

"Do you know who it was from?"

"The note?" The elderly lady searched in her pocketbook and with-drew a piece of paper. "A Mr. Saito. Here's his number."

"Where did you get this?"

"From Helim's room when I went in looking for her. She'd left it on the table, so I picked it up."

"You didn't tell the police about this?"

"They didn't ask."

"Do you know this Saito?"

"Never heard of him."

"Thanks very much, Mrs. Kim," Mori said, rising and bowing. "You've been most helpful."

MORI SEARCHED HELIM'S room next door. Nothing had been disturbed. He went out to the garden. He tried the door and found it slid open. The grass was cut short, and the ground underneath was soft from the storm. He examined the area around the door, but could find no clear footprints. However, the door lock showed scratches.

The policeman at the front of the inn confirmed that the door had been found open. Although this in itself was not conclusive evidence, it raised Mori's suspicions.

"Could there have been forced entry?" Mori asked. "Were any maids on duty this morning who went home before the police arrived?"

"I don't know if we checked that," the officer murmured.

"Was anything missing from the room, or did you forget to check that too?"

"A sheet. A maid told us it was missing from the closet."

Mori glowered at the officer. "Why didn't you tell me that earlier? Get the owner out here again."

Mori learned that a part-time maid had been working at the hotel that morning. Since she had been assigned upper floors, the police hadn't bothered to question her. Mori ordered her picked up and driven to the inn immediately.

The maid could recall only one thing out of the ordinary. Working in a second-floor room, she had looked out a window about twelve o'clock and seen a foreigner crossing the carp pond. She thought it strange at the time, since few gaijin stayed there. But the foreigner had waved at her, and she had assumed he was a guest. He was tall and broad-shouldered.

His head was shaved, and she thought his eyes were blue. Yes. Light blue.

STEVE JURIC HAD received first aid for his cuts and was in a holding cell when Mori arrived. "How did you get those cuts?" Mori snapped as the cell door banged closed behind him.

"The crease on my forehead is courtesy of your police. They shot at me."

"Our police?" Mori stared at the bandage on Juric's forehead.

"Yes. The rest were by that bastard. He cut me."

"Who? What bastard? You mean your friend?"

"He's not my friend! Jesus. The guy was after Helim. I was trying to stop him."

"How do you know he was after her?"

"I think it was the same man who attacked Helim in Los Angeles."

If he was an accomplice of the killer, why would he admit this? Mori pondered. And why would he and the killer not have escaped together? "We would've let you go soon as Helim Kim cleared you. Your passport shows you haven't been in Japan for the past six months. So why the hell did you run?"

"Your people were shooting at me and you wonder why I ran? Besides, he plastered your guys. Bastard was getting away. I followed him."

"You kill that poor fisherman and his wife?"

"Hell no!"

"You steal their car?"

"No, dammit! This is crazy."

"Why'd you resist arrest?"

"I didn't. Your people just started clubbing me."

Made sense, Mori decided. The local police weren't known for their finesse. The murders had been cold-blooded. If Juric was an accomplice, why not stick close to the killer, who had a car and was now well on his way to possible freedom? Why stumble into the Manazuru police like an amateur? No, the accomplice theory didn't make sense. Nor was this man a cold-blooded killer.

"You wasted our time," Mori said. "Helped us lose the real killer. And jeopardized the life of Helim Kim! Technically, that makes you an accomplice if I want it to."

"Look, Helim is my . . . good friend."

"So that's why you swam out into a dangerous sea after the killer? In that storm?" This was the hardest part for the local police to believe. Only a desperate man trying to escape the law would have tried to swim that sea, they argued.

"I used to surf. Rough water doesn't bother me. I didn't want him to escape."

Perhaps this American was telling the truth. That made him either very brave or very crazy. A request for a background check had been sent to the L.A. police, and it would provide final evidence. "Your friend may be in danger. I think you can fill in some missing pieces."

"If it helps Helim, I'll do anything."

"You're not cleared, understand," Mori said. "We're checking you still. But if you cooperate, I'll see what I can do. Stand up. You're coming with me."

59: THE ACCIDENT Niigata City: Wednesday, 7:50 P.M.

"TOMÁS VELAQUEZ WAS picked up by a pleasure boat and turned over to Japanese harbor police this afternoon." Joe Pipe's voice was calm. "He was in a state of shock and exhaustion. Nearly drowned, and looks like he'd been tortured."

DeCovasi knew there was more. He didn't need to ask.

They were having an American-style dinner of T-bone steak and baked potatoes in a restaurant.

"The Japanese are holding him for illegal entry," Pipe continued. "He thinks he's in North Korea. Doesn't believe anybody."

DeCovasi chuckled. "Perfect."

"Yes. Wants to see a UN representative."

"Poor bastard. Gonna die when we show up."

"They have him in a high-security room at the Red Cross hospital."

"His lucky day."

Pipe cut his steak into squares, tucked a piece neatly into his cheek. "My guess is we were wrong about him."

DeCovasi shrugged agreeably. "Maybe he fell off that North Korean ship."

"Looks like they beat him up pretty bad. Not a sign he was working for them, hey? Like your boy Park told us?"

"We'd better hear what Velaquez has to say. Like to know where Helim Kim's gone off to."

"She's disappeared?" Pipe asked. "Where'd you get that?"

DeCovasi stuck a forefinger in his mouth to extract a piece of meat stuck between two molars. "Park's in town. Contacted me to say she disappeared from a Japanese inn near Tokyo earlier today. Says she was kidnapped, but it could be a ruse. Police say her disappearance is connected to two dead bodies and a stolen car. A foreigner's the suspect. Park gave me the stolen car's license number. Maybe Tomás knows something about it—if he's connected."

"I don't think so. But whatever he has to say could be useful to the operation."

THE INCANDESCENT LIGHT overhead made bands of color shimmer across Tomás's eyes. There was a green tray on a white table next to him, but his head exploded each time he tried to look at it. His clothes were gone. He was wearing a white gown with gray ties and a white plastic bracelet on his wrist with a number that was too blurred to decipher.

"Mr. Velaquez?" He tried to move and wondered vaguely what hurt so terribly. Who was calling his name?

"Can you hear me?" A pause. "Good, he's coming out of it."

He strained to see. A hand touched him gently and turned him; the pain subsided. The hand was connected to a face floating above him. Nurse. Asian face. Not Miss Suk's. A kind face. Holding a syringe. No. No. He tried to rise. "Be calm," the voice said. "This is for the pain. Broken ribs."

Something pricked his arm. He slammed his eyes shut. Shit, not again. No. This was North Korea. Definitely.

"You'll feel better." The voice trailed away, and he could hear a door shut.

He waited. Yes, much better now. He drifted.

The face returned later. Large Asian eyes inspected him. The pain did not return.

"Okay," the nurse said to someone out of his range of vision. "Five minutes only. Then the doctor wants to see him."

Another face replaced the nurse. Caucasian. Male.

Familiar, he thought. Somewhere in the past. The lights made halos around everything. Aviator glasses. A cocky grin.

"Can you hear me, Mr. Velaquez?"

He waited for the torture to begin, the pain to attack, but it did not. He let out his breath.

"You're going to have to relax a little here. Looks like you've had a rough time."

This was an American accent. Where was he, then?

"I'm John DeCovasi, with a U.S. intelligence agency." He paused for the Costa Rican to accept that.

"U.S intelligence . . ." His mind went back to Vienna. Two Americans asking questions. Long, long ago.

"Yes. We're with the FBI."

Tomás wanted to speak, but no words formed.

"I read the report about your accident. You were pulled out of the water yesterday. Nearly drowned, I understand."

Accident? Tomás thought. I was tortured. Held captive.

"How do you feel?"

Terrible, he thought.

"This will just take a minute. We want to know if you can remember what happened. We believe you were on a North Korean ship. This correct?"

A word emerged. "Ship?"

"Let me rephrase that. What nationality was the ship you were on? You know?"

"North Korean."

"You had bruises and burns on your body when you were taken out of the water. How did you get them?"

Tomás turned away.

"Look, I know this is difficult, but there's little time. Can you describe the people who did this to you? We won't hurt you."

Tomás opened his mouth. Nothing came out. He tried again. "Alpha."

The face above him jerked to look away. "You said Alpha?"

"Yes."

"That bastard tortured you?"

"Yes."

"Can you tell me why?"

"No."

"Head of their intelligence," DeCovasi said to no one in particular. "Why did they torture you? There has to be a reason. Please answer that. Then we're almost finished."

Tomás thought. "Helim," he said.

"Helim was the reason they tortured you? Helim who?"

"Kim?" asked another voice. Tomás couldn't tell who had spoken.

". . . kill her," he said.

"They're going to kill Helim Kim?" DeCovasi asked.

Tomás felt tears welling in his eyes. "I told them."

"Shit, he's crying," the unknown voice said.

"Why are they going to kill your girlfriend?" DeCovasi asked.

"I told them."

"Told them what?"

"Park . . . and she. Together."

"Park Chung Il," DeCovasi said.

"Yes."

"You told them she had a connection to Park Chung Il? That right?"

"Park," Tomás said, because the name had become embedded in his soul. He hated that name. "Switched plutonium."

"Son of a bitch!" DeCovasi stood suddenly, moved out of Tomás's sight.

A nurse stuck her head in the door. "No more time, sir. I'm sorry. He's still weak."

"A minute or two more is all we'll need," Pipe said.

Tomás thought he recognized that voice, which now said, "No time left, Thumper. Go to the two-minute offense."

DeCovasi's voice was harsh: "Park switched the plutonium? That right, Tomás? That what you want us to believe?"

"Helim did for Park."

"Yeah, right. How long have you been on the ship, Tomás? Since Hong Kong?"

"Yes."

"Did you see any high-ranking military on the ship with Alpha? A general, maybe?"

"Yes." He held up one finger.

"Could be our number two target." DeCovasi turned to the person Tomás couldn't see.

"I hope to God he's right," the voice said.

"Helim Kim, Tomás. Do you know where she is now?"

"No."

"We can help save her life if you tell us."

"Can't remember."

The nurse came back, "I'm sorry, no more time. He's very tired."

"Just one last question, nurse," DeCovasi said. "Alpha was trying to find out who switched the plutonium, then? You sure?"

"It was Park."

"Why, Tomás?" DeCovasi asked. "Why did Alpha want to know?"

Something was wrong. The tone of this man's questions. His lack of grief. His anger about the plutonium. The eyes studying him clinically now like those of the one who tortured him on the boat. Perhaps government people were like that. He was alert now. There was danger.

"Sorry," the nurse said and took DeCovasi's arm forcefully.

The American stood, touched the bed with his hand as if to comfort Tomás. "Thanks for your help," he said. The pain returned with his touch. Tomás wiped the tears away from his eyes.

OUTSIDE, DeCOVASI STOPPED abruptly and slammed his fist into the wall. *"Son of a bitch!"*

Pipe put his hand on the younger agent's shoulder. "Not here, John. Later."

DeCovasi swung on him. "Did you get all that? All the fucking implications? There isn't going to be any assassination attempt, right? This whole deal was a figment of Park's imagination. No coup, Joe. Nothing. He blew smoke up my ass, and I inhaled it. Hook, line, and sinker. And this Kim woman. Man, would I like to get hold of her. Jesus!"

"We'll talk about it later." Pipe's hand squeezed more firmly on DeCovasi's shoulder. "Somewhere secure. We all bought a piece. Cool it."

DeCovasi shrugged his hand off. "Park is my responsibility. I'm his handler. I bought him. Sold him to you and the director. It's not your ass, is it?" He began pacing furiously.

"He conned us all, Thumper," Pipe said. "Lighten up. My ass is in the sling too. Doesn't mean we're both finished though, does it?"

"I don't believe this," DeCovasi went on. "He conned me into setting up the entire operation so we'd take out his opposition. You understand what Tomás told us, Joe! Park set up that plutonium switch, using Kim. Then convinced us it was the hard-liners in Pyongyang who wanted a coup who did it! You know what I'm gonna do when I find that double-crossing son of a bitch?"

"I wouldn't want to imagine," Pipe said. They reached the elevators. DeCovasi punched the down button as if he were trying to drive it through the wall.

"He conned us, Joe. Into this huge fucking operation. But we can't back off now. Can we?"

Pipe stepped inside after DeCovasi and pushed the first-floor button.

"Maybe we don't have to, eh, Thumper? Maybe it's for the good of our flag, forefathers, and the country? That what you're trying to say?"

"Yeah. Only three people besides us know. Park, who planned the plutonium switch to set us up. Helim Kim, who did it. Tomás, who found out about it. Before I go after Park, I need to find Helim Kim."

"Helim Kim? Why?"

"To see if Velaquez was programmed by someone to tell us what he did so convincingly. Maybe he lied. She'll know the truth. After all, she's the one he says switched the plutonium."

"And if Velaquez wasn't lying?" Pipe spoke as if he knew DeCovasi was desperate to find any way out.

"They're all expendable players, Joe, in the greater scheme of things. Tomás. Helim Kim. Park. We have to get rid of them all."

"Can't do that. We're the true blues, remember? The white hats. No, absolutely not."

"Talking qualitatively, that's all. We're not going to harm anyone. Lordy, of course not! Just make sure Helim Kim gets on that boat to North Korea and stays there, that Tomás Velaquez stays in that hospital until he has no memory, and Park ends up in a ditch somewhere and has to hitchhike back to Finland. No more money from us! Wouldn't be the first time, either. You're in this too, Joe, like you said. It could be your career and pension too when they sort responsibility."

"I know that." Pipe thought a moment. "Yes, let's talk to Helim Kim. I'll buy that part of your plan for openers."

"Okay!" DeCovasi made a fist and slapped it enthusiastically in his other hand. "How do we find her?"

"Park told you she disappeared from some inn outside Tokyo. He gave you a license plate number."

"Right. Bet you anything, Pipe, they're bringing her here."

PART SIX

Beware beautiful women
as you would red pepper.

Korean proverb

60: ARRIVAL Niigata City: Thursday, 1:18 A.M.

STEIG PULLED INTO the empty parking lot near the train station just after one o'clock early Thursday morning. No trains ran that late. He checked that Helim was still tightly bound and locked the car while he called the number at the Otani Hotel. When the hotel operator answered, he asked for Aleksei's room.

A Russian voice answered. "Romanov speaking."

"It's me," Steig said.

"Good. Wonderful. You have the woman with you?"

"In the car."

"Bring her to the hotel. Pull up in the rear. I'll meet you there."

WHEN THEY FIRST entered the city, Helim had been able to see tops of buildings and hear occasional passing cars. She hoped an escape route would occur to her. When it didn't, she dove into the twilight of her subconscious and summoned the spirits from the other world to her side. The snow-white tiger appeared, and she felt her confidence return. Something good would happen.

The sheet bound her tightly, and she could not sit up. Finally, she was able to raise her head above the window, see cars and streets. But the long ride had dulled her senses. She did not notice a car parked by the side of the road flick its lights and, shortly after, another pull out of a side street one block ahead of them.

While Steig was making his call, a Prince GT with its lights off drove slowly into a parking place near the entrance. The driver spoke into a handheld phone-radio. Other cars were forming an impenetrable cordon.

When Steig returned and pulled out of the parking lot, they followed. The target headed south toward the sea, where the major Western hotels were located.

STEIG PARKED BEHIND the Otani Hotel as the Russian had ordered. The Russian strode out of the night and slid into the front seat. He held out his hand. "Give me the keys."

Steig did as he was told. Aleksei slapped a room key into his hand. "This room's been booked for you. One night, and no need for you to check in. Now get out of the car and walk directly through that rear entrance and upstairs to your room. Do not turn around or talk to anyone. I'll drive the girl where she needs to go. Then I will call you in the morning."

"Why not let her stay with me tonight?" The girl had become totally dependent. Captives often fell in love with captors, Steig mused. He was sure she wouldn't resist. And if she did, so much the better.

Aleksei chuckled. "Because she will have a busy schedule tomorrow. Eventually, you might get some time with her after the others are finished. First we have more important chores for her to perform."

"What kind of chores?"

"Not your concern."

"I've fulfilled my part of the bargain."

"Yes. And all has been arranged as I promised." He paused, waiting for Steig to get out.

ALEKSEI DROVE THE Toyota slowly from the rear of the Otani Hotel. At the broad street in front he paused to look both ways for traffic. There was little. He turned onto the broad four-lane, two-way street. A parked car with lights off and engine running began to move. The car kept well behind as it followed. Traffic was light at this time of the morning, but three other cars were moving in the same direction as Aleksei's, one ahead of the Russian, one just entering from a side street, and another behind.

A stoplight at the first intersection turned red as the first car approached. It stopped, and the second car took the outside lane. Aleksei pulled up on the inside lane behind the first and, too late, saw the cars behind him roar up and brake sharply: one behind, the other to his side, another front. His mind shouted a warning. They'd boxed him in!

He reached for his pocket radio, but before he could do more, men had jumped from nearby vehicles and opened his door. They roughly hustled him into the first car. Three men got into the Toyota and drove it away, tires screeching. One checked the inert body bound by a sheet on the backseat and confirmed by radio that it was Helim Kim.

In the first car, DeCovasi grinned at Aleksei and held out his hand. "Nice to see you, stranger."

Aleksei ignored the hand. "I'd heard you left the Tokyo office."

"Don't be angry. We're going to make a deal with you."

"I am going to report this to my government."

"What? That you kidnapped an American citizen named Helim Kim? Who you bullshitting, Aleksei?"

"I have official status here. You've forcibly abducted a consul of the Russian embassy in Tokyo. It will have repercussions."

"Well, we wouldn't want that, would we?" DeCovasi grinned. "Let's get serious. Here's what is going to happen. We need the girl to clear up certain, let us say, irregularities. We know she is a double for the North Korean government. Technically, since she is also an American citizen, she's a traitor. But as we are a benevolent democratic state like your own, we stretch the lines sometimes. You following?"

"May you drown in your repugnant lies."

"Good, you understand, then. The deal is this. We get to keep her overnight. You have an embassy car at our compound tomorrow at noon. Don't tell me you don't know where it is."

Aleksei's eyes began to show interest. "We know."

"Helim Kim will be turned back over to you at that time."

"You wish to tell me why?"

"Our laws would only slap her hands. She's damaged goods, Aleksei. An embarrassment. We know you and your Russian friends will take good care of her future."

THE PHONE RANG at exactly eight o'clock next morning. "Yes?" Steig answered.

The voice was Aleksei's. "Good morning. In half an hour I will knock on your door. Be ready to leave. Your hotel bill has been taken care of."

THE RUSSIAN'S BREATH stank of strong mouthwash, sure sign of a morning drinker. And the car that was waiting outside the Otani Hotel flew the flag of the Russian consulate in Niigata City.

"I've made preparations for you to leave Japan this morning." Aleksei said this cheerily, as if Steig would be a Sunday attraction for a weekend party.

"Where to?"

"North Korea. All arrangements have been made."

"You promised I was going to Russia!" He should have expected this, Steig thought. They knew he was powerless, had no choice.

"In time, Steig. You're too impatient."

The car pulled out of the hotel drive and turned north, heading up the coast away from the city. Neither man spoke. However, all of Steig's senses had come fiercely alert. His mind was whirling the dials of a safe, trying to unlock a combination. He had badly underestimated the Russian. He never should have trusted him.

It was Aleksei who finally broke the silence with what sounded like a prepared statement.

"You have to leave Japan somehow, don't you? The Japanese police are watching all airports. They have a computer composite sketch that is a remarkable likeness, if I do say so. Even with your new haircut. Such clever people. I've arranged for some North Korean friends to take you in, so to speak. It happens they have a ship in the harbor. Several of my contacts are aboard. The formalities here are rather lax. You'll be boarding the vessel courtesy of some patriotic locals who have a powerboat"—here Aleksei scrutinized his watch—"in about another hour or two, yes? You will sail soon. Only two days to destination. And on the way, you can have a nice chat with their people. The head of North Korean intelligence is fascinated by your background. We all have to sing for our supper, my boy."

"North Korea for how long?"

"Say three to six months for us to arrange a new life for you in Russia, Steig. You will need credentials, a job, a wife. Already I have started procedures."

"What if they find out I've been killing all those North Koreans?"

"It was at their orders, Steig. I can tell you now that, in fact, your entire operation was for my Korean military intelligence friends. On both sides of the thirty-eighth parallel. Believe me, they'll welcome you. I'm simply the middleman. I found you, introduced you. They've been very impressed with your thoroughness during the entire operation."

"Both sides?"

"Patience. Everything will become clear in good time. In the meantime, we're almost there, and I have something for you. A gift." He handed Steig a box.

Steig held the small box to his ear and shook it. There was no sound. "So you're working with people in North and South Korea?"

He turned to see Aleksei's face, for he was more interested in the effect of his question than in the Russian's answer, in which he had little trust.

"Intelligence has changed since the Stasi closed down. In even that short time you'd be amazed what's happened. The KGB tries to keep abreast, difficult as that is. Friends on all sides, now, yes. The new wave. So what do you think is in the box?"

"Solid. Electrical."

"Very good. Open it."

He did. "An electric shaver?"

"Yes. Battery-operated. Works very well. Dutch-made. Highest quality. One-year warranty. Present. Try it."

Steig turned it on and ran the shaver suspiciously over his jaw. "Very good. Thank you. A bit heavy though, I should say. Electronics inside, I would guess."

"Top marks." Aleksei clapped his hands. "Concealed inside is a high-frequency receiver and sender. Today we are mainly interested in sending. This button here." Aleksei touched a yellow button on the bottom of the shaver.

"What for?"

"Where we're going, they will explain. It's so you can keep in touch while you're in North Korea."

Did this radio mean he would be an agent for South Korea working in the North? When the time came to leave, what then? Steig wondered. Tip off the North, let them arrest him? Save lots of trouble. Bye, thanks for your good work. "I won't stay in North Korea forever. You said only three to six months."

"Ah, good. Then you approve! We were afraid it might offend your German sensibilities."

The car turned right toward the ocean and stopped before a high-barred gate. Three Korean faces peered in. The driver got out, pointed at the Russian flag on the fender posts, then was asked to open the trunk. The security men scrutinized Aleksei and Steig and spoke into handheld radios. Finally, they saluted and allowed Aleksei to drive on up a winding drive through dense pine.

"Where the hell are we?"

"A house on the seacoast, Steig. Owned by one of the more prosperous immigrant Korean fishermen of the area. He's done well in import-export. South Korean patriot, of course. Owns a speedboat. Tried it out once. Special design and painted matte black. Almost invisible to radar and sonar, so it's hard to spot during duty hours. Suits their work. Quicker than the police ones, don't you know." He glanced at Steig. "Be sure you hold on to that shaver. They'll tell you how to use it, the frequencies, the codes. I'll see you on the ship this afternoon for the question-and-answer period."

"This isn't another operation, I hope."

"Of course not. My South Korean friends just want you to be a channel to their friends in the North. Keep in touch. Debrief you. Please act overwhelmed. You'll be meeting the local head of South Korean intelligence here. He'll get you to the North Korean ship. I mentioned that you were a pupil of Markus Wolf. He was very impressed. Now I must leave you here to meet a very beautiful Russian lady with whom I have a nine-o'clock engagement."

ALEKSEI PICKED ELIZABETH up, and the Russian embassy car drove them to the Prince Hotel. He led her to the elevators, carrying the large bouquet of Niigata roses he had brought, because, he explained to her, they were much too cumbersome for such a beautiful woman. In fact, she had once been beautiful and still had a tall, elegant figure and a presence in her walk that made strangers look at her.

"Good luck," Aleksei said as the elevator doors opened. They had talked in the car, reviewed all the details of what should be said. Aleksei had even role-played for some of the worst-case questions she might be asked.

She did not look back as the doors closed. Her mind was elsewhere. She ascended calmly to the top floor. The doors opened at the penthouse, where two American Secret Service agents stopped her and asked for an ID. They waved her on when she showed them a Russian diplomatic passport. She walked down the carpeted hallway toward an impressive burgundy double door with gold appointments. It was at this point that she checked the flowers to make sure they looked as they should. Beautiful though they were, the bouquet of Niigata roses seemed too large, she thought. Perhaps it was her imagination playing tricks.

Two more Secret Service agents met her in front of the door, and Elizabeth again showed her passport. She was ushered into a large ante-room full of flowers in baskets and bouquets with silk greeting banners in Japanese and English. Agents stepped forward, and Elizabeth showed her ID yet again. Security was tighter than even she had imagined.

"We'll have that." An athletic woman who introduced herself as Al-ice, wearing a navy dress and a look of permanent distrust, took the bouquet from Elizabeth and then passed it to one of the men, who placed the roses in a gray scanning machine. A door entered onto another room, and Elizabeth could see that there were more rooms extending from it. The suite must take up half of the hotel's top floor, she marveled

Alice subjected Elizabeth to a body search, and when it was completed led her through the second room, where there was a long table with miniature American and North Korean flags and legal notepads arrayed before the six leather armchairs on either side, into a carpeted study be-yond. Four Secret Service men had followed her into this room and stood quietly as Alice lifted a belt radio and spoke hurriedly into it.

Another door opened.

A terrier dog scampered out, followed by former president Sherman Whitlow. Elizabeth felt weak for a moment, then steadied herself. He still had a rugged handsomeness about him. She felt the hatred within her gather and build. Handsome and distinguished though he was now, he was the man who had destroyed her life.

STEVE STAYED LOCKED in a room overnight at Mori's place and blissfully shaved and showered in the morning. Mori's mother had insisted on pressing his wrinkled slacks. Mori had lent him a shirt. He had no jacket.

Over breakfast, Mori's wife was discussing something intently with the inspector. Steve ate in silence, wondering what they were talking about. He'd heard that Japanese women were shy and submissive, but Mori's wife certainly didn't seem to be. As Steve's mother used to say, they were having a "frank exchange of ideas."

After leaving the house Mori and Steve took the Seibu express from Kawagoe to Shinjuku. Steve asked if everything was okay between the inspector and his wife.

Mori waved a hand. "Oh that," he said, and asked if Steve had ever been married. Steve said he had, but it hadn't worked. Mori explained that divorce was not yet popular in Japan, except among younger couples who liked to imitate the United States. For the older folk, he declared, marriage was considered lifetime employment. "We put up with it the best we can," he said with a sigh. "And as for this morning's discussion, it was nothing really. We were discussing the possibility of adopting a child."

"You've decided to do this?"

"My wife is reluctant. You see, the boy isn't Japanese. But my mother thinks it's a fine idea. And so do I. In the end we reached a compromise. We'll take the boy in. My wife will not have to take care of him. My mother stays at home and will look after the boy."

"And this is all right with you?"

"Yes, because I know my wife. At first she'll complain my mother isn't feeding him proper food and his clothes should be more stylish. Then she'll start bringing home food for him, and accessories. Within months, she'll be taking over the boy's upbringing and telling everyone else how little they know about it. She'll come to love the boy as his own mother once did, may the gods rest her unfortunate soul."

WHEN STEVE AND Mori arrived at the Public Security Bureau office, Ayumi was already working.

"I heard you were up all night at the hospital," Mori scolded.

"Helping the wounded, sir," Ayumi replied. "And praying for Oishi's soul."

"You could've taken the day off."

"Everyone wants Oishi's death to be avenged. I want to help."

"He'll be avenged, Ayumi."

She handed him a fax copy. "A reply to your fax regarding the gaijin." Her eyes slid to the foreigner who was sitting in one of the lounge chairs reading an English-language *Japan Times.*

Mori quickly scanned the page. It was from Los Angeles Police Department headquarters.

STATUS: Confidential
SUBJECT: Steven Juric
DATA: Your 6/18. Subject questioned 6/14 regarding murder case #13-15987/Volpe. John. Superintendent La Vista Condominiums, Westwood, California. Subject is friend of one Helim Kim same above address who was with deceased at time of attack. Kim has disappeared after agreeing to cooperate on case. Juric not held and

no charges pending or being considered current. Please advise if any knowledge of Helim Kim. Juric runs law office 1789 Lincoln Ave. No offenses registered.

XXBT LAPD

Mori looked at Juric. "Seems you're in the clear."

"Then I'd like a favor."

"What is it?"

"Does the FBI have a Tokyo office?"

"Why?"

Steve explained that he had a friend with the FBI who was in Japan somewhere on assignment. He'd like to get in touch with him if he could.

Mori buzzed Ayumi's line. "Take care of Juric's release forms, Ayumi. And get me the local FBI office."

He spoke for several minutes. Steve heard his name mentioned a few times. Mori turned to Steve. "What's your friend's name?"

"Uemura. Ron Uemura."

"Japanese?"

"Japanese descent."

Mori completed his call. "They said they'd see what they could do. That usually means don't get your hopes up."

"It's okay. Thanks for trying."

Ayumi came into the office to pick up the fax. "I checked that number you called in yesterday, Mori-san. A Mr. Saito?"

"Yes, I'd forgotten completely. The man who contacted Helim Kim just before she disappeared. What did you find out?"

"He's private secretary to Kenzo Tanemura."

Tanemura! Mori's brain exploded with possibilities. Why would Tanemura's office be in contact with a double agent? "I certainly hope Yuka can explain."

"Shall I leave?"

"No, stay. It's your case too, after all. . . . Have you seen my report?" he asked when Yuka came on the line. "I faxed it to you last night."

"It was on my desk this morning."

"Then you know a foreigner was seen at the inn where Helim Kim was staying shortly before she disappeared. And that she received an urgent phone call from your father's secretary, a Mr. Saito. A description of the foreigner in the garden matches the suspect we're seeking in the firefight at the Kami-Hai complex and the North Korean killings."

"The one you let get away?" Her voice was cool this morning.

"Where are you going with this, Mori? I should tell you a crowd of people here want your head. And mine. You let me down."

"It's not over yet. Trust me. Want to tell me why your father's secretary would put in a call to Helim Kim?"

"I don't really know. It's not related or important, I'm sure."

"Why don't you find out? You're the one with a father who's about to become a prime minister."

"And you're not in a position to be giving orders."

"All I want to know is what Saito was doing calling Miss Kim yesterday morning. Could be a clue to her disappearance. I won't say anything to anyone. I'll honor our agreement." Mexican standoff, Mori thought. She's mad enough to can me, but she also knows I could embarrass her father.

"I'm not getting the point here."

"The point is that we're pretty sure a Japanese politician is protecting the flow of money from Japanese pachinko to North Korea. Amounts are huge, so the politician could be pocketing a fortune. Campaign fund, of course."

"Are you implying that my father—"

"Absolutely not." Mori believed that lies, if used properly, could be more valuable than truth. "Just following up a lead in the disappearance of a young Korean woman . . . who happens to be involved in cleaning up the pachinko industry, and who your father apparently has some connection to."

Yuka sighed. "I don't feel circumstantial evidence makes this call worthwhile. Frankly, I'm disappointed. Look, sorry, I have to go."

"Yuka, listen. I don't want to screw up things for your father, but I have to tell you this. I am pursuing this investigation. Whatever happens."

The prosecutor paused long enough for Mori to understand he had gone too far. "Then I should tell you that Director Aoyama called my home last night and explained the debacle in Atami. He was very apologetic. Both foreigners escaped, I understand. And one of your people is dead."

"I admit it was unfortunate. However, we're closing in on them. I can explain."

"No, you can't. Not anymore," she said curtly. "Better that you hear this from me than your superior. It's over. I've withdrawn my support for your operation. Aoyama will be confirming this shortly. Continue the investigation and you'll be fired. Flat, no retirement, nothing. It's that simple. My office is now assigned this case and the entire pachinko investigation. You're to hand over all files and data. And take no more action. Don't pursue the North Korean murders. Or any of this other nonsense. Including the Saito phone call. I'll take it from here."

"Would you like to tell me why?"

"After bungling the capture of the foreigner in Atami? I'd say you're lucky to get off so lightly. By the way, as you mentioned, my father will most likely become the next prime minister. He's heard good things about you. From guess who. Don't make me change my opinion. If he becomes prime minister, a promotion will be in order."

"I get it. Don't rock the boat."

"Right now, I'd keep my head down if I were you."

Mori slammed the phone down.

"Do a full-scale search of Kenzo Tanemura's background. Where he was born. Who his parents were. Where he grew up. The works."

"Right away," Ayumi said, turning to go. The foreigner was rather handsome, she thought, as she scurried past him.

ON HER DESK Ayumi found another fax for the inspector. She read it and entered his office again. Mori and the American were talking in low tones.

"I have been taken off the case," Mori was saying in English. "I'm not feeling too good about it. We'll have an early dinner and I'll put you on a plane back to America tonight. Now if you'll excuse me, you can stay in an office here today, but I've got some other work to do." He turned to his assistant. "Yes?"

"Another fax," she said, expressionless.

Mori took the fax without looking at it. "Will you get Mr. Juric's file, please. And a one-way ticket to Los Angeles in his name, reimbursable to us."

"Perhaps you should read the fax first, sir. It's from Niigata City. Captain Homma."

Mori read it. Then read it again. The message was addressed to the Atami police, with a copy to Mori's office dated this morning. A stolen Toyota sedan with Manazuru plates had been located on a side road outside Niigata City. The car had been impounded pending further advice and was being dusted for fingerprints. Plates matched those of the stolen car they were looking for.

Mori clapped his hands together. "Of course!" he cried. "Niigata City!"

Juric looked up in surprise and opened his mouth to speak, but Mori was already on the phone to Homma.

FORMER PRESIDENT SHERMAN Whitlow strode toward Elizabeth, his eyes alive with curiosity. "I've been trying to place you. But the one Elizabeth that I can remember died a number of years ago."

"Yes," Elizabeth said. "In the war."

"So you know about her? Shall we sit down? Then you can tell me what this is all about." He liked her perfume. It reminded him of . . .

"First let me give you a gift of flowers and my wishes for your success." She handed the roses across to him.

"They're certainly beautiful." He gave them to Alice. "Will you see these are properly cared for?"

"I certainly will, Mr. President."

She went into another room.

Whitlow showed Elizabeth to an alcove where there were comfortable armchairs and a low table. Four Secret Service agents followed them. Two stood directly behind Elizabeth's chair, the others flanked her, eyes watchful. One fixed his eyes on her hands and upper body for any significant twitch, the other on her legs and feet like a guard dog.

Elizabeth stifled a snicker. A woman her age could do no physical harm. But there were other kinds of harm, weren't there?

Alice returned with the roses in a crystal vase and placed them on the table. The bouquet was harmless, of course. But another similar bouquet would be presented later today. At a dockside ceremony when these same Secret Service people would be watching their former president greet Park Tai Jin.

Whitlow held out his hand, and Elizabeth took it. She was surprised at how warm and firm the famous man's hand felt. "I've seen you many times on television," she said, feeling suddenly awkward. She calmed her mind and fixed her thoughts on what it was she had to do. Plant the poison that would eventually tarnish this man's reputation.

"What is it you wish to tell me?"

"It is about Harbin," Elizabeth began.

"What about Harbin?" Whitlow's voice changed only imperceptibly.

"I was there when you were—before the war."

"I knew an Elizabeth then," Whitlow said. "Blond, wavy hair." He was staring at her.

"I used to be a blonde, and wavy hair was the style in the late thirties."

Whitlow's eyes searched the past.

"You worked for the American government—they didn't tell me in what capacity. I was with the Red Cross taking care of the many refugees. A nurse."

Whitlow barely stifled a gasp. "But is it really you? I was told you'd been killed at the outset of the war. You disappeared just before Pearl Harbor. How wonderful to see you after all these years!"

She said coldly, "Really? We had an affair. Do you remember?"

Whitlow flushed. "We were both young and emotional. In a dangerously romantic situation. A war was imminent. It was like living the movie *Casablanca*. Only it was in Harbin, China."

She glanced at the bouquet of roses. "I loved you very much."

"And I suppose I loved you too." Whitlow glanced at the stone-faced Secret Service team and wondered if their discretion was absolute. If this woman was who she said she was, then she had changed a great deal. And wasn't her passport Russian? He wondered how she could explain that. He was suddenly glad the Secret Service men were present. He reached up and scratched his right ear, a signal that the conversation should be taped. Then he turned back to her. "But you disappeared. I couldn't find you. Later I heard you were dead."

"I wanted to explain why I disappeared. I've wanted to for many years."

"It was long ago."

"The Japanese Narcotics Monopoly," Elizabeth said, finding her place. Knowing what she wanted to say. "That was your assignment, wasn't it?"

Whitlow hesitated. "Yes. Their office was on Uchatskovaya Street. I used to hate their guts."

"So did we all. Because the Japanese made those they conquered pay for the cost of occupation. They weren't a rich country and had studied the British example."

"In those days, the Japanese were out to poison the world with drugs. To pay for their wars and weaken their enemies. My job for the government was to find a way to stop them. But how did you know that?"

"After the war, I did some research. Pieced it together with what I knew. You were successful."

"I discovered what they were doing and reported it to the League of Nations." Whitlow's voice smoldered with the memory.

"Yes," Elizabeth said evenly. "They were forcing farmers in occupied areas to grow opium poppy instead of soybeans. Manchuria had become one of the largest opium suppliers in the world by 1939. In Harbin, Tientsin, and other cities, factories manufacturing morphine, heroin, and cocaine were built. Japanese ships transported the drugs disguised as military supplies to consulates and embassies throughout Asia. Opium dens were set up everywhere. Japanese dope peddlers encouraged addiction in schoolchildren in occupied areas. In Harbin I saw Russian and Chinese children—" She stopped suddenly.

Whitlow was looking at her with troubled eyes. "Why bring up the past now?"

"Because some things we should not forget. The Japanese wanted to stop you. They found out you had a girlfriend. They kidnapped her."

Whitlow grimaced. "I remember," he said softly.

"They asked for a ransom, didn't they?"

Whitlow motioned to the head of his security team, and they immediately vacated the room. Taking out a handkerchief, he wiped his forehead, then stood and started pacing in front of her. "It was my job, Elizabeth. I was doing my job."

"They wanted you to tear up your report, to leave Harbin, in return for my release. You refused."

"We mounted an operation to find you. I was sure—"

"You failed. I was drugged. Became dependent on their heroin. You traded my life for a piece of paper."

"It wasn't like that at all."

"Really?" Elizabeth's voice rose suddenly. "Tell me what it was like, then, and I'll tell you what it was like to be a prisoner of the Japanese for five years. A sex slave. To suffer their tortures and brutality. To be liberated by the Red Army."

The impact of those words made him blink as if he'd been struck. A shudder ran through his frame. He lifted his eyes to hers. "You're the one all this publicity is about, then? The American . . . that really happened to you?"

"The American comfort woman. Yes. Eventually, I married. A Russian who worked for the Soviet government. My name is now Kayanskova. Elizabeth Kayanskova."

"And you live . . ."

"In Moscow. I'm a consultant to the new Russia. There are many American consultants there now. My husband died in the Afghan war."

Her words collided like planets exploding inside his head. She'd married the enemy during the cold war? Why had she come? Was she trying to destroy him? "I'm sorry to hear that."

"I'm in Japan on business. Developing joint ventures with Japanese firms for the Tumen Delta area. A new trade zone being established in North Asia. With Japanese cooperation."

"I know the project. Listen, I looked everywhere for you, Elizabeth. Really I did."

"You were working for the U.S. government. You had to obey their orders. I can understand that now. Then, it was more difficult. I forgive you, Sherman. But there is one favor I'd like to ask."

"Certainly."

"Not here and now. Perhaps we can meet again? As before."

"Yes. Perhaps. I have a busy schedule."

"By the way, I'm very sorry about your wife." She rose, and Whitlow stood with her. He nodded silently. "Thank you for seeing me today," she said. "Since you changed my life, I thought I should at least try to return the favor. No need to see me out."

In the elevator, Elizabeth took a deep breath. It was done! Already their computers were searching for her background. Who was this woman that the former president had been intimate with? Who married a Russian soldier. Whom he had reluctantly agreed to meet again. It would only be a matter of time before they discovered what she had really been doing since they'd parted. That both she and her dead husband were employed by Soviet intelligence. This meeting today with the North Koreans, the rest of it, would be in ruins. The elevator doors opened on the first floor. Aleksei was waiting for her. One look and he knew her part of the operation had been successful.

61: THE DEAL Niigata City: Thursday, 10:00 A.M.

THE AMERICAN REMOVED his dark glasses and grinned. It was the first time Helim had seen his eyes. They were dark blue, like the American flag. Resolute, as though he'd placed a large bet and won. With him was a dour older man with bushy eyebrows introduced simply as Joe Pipe. DeCovasi spoke first.

"We wanted to ask a few questions, Helim. And talk about your politics."

DeCovasi motioned her to a chair but didn't take one himself. The room they had placed her in last night was at the rear of the building. The lone shatterproof window had a fine wire mesh that triggered an alarm if it was broken and could not be opened except by key. The door could not be unlocked from the inside. The furniture was spartan. She was a prisoner, she understood. This time of the Americans.

"What about my politics?" Her voice sounded strained to her ears. She was trapped by men again. As she had been all her life. Men who wanted to control her, she thought, and remembered that horrible ride yesterday. The killer wanted to control her as well. Even Tomás. Only Steven was different. However, she could not trust him either now. When she needed him most, Steven had turned his back. Deserted her. She was never going to see him again.

She bit her lip to prevent it from quivering. The inner struggle to maintain her balance had taken its toll. Last night, when they'd first brought her here, she had struggled and screamed at them until an orderly had given her a sedative. This morning she had awakened feeling light-headed. Food had been brought: a gruel of rice and meat, kimchi, a fried egg, fresh sardines, and Japanese tea.

"We work with the U.S. government," DeCovasi said. "We're the good guys, Helim. Relax."

316

"I'd like to believe that. But why was I locked in this room? And what are you doing working with that monster who kidnapped me?" She felt the tides rising and falling inside her, competing for loyalty.

"What monster?" Joe Pipe stepped forward. "As I recall, a pleasant Russian drove you partway here last night and handed you over to us, no questions asked." Pipe shrugged. "You had disappeared from a delightful inn on the Japanese seacoast, the Japanese police are looking for you, and you are an American. We, of course, are concerned for your safety."

"I was kidnapped at the inn by a different man. The same one who attacked me in L.A. A very large man. He'd shaved his head. Light blue eyes. I was driven here and handed over to the Russian. That's what happened!"

They didn't believe her, she thought. America was her adopted country, a foster parent. She was like an orphaned child who discovered her biological parents were alive, and realized that maternal love was deepest.

"An investigation is under way by the Japanese police," DeCovasi said. "I'm sure they'll bring any wrongdoers to justice."

"What are you going to do with me?" she asked. How could she escape? How long would they hold her here? She'd have to act quickly. Americans would never understand her heart.

"We'll just have to see." Pipe had turned, as if to give her question some honest thought. "I'll agree the KGB—every side—has its own methods, though, doesn't it? But please understand that the KGB cooperates with us now."

"Is my grandmother okay?"

"She's fine," DeCovasi answered. "It's you we're really worried about."

"I want to go back to my grandmother. Now!" Helim said, raising her voice. At least she was better off with these people than with the Russians, she decided.

"In a hurry, are we?" Pipe's tone hardened. "Okay. Let's talk politics, then. Have you ever engaged in any acts of terrorism or been the agent of a foreign government?"

Yes, she thought. I have. Many things that I was forced to do. Yes. Yes. Take me. Arrest me and cross me off your lists, a voice inside her was screaming. "No," she said. "I have not."

"There are serious penalties for U.S. citizens who perjure themselves. Do you know what terrorism is, Helim?"

She could feel her body trembling. The enormity of what she was doing crushed her voice and made it feeble. "Yes. I know."

"You don't have to blow up a building," DeCovasi said gently. "If you're working for a group that's dedicated to the overthrow of a foreign government with which the United States has relationships toward building the peace. That also is considered terrorism."

"I'll keep it in mind." She didn't hate these men, she decided. It wasn't their fault. They were doing a job in order to preserve a way of life. But you had to save your life in order to create a way of life, didn't you? Or was that too subtle a thought for these two?

DeCovasi said, "Do you deny switching the plutonium sample in Hong Kong? To embarrass the current leader of North Korea?"

"I have no idea what you're talking about." She hadn't switched anything. Her orders had been to get the sample. That was all. She'd done that. No one had said anything about switching.

"Let's start with Park Chung Il." Pipe moved in close.

"He wants democracy. That's all. He wasn't involved." Poor Park, she thought. Untrustworthy bastard that he was. Doomed now—she could hear it in their voices. When you wanted something too much, you never got it. First rule of life.

"Wasn't involved, you said." Pipe leaned closer. "Which implies you know who was. Your hardball friend then—the head of North Korean intelligence? Alpha. He playing the traitor, is he? Wants to knock off Dear Leader?"

"Are you sure you're talking to the right person?"

"Quite sure," said DeCovasi. "From what we can piece together, you've had a busy time working for both Park and Alpha. We know you're a double and that you're the least trustworthy type of individual on earth."

"No," she murmured, fighting back tears. It wasn't fair. She hated Alpha more than anyone in the world. Alpha had destroyed her life.

"Bit harsh, Thumper." Pipe raised his hand. "Alpha had a motive too, if we read our tea leaves right, Helim. To want the plutonium switched, that is. So did he order you to switch it?"

"I don't know about any motives." She fought the terror creeping up her back. Peering over her shoulder. No, she said fighting it. Not now. She wondered how they'd found out so much. What had gone wrong? Remember whose life is at stake here, she reminded herself. Don't let the terror in. It was what all men wanted. For you to hurl yourself into their arms.

"Here, let me just slip this on you." DeCovasi was walking toward her with a small case.

"What's that?" Helim recoiled.

"Takes your blood pressure, Helim. Worried about your health."

"Is it a lie detector?"

"Yes. Latest gadget," DeCovasi said.

She did not resist as he slipped the cuff over her arm, opened the case, and punched three keys.

"Amazing what genius can do." A screen glowed green, and a number of lines appeared. They had agreed that each time Helim lied, DeCovasi would cross the fingers on his left hand.

Pipe backed into a corner of the room and brooded.

"Are you working for the North Korean government?"

Helim did not reply.

"The switch was made by their order, right?"

Silence.

Pipe chuckled. It was a low, soft sound as if intended only for himself. "Hard to know who your friends or enemies are sometimes, isn't that right, Helim?"

"Yes. It certainly is."

"We're your friends, Helim," DeCovasi said, as if representing all decent people the world over. "You help us, we let you see Steven. He's very worried about you."

Helim jumped up, nearly overturning the device. "Where is he?"

"Whoa." DeCovasi smiled. "Got a hot button there."

"Good. That's the attitude," Pipe said. "Now try the Tomás button, Thumper."

DeCovasi turned serious. "I can offer you a trade, Helim. Let's just say we've had a deep interest in Tomás since that plutonium sample came back from North Korea all fucked up. It's connected to other recent events in which you have participated, yes?"

"I don't know anything about that."

DeCovasi crossed the fingers of his left hand.

Pipe's voice was suddenly loud. "You know everything about that, Helim. Please don't lie to us anymore. You switched the plutonium to make sure it failed the tests. Let your friend Tomás take the blame. Wasn't very Christian, now was it? We want to know whose orders you were following."

She stared at a spot on the floor. The terror had her now. She couldn't speak. She was afraid she'd confess to everything. Beg the chauvinists to take her back. No, a voice inside her pleaded. Never.

"Park came to us and explained it was an age-old trick Alpha used," Pipe continued. "According to Park, Alpha paid a bellhop to say he was approached to steal the plutonium. Approached by a Korean matching Park's description. We bought Park's story, Helim. Why not? He's on our side, isn't he? All we want is for you to confirm that. Authentication is what we call this procedure. Painless. Guarantee it. Get you a lot of points. Steve, for example. Maybe Tomás."

"Who did he say switched it?" In the fearful darkness of her mind, a sudden light switched on. Confusing in its clarity. Unrelenting in its direction. Can't do it, she thought, but knew in the end she would.

"He said you did. Under Alpha's orders!"

"Park told you that?" The anger was cleansing. Sweeping away logic. Steadying the light. Park had betrayed her then, as she'd known he would. As all men did. Whatever they stood for.

"Sold you down the drain," DeCovasi said matter-of-factly. "So was it Park that set it all up? Then sold us a bill of goods? Or Alpha that ordered you to switch?"

Helim crossed her legs. The moment had come, but she could not face it. She felt herself staring at nothing as if trying to accustom her eyes to the dark. The darkness of this new life she was about to enter. "What's this deal you mentioned?"

"Ah yes," Pipe said. "Hoped you'd ask that. The trade is this. You tell us who ran the switch and the charges against you are dropped. Plus you get to see Steve."

"What charges?" She was stalling to give her stomach time to unravel itself and her pulse rate to drop below five hundred. She wondered if she'd ever be able to feel anything again.

"Why, treason, of course." DeCovasi sounded hurt. "In addition, we get you out of Japan somehow with immunity from any U.S. government anger, although that might not be as easy as it sounds. Once you're back in the U.S.A., we'll probably want to debrief you, so you can tell us what nice little things you've been doing in the United States for the North Korean government. We may even ask you to go triple when you get back so we can run down the North Korean espionage net you were part of in Los Angeles. Right? We may think up a few more things along the way. Fair enough?"

Helim was numb with horror at what she'd heard. The chasm was bottomless. There was no future. No feeling from the neck down forever. How could she decide what was "right"? Nothing was, she decided.

"Right" was the excuse people used to take from you. Take money, free-dom, pride. She rode down the tunnel of her shaman spirituality. Begging it to blow up her soul. Destroy her. Anything. Nothing happened.

Pipe wearily pressed his sinuses. "If that sounds like a steep hill to climb, I'd like you to think a minute. What it boils down to is this: you've got to decide who you really are. What you want to be. You and many other immigrant Americans like you suffer from a kind of multiple per-sonality. Your homeland is North Korea, you were born and raised in Japan, and you're a naturalized American citizen. Can't have us all, can you? What we're asking you to do isn't that difficult, I should think. Sooner or later, you would have had to make this decision, after all."

Helim selected a strand of her hair and examined the end for splits. She was waiting for her rage to rise. To galvanize a final furious assault and perish at the head of the charge. Again, nothing came. Maybe that's the answer, she thought. I don't know who I am. Unexpectedly, she started to weep.

DeCovasi's eyes were fixed on his screen. "C'mon, Helim. No acting. Whose side you really on? The United States of America's? North Ko-rea's? And I don't mean only those bad guys in Pyongyang, some of whom may not be so bad after all. I also mean your loyalty to a Koreans for Democratic Action movement run by a do-good countryman of yours who claims to be promoting democracy in North Korea but is maybe only promoting himself. That's what we're trying to figure out."

Helim wiped her eyes and tried to protest, but Pipe held up his hand.

"I should remind you that Americans have given this planet the first real peace in its history. And that we've popularized democracy and want to see it in North Korea, China, Cuba, Iraq, and everywhere else too, but not at any price. Given time, it'll come. So make up your mind, Helim. Who are you? An American or somebody else?"

"I don't know," she sobbed, then stopped as quickly as she'd begun. She looked from one to the other of the agents as if seeking some com-pelling answer. What came was almost too simple. Without love, her future would be a farce; it would gain meaning only from some final definitive act.

She took a deep breath. "It was Park," Helim said. "I did it for Park." She blinked back tears, which quickly returned. From relief, she thought. From knowing she'd had no other choice, and that she'd finally got it right.

DeCovasi glanced at the machine. His fingers were not crossed.

62 THE RUSSIAN OPTION Niigata City: Thursday, 10:25 A.M.

AFTER HELIM KIM had been escorted from the room, an agent came in with a note for DeCovasi. Pipe let him read it, then said, "Nice interrogation, Thumper. Couldn't have done it better myself. What's in the note?"

"The Russian car will be here at noon to pick her up, Joe. We're ready to turn her over. I say we go ahead! Get her out of the way. Too late now to stop our operation."

Pipe held out his hand. "Give it to me, John."

DeCovasi held out the note.

Pipe read it. "We're not giving them the girl."

"You gone crazy, Pipe?"

"No, I've gone sane. I'm going to call Washington, lay it all out. We can't run this operation if Park set us up. And that's what we just heard from Helim Kim. Tomás's story confirmed. Two sources, Thumper. That's the rule. There's no justification—no attempt on Park Tai Jin by the hard-liners. Like you said at the hospital, Park Chung Il set us up to do his dirty work for him. Get rid of the hard-line boys in the Pyongyang tribunal. So he can go back home. Now we know they're not planning a coup or anything else, I'm calling our operation off."

"Calling it off!" DeCovasi's voice rose to a shout.

"It's the only way."

DeCovasi slammed a fist into his thigh. "No, goddammit. How do we know for sure? You're guessing. What if you're wrong? Think about that. Nobody in Washington would believe this whacked-out IAEA guy or this double spy Helim Kim, would they? So why should we? At least set the plan in motion with a stop-order scenario so we can turn it off anytime."

Pipe mulled the words. "Understand how you feel, and wish I could tell you you're right. But remember that song about the gambling man and his cards? You got to know when to hold 'em, know when to fold 'em and know when to just plain run. It's time to run. Believe me."

"Not if we've got balls."

"Not our decision."

DeCovasi folded his arms across his chest.

"Look. We've put in a lot of miles together. I admire and respect the hell out of you. When you came in a couple of months ago, the director said he was considering you for the top SIG slot when I retire. I've been thinking of retiring soon. Real soon. Don't change that."

DeCovasi straightened himself. "I'm not trying to cover my ass. This is what *should* be done! When will we or the world get another chance to move North Korea away from communism to democracy? What if during the Gulf War we'd gone all the way? Taken out the thief of Baghdad?"

"I hear what you're saying. But admit it—you *are* covering your ass."

DeCovasi ignored the issue. "Chance like this comes along only once in a career. To make a significant impact on the future of the world— Chrissake, don't you see? We'd be real heroes, even if we get hanged for it."

"Tell you what I'm willing to do. Let's talk with the boss. Air it all out. He's the one who has to decide."

"Take too long. It's this minute or never."

"Look, Thumper, *if* we get this wrong, you and me could trigger the first nuclear war. So it's not just our asses. If it were, I'd buy your program without a blink and never look back. I hear what you're saying, and I agree Americans think of us and the CIA as some kind of comic relief. But we can't set that straight with one swing of the bat. Lot of good Americans counting on us." Joe Pipe kept his eyes on DeCovasi as he picked up the phone. "It's their asses too."

DeCovasi remained silent.

"Sometimes we get the bear," Pipe said. "Sometimes the bear gets us."

He punched the director's secure number in Washington, D.C.

63 THE TRIP Niigata Prefecture: Thursday, 10:45 A.M.

STEVE LOOKED DOWN through the helicopter's Plexiglas window at the mountains of Niigata below. He was cold in spite of the spare jacket Mori'd loaned him.

"So what's this place we're heading for look like?"

"Niigata City?" Mori said. "It has a beautiful seacoast. Some interesting historical sites. Excellent food. And about an hour offshore is a place where I often vacation. Sado Island. Secluded, and not many tourists. Only one jetfoil a day. And has a Taiko drum school run by a friend of mine."

"Taiko drums," Steve said. "Oh yeah. Those people with headbands who beat on a pile of huge drums."

"Well, not quite." Mori grinned. "It's an art. Involves Zen. You ought to go there and try it sometime. Good for the soul."

Steve nodded, unconvinced, and dug his hands into the jacket pockets to keep warm. One hand felt an object and he pulled it out. Only a cheap plastic lighter.

The radio crackled with a message. One of the crewmen handed the inspector a transcript, which he quickly read. "Tell Homma I'll follow instructions," he said and turned to Juric. "Just received a message from Captain Homma in Niigata. Seems like your countryman is in Niigata and wishes to talk with you."

"Who?"

"The FBI agent, Uemura. They have a compound on the outskirts of Niigata City."

Steve felt something churn in his stomach. "They say about what?"

"I'm not sure. You seem to lead a complicated life."

"Okay, fine. I'll talk with them."

• • •

"SON OF A bitch, Steve. Your call took me by surprise. What have you got yourself into this time?" Uemura grabbed Steve's hand as if he were going to arrest him. The wash from the helicopter lifting off made them squint. A group of men in dark suits closed around the two friends. They walked, huddled together, toward the low-lying stone buildings.

"Man, where'd you get that jacket?"

"Long story. It's borrowed."

"Yeah, well, I was hoping you hadn't gone color-blind." They walked between two rugged one-story buildings that looked like ranch houses crossed with bunkers. The windows were tiny and filled with opaque and mesh-enclosed glass.

"What is this place, anyway?"

"A facility we are going to ask you to forget you ever saw. That okay with you?"

"Sure."

Uemura led him into the next building. One of the dark suits walked ahead and opened a door. Inside was a small room with a desk and two chairs. Someone closed the door behind them so they were alone.

"My boss is pissed because he thinks I told you where I was," Uemura said. "Broke security regulations."

"I'm sorry, Ron. Guess I didn't consider that when I called."

"Yeah. Here's the deal. You got me into hot water. Now you can help me out."

"How?"

"I'm going to ask you to sign a confidentiality agreement. Nothing you hear or see during your time with us can be discussed with a third party. That sound reasonable to you?"

"Okay. What's up?"

Uemura reached behind him for the document and handed it to Steve. "Like you to sign and date this thing first. Here's a pen."

Steve noticed the strain in his friend's voice. He took the pen and signed the document without reading it, something he had never done before in his legal career.

"Seems this girlfriend of yours has a complicated background," Ron said.

"Helim? I could have told you that."

"Not quite, I don't think. She's been working for a gentleman who also works with us."

"Helim's an agent for the U.S. government?"

"That's the good news. She hasn't admitted as much, but we know she's also working for the other side. Pyongyang."

"North Korean intelligence?" he said incredulously. A chill passed through him. That couldn't be. *Traitor.* The word echoed through his brain.

"Yep. Nice, huh?"

"Helim is complicated," he said, as if he himself were not. "Must be some mistake. Not Helim." He summoned the defense to plead her case. They were partners. Lovers. Cosigners for their souls. She'd explored his psyche, held up lights and mirrors for him to ponder. He needed her, if only to save himself. No traitors allowed. "You shouldn't judge her. If we knew all the facts . . ."

"Exactly what we hoped you might be able to find out. Maybe we're wrong."

That hit a resonant chord. He'd do anything to clear her if he could. "But she's on the other coast of Japan. I couldn't find her."

"You're in for a little surprise."

"You mean she's here?" New life flowed through his veins.

Uemura nodded silently.

Steve tested his soul for wounds and found it whole. She was the best, whatever else she was. The distant star he'd been following without knowing. The one matchless lover every human being is granted and appreciates too late. He gathered his scattered emotions and tried for a defiant straightforwardness. "What's the big deal, then? I mean, why all the formality?"

"I told you I was on a special assignment. It involves protecting an ex-president. And the leader of North Korea."

"Helim's involved?"

"In a plot to assassinate Park Tai Jin."

"You're joking!" He refused to budge. He could not believe that others had better answers than he did. Not when it came to Helim. She couldn't assassinate anyone.

"Not directly involved, maybe. She might not know what's really going on. But we need to understand everything she does know. Anything could be helpful. She's not saying much. Prefers to remain silent, which is her right, of course, as a U.S. citizen."

"So you want me to talk with her?"

"Yeah. Just be natural. Talk about whatever you want to. See where it goes."

"Sounds okay. But I won't do anything to hurt her."

"Listen, she's in shit so deep it couldn't possibly be worse. If she'd loosen up we might be able to help her. As it is now, anything she tells you will help, believe me."

"All right, then." His commitment was to Helim, not anyone else. If he could get her out of this, he would.

"You'll have only forty minutes with her. Then your Japanese police friends want you back."

A COOL AFTERNOON breeze from the mountains toyed with Helim's hair. She was standing on a stone patio behind one of the low buildings.

Helim didn't see him at first. Then she turned, and, with a shriek, she rushed into his arms. "God, Steve! What happened to you? Where have you been?"

"A long story."

Perhaps it was the tone of his voice. "I know," she said, and started to cry.

An agent came over. "You have until noon, Miss Kim. Use the patio chairs if you like."

Although they sat close to each other, Steve could sense her hesitation. The men watching them were intimidating. "First I should thank you for the idea," she said formally. "I gave the interviews. They'll be aired soon. It went much better than I thought. I believe we'll succeed."

"Congratulations." Steve tried unsuccessfully to sound enthused. He glanced around at the security. Four men were stationed in corners of the patio. Uemura was sitting in a chair reading a magazine. This wasn't going to work, he thought. You can't feel intimate with a bunch of Fibbies eavesdropping.

Helim continued to talk as if words would ease the awkwardness they both felt. "The Japanese network's making a big promotion out of the comfort woman issue, too. They're offering a million dollars to anyone who can identify the American woman. Whether she's dead or alive. I wish I knew her name."

"One million dollars," Steve said, trying his best to exude optimism. They could start a new life, buy a new identity, hide forever. It was the first time he'd felt like escaping.

"But why didn't you come?"

He explained all the ways he had tried to reach her. When he told her how he'd followed the foreigner who attacked her and how the sea had defeated them both, tears filled her eyes.

"Forget the past," she said. "Trouble with us, Steve, is we still be-lieve in justice."

"So what are you doing here in FBI custody?" It sounded false, and he knew it. He couldn't play the role of interrogator. He was on her side. His commitment was not based on sound logic, the prosecutor inside him warned. She was his liberator from the chains of logic, defense rebutted. His Princess Jingu and sex siren. He had shared her bed and now he had joined her revolution.

"Didn't they explain it to you?"

"Yes. But I wanted to hear it from you." He breathed in her scent and felt free.

"They think I work for the North Korean government."

"A mistake, right?" He said this too fast, as if knowing the hope could not be fulfilled. Uemura had told him, and Uemura never lied.

She studied her hands, then looked up at him for a long moment. "Yes."

"So what happens now?" She was learning, he thought. Denial was always the starting point for a good defense. He would help Helim beat this, whatever their case against her.

"They'll send me back to the United States."

"Can you leave with me?" He put his hand on her leg. She didn't move.

"I can't." Seeing the look in his eyes, she added, "You see—in some ways I was helping the North Korean government."

He wanted to stop her. Warn her that self-incriminating tape record-ings could be used in California courts. Even if she hadn't approved their use. But he noticed she was watching him. Oddly, it reminded Steve of the time he'd visited a friend who'd been in a bad accident and they'd just taken off facial bandages. Helim had the expectant look of an accident victim searching for a reaction in the eyes of someone trusted. He tried not to overreact.

"We can make a good defense," he said. "Don't worry. I'll work something out." Be reassuring, the doctors always advised. Even if you wanted to turn and run. A traitor's scars were permanent and disfiguring.

"I worked for Park too, when I could. There were reasons. I had no choice." She was relieved, he could tell from her voice. The scars didn't show, she was assuring herself.

"We all have a choice, Helim."

"I didn't. Remember, once I told you there are many kinds of love?

In the Korean language, over thirty. This was for one kind of love. Very deep."

"Who was it? Your former boyfriend, Tomás?" He immediately regretted his tone. She deserved a hearing, and he wasn't allowing her one. He drew a deep breath and waited.

"A . . . a relative."

"Who?" He couldn't breathe. An icy stillness had descended on his heart.

"It's very complicated."

"Tell me."

"No!"

"Please. I want to help you. But I need to know the truth."

"Oh, God." She sighed. "Oh hell. I guess it's better you know who I really am. I owe you that much. I owe . . ." Her eyes focused on some distant time and place. Then she began to speak.

THE WAY HELIM found out was pure chance. Or so it seemed at the time. Her tutor at college suggested she take a trip to North Korea. He showed her how it could be done without anyone knowing. Her parents. The U.S. government. So she went.

"You actually went to North Korea alone? In your second year of college? Why?" Steve asked.

"It's my country. I'm Korean more than American. I felt I had to go."

"So you went," Steve said, realizing he didn't really know Helim very well at all.

"The trip started with a flight to Hong Kong. A message waiting for me in the transit lounge: 'Meet you in Beijing. Park Chung Il.' I had no idea who on earth he was. Never heard of him. But three hours later at the Beijing airport, sure enough, Park grabbed my arm as if I were his long lost sister. He knew me on sight, although I had no idea how. He was handsome then. Before they broke him as they broke everyone. His eyes held passion and mystery in those days, as if he knew secrets of great importance. I suppose he did. I found out later he had worked for North Korean intelligence. Until he broke with them and formed a pro-democracy movement.

"Nine other students were introduced to me in Beijing: two Thais, one Indonesian, three Malays, an Indian, and three Sri Lankan Tamils.

Three women, six men. We stayed overnight at a hostel. My roommate was a Tamil girl named Jaret. She talked about the Tamil cause in Sri Lanka half the night. I heard she blew herself up outside an army barracks in Colombo two years later. Killing five Sinhalese soldiers and herself.

"Park explained the schedule. Three days in Beijing, then on to Pyongyang for a week and back for the wrap in China. He had a wonderful way of explaining everything believably, even though it was party line. He became our safety net. Whenever there was a problem, he would solve it immediately, casually. By the end of the tour all the girls were madly in love with him. So when he singled me out in Pyongyang, naturally I was flattered."

Steve shifted positions. He'd lost his capacity to be surprised by her.

"Pyongyang was very clean, with few vehicles but what seemed like a million bicycles and red-and-white trolley cars that ran everywhere on electric rails. There were massive buildings in the city center that seemed like the set of a movie because the rest of the city structures were so vastly smaller. The people were well-dressed and apparently happy.

"We were fed too much food and driven around in rickety old buses, but no one minded. We saw Kim Il Sung's birthplace, a number of factories full of workers chanting slogans about their leader, nurseries with happy children, and schools with students singing patriotic songs.

"The third night in Pyongyang, Park knocked on my door. I opened it without unlatching the chain.

" 'You are to feel greatly honored tonight.'

"I stared at him and could not find words. Perhaps I felt an unreasonable fear.

" 'Someone of importance wants to see you. Now.'

"He didn't allow me to refuse. So I changed into something decent and met him downstairs. A Russian car drove us up into the nearby mountains. On the way, Park said I was the only true North Korean of the lot and that my grandmother was special. Everyone in Pyongyang knew of her work. I wondered how he knew about her. He'd been well briefed.

"As a reward for the quality of my family, this meeting had been arranged tonight, he said. I was not to tell the others. I felt proud and excited. We arrived at a huge building. I could tell it was a hospital right away.

"An elevator took us to the third floor, and we waited in a small room. Park said it would be just a few minutes.

"Already I was feeling disappointed. I'd thought I'd meet Kim Il Sung or at least his wife. But the man that entered the room was a general. Scar under his right eye. Lots of medals.

"He asked several simple questions. Where I was born. When. What my grandmother looked like. Finally, about my mother. Did I remember her.

"Instead of answering I opened the locket I carried around my neck and showed him the only picture I had of her.

"He spoke about the ultimate victory of communism. About Juchi, which was the philosophy of the government. 'Now we have a surprise for you,' he said. 'Prepare yourself.' He got up and left the room. It was then I began to feel nervous. I had a premonition. I turned to Park for support, but he would not look at me. I called my spirit animals as grandmother had taught me. But they would not come.

"The door opened, and a man in a white coat entered. He looked much older than I remembered him when he took me and my mother to the zoo. His face had become pockmarked—I later found out this was from the burns of plastic explosives. I came to know him as Alpha.

"I remember thinking that he'd changed. Something had changed him. It didn't occur to me then it was power. All I could think was what an arrogant bastard he'd become. What could my mother have seen in him?

"A woman came into the room.

"It was clear she was part Caucasian. Like me. There was sadness in her eyes. She held out her hands. 'Helim, my child . . .' Her voice was soft and low. Just as in my dreams. It must be a trick, I thought.

" 'Do you remember your favorite animal?' I said.

" 'The monkey, of course. You liked them too.'

" 'And the worst animal?'

" 'For me it was the bear. Bears you never could trust.' She began to cry. 'I'm so sorry, Helim.'

"I was trembling all over and could not breathe. The face was spinning before my eyes. Something inside my mind was screaming out, but I could not understand the words. Inside my brain, lightning was flashing. I heard the words more clearly. 'This is my mother! This is my mother!'

"Then the floor came twirling upward, and Alpha grabbed me to break my fall.

"When I came to, I felt angry. My mother was gone. Alpha was there, talking with Park. I shouted obscenities at them, tried to hit them, but there were ropes around my waist and clamps on my wrists and arms. It was from that day I hated all men who tried to control me.

"Alpha spoke softly, as one would to a wild animal. Gradually I calmed down and listened. 'It was your mother's decision,' he said. 'To come to North Korea and to stay. You were only a few years old when your grandmother's sister in Pyongyang fell very ill. Your mother had agreed to make the trip and bring the special medicine from Japan. A one-week trip only. Your grandmother had business problems with the pachinko halls and could not come herself, we later learned.'

"After my mother arrived, her aunt suddenly took a turn for the worse. My mother could not bear to leave the dying woman, and so she stayed. Looked after her even though her visa finally expired. It took some time until the aunt finally died. By then, many things had happened. My mother decided not to return to Japan. Part of the reason was that she'd been having problems with my father. He was a womanizer. He drank. Ran with the bar girls.

"So rather than explain all this, Alpha sent my grandmother a cable saying that my mother had died in an unfortunate accident while hiking in the mountains north of Pyongyang. Naturally, my grandmother wanted to go to Pyongyang immediately, but unfortunately the government had banned any more tourist visits that year. An urn was sent to Tokyo with someone else's ashes. And so, as far as my grandmother and father knew, my mother died in an accident. Alpha forbade me to tell anyone the truth. Today is the first time."

Helim stood up and started to pace. Uemura watched her silently.

"So that's how it all started," she said.

"And why you began to work for them?" Steve asked.

"I had no choice. They said if I didn't follow their orders when I returned to L.A., my mother would be hurt."

"And what about Park?"

"Park asked me to go along with Alpha for another reason as well. To work from within and help overturn Alpha and his hard-line clique. When Park succeeded, my mother would be set free, he promised. So I agreed to work for him and Alpha, thinking it would help my mother and my homeland. Later, Park explained how my mother had been tricked by one of the oldest games intelligence services play. Target a candidate. Make her fall in love with you. Persuade her to defect. Then when she realizes what has happened, it is too late."

Tears flowed down Helim's cheeks.

Steve said, "You mean they held her like a hostage? All those years?"

"Alpha told me she wanted to stay. But I never believed that for a moment. My mother's Japanese was perfect. She knew English. She had knowledge of everything Japanese. American. She couldn't possibly have wanted to live in Pyongyang."

"Is she still alive?"

"They tell me she is. I haven't seen her in six months." Her tears increased. "That is all I can tell you now."

"But what happened to Park? He still works for North Korean intelligence too?"

"No. Five years ago he was deported for his democratic leanings. Sent to the North Korean embassy in Finland. One day he hopes to return. But lately he's changed. I think he may be just like the ones he tries to replace. Someone who thirsts for power."

"And Alpha?"

"His clique won the last struggle, but a new one has erupted in Pyongyang. That's why Park has increased his activity. Why we are trying to get the pachinko company listings. He feels the time to topple his enemies is now."

"I understand why your life is in danger. Let me help."

"There's nothing you can do. I'm sorry I haven't been honest with you. I was going to tell you. Now you know why."

"It doesn't matter." All these years she's been a slave, Steve thought. Little better than a comfort woman. Used by both sides. He wanted to hold her, protect her, end her bondage to governments. "I want to marry you, Helim," he said impulsively.

Helim shook her head sadly. "I've agreed to work with American intelligence. I must do as they say. I will have no freedom. They want me to—"

"No more time, Helim." Uemura strode over to them. "That's enough."

"Wait just a damn minute." Steve stood. "What are you going to do with her?"

"Not up to me." Uemura pointed at three agents who had come out of the building and were walking toward them. One was carrying an overnight bag.

64: A PLANE OUT Niigata City: Thursday, 11:00 A.M.

THE INTERNATIONAL SEMINAR on the Asia Tomorrow Project was being held at the Okura Hotel in Niigata City. It included delegates from the Tokyo embassies of South Korea, China, Russia, Singapore, Taiwan, Malaysia, and Indonesia. Also attending were prominent Japanese and Korean businessmen. Kenzo Tanemura opened the conference. Everyone in the room expected him to be the next prime minister of Japan. A simple matter of a party election next week.

The Asia Tomorrow Project, Tanemura began, was a free trade area on North Korea's northern border that had been recently catalyzed by the signing of an accord among North Korea, China, Russia, South Korea, and Japan.

With growing interest in peace on the Korean peninsula, Tanemura continued, economic cooperation had begun to take shape. The project would utilize the vast pool of North Korean labor, the huge resources of northern China and Siberia, the know-how and financial backing of Japan, South Korea, and other Asian states.

Tanemura explained how countries of the Japan Sea area had long played a role in promoting peace and prosperity. "Now I see a new chance to ensure a nuclear-free zone in Asia. It will start with cooperation. While the past cannot be forgotten, the future must be foremost in our minds. While a wall still separates the two Koreas, we must keep everything in perspective. I urge all Asian nations to build mutual trust, friendship, and peace in the Japan Sea area."

The audience burst into applause.

Aleksei Romanov, listening from the first row, applauded harder than most. For he saw in the Asia Tomorrow Project a unique opportunity for Russia. He had already spoken with a number of Japanese companies about joint ventures. One, a producer of MagLev trains, could supply European Russia's markets with finished goods from the free-trade zone in hours rather than days and carry supplies of raw materials to the free trade zone from the vast Russian resources in Siberia. He now had ten negotiations under way for Japanese money to assist in developing Siberia's mineral and timber wealth.

He understood that if Russia could succeed as partner to the Japanese in the Asia Tomorrow trade zone ventures that benefited North Korea as well as the region, then Russia was in a good position to regain its lost influence in North Korea. Or at least prevent a United States or Japanese hegemony. Whoever controlled North Korea controlled access to Siberia and China, he reminded himself. Power was fear, was it not? Respect. It was time the Chinese and Americans regained their respect for Russia. Aleksei checked his watch reminding himself that at noon he must pick up Helim Kim at the FBI compound. He would leave soon.

WHEN HE FIRST arrived at Homma's office, Mori had thanked the Niigata police team who had spotted the stolen Toyota. It had been stolen, he explained, by a foreigner who had killed eight North Koreans, three Atami police, and a member of the Public Security Bureau. "I'm sure he'll try to board the North Korean ship in the harbor illegally," Mori concluded. "There may be an American girl of North Korean descent with him. He abducted her or she's working with him. I need to prevent them both from escaping."

"We make a trade then, Mori. You're going to help me with my stolen cars, yes? And at the same time you can look for your killer. Two birds with one stone. Remember?"

"Agreed!"

Homma began to lay out the details of his plan.

JOE PIPE COULDN'T reach the FBI director at Washington headquarters directly. It was late there, and all evening calls to the director were screened by the night security chief at the tenth-floor communications center. After Pipe provided his identification number and advised it was a 237 Code Red meaning Urgent Highest Priority and Black Op sector, the officer asked for Pipe's secure phone number in Niigata and then requested a topic succinct.

"Tell him it's about permission to abort."

After he'd hung up the phone he turned back to DeCovasi. "I want Uemura to personally see that Helim Kim and the two escorts get to the airport," Pipe ordered. "She's going back to the United States on the next plane. Your other men are to take Juric back downtown to police headquarters. And then tell that damn Russian car we've had a delay. We'll consider turning Helim over in a day or two. Stall them any way you can until she's out of the country."

DeCovasi turned on his heel and strode away to carry out Pipe's orders. After that he'd drive into Niigata City. A possibility had occurred to him.

The Russian limousine was parked in front of the low stone building. DeCovasi rapped on the rear window as he came up to it. The door opened and Aleksei got out.

"Where is she?"

"There's a small problem."

"No time for your problems. Where is Helim Kim?" Romanov demanded.

"Your man kidnapped her, she says. There've been some related killings. Including a member of the Japanese intelligence branch. Your boy got sloppy, Aleksei. The local police want to question her. It'll just be another day or two. Then you can have her. What's your hurry?"

Romanov glared at the American. "Out of the question."

"It's not negotiable. Sorry."

"Then I must talk to her here."

"No."

"I will talk to your superior."

"Don't be difficult. He'll tell you the same."

"I cannot be responsible, then. I have my orders."

"Get the fuck out before I throw you out."

Without taking his eyes from DeCovasi, the Russian flung himself back into the car, slammed the door. "You will be sorry for this."

The wheels dug into loose gravel, and the car gained speed as it headed for the outer gate.

DeCovasi reached for his radio and punched Pipe's number. In the meantime he headed for the parking lot.

"Pipe here."

"Helim's about to leave for the airport. Juric downtown. I just kissed off the Russians—they're pissed. What did Washington say?"

"Still haven't heard. Hold your water."

"I'm heading over to the hospital then."

"What for?"

"Few more questions for Tomás Velaquez. We got kicked out before we finished our interview. Can you call Homma, let the hospital know I'm coming?"

"Sure. I was about to call the police chief and put our entire operation on hold. When you finish with Velaquez, check in. Lots happening this afternoon."

ALEKSEI ORDERED THE driver to pull over a half mile from the American gate. The road ahead was hilly, and tall pines crept close to the shoulder.

"Get me the colonel," he ordered the driver.

A woman's voice answered.

"They are stalling about the girl," Aleksei said. "Tomorrow or the next day now. What do you want done?"

"We've been monitoring the Americans. A call was placed less than an hour ago from the American compound. A seat on the one-fifteen All Nippon Airways flight to Tokyo in the name of Helim Kim. Onward booking to Los Angeles. Two escorts."

"What?"

"She cannot leave on that plane. Those are my orders."

"I understand. I may have to use force."

"Do whatever is necessary. They took her from you by force, didn't they?"

Three burly Korean men listened carefully as Aleksei explained what he wanted done.

RON UEMURA SAT in front, with Helim Kim and her two escorts in back.

They were traveling on a hilly road a mile from the compound when the car suddenly lurched to the left. The driver fought the wheel expertly to bring the car to a safe halt on the shoulder. "Damn!"

"What's wrong?" Uemura punched a button on his radio. "Car fifteen with a problem mile out on the exit road en route for the airport. Be prepared to send another car. Back to you if we can't fix it shortly. Over."

"Flat," the driver said. "Right front, it feels like." He and Uemura got out. A car was coming up the road on the other side.

"How long to fix it?"

The driver was staring at the tire. "Couple of minutes. Funny. It looks like a puncture on the side." The driver took off his jacket and went around to the trunk. "Sorry, everybody out."

Uemura went over to take a look as Helim and her two escorts got out. The approaching car slowed.

"That's not a puncture," Uemura shouted suddenly. "That's a bullet hole."

The approaching car stopped. A tinted window rolled down. "Throw away your weapons. Nobody gets hurt." A metallic snout appeared. No faces.

Uemura shouted, "Take cover, everyone! Run for it!"

Another tinted window had rolled down. "Don't do it!"

The Japanese-American cleared his pistol but had no time to fire. The automatic weapon chattered. He felt searing pain. The last thing Uemura heard was Helim Kim screaming.

65: STOLEN CARS Niigata City: Thursday, 12:16 P.M.

HOMMA WROTE THE Korean word for "fire" in romaji and handed it to Mori. "Memorize this. You may need it." Earlier he had had Mori try on the clothes he would use to make sure they were a proper size. He showed the inspector how the smoke canisters the Americans had given him fit into a specially constructed work kit. Finally where the goods-delivery documents should be signed by a ship's officer. At the moment, they were consuming a quick lunch in Homma's office.

Homma's assistant placed several phone messages on his desk. One was from Joe Pipe.

Homma did not phone the FBI complex until he'd finished his lunch.

"You're canceling, Mr. Pipe?" Homma said. "But why? You can't do that."

He listened, his neck growing red. "Okay. I understand. But we need your diver. The diver is important."

Homma listened again, scowling. "Then we'll take care of it alone. We're leaving in a few minutes ourselves." He slammed the phone down.

"What was that all about?" Mori asked.

"The damn Americans are untrustworthy, I should have known. The ship is technically foreign territory, so it can't be boarded as we would a Japanese ship. I was to provide the team to execute the boarding plan. They were to provide divers, canisters, and a team to help secure and search the ship. Now they've pulled out, leaving us to go it alone. They must've found whoever it was they were after."

Homma returned to several final points of his briefing, the sequence of events that was to begin in several hours to recover the stolen cars from the North Korean ship.

. . .

THE TURTLE-BOAT PACHINKO Parlor was located two blocks from the Niigata City dock area. Like some tawdry lady of the night, it glittered cheaply in the daylight.

A Russian embassy car swung into the pachinko parlor's parking lot. Helim was led through an entrance by Aleksei Romanov and three Korean men, professionals from the North Koreans' special services team. Her eyes were red from the terror she'd witnessed. Her dress was streaked with dirt.

"Where are you taking me?" Helim asked.

Aleksei held her arm. "Almost there, love. To meet several of your friends and the one who gives me my orders."

They hustled up two flights of stairs, the noise of whirling pachinko balls, rap music, jackpot sirens, and air-conditioning swirling around them. On the third floor they entered an outer office. A Japanese secretary greeted Aleksei with a bow and spoke into an intercom. "They are here."

A door buzzed and unlocked. The girl gestured them onward. Aleksei pushed open the door for Helim. She stepped into the next room.

The curtains were drawn, shutting out the sunlight. White carpeting was lit by TV consoles that filled one wall, monitoring the floors of the parlor below them. Four black chairs were pulled up before a kidney-shaped desk. On the desk was a Waterford vase filled with champagne-colored roses. At one end of the desk was a computer workstation, and behind it sat a slim, sharp-eyed Caucasian woman. Helim could not tell her age, though she was not young. She could have been seventy or forty in this lighting.

Helim stepped closer. The Caucasian's fearless blue eyes were remote and masked to hide emotion. She wore a dark suit, a single strand of pearls.

Aleksei introduced her as an American would. "Helim, I'd like you to meet my boss. This is Colonel Elizabeth Kayanskova."

A Russian intelligence officer with an American first name?

"Tell me what happened first, Aleksei," the woman demanded. "I am getting reports of an American agent killed. Are you insane?"

"He drew. One of our Koreans fired. Our man was just defending himself."

"That's not good enough! This jeopardizes everything."

"But—"

"I know what I said. Use force. But not deadly force, you idiot!"

Aleksei stepped forward. "I ordered him to drop his weapon. He ignored me. He knew the choice he was making. Our man was following the book—our rules of engagement."

"Then he's brain-dead, Aleksei. Follow the book? Who follows the book these days?"

"You shot him in cold blood." Helim stifled a sob.

"I want that Korean arrested and turned over to the Americans." The KGB colonel's voice was shrill. "I am going to have you driven directly back to the consulate in Tokyo. Before you can cause more problems. A hearing will be held when we are finished here. You'll have to answer for this, Aleksei. This isn't the old days. Now go!" She clapped her hands, and the doors opened. Two Russian agents entered and led Aleksei out. He looked pale and shaken.

When Helim was alone with the woman, she felt relieved. Her legs were trembling from exhaustion.

"You've had a difficult morning," the colonel said in a pleasant voice. "Please sit down." Her English was perfect. "I understand the Americans didn't treat you very well. We felt it necessary to extricate you. Our apologies for the way it happened. I hope you are not too tired from the ordeal."

The woman was clearly sorry, Helim saw. It had all been a terrible mistake. And they had freed her from the Americans. She wondered what this woman wanted. She decided to wait and see. To keep an open mind. She was curious about this person she had been prepared to hate.

"Why didn't you leave me with the Americans?"

"I'm on your side, Helim. I know all about your good work for Asian women's causes. I am also one who wants to help elevate the position of women in Asia. In Russia, women are equal. A strong Russia is important to Asia. With the help of our actions here in Niigata, and in future days on the Korean peninsula, we will return to our former glory soon. But first I would like you to meet two friends. I have a surprise for you."

She pushed a buzzer, and two Koreans emerged from the shadows. One was swarthy and tall and wore a pigtail. Some would call him handsome in a brutish, masculine way. The other was middle-aged, short and stocky, with a square jaw and hungry eyes. He wore a general's uniform.

Helim gasped. "Alpha! What are you doing here?"

Alpha lifted his hand toward the general. "You haven't met, have you? Let me introduce General Myun Chun Kuk. He's been trying to

have you assassinated for several weeks, he tells me. We've come to apologize."

She tried to confront these new facts. Before, she'd wondered what
was going to happen to her. Now she didn't care.

"I didn't know the full story of your activities, Miss Kim. My apologies." The general made a mock bow. "You live a very dangerous double—or is it triple—life."

"What's going on?"

Alpha waved at the Russian woman like a lion tamer introducing his
favorite lioness. "KGB Colonel Kayanskova can explain it far more elo-
quently than I can."

The colonel glanced at some notes on her desk, then beamed at Helim.
"You have played an important role. Congratulations. You did brilliantly.
From the KGB's man inside the FBI compound, we learned that they're
calling off their operation."

"Why? What operation?"

"To stop an imagined coup. Your action defused the situation. We
are going to reward you."

"You did well," Alpha agreed.

"Then you gave Tomás a contaminated sample in Yongbin?"

"Exactly the conclusion I reached," the general chortled.

"Why did you want me to lie about Park?" She didn't want to think
anymore. Alpha and Park played their clever games for the same reasons.
They deserved each other. They both wanted power. And went to any
means to get it. Cheating, killing, not caring about the cost to others. She
never wanted to see them again. Or the toad general. She just wanted to
curl up and sleep.

"To destroy Park's credibility with the Americans, of course," Alpha
said cheerily.

"What a charming, bright woman!" The general spoke in a low hard
voice. "I understand why you wanted her alive."

Helim dismissed the repulsive figure leering at her by turning to the
woman at the desk. "What is to become of me now?"

The colonel lifted her eyes to Helim's. "For your courageous patri-
otism in the cause of your country, your fate and mine have been united.
You will be honored greatly, my dear. Come over here. Let me show you
what I mean."

Helim advanced until she stood directly opposite the woman on the
other side of the desk. The perfume from the champagne roses on her

desk was heady and sweet. Her feelings became more intense. That secret faith without which people cannot live burned like a flare in this woman also. Helim wondered what she had overcome.

The colonel caressed the roses with her slender, tapered fingers. Helim noticed that there were no rings. "Do you like flowers?"

"Of course. And these roses are very beautiful."

"Unique. Bred locally by an expert. Niigata roses. Their scent is said to be stronger than any other." She took a rose from the vase and handed it to Helim. "A bouquet has been made up for you to present to the leader of North Korea at a ceremony in one hour. It is a great honor for you!"

"Me? One hour?" Whose insane idea was this? Yet the woman seemed sincere. She was not like the brutish men in the room.

"He is someone you have long wanted to meet." Colonel Kayanskova beamed. "Is it not so?"

"This is very kind. But I'm too tired. I'll have to decline."

"Please sit down, Helim," Kayanskova entreated her softly. "I want to tell a little story so you will understand who I am better. Why I am here. It is not very long. Just listen. Perhaps it will take your fatigue away."

Helim sat down. This mysterious Russian woman intrigued her despite her doubts.

"The story begins in China," the woman murmured. "Many years ago, when I lived in a beautiful city, built mainly by the Russians, called Harbin."

Helim flushed. It was as if an ominous penumbra had invaded the room. Perhaps the name Harbin raised her fears.

While there, the Russian continued, she met a beautiful young Korean girl from Pyongyang. They both worked for the Japanese at the same . . . job. They got to know each other.

"What kind of job?"

"The Japanese imitated the British principle," the Russian woman continued. "The British conquered nearly half the earth and always made conquered countries pay for the cost of the conquest. The Japanese did likewise. They granted monopolies to trustworthy individuals, mainly expatriate Japanese. One was the Official Prostitution Monopoly. This provided girls for the military and public brothels—anyone could place an order for girls. There were one hundred seventy-two brothels, fifty-six opium dens, and seven hundred ninety-four narcotics shops in Harbin. I was working for the American Red Cross helping refugees when I was drugged and forced into one of the military houses, where your grandmother was. A brothel."

"You knew my grandmother?"

"I was *there*, Helim."

"No. It's impossible." Helim stared at her as if willing her away. "You're making this up," she whispered savagely. Her heart was pounding as if she were pursued by an enemy.

"My name was not always Kayanskova."

Helim's mind flew over the pages of her grandmother's diary. "Elizabeth with a Z?"

"The very same."

"How can I be sure you're not lying!?" she asked in a voice that echoed in the still room.

"Call your grandmother, then!" the lady said. "Here's a phone. Have her ask me any question you wish. I lived in that past. The filthy rooms we were forced to perform our acts in. The name of the doctor who examined us. Dates, places in the city that no longer exist. Units that we serviced." The colonel's voice choked, strangled by memories too vivid and permanent ever to fade. She bent over as if physically ill, her fists knotted against the shiny surface of the desk.

Alpha approached her. "No," she said, waving him away. "I'm all right." Gradually, her color returned.

She's telling the truth, Helim thought. And if this is true, then she is one of us. The legion of women used by men. Used and tossed aside. But why is she Russian? Why is she mixed up with this group? Where is her soul?

"So, you're the American comfort woman of my grandmother's diary," she said.

"Yes. In another life."

Helim swallowed, her thoughts engulfed in a turbulent sea. "But now you are here? What happened to you?"

"Many things, my child."

Helim stared at the woman as if trying to see through her. "My grandmother told me the Russian army occupied the city for a time after the war."

"They did. And I tried to kill myself. The Russians found me and were kind to me. They got me off drugs the Japanese had forced on me. They made me want to live. Offered me a new life. Eventually, I came to love their country as my own."

"But you work for men like him?" She turned with loathing to Alpha.

"They saved my life. Gave me back my self-esteem. And a new identity with which I could live. We all have to choose, Helim. Women can only love one country at a time. Not like men. This is the first time that I have ever told any American what I once was. Everything of my past was discarded, except for my first name. I wanted some link to the past." Her eyes seemed to peer over the horrific precipice that was her past. "So you see, we're very much alike." Her voice seemed to reach out to Helim and embrace her. "In the eyes of the United States, we are—both of us—traitors."

The room was very quiet.

Elizabeth Kayanskova broke the spell. "My dear, I know your feelings, I truly do. And I'm here to help you as I was once helped. It's about your future. I can understand you're torn in several directions. Once I was too. But it's time you made a choice. We want you to come over to our side. The side of the future. It includes Russia, the two Koreas, China, and Japan. A pact will be reached for a new era of cooperation. The United States will be replaced by a consortium of countries that will dominate the next century. So tell us you will commit to us and we will make you a promise."

"What promise?"

"That your mother will be released. To live with you wherever you wish."

Helim looked at Alpha. He was beaming.

IN A CAR outside the pachinko parlor, Aleksei Romanov and the two Russians who had led Aleksei downstairs had been listening to the conversation. They turned the speaker off, slapped each other on the back, and passed a bottle of vodka around. "She's going to do it," one declared. "Elizabeth's a genius." They toasted the new Soviet Union and the colonel. "So what happens to the Korean who pulled the trigger?" Aleksei asked.

"Oh, him." The driver smirked. "He gets to shoot Helim Kim if she doesn't deliver the flowers properly like she's told."

"Excellent plan," Aleksei agreed. No one could be possibly blamed. Except Helim Kim. And the Americans. The driver started the engine and pulled out onto the road toward Tokyo. The charade had worked.

• • •

THE POLICE LAUNCH had, among other amenities, a bulletproof cabin
that seated six and portable Volker heavy machine guns fitted into mounts
on the forward and aft decks.

As they pulled away from shore, Steve's thoughts returned to Helim.
Her flight would be in the air now, and he prayed silently that she was
safe. He had been turned over to Mori by the three American agents and
introduced to Captain Homma just as they were leaving headquarters to
board the launch.

Mori had explained to the police chief that Steve knew what the
foreign killer looked like. That his girlfriend had been abducted by this
man and he could help them to locate both: Helim and the killer. Steve
listened silently. He could not reveal that he had already found Helim.

"Just remember, gentlemen," Homma said, "the *White Swan* can't be
searched officially. Any foreign vessel—even though it's in our waters—
has territorial integrity. That is, we can't board without permission."

"I know that already," Mori said. "You've figured an ingenious way
to get aboard so we can search for the cars. I'll admit that much."

"And your killer, right?" Homma added. "We're positive the cars are
on board. About your killer I can make no guarantees."

"Cars?" Steve asked.

"Yes. Stolen and winched aboard someplace off the China coast."

Mori changed into a dock worker's blue outfit with a yellow hard hat.
Slung over his shoulder was a canvas tool bag.

"What's this for?" Steve asked.

"You'll see soon enough," Homma said. He began to review for a
final time how Mori was to board the North Korean ship.

A radioman handed Homma a document from the harbor master.
"The final piece just arrived," the chief said. "We're getting close, Inspector."

ALPHA WENT TO a table against the wall and lifted up a large bouquet
of roses. "As a symbol of your commitment to our cause, we wish you
to present these roses to Park Tai Jin," he told Helim.

Helim was pleased. Then she looked down at her wrinkled clothes.
"I can't. Not like this."

"Of course not," said the colonel. "We have a changing room next
door with three choices of suits. You can take a shower, wash your hair.
All the amenities. After that you can rest. We don't have to leave for one
hour."

The roses were tied with a pink ribbon. Aluminum was wrapped around their base. A card was attached. Helim read, "In honor of His Excellency's first trip to Niigata City. The Korean Association."

"Does that please you?" the Russian woman asked. "You can refuse if you wish. You don't have to do this if you are too tired."

"No," Helim said. "I want to meet him." In truth, she did not know how she felt. But she understood this was what they wanted to hear. That if she did not agree she might be imprisoned or worse. And perhaps, just perhaps, it offered her a way to escape. A way out that could also free her mother. She wondered, finally, what this woman had to do with pachinko in Japan.

66: THE CONFESSION Niigata City: Thursday, 1:25 P.M.

THE NURSE APOLOGIZED when she came in to take Tomás's lunch dishes away that afternoon. Yesterday the two foreigners had upset him, hadn't they? Normally, doctors did not allow the authorities to question patients during their stay in the Red Cross hospital. It was considered a sanctuary.

"Thanks for your concern," Tomás said, knowing he had been changed by what had happened and would never be the same again. But already he was beginning to regain his vigor. "How long will I be here?"

The nurse picked up the tray. "The police say you may be held here for some time."

After she'd left, he considered the hopelessness of his predicament. The authorities were claiming he'd entered Japan illegally, even though he'd explained he had been abducted by North Koreans. They said they had contacted the IAEA, but the case was complicated. They said it might take many days, even months, to decide what to do with him. He sensed they had another reason for holding him, a political situation in which he was a pawn.

He opened the door. A Japanese plainclothesman was sitting on a chair near the door reading a magazine. The Japanese looked up. "Dame, dame," he said, shaking his head. No good, no good.

Tomás closed the door, swearing under his breath. Then he went to the window and examined the lock.

Tomás froze. Someone was talking with the guard outside. The door opened. A Caucasian man entered.

"You look a lot better today. You remember me, Tomás?"

"Yes."

"I'm here to help solve your problem." DeCovasi's eyes were hard and cold. "You can be free soon."

"I don't believe that."

"You'll have to cooperate."

"How?" Tomás sat in the visitor's chair

"We make a trade," DeCovasi answered. "You tell me what I'd like to know, I'll help you get out of here. That's our trade."

"What do you want to know?"

"Let's start with Helim Kim. She ever tell you she switched the plutonium?"

"No. And she doesn't like being a pawn. She said so."

"I don't think she did either. Someone taught her how to lie pretty good, though."

"She tells men what they want to hear sometimes. To her it's not lying—she doesn't look at it that way. You could call it her weakness. But to her, life is a chess game dominated by men. The game isn't fair. So maybe she cheats a little. Look at the game itself, she told me once. Kings, rooks, castles, and knights, all male. One female, the queen. Only pawns aren't gender-specific. 'How many female chess champions are there?' she asked me."

"So she tries to get even. Okay. Good. Now tell me again how it was you escaped from that North Korean ship. Explain to me exactly how it went."

"I'll tell you what I remember." Tomás shuddered at the memory. "I was strapped to an operating table in a small room."

"Yes. A gurney."

"Next to the table was a transformer with wires they attached to my testicles. The torturer had left the room."

"How nice. Alpha was his name, you told us. What did he look like?"

"Big man. Pigtail. Pockmarked face. But they had given me drugs. I can't really say more."

"What happened after he left?"

"A Korean woman stayed in the room, his assistant. Not very smart."

"How come?"

"She turned her back to me. I was able to move close to the transformer. Then when I explained my skin itched, she came close. That's when I . . ."

"Yes?" DeCovasi leaned forward.

"I took the clamp and fastened it to her neck."

"Good boy! And . . . ?"

"I turned the transformer to full power."

"Jesus," DeCovasi grunted approvingly. "That must have smarted. Knocked her out, did it?"

"Both of us. When she revived, she pulled a pistol."

"Then what did you do?"

"I pushed the gurney over onto her. The gun spun away. I picked it up."

"Nice. Let's hold up a minute." DeCovasi was squinting now, like a movie director trying to get a scene right in his head before shooting it. "You had a couple of breaks there, didn't you?"

"What do you mean?"

"Well, it must've taken a little time to get that clamp clipped on this woman's neck. I mean, she just sort of let it happen."

"I don't remember everything exactly." He wondered what the American meant. It was as if he doubted everything Tomás was telling him.

"And when you pushed that gurney over on top of her. Must have taken a little struggle to get it tipped over, right? I mean, you weren't exactly Arnold Schwarzenegger by this time. Meanwhile she's aiming this thing at you, grinning and whistling 'Dixie'?"

"What is Dixie?"

"Never mind. So where do we go next?"

"To the door. It opened before I could get to it. A soldier was standing there with a gun."

"*Perils of Pauline,* wasn't it? Dear me, one thing after another. So?"

"I aimed the gun I had . . ."

"The woman's, yes."

"I fired first. It hit the man in the thigh."

"Quick. You must have been very quick."

"No. It seemed it took me half an hour to pull that trigger."

"So the soldier just stood there and let you shoot him?"

"I can't remember. I was just trying to escape."

"And you did, didn't you? Ever hear of mental programming?"

"No."

"Used in espionage. Find someone who'll make an unimpeachable, believable subject, then fill his head with data you want to pass to the enemy. Misdirection. Wonderful technique. Then you allow him to escape."

"I don't understand."

"Don't worry about it. So where did we go from there? Run to a railing and jump ship, did we?"

"No. I hid in a car in the hold."

"A car in the hold?"

"Yes. It was full of them."

"Really?" DeCovasi scratched his chin. "The bad soldiers search for you?"

"Yes. But they couldn't find me. Until I went to this door in the hull. I think they used it to drive the cars through. Then one soldier came up from behind and hit me."

"How did he hit you, Tomás?"

"He knocked me out the door with his rifle butt and I fell into the water."

"But he had a weapon. Why didn't he grab you or shoot you?"

"I don't know. I was lucky, I guess."

"So we're in the water. A mermaid come by and pluck you out?"

"No, I was knocked out momentarily when I hit the water. When I came to, I was in a boat."

"Your lucky day. Describe the boat, can you?"

"Black. Everything was black. The hull, cabin. Maybe thirty feet long. Inboard engine."

"They spoke Japanese?"

"No, Korean."

"Really? How brilliant of them! And they took you safely to the police, who brought you here. End of story?"

"Yes."

DeCovasi stood. "Tomás, I've changed my mind. Sorry. I want you to stay here. And you can have that old job of yours at the IAEA back if you can stomach it. In fact, I may need you to tell others the same thing you've just told me. But not for a day or two. I promise I'll come back and get you out of here. Right now, I really have some things to do."

Before Tomás could protest, the agent had disappeared.

FORMER PRESIDENT SHERMAN Whitlow was in the bedroom of his suite when the phone call came.

"Sir, you have a call from the FBI, SIG, John DeCovasi."

"Put him on."

"Mr. President, I'm sorry to disturb you," DeCovasi said. "I know you're about to have a meeting with Park Tai Jin. Would you push your scramble button, sir."

"Done. I had a call from Agent Pipe thirty minutes ago. Now you. What's this all about?"

"Your schedule with Park Tai Jin, sir. Where are you meeting him?"

"At the pier, then we drive to my hotel."

"At the pier, what's the procedure?"

"I say a few words, he says a few words. A Japanese band plays his national anthem, then ours."

"What did Joe Pipe tell you?"

"He said there was an all clear on an alert. No attempt on Park Tai Jin's life is expected now."

"I'm afraid he's wrong."

The former president was silent a moment. "What do you mean?"

"North Korea set up an operation to make us believe there'd be no assassination attempt. We bought it. Any procedures at the pier seem out of the ordinary to you?"

"Not that I can think of. There was to be a bouquet presentation by some local Girl Scouts. But that's quite normal, isn't it?"

"Yes sir. Thank you, sir. Sorry to bother you."

When he'd hung up, Whitlow clicked his receiver.

"Yes sir?"

"Get me Joe Pipe."

"We're calling Mr. Pipe right now, sir," the Secret Service agent replied. A moment later, "I have him on the line. Please go ahead."

"Mr. Pipe?"

"Yes, Mr. President. What can I do for you?"

"I've had a call from one of your people, John DeCovasi."

"Really?" Pipe paused. "I was just looking for him. He's not answering his radio calls."

"He had some contradictory news, which I wanted to confirm. Said there *was* going to be an assassination attempt on Park Tai Jin."

"That is incorrect, sir," Pipe said immediately. "I've just spoken with my director in Washington. There will be no assassination attempt, and he gave approval to withdraw our team immediately."

"So initially you did believe that there was going to be an attempt?"

"Yes sir."

"What made you call if off?"

"Information we received yesterday from an unimpeachable source and confirmed earlier today. We don't like to admit it when we've made a mistake, but in this case we have."

"What about this DeCovasi?"

"He was completely out of order, sir. Earlier today, he indicated to me he wished to see the counteroperation carried out regardless of our director's orders. His call to you was an act of insubordination. Therefore I am issuing an order for the Japanese police to arrest and hold him. Sorry to trouble you with this, sir."

"Okay. Let me know if there is anything I can do."

After he'd hung up, Whitlow felt a pulse of fear tug at the pit of his stomach. Good Lord, he hoped these people had got it right. What if . . . No, that was impossible. They were professionals. He'd have to trust their judgment. He picked up his speech and tried to concentrate. In five minutes he had to leave for the pier to meet the North Korean president.

67: **THE UGLY DUCKLING** Niigata harbor: Thursday, 1:45 P.M.

THE LIGHTERS LOOKED like ugly ducklings, roped alongside the North Korean oceangoing mother vessel. Cranes on the ungainly black barges for loading and unloading ships winched the loads of supplies aboard: rice from Niigata, soy sauce from Nagoya, vegetables from the Kanto Plain.

The loading would last right up to departure at nine o'clock tomorrow night. They would finish loading by then—on schedule, so the big Korean vessel could sail as planned.

The *White Swan* was a fifty-thousand-tonner. Top speed was thirty-five knots, about the same as a destroyer. It had a substantial forward cargo hold, a smaller one aft. Engines and storage tanks were amidships. The ship was constructed with twenty guest cabins; facilities for crew were below. Sleeping quarters for a platoon of thirty elite troops had been added forward. The main mess for crew was belowdecks aft, and an officers' canteen and meeting rooms were on the first and third decks.

Homma said, "You'll go aboard the lighter in another twenty minutes while everyone is watching the dockside ceremony. You'll begin to execute the plan after another fifteen minutes."

"Right," Mori said.

The radioman handed Mori a fax. "From your head office in Tokyo, sir, just received. Marked urgent."

It was from Ayumi:

> Attention: Mori-san
>
> This is a summary of data you requested regarding Kenzo Tanemura.
>
> Born Kanagawa Prefecture, second son to Aiko and Kenji Sakamoto, farmers. After serving in China with the intelligence branch

of the Imperial Army entered into arranged marriage to Sachiko Tanemura. Her father was member of postwar Diet and large land-owner. Daughter was an only child. Sakamotos were approached by Sachiko's parents offering their daughter's hand provided their son took Tanemuras' name. In this way the name would be continued. The Sakamotos agreed and Kenzo Sakamoto became Kenzo Tane-mura. For further detail (which I think you will find most interest-ing) refer to Kim diary, July 9 to 12, 1941.

In his briefcase, Mori found the copy of the diary. He opened it to the pages and read them quickly again.

Jonquil Kim
Pyongyang, Korea
July 9, 1941

I will one day become a great nurse or doctor. A healer of spirit. A guide to the vast galaxy of modern medicine through which the sick wander confused. This summer vacation, I planned to work as their helper at the Japanese Imperial hospital in the city. However, today I had exciting news. A Japanese officer of the Medical Corps will visit our school for special job interviews. I have been selected to meet him tomorrow.

Since the Japanese governor outlawed and closed the churches, it is rumored that Principal Chong fears all Christians, so I was sure no awards or privileges would come my way this senior year. Wrong again!

Because the Japanese have occupied Korea for so many years, my parents worry we Koreans will never be a free people again. I have mixed feelings, I must admit. Particularly today!

July 10, 1941

At 4:00 P.M., I met a Japanese officer in the principal's office. It was terribly warm and the great overhead fan turned with agonizing slowness. The palms of my hands were moist and my legs shaking. There were several men in the room when I entered, and I felt my face go hot from their stares. Everyone spoke Japanese, since no one is allowed to speak Korean anymore in public.

"Miss Kim," said Chong, the principal. "This is Lieutenant

Sakamoto of the Kempeitai, the Thought Police. He is visiting us from China."

The Japanese lieutenant was handsome and young, his hair pomaded straight back in the current style. He smelled of a perfume not available in Korea. "So, this is Miss Kim," he said. "Yes, I can see she is attractive. And a Christian too?"

I blushed. The lieutenant walked around me, examining my figure. In spite of the fact that I was wearing the school's blue uniform—a long pleated skirt and a loose blouse—I could feel the Japanese officer's eyes undressing me down to my skin. I pretended I did not mind. After all, I am a senior, and already eighteen.

"We may have a special assignment for you," the lieutenant said. "If you can pass the tests, of course."

"What kind of job, sir?" I could barely keep my voice from trembling.

"In . . . nursing. The Imperial Japanese Army would like you to come into the city for these tests tomorrow."

I did not know what to say. It sounded like such a huge honor that tears came into my eyes. I thought how silly my parents are. How wrong they are to hate the Japanese, say terrible things about them.

July 11, 1941

As I bicycled into the city, I marveled again at how Pyongyang has become such a beautiful place under the Japanese authorities. New buildings are being constructed every day. Not only are the hospitals modern and clean but we now have wonderful new brick office complexes, beautiful parks, paved streets, grass in front of great homes. Our school, on the outskirts of the city, is near the shiny new rails on which the modern trains arrive right on schedule. The Japanese have done so much for Korea.

I was interviewed at the Pyongyang Imperial Army command center by a Colonel Sato, who claimed to be a sculptor in his spare time. He spoke in a deep voice. "So you want to be a nurse." My school records were on the table in front of him.

"Yes. It is my dream."

He began to interrogate me on my opinions and experience. The questions he asked so casually became more and more intimate. He asked if I had ever had sex. I said no. He asked if I had a boyfriend, and when I blushed he knew the answer was yes. When, at its conclusion, he said I had passed the mental exam and would do wonderfully, I was very pleased and excited.

A Japanese doctor touched me in places I have never been touched before, even by our family doctor. At one point he cupped his hand over my bare breast to check my heartbeat.

When he was finished, he declared me a wonderful specimen. Perfect health. He wrote this in a medical record. At some sacrifice to my pride, I have passed all their tests.

Tonight, instead of taking me back home, they have put me in a barracks with other teenage girls as confused as I am. What is happening to us? They still have not explained what kind of nursing we are to be trained for.

July 12, 1941

In the middle of the night, a rough hand touched me and I awoke frightened and trembling. A soldier pulled me out of bed, threw a coat at me to cover myself with, and led me outside. Lieutenant Sakamoto was there. Apparently he'd been drinking. His breath smelled like Father's on celebration days. "You are to come with me," he said, and he led me to a car. He drove to a house nearby and took me inside.

There he undressed me and made me perform acts on him that it makes me sick to recall. When he became large, he placed his manhood against my poor virginity. Suddenly he tore into me, and though I screamed and tried to hit him, he raped me again and again for the rest of the night. I didn't know humans could be so cruel. I can't believe what has happened to me. For the rest of my life I will be ashamed of that night. In the morning I was given olive drab slacks and shirt and driven by a soldier to an airport. Then I was pushed onto a plane full of soldiers where there were also several of the girls from the barracks. I have never felt so sick and miserable in my life. We were told the plane was going somewhere inside China.

"Mori!" Homma's voice brought the inspector back to the police launch. They were approaching lighters tied up to a large white-hulled ship.

"Right." Mori slipped the diary back in his briefcase, the taste of its words souring his throat.

"Better get ready. We're here. What're you reading?"

"A little history that makes me angry about powerful people; how they get away with things."

"No time to right wrongs now."

"Yeah," Mori said, a hard light entering his eyes. "Maybe later."

MOTORCYCLE POLICE LED the cavalcade of five limousines as it proceeded slowly along the waterfront and turned into the dock area. There was a fence separating the loading areas from the public. The cavalcade drove through a gate and pulled up near steps leading down to a captain's launch that had just tied up at the dock.

Several hundred Asian businessmen holding North Korean and Japanese flags were waiting for the ceremony to begin. Later, a launch would ferry them out to the Korean ship. These were dignitaries invited to the ceremony who would later attend the afternoon aboard-ship session of the Asia Tomorrow seminar.

Police had cleared an area around microphones set up on an elevated platform covered with red carpeting and backed by national flags. A group of pomaded Japanese politicians and VIPs spoke together, occasionally glancing toward the Korean launch, which was now unloading an elite Presidential Guard team. Three TV trucks decked out with small satellite dishes added to the sense of excitement. Those present knew something momentous was to happen. Park Tai Jin was about to meet a former president of the United States and the expected next prime minister of Japan.

The motorcycle policemen dismounted and formed a protective rank around the lead car. Americans popped from cars and limos to take positions around the former president's car as well.

The two hundred businessmen and diplomats fortunate enough to be invited to the ceremony craned their necks to see who was the center of attention. Sherman Whitlow stepped out first, followed by Kenzo Tanemura, to a burst of applause and cheers. From other cars, aides to the former president and the Japanese politician emerged.

They were quickly surrounded by U.S. and Japanese security men, who led them to the platform where the microphones had been set up. A red carpet led from the platform to the edge of the dock and down steps to where the covered launch from the *White Swan* had been tied up. Whitlow and Tanemura marched over to the microphones. Standing ten paces from the steps that led to the launch, Helim was looking around nervously. Korean guards from the ship were stationed on each side of her.

Weapons were presented. A group of high-ranking North Korean military officers marched up the steps from the launch. Behind them in a dark blue business suit walked a youthful-looking, handsome Asian man with a full head of hair. He smiled and waved at the applause from the crowd, many of whom waved small North Korean flags.

Whitlow and Kenzo Tanemura applauded. Helim joined in. Near her, a group of Japanese Girl Scouts had formed, their leader whispering last-minute instructions. They would present a bouquet to the former president, Helim had been advised. Then she would present her bouquet to Park Tai Jin. She smoothed her hair against the wind, adjusted her new dress.

The North Korean leader walked onto the platform and stood looking straight ahead. All TV cameras swung to get better angles of the man on his first trip to Japan. Kenzo Tanemura went over, bowed, and shook hands with Park Tai Jin, then with each of the generals. He introduced the Korean leader to the former American president, and they too shook hands as flashbulbs popped and TV cameramen moved in.

Helim watched, feeling proud of the youthful leader of her homeland. And of the former president of the United States of America. They were both taking risks to do this. But as her face studied Kenzo Tanemura, her eyes filled with loathing. She recalled the phone call from his assistant. Tanemura was the man behind the pachinko money-laundering. No doubt he was corrupt. She wondered how such a man would lead a nation.

68: THE LIGHTER Niigata harbor: Thursday, 2:00 P.M.

THE POLICE CRAFT tied up against lighter three.

"I'll have a diver ready in case anything goes wrong," Homma told Mori. "He should be arriving any minute."

"Diver?"

"Did I forget to tell you?" Homma scolded himself for his forgetfulness. "I asked the Americans for a diver just in case."

"What could go wrong?"

"Nothing, of course. But as I mentioned, my friends in the FBI canceled a cooperative effort with us at the last moment. It was supposed to be a joint operation. Now we're on our own. They agreed their diver could still participate, however. It's better to be prepared for anything."

The lighter was bobbing against the *White Swan* as Mori boarded it in the afternoon chop. Overhead, the sky was beginning to darken with clouds, harbinger of a front forecast to move in later tonight. As agreed, Steve stayed aboard the police craft for the first phase. He'd been assigned to board the *White Swan* with the first police team if stolen cars were found in the *Swan*'s hold. His job would be to help locate the foreign killer and point him out to police.

Another police craft arrived and pulled alongside the first. The American diver jumped aboard, holding a diving mask. He settled in the stern, where he began to fit a weight belt and shrug into an oxygen tank. Then he tied a kit to his belt, put on his mask, and slipped over the side. Behind the lens of the mask, Steve had seen calm eyes.

Mori's official job was to stand on the deck of the North Korean ship and record each winchload of supplies, which hatch it was lowered into, and the time. Fifteen minutes after boarding, exactly on schedule, Mori removed his yellow hard hat and placed it on the deck, turned from the hatch, and strode off, clipboard in hand. As he turned into the companionway that led to cabins and upper decks, an armed North Korean soldier stepped in front of him. Mori pointed at the clipboard, the lighter badge fastened to his lapel, and the bridge, then made a signing motion. "Finished loading." The guard waved him on.

His dark blue shirt and trousers nearly matched the uniforms of the Korean naval officers. To a casual observer he looked like one of them. Captain Homma had been given a courtesy tour on one of its earlier visits and had provided Mori the ship's layout. The bridge of the *White Swan* sat atop five floors of cabins and equipment rooms. On the first deck, rooms opened off each side of a long corridor. Midway, Mori found a door that Homma had told him opened to a toilet next to the officer's canteen.

The only problem was that half a dozen security men stood smoking in the corridor, automatic weapons slung casually. One started to amble toward him. Mori straightened and walked confidently up to the soldier, then pointed at the toilet. The soldier noted the tag on his lapel and said something in Korean. Mori strode into the lavatory.

That was too close, he thought. There was too much to do in the next half hour for any slips. It would be hard to explain to his Tokyo office and the public prosecutor what he'd been doing wandering around a North Korean vessel if he got caught.

Sweating now, he selected a stall that he knew shared a wall and a ventilation duct with the canteen where the ship's officers gathered for meals. He took a canister from his tool kit and placed it behind the toilet against the wall where it could not be seen. He flushed the toilet and walked out, away from the officers' mess, then retraced his steps until he reached an open door beyond which a narrow steel stairwell led to the lower levels of the ship.

The hardest part came next.

Homma had told him the stairs led down two decks to a catwalk that ran toward the bow of the ship. It would be the quickest way to the larger hold. That should be where the cars were kept. At least that was what Homma figured. Mori hoped he was right.

The steps rattled as he hurried down to the catwalk. Several sailors saluted, thinking he was an officer.

If the cars were aboard and they were in the large forward hold, several things could go wrong. He could get lost in the hold of this huge ship, or someone might stop him if the areas were restricted. He'd just have to chance that. Below was a huge engine at least fourteen meters in length and five meters high with a large brass TOSHIBA MARINE nameplate proudly displayed. It pulsed softly, like a resting giant. Mori walked the perforated catwalk above it. An incomprehensible maze of valves, manifolds, pipes, springs, polished copper tubing.

Occasionally, more young crewmen passed him and saluted. Like its masters, the ship's crew and engine have no individuality, Mori thought. They did not recognize him, yet they saluted the image. The system was soulless.

The engine slowly increased in pitch, then decreased, as though testing itself for the voyage ahead. From his work kit, Mori removed another small circular canister and set a dial for twenty-five minutes. Then he placed the magnetic device gingerly against the wall in an alcove where it could not easily be seen. Mori took a quick picture with a pocket Minolta, then headed toward a hatch in a bulkhead at the far end of the catwalk.

He entered an area that led past green diesel tanks numbered in large white letters. The amidships hold. At intervals were fire extinguishers and instructions in Korean explaining their use. Signs every five meters prohibited smoking. Mori took out another canister and set it for twenty-four minutes. He hid it near an extinguisher next to the alarm system. He worked quickly, hiding more canisters as he went.

Now he was nearly there. A spiral staircase led upward to another door. If he was not mistaken, it should open on the large forward cargo hold. If there were any cars, they would be there. He spun the locks and opened the door. The space ahead of him was cavernous and dark, reverberating with echoes of people moving about.

There were no portholes. Insufficient electric lights were spaced at intervals of ten meters in wire mesh cages high on the steel sides of the ship's hold, throwing an eerie light over the vast scene. Ahead of him, a door on the port side had been swung open, allowing a shaft of light to penetrate the gloom like a movie projector's beam.

Gradually his eyes adjusted enough to distinguish that the hold was full of polished steel. Car roofs. Grilles. Hoods. Mori swung his amazed eyes over the cars. There had to be a hundred or more. Rolls, Mercedes, Alfa Romeo, Porsche, Bentley. An exclusive parking lot. Damn!

He strolled along the catwalk, his attention entirely on the amazing scene below. He placed more canisters, took pictures of the cars. Two passing crew members looked at him curiously.

Mori knew there was not much time to get off the ship. The first canister would do its job in a few minutes. He headed back the way he'd come. The only thing he had failed to do was find the foreign killer. He would have to leave that to Homma and Steve. He heard a shout. The crew members who had passed him had turned and were coming back toward him. They had noticed something.

Mori pretended not to hear. He reached a door and opened it. He had completed the hardest part of the mission. All the canisters were planted. He began to run, wondering what Aoyama and Public Prosecutor Tanemura would do if they knew what he was up to. That made him grin.

Mori opened another bulkhead door and slammed it shut behind him. He turned the screws so it couldn't be opened from the other side and started to run again. He passed the diesel tanks in the amidships hold and reached the stairs to the engine, hearing pounding on the bulkhead door. He tore past the giant engine, bounded up the final flight of stairs, and, out of breath, found himself again in the main cabin corridor. Here he stopped, trying to look casual. Then he stared at his watch. It couldn't be!

In three minutes the lighter would leave without him. Without appearing to hurry, he headed toward the outer deck. When he was five meters from the outside main deck, three men came around the corner toward him. A Caucasian talking with two Asians. The Caucasian was powerful, with a shaved head and eyes like a wolf's. He was dressed in dungarees and a blue shirt open at the neck. Mori would have recognized that face anywhere. The killer's face.

Damn you to hell! His mind unleashed a volley of curses. He needed to get off the ship, but now he wanted to stay. His muscles convulsed with the vehemence of his anger, the mayhem of his thoughts: Attack him here. I have no chance. So what, he will die. Even if I kill him, there are too many others. He will die badly, I will die well.

Irrational demons argued in Mori's head. He wavered.

The first of the Asians was middle-aged but still powerful, with a grizzled face and short iron-gray hair. A scar under the right eye. He wore a military uniform with many stars on the red epaulets. A high-ranking North Korean officer. Probably a general. The face was in his files, but the name did not come to him immediately. The second Asian wore a dark civilian suit and had his blue-black hair tied in a pigtail. Damn! Mori said silently to himself. Damn!

They were walking toward him, engrossed in their conversation, blocking his path. The language was not English. German perhaps. Mori turned back down the corridor and tried the handle of a door. It opened, and he stepped inside. The cabin was dark, the porthole closed, and he could hear someone breathing regularly. A person asleep. Outside, steps passed by the door and receded. Mori could hear his own breathing now. He held his urge to overtake and kill them. Not now, he warned himself. More important things to do.

Quietly, he opened the door in time to see the three enter a door marked OFFICER CANTEEN. Two soldiers burst through the stairwell bulkhead door he had come through moments before, the same two who'd tried to stop him in the hold. Shit! He closed the cabin door and heard them race past.

Less than a minute left before the lighter departed. But now he had a new decision to make. The killer was aboard. But also the big pigtailed Korean. He fit Tomi's description of Alpha, the head of North Korean intelligence. And the name of the general came to him. General Myun Chun Kuk, deputy chief of staff. A leader of the hard-liner clique in Pyongyang. Why weren't they ashore at the ceremony? he wondered. Perhaps they knew something was going to happen.

Too much time had elapsed since Mori had boarded the *White Swan*. The canisters would blow in another few seconds. Several might have already begun. He was stuck. He pulled the small transceiver from his pocket and pushed a switch. Steve's voice sounded loudly in his ear.

"Juric here. Did you find any cars?"

"Yes. Must be a hundred of them."

"Where are you?"

"In deep shit. Just saw the killer talking to the head of North Korean intelligence. But I'm stuck. I can't get off the ship. Can you see any smoke yet?"

"Not yet."

"Is Homma there?"

"Yes."

"Okay. Tell Homma I found the items he wanted. In the forward hold, third bulkhead door on first level, then past the engine room and fuel storage. Tell him to get his boarding party here as soon as the canisters go and I'll hang on as long as I can. I might head for that forward hold if I have to. Safest place. Canisters are set to start any time now."

"How about I come aboard now?" Steve said.

"That's suicide. And it'd tip our hand and ruin everything. Wait until the canisters go. Then Homma's fire control team will get permission to board. They'll order an evacuation of the ship. All hands. Our killer will be forced onto the open deck, where we can take him. You can point him out to the police team. I'll try to help. Understand? That's the plan. You come aboard with Homma. Otherwise you don't have a chance."

"Okay, okay," Steve said. "I'll make sure the diver's around too. Just in case you have to jump."

"Don't even think that," Mori said.

THE OFFICERS IN the canteen came to attention as the three men entered. "At ease," the general barked. The room was surprisingly large and luxuriously furnished, Steig noted. There must have been twenty tables with armchairs, about a third of them occupied. It reminded him of a first-class waiting lounge at Narita. They selected a table where they could not be overheard.

"The operation is nearly completed," Alpha said. "Only the final phase."

"Where is Helim?" Steig asked.

"There was a little problem," Alpha said. "The Americans took her by force from Aleksei after he left you. I tell you that now, because Aleksei returned the favor. It cost the American FBI one of their agents. Japanese-American named Uemura. Pity."

General Myun Kuk guffawed. "We have a role for her to play on-shore. Then she'll join us here."

"What role?" Steig asked.

Alpha looked around. "Since there is no chance for you to leave us, you can be told now. She is about to assassinate Park Tai Jin. Unwittingly, of course."

"The flowers," General Myun agreed. "In less than a half hour more."

"Flowers?" Steig said. "How?"

"A syringe device inside them which injects a deadly plutonium poison into anyone who grasps them at a certain place."

"What if it doesn't work?"

"It will. If it doesn't, one of our men will kill Helim Kim with a silenced weapon, the poison device will be exposed, and the Americans will be blamed. Either way we win," Alpha said. "If it works, I'll interrogate Helim Kim tonight after Park Tai Jin has died and we have put out to sea for the emergency return to Pyongyang. Extract her confession."

"What do you expect her to confess?" Steig asked.

"That she's a traitor and assassinated our leader, of course. That she works for one. Park Chung Il. Second, that her grandmother is a high priestess in a cult controlled by revisionist women. Helim Kim uses it for political ends."

"What will you do with her?" Steig seemed anxious to know the answer.

"When I'm finished, we shall let the officers have a turn with her. Including you. Such things run in her family." Alpha snickered. "Perhaps we'll let her live. Let's see if she wants to tomorrow."

"I've promised her that I'd spend some time with her when you're through. I'd hate to go back on my word."

The general laughed. "There might not be much left of her private parts by that time. Alpha's found electric shock of the genital area an effective treatment for women. Also techniques with the barrel of his gun."

69: STRICKEN SHIP *White Swan:* Thursday, 2:25 P.M.

MORI COULD SEE to the open deck from the corridor. The sky was darkening. The lighter had departed the ship seven minutes ago. There was no reason for him to be on the damn ship! He had to look busy, as if he belonged here. The first canisters in the hold must have gone. Why didn't he see smoke from the toilet?

The threesome were still in the canteen. No way he could get inside—there was a guard on the door. But the longer he hung around here the greater was the chance someone would discover him. The guard saluted and held the door open. A foreigner came into the corridor. Shaved head, blue eyes. A giant.

The sight of him rocked Mori's brain. The composite picture flashed before Mori's eyes—no doubt, this was the killer! Molten anger flooded his senses.

"You," Mori shouted.

Steig saw Mori. His arms tensed, the hands came up knotted in huge fists. Simultaneously, a cloud of smoke erupted from the lavatory door next to the canteen. An alarm sounded. "Shit," Mori spat and looked around for his best advantage.

The killer advanced toward him, his eyes widening with recognition. "You bastard!"

Mori flew at him, striking with straight chops and leg kicks. The German blocked them almost carelessly.

Alarms began to sound throughout the ship as other smoke canisters exploded. Sailors rushed into the corridor. The bedlam separated Mori and Steig. Crew were pouring out of the doors that led below, since the smoke was thickest in the hold.

Mori backed toward the outer deck with the excited sailors. Space was necessary in a fight, he told himself, and the corridor was crowded. Homma would soon be boarding with police reinforcements; this was not the time or place to fight the giant. Before he could reach open air, a soldier came around the corner from the main deck, his weapon slung.

"Soldier, stop that man!" Steig screamed. "Don't let him escape! He's mine!" The soldier only stared bewildered at the foreigner, not understanding what the big man was shouting. Steig hesitated.

In that moment of Steig's indecision, Mori yanked open a bulkhead door the grimy engine crew had used to escape the lower decks. "Fire!" he shouted in Korean, as he slammed the door shut behind him. He spun the lock handles and ran down the stairs for his life.

STEVE SAW SMOKE pouring from portholes. He turned, but Homma had already barked orders. The police craft roared toward the *White Swan*.

Steve saw that there were at least five other craft simultaneously steaming for the North Korean vessel: three red fireboats and two dark-blue-hulled police craft had miraculously appeared. Homma's vessel fastened alongside the *White Swan* ahead of the others, and the first team of police that clambered up ladders to board the vessel was led by the feisty police chief himself. Steve climbed up with him. He felt his adrenaline pumping. They had to find Mori. The killer was here somewhere too.

North Korean crew were lining up on deck. Steve searched the faces, but could not see Mori. Homma shouted orders to his men. Steve mentally reviewed the ship's layout. Mori had seen cars in the forward hold. Through the third bulkhead door aft. Engine room, storage tanks, forward hold. Maybe Mori was there. A large hold, Mori had said. Full of cars.

The captain of the ship appeared. He and Captain Homma began to untangle the legalities. Jesus, Steve thought. If this was a serious fire, the ship would have gone down long ago. He looked around the growing crowd on deck. Where the hell was Mori?

MORI DOVE DOWN the stairwell. Smoke was curling up the stairs. He could hardly see ahead of him. There was a growing clamor in back of him. To his left, the dim form of the giant engine appeared through the smoke. Good. He was on the right catwalk, the one he'd taken before.

Smoke was swirling around him now, pouring from the canisters he had placed there earlier. He heard someone shouting in German. The foreigner. He slammed into a metal door. A gash opened above his right eye. He felt sparks of pain shooting though his forehead.

Cursing, he pulled open the door and entered the midship hold that contained the diesel tanks. Several panic-stricken crew raced past him heading the other way. Mori went blindly now, bumping into railings, until he reached the spiral stairs that led up to the door to the forward hold. The smoke was catching in his throat, and he started to cough.

He climbed up the spiral stairs and leaned gasping for air against the door. His strength was draining. Behind the door was the main hold, he told himself. If he could reach it, maybe he could escape. Behind him he could hear the shouts of the German and his other pursuers. He wrenched at the door handle, his mouth dry from fear. The heavy metal door opened and he heaved himself through. Then he slammed the door shut.

He ran directly into a soldier leveling an AK-47 at him.

Instinctively, Mori swung a forearm against the barrel and drove a fist at a point where the chest bones met. He heard a crack and the soldier screamed, dropping the weapon. Mori picked it up and raced down the catwalk.

The smoke canisters had no effect here. His pursuers would see him clearly, except that the hold was vast and dark. He was again above the cars, only this time he had no time to admire them. Several engines were running, Mori noted, as he half slid, half fell down stairs and ducked in among the rows of vehicles. The mechanics who had been working on them had disappeared, scared off when the alarms first sounded.

Mori saw the reason why there was little smoke here. Portholes had been opened to allow exhaust fumes to escape. And a large forward door was open to the sea, allowing daylight to pour in. Cars near the door were draped in coverings. He headed in that direction.

A figure suddenly loomed ahead of him. He slid to a halt. The German came toward him slowly.

THE DISCUSSION BETWEEN Homma and the captain wasted valuable minutes. Steve waited impatiently. The sky was dark now and the wind strengthening. Steve could see the fireboats playing water on the hull of the ship, directing streams to open portholes. Their hoses were probing the North Korean ship's hull and superstructure, from which smoke

poured. More boats had been attracted to the scene. There must have
been two dozen already crowding around.

Soldiers were lined up with weapons held at the ready, preventing
any foreigners from entering the ship's corridors. The police stood in
disciplined ranks on deck awaiting orders. Three teams from their boat
had climbed aboard, plus teams from the two other police craft; over thirty
Japanese officers were on deck with fire-fighting gear and weapons.

Homma was explaining through an interpreter that since there was a
fire in the main hold of the ship, the law of the harbor prevailed. The
captain disagreed.

It was an emergency, Homma said. Under such circumstances, the
safety of those aboard and the ship itself passed to the Niigata police and
firemen. North Korean territorial integrity was waived. The North Korean ship was a threat to other shipping in the harbor. He showed a
document from the harbormaster. It apparently did not occur to the captain that the document had been produced with remarkable speed.

If necessary, Homma continued, he could request the North Korean
crew to abandon ship. He stared at the crew now lined up on deck.
Eventually, the captain acquiesced. Homma shouted an order to his police
team and they began to fan out.

Steve knew they had very little time. The North Koreans would
quickly discover there was no fire, only smoke canisters. He had to find
Mori and the killer before that happened. Remembering Mori's instructions, he started down a companionway looking for the doors that would
lead to the forward hold. A thought suddenly occurred to him. They
needed time, didn't they? What if there was a real fire?

MORI HEARD DOORS above on the catwalk open and the shouts of reinforcements arriving. He jumped to the trunk of a car, then leaped from
one car to another, trying to move closer to the open door and the sea.
The German ran with him. Mori realized he could not escape. He turned
and with a yell leaped at the man.

The huge man threw Mori off arrogantly, driving an elbow into his
face. Mori felt an explosion between his eyes and felt the flow of blood
in his mouth. His nose was broken, he knew. Other soldiers had reached
them now, but the killer waved at them to keep away. "He's mine," the
German bellowed.

Mori drove a fist toward the leering face, but Steig flicked it aside.

He advanced, and Mori slowly backed away, blood pouring from his nose. Korean soldiers formed a circle around him, pointing their rifles. Mori leaped to the hood of a Rolls-Royce and then dove again, driving a leg kick that struck home and sent the killer reeling off balance against a Mercedes. He quickly recovered and gestured for Mori to come forward. Try that again.

But Mori backed away. Someone prodded him with a weapon, but Steig shouted, "No. Let him alone. Mine."

The man was like some wild beast, Mori thought. A huge invincible ape.

The German unleashed a series of blows that drove Mori reeling down the narrow lane of cars. Soldiers howled with delight and regrouped around the two men again. Another gash had been opened on Mori's cheek. His right arm was numb. He knew it was hopeless now. His strength was ebbing. Enough adrenaline left for one last charge, that was all.

Mori hurled himself at the huge figure, landing a glancing kick to his thigh. The German narrowly missed taking Mori's head off with his own leg kick, but quickly turned and drove a fist into Mori's chest. Mori grunted, the air gone from his lungs, and crashed against a Lamborghini. He had backed almost to the end of the row of cars and could feel the sea air behind him. He did not dare look.

Don't give up, he urged himself. Remember Oishi. Remember Tomi. His chest burned, and he gulped for air, gathered the last dregs of his remaining strength. Now, he told himself. With sudden quickness, Mori exploded in a final fury of karate moves that were faster than the killer could follow. Two legs shots doubled the huge man, and a blow to the forehead split skin. Steig sank to the floor. The soldiers hesitated.

In that instant, Mori catapulted to the top of a car, rolled over it and into the next alley. Then up and over again, quickly putting two rows of cars between him and the squad of soldiers.

He heard a purring sound and felt a vibration. He was leaning against a Mercedes with its engine running! Mori fell into the driver's seat. The smell of leather surrounded him. He shifted the car into gear; pulled out into the narrow alley between rows of cars. Through the rearview mirror he could see a squad of soldiers racing toward him. He floored the accelerator and the Mercedes backed suddenly, careening as it picked up speed amid a volley of bullets. The soldiers scattered.

Mori braked, hearing the tires screech as they clawed for traction on the metal grate. He shifted into drive, then again floored the accelerator. The Mercedes shot forward. A bullet pinged off the rear window, turning it to cracked ice. Mori could see the door leading to the water. It looked very small. The buildings of Niigata City rose in the distance. He prayed.

Blocking the exit was a yellow wooden warning barricade with black stripes. His mind furiously tried to calculate options. No time to think. Just to hope that the door was large enough. A door used to drive cars on and off the ship when it was in dock. But they were not in dock now.

He crouched low beneath the steering wheel, keeping the accelerator jammed against the floor. The engine spun the heavy car into a cannonball of fury as it splintered the wooden barrier, tore though the door in the hull, and burst onto a short ramp that became his catapult.

The last thing Mori remembered was the sensation of seawater rushing into the car, engulfing him.

STEVE RAN THROUGH a door and down a smoke-filled spiral stairwell, descending into the bowels of the ship until he reached a catwalk. He began to sweat and took off Mori's jacket and shirt. He knotted the shirt so it would burn if soaked in oil. When he reached the engine room, he glimpsed several pools of oil and waste on the floors. He soaked the shirt in a puddle of oil. Then found the plastic lighter in Mori's jacket, and lit the shirt. Almost immediately, the material exploded in flames. He torched the first oil puddle, then moved to another. After five blazes were going, he dropped the shirt in a bucket of waste and dumped the entire mess onto the floor. Flames shot up. Fires were beginning to catch hold. Racing back upstairs, he headed forward, past the engine room, then into an amidships hold where large diesel tanks were located. Here the smoke was thick, and he could barely make out anything except the tanks. His pace slowed. By the time he reached the doors to the next hold, he was gasping for air. His lungs burned from the smoke and exercise.

He turned the door handle, beginning to feel dizzy from smoke inhalation. No good. He stopped to put his head between his legs. Damn smoke. There was going to be a lot more real soon. With great effort, he flung the door open.

He emerged on a wide catwalk over a huge hold and stopped for a moment in amazement. The air here was relatively clear, and he could see. The hold was full of cars. He was alone. No police. No Koreans. He wondered if Homma's negotiation had hit another snag. No time to find out now, he thought. And too late to stop those fires.

He heard a bulkhead open somewhere and steps coming toward him. Steve looked back the way he'd come, hoping it was the Japanese police. Instead he saw the dim khaki uniforms of North Korean soldiers. The Elite Presidential Guard. Hurry, Steve told himself.

He ran toward steps leading down into the huge hold. Suddenly soldiers appeared from that end as well. They raised their weapons but did not fire. A Caucasian behind them had held up his hand and was limping slowly forward to study Steve. His head was shaved, and blood ran from a cut on his forehead that he didn't seem to notice. Steve felt his heart start to pound, knew this was the killer he'd faced in the seas off Atami. Only now Steve was outnumbered. He'd have to take them all on. Or surrender.

"It's the swimmer, I believe," Steig said casually, coming closer.

His right leg, Steve noted. He can't put much weight on it.

"The boat's on fire," Steve said. "It's going to sink."

Steig looked around as if unsure who was being addressed. "You have a sense of humor. Good." He took several more steps toward Steve and held up a metal object. "See this? Smoke canister. Found in the central hold. We look more, we find more, yes? Planted by that bastard of a policeman."

"He got away?"

Steig shrugged at the American. "No chance for you to escape, however. Or do you want to try your luck? One on one?"

Mori had somehow escaped them. He only had to worry about extricating himself. "You're the bastard who tried to kill Helim, aren't you? Why?"

Steig suddenly roared with laughter. When it subsided he asked, "So that's it? Girlfriend, is she? Well, you should have told me. She'll be on board in a little while."

"You're lying."

"I have an impeccable source."

"So do I. She's on a plane heading for the U.S.A."

"Wrong. She took a detour. In fact, she's about to meet Park Tai Jin dockside. After which she'll join us on this ship for a party. Surrender to our soldiers and you'll meet her again. Otherwise . . ."

"You're lying. I saw them leave. Three Americans took her to the airport."

"One American resisted. He was killed."

"Nonsense."

"Trust me. An agent named Uemura. Japanese-American."

Uemura dead! The words triggered a volcanic fury. Helim captured! His left hook smashed against the surprised face. He threw a right. Another left, punching in manic combinations, his mind suddenly crystal-clear. Like riding the waves at Waianae and Banzai Pipe. Like at the Kami-Hai compound, hiding in the grass. No more hiding. His right again mauled the killer's eye. Like the old days, boxing light-heavy.

But even under this furious assault, Steig only blinked, shook his head, took two steps backward. Then, like a bull, the big man charged.

A knotted karate fist missed. Then a second took Steve's wind away. Steve backpedaled, used footwork and a left jab to keep the limping man off him. The fellow had a chin like stone. They moved along the catwalk, Steve's fists high, whipping out at will, damaging the killer's face, raising purple welts. But Steve knew he couldn't knock him out. Steig scored with huge blows, staggering Steve twice, but Steve kept doggedly punching with the precise left—one two three, then bam, another right. His huge opponent caught Steve with a karate chop that sent him reeling. He grasped the railing and pulled himself to his feet. Steig put his hands down and signaled to the soldiers on each side of him.

"Enough entertainment. I could kill you, but I want you to meet some friends of mine first. We can have another round tomorrow. Helim can watch."

Soldiers closed in from each end of the catwalk.

Steve searched overhead for some way out. His eyes found a wall ladder that led upward toward a landing and disappeared into the murk toward the roof of the cavernous hold. He took a good grip on the first rung, then furiously started to climb.

As he clambered up the ladder, he heard shouts below. His legs cramped, felt as if they were on fire. He reached the first landing and looked down, the scene below spinning before his eyes. His calves hurt as if someone was grinding knives into them.

Below him, the North Korean soldiers had not tried to climb. Steig was laughing in great bellowing roars, looking up at him. He willed the pain in his legs away, shook his head to clear it, then with a deep breath started upward again. As Steve climbed higher, he wondered why the North Koreans weren't coming up after him. Maybe they knew something he didn't. Near the ceiling of the hold, the ladder reached a small door. Steve opened it and peered in. His hopes of escape suddenly evaporated.

A STRONG ARM wrapped around Mori and he came to. He felt himself being pulled from the submerged Mercedes and lifted toward the surface. An object was placed over his mouth. He inhaled, and oxygen poured into his burning lungs. He and his rescuer broke the surface.

"It's okay, Mori," said the American diver, removing his mask. "You made it."

The diver's identity stunned him. "DeCovasi! What the hell are you doing here?"

"Odd jobs. This and that. Now I want you to just relax." Mori allowed himself to be towed to the police patrol boat, where he was hauled aboard.

An ominous darkness had descended over the harbor in the face of the impending storm. The American agent came into the cabin, still in his diving gear.

"How are you feeling, Inspector?"

"Lousy but alive. I haven't thanked you."

"No need to thank me. Just doing my job. You're going to have a couple of black eyes from that broken nose, if you don't watch out. Here, let me have a look." He reached into a kit, found several cauterizing sticks to stop the bloodflow from Mori's nose.

"Like to repay you, DeCovasi," Mori said, seeing that they were alone. He found his briefcase, which had been stashed in the cabin, and came up with the copy of the diary.

"Like I said, comrade, no need."

"It's something I can't use myself. Personal reasons. About Kenzo Tanemura, who's supposed to be the next prime minister of Japan."

DeCovasi's eyes became alert. "Go on."

"You know how our politicians live or die by scandal. Takes the place of assassinations in our more civilized society, I suppose. Used to be somebody'd run an opponent through with a sword. Now they do it with words."

"Very civilized. Yes."

"Seems like Tanemura wasn't from a wealthy family. But he was smart as hell. Lived in a farming district outside Tokyo, wanted to be a politician. During the war he served in the Kempeitai in Korea and China. One of his sidelines was lining up girls for the military brothels. Perk, you might call it. His name wasn't Tanemura then. Born name was Sakamoto. When he married he took the name of his bride, because the family was rich and the father-in-law was an important politician. Tanemura, his bride's name was. Greased the way for his political career. Read this and you'll see he had a penchant for young Korean girls. Would make interesting viewing on your news telecasts, but I believe you'll come up with a better use! Add to it the fact we suspect him of masterminding the protection of this Korean pachinko laundering operation and you might say his future is in your hands. Naturally you have to do a little research. Start with this."

DeCovasi took the proffered diary. "Very kind of you."

"It evens a score. But I do have one condition."

"Of course."

"You do not name the source. And you let Tanemura stay in power."

DeCovasi grinned. "Assuming he wins the prime minister's job, it would be stupid to rock the boat. We can just exert a little influence here and there. Nothing extravagant, mind you. A tweak or two to get him pointed in the right directions."

"Exactly. I believe I feel about the same as you do. You've eased my mind."

"We're even then." DeCovasi folded the diary and put it in his kit. "And friends for life."

The police boat had pulled away from the Korean ship again. Mori could see that the *White Swan*'s launch had returned from delivering Park Tai Jin dockside to the mother ship and was now being made ready again alongside the North Korean vessel. DeCovasi looked at it a moment. "Sorry, Inspector, I have to go now."

"Where to?"

"To finish what you started."

He dove off the bow of the police boat and disappeared in the direction of the *White Swan.* Ten minutes later he returned dripping wet and retired to the lower cabin to stow his gear.

STEVE GLANCED DOWN the ladder into the hold, not believing where he now found himself. The anchor room was for the huge chain that wound around an enormous drum. Each link was three feet in length, and when he tried to heft one it could not be budged. The anchor had been lowered, so there was plenty of room. If the ship hauled anchor . . .

He shut the door and held it tight. He was trapped. Worse, there was no lock on the inside of this door. He looked at the hole in the hull for the huge anchor chain. How far to the water? he wondered.

A roaring noise suddenly filled his ears. The drum had started to turn, and the chain clanked and hummed as it snapped taut and began to wrap its great links around itself like a python around a victim. Suddenly, it stopped.

"Come down," the killer bellowed, "or I'll have the bridge raise the chain again until you surrender or die." If they weren't bluffing, Steve told himself, the chain would fill the remaining space in the tiny compartment. He'd be crushed.

"Bastards!" Steve shouted. Maybe they were bluffing, but he didn't want to take that chance. Anyway, he couldn't stay here.

Bracing himself as he wriggled out through the opening feet first, Steve slipped, felt the links tear his skin. He hung precariously on the chain for a moment, looking down. The water was too far below. Much too far. Then he let go.

He tried to hold himself rigid, his feet together. The water hit him with the force of concrete. The shock of the impact knocked the wind out of him for a moment, and he found himself ten feet under water when he came to his senses. He fought his way to the surface. The bow of the ship towered over him. He started to swim as fast as he could toward shore.

MORI HAD BEEN on the launch barely long enough to recover when Homma clambered back aboard, checked orders with the boat crew, and then came over to congratulate him. "The crew told me about the crazy stunt you pulled. You wrecked a perfectly good Mercedes. And got a broken nose in the bargain, it looks like."

Mori felt his face. "I got a perfect ten from all the judges except the

North Korean one. To be honest, the car was a clunker—the air bags didn't work." A surge of pain flooded through him. "Your show now, Homma."

"You did a great job." The police chief put his hand on Mori's shoulder. "However, they found the smoke canisters."

"Damn! So fast?"

"That's the bad news. The good news is that a real fire is now raging in the engine room and they've decided to let our firefighters go in. They may really be forced to abandon ship this time. You know anything about that?"

"I swear I don't. How'd it start?"

"Nobody knows. None of my people. We've just sent the firefighters in, but I've told them to take their time. The captain has still refused to allow our men into the forward hold. We're going to let that fire burn awhile until he does. Forward hold's being guarded by a team of their soldiers right now. I think your friend went in there and they're not going to let him come out. They've got their stolen cars in there. I hope your foreign friend can take care of himself. He's not going to get any help from us, I'm afraid."

Mori considered what could be done. If Steve was captured, he'd become another pawn in the game that was being played. "I'll go back on board after I catch my breath. Give me a little longer to recover. What are your plans?"

"We'll try and flush the people you want off the ship. But it's not looking good. Too many places they can hide." The police chief looked up at the big ship. "I'm going to get fired for this, I guess. Tanemura and his cronies at the dock over there will be pissed." They both turned in the direction of the international pier where the ceremonies were being held. It was less than a thousand yards away; through the overcast, they could catch a glimpse of the crowded ceremony already under way.

"I wouldn't worry about Tanemura." Mori pulled a camera from his belt pouch. "I took pictures of the cars."

"Might help. We'll see."

Mori turned back to the ship. "Try and locate the North Korean intelligence chief," he said. "And the killer. Have your people on board find them if they can."

THE WELCOMING CEREMONY had run overtime, but no one seemed to mind. Park Tai Jin had spoken first, and his comments alone had taken nearly forty minutes. He promised to consider the U.S. position on oil and other matters. A document would be drawn up that both could sign and release to the press. He'd made a good impression on the Western media, discounting the picture that had been painted of him as a reclusive and introverted egomaniac.

Tanemura had also spoken at length, for he understood the ceremony would be on all the important evening news shows.

Now it was the former U.S. president's turn. Sherman Whitlow proposed a new beginning. A bridge to peace. A linking of hands across the Pacific. The opening ceremony was now an hour over schedule.

ALTHOUGH THERE WERE no witnesses, the rental car had apparently been traveling at very high speed when it plunged over a retaining wall and into a deep channel that cut inland from the Japan Sea. The lone occupant was trapped inside and drowned, although there was a nasty blow to the back of his head that could not be readily explained. The rental agent said that three Asians had rented the car, using Park's passport and license. The spot where it occurred had been the cause of accidents in the past, so no one was overly surprised. The officers sent to investigate did note that the crash happened at a time of the afternoon when the light could glare off the water, which might have affected the driver's vision. The fact it was overcast did not seem to matter. The driver was pronounced dead on arrival at the local hospital and a notification was sent to the Finnish consulate of the North Korean government in Helsinki. The tragic accident involving their consul, Park Chung Il, had apparently been caused by driver error. There were no witnesses. A short obituary appeared in the evening papers the next day, noting Park's death and the fact he was believed to be a distant relative of the current leader of North Korea, Park Tai Jin.

71 : **FINALE** Niigata harbor: Thursday, 3:00 P.M.

THE GIRL SCOUTS were sitting on a curb along the quay where Park Tai Jin had disembarked. Helim leaned against a railing to take the weight off her tired legs. The sky was overcast, and she wished it would rain so that she could get this over with.

The roses still looked fresh. She wondered if she looked the same.

Elizabeth Kayanskova was twenty yards away, watching her. Afterward they were to go for dinner, a prospect she was not looking forward to.

They had given her specific directions for handling the flowers. A black line had been drawn around the foil. She was to hold the foil below the line and present them so that the North Korean leader would grasp them above the line. This was the formality—never let a head of state grasp flowers or other gifts below your hands. It was politically incorrect. Elizabeth had been very clear. "We can't have bad manners, now can we?" she had said emphatically.

It seemed odd that it mattered how you deliver flowers to another human being, but she had no practice in the art. Still, the way Elizabeth insisted made her somehow suspicious. Would they harm someone in front of all these TV cameras and media? It didn't seem likely. She wished she could think. Her brain throbbed with fatigue. She must get some sleep. She imagined herself in a bubble bath surrounded by candles. Roses were harmless, weren't they? Then a thought occurred to her, and she studied the flowers more carefully.

They certainly were beautiful. She rearranged them a little, and in so doing peeked down inside them. The stalks were squeezed together by the aluminum. But something caught her eye. Shiny, way down there hidden in the foil just above the level of the black line. Like needles. Maybe just her imagination. She looked at the colonel.

Elizabeth was staring at her, so she tried to appear nonchalant. On either side of Elizabeth were two tough-looking North Koreans. The colonel had asked her to join their group. She couldn't. Never. Only she couldn't let them know. Whose group will I join? she asked herself. None. I'm the great nonconformist. That made her laugh to herself.

She hoped Sherman Whitlow wouldn't end his speech soon. She needed time to think.

SECURITY WAS WATCHING the crowd of onlookers seated in front of the speakers rather than the water. Therefore it was not surprising that the figure that clambered onto the stone landfill of the dock area some one hundred yards away was not immediately noticed. Helim happened to be facing that way.

The figure was obviously a man, somehow familiar to her, walking along the bank, approaching Elizabeth Kayanskova and the other onlookers from the rear. The crowd began to applaud. She turned back toward the podium.

To her horror, Sherman Whitlow was bowing. He had finished his speech. The leader of the Japanese Girl Scouts rallied her group together. Huddled as if for protection, they approached Whitlow and presented their bouquet. The three famous men were standing close together at the front of the podium. Kanemura said something to Park Tai Jin, and they both applauded as the Girl Scouts retreated, mission accomplished.

Helim glanced at Elizabeth, who nodded. The time had come for Helim to present the roses. Yet all the questions were still unanswered. Was this woman really who she said she was? Would they really set her mother free? Why had they asked her to deliver the flowers? What was going to happen to her if she returned to the United States? She didn't know. She had no answers.

She summoned her power animal. The snow-white tiger arrived, shaking itself as if just aroused. She went deeper inside herself. To an altered state of consciousness. A humming noise filled her ears. Overhead the sky became brighter. Violet hues formed in an expanding hood over her head. Within her celestial grotto, she could suddenly see an iridescent waterfall in which dim figures writhed. A huge crocodilian head thrust itself through the waterfall. From its mouth gushed a torrent of blood-red water. She stared transfixed. The head became Tanemura. A claw emerged, holding flowers that grew into a grotesque bouquet. The flowers were purple and black—Poison and Death. Other creatures emerged from the waterfall and danced around the flowers. Then the scene disappeared. Everything returned as it had been. Yes, she thought. She understood.

Helim began to walk toward Park Tai Jin. The snow-white tiger prowled alongside. All eyes watched. The TV cameras picked up her elegant stride. Somewhere in the distance, she heard a voice calling her name. But she kept walking, blocking out everything except the three powerful men who stood together on the platform directly in front of her now. Smiling and waiting. Chatting with one another. Unaware that death was approaching them.

MORI STEPPED TO the railing of the police boat. "So what do we do?" he asked Homma.

"I don't know. We can't locate Steve Juric, your killer, Alpha, or the general on the ship. There are too many hiding places. But that fire's still raging, although we can control it now. And the harbormaster has refused a request by the North Korean ship captain to change schedule and depart tonight. They've referred the matter to Park Tai Jin, who's meeting with Sherman Whitlow in the city and is due back tonight on the launch. Anyway, the fire's caused enough damage to require some repairs. Don't understand why the captain's insisting on leaving."

Mori squinted at the *White Swan*, where the captain's launch was being made ready for departure. "If we can get my pictures developed tonight, and submitted to a local magistrate, we can prove they have cars aboard and impound the ship and crew tomorrow. I've requested an arrest warrant for the intelligence chief, Alpha. And the German who goes by the name of Helmut Stern. We have them cornered now. The rest is up to you fellows in the local police."

DeCovasi came forward. "You're going to have a couple of black eyes, Inspector. In spite of my good work."

"Don't worry. I was lucky to get off with that."

Homma looked at them. "You two friends?"

"He saved my life, Homma," Mori said. "Guess you could call us friends."

He stiffened. Three figures were racing down the canopied stairs to the captain's launch. The lead figure was tall, his hair tied back in a pigtail.

Behind him was a Korean in a general's uniform. And behind them a tall powerful Caucasian. Unmistakably the German killer.

Mori pulled out his radio and punched in a frequency. There was no response. He looked around helplessly, but Homma had already dashed into the wheelhouse and was issuing commands. DeCovasi had gone to the railing and was leaning over it, studying the trio. Then, as if satisfied, he sat down and examined something in his hand.

The launch crew cast off ropes, and the boat gunned away from the *White Swan.* From the wheelhouse, Homma directed the police patrol boat to follow it. They started toward it, but their craft was clearly no match for the launch. It lunged away, easily outdistancing the police. Homma turned the boat and headed for the dock. He radioed other police boats in the area to take up pursuit.

The launch headed north up the coast, disappearing and reappearing in the humidity and gloom. Suddenly DeCovasi stood and flexed his hand.

There was a blinding flash.

Mori turned just in time to see it. There was the explosion, then a fireball, and the captain's launch simply disappeared. Out of a white castle of smoke flew sparklers in gold and silver, like a unique fireworks display for an Independence Day celebration. And following that, like comet tails, blazing pieces of white-hot metal twinkled against the low-hanging clouds.

HELIM HAD STOPPED in front of the North Korean leader. "Welcome to the peace negotiation," she said in Korean. "May you and those like you in North Korea live forever." Her hand hesitated above the forbidden black line and moved upward to pluck one flower, which she handed to Park Tai Jin. "Love is symbolized by one rose, not many. This is for the love from all Koreans."

"Why, thank you." Park Tai Jin was clearly moved.

Helim turned to the Japanese leader standing beside him. "Tanemura-san, may I present this bouquet to you with gratitude from the Korean Association for your protection and kindness." She grasped the flowers well below the black line and held them out to him.

The explosion in the harbor made everyone gasp and turn. A woman shouted, "No!" Helim turned and saw a Secret Service agent grab a gun in an assailant's hand as they wrestled to the ground. Helim's eyes widened with horror. The gun had been pointed at her. There was shouting and confusion around the platform. Soldiers raced to surround the North

Korean leader and hurry him away. Other security hustled Whitlow and Tanemura safely toward their cars. Helim waited until she'd regained her calm. Then she turned, still holding the flowers, and walked through the confusion toward the voice she'd heard shouting her name. She recognized that voice now. The snow-white tiger beside her protected her from harm. It nudged Helim away from the crowds toward the edge of the dock and the open water of the harbor.

HELMETED SOLDIERS BLOCKED Steve's way. He shouted her name again, but she'd disappeared. A surging crowd of security had rushed between them. Where had she gone? He'd seen Helim glance at an elderly Caucasian woman, seen the woman nod, seen Helim walk toward the leaders on the podium. He'd craned his neck and watched as she'd handed the North Korean leader a single rose, then turned to a Japanese beside him.

Then chaos. Something exploded in the harbor, then a sudden disturbance right in front of him. Seeing the metallic flash of a weapon, Steve instinctively dove at the man and tackled him. Others piled on. By the time Steve struggled free, a swarm of security had rushed between the leaders and the crowd watching. Helim was gone.

Gradually order was restored. The area slowly cleared. Although Steve searched desperately, it seemed like hours had passed before he caught sight of Helim again.

She was holding the bouquet of roses in her hand, standing apart by the edge of the dock, staring out to sea. She raised the flowers to her face as if inhaling victory, then cast them into waves made turbulent by a police boat that had just arrived and was tying up.

"Helim!" Steve shouted. She looked in Steve's direction. A man emerged from the cabin of the police boat and jumped ashore.

"Miss Kim!" DeCovasi said, coming up to her and taking hold of her arm. She turned in fear and tried to pull away. "No," DeCovasi said. "Wait!"

Steve raced up to them, recognizing the diver from the boat. "What's going on?"

"Those flowers," DeCovasi said to Helim. "Why did you throw them away?"

Helim looked from Steve to the diver. "It's okay," Steve said. "He's a friend."

"There was poison . . . then a man tried to shoot me. Someone stopped him."

"They set you up." DeCovasi studied her a moment. "Get on the boat, quickly."

"Where are we going?" Helim asked, holding on to Steve's arm.

"You're going to disappear," DeCovasi said. "I'm going to help you do it."

They clambered onto the police boat.

Mori waved at Steve as he came aboard. "How did you . . . ?"

"I swam," Steve said, noticing Mori's blackened eyes. "Glad to see you got out too."

"I need a last favor," DeCovasi interrupted as Captain Homma came over.

"Okay," Mori answered for both of them. "You've earned it."

"She has to disappear. Can you organize that?"

"I have a friend who can take her in for a while," Mori said. "On Sado Island. She won't be bothered there. I'll see to it."

"Perfect," DeCovasi said. "And forget you ever saw her."

"What's going on? Who is she?" Homma asked as he gestured at his men to cast off.

DeCovasi jumped back ashore. "Explain everything later. No time now. And Helim, forget about coming back. Ever."

Homma gave the order. The boat headed into the harbor, sped up the coast, then swung out into the Japan Sea.

HELIM CLOSED HER eyes and tried to sleep. Suddenly she opened them. "That diver was one of the men who interrogated me!"

"Could be," Steve agreed. "He's with the FBI."

"Are they letting me go?"

"Guess so." Steve put his hands on her shoulders. "But he wants you to lie low for a while."

"I can deal with that." She hugged him tightly, passionately.

He kissed her neck. "Now about that conversation at the compound . . . let's forget we ever had it."

"Agreed," Helim said. She paused a moment, smiled, and then looked up at him with eyes shining. "Except for one part—I've changed my mind. The answer to that question you asked me? It's 'Yes.' "

EPILOGUE

THE MOST SPECTACULAR feature of the blast was its light, DeCovasi would later recall in his debriefing at FBI headquarters in Washington. Like a star exploding, others who saw it later agreed.

An FBI investigation into the attempted assassination ended inconclusively. The gunman, the disappearance of Helim Kim, and Park's death left no grounds for Pipe's insubordination charges against DeCovasi; they were dropped. Park and DeCovasi's theory, a coup attempt by North Korean hard-liners, was considered the most plausible, although this finding was never made public. The gunman swallowed a cyanide pill after being overpowered and could not be positively identified. The fortuitous timing of the *White Swan* launch explosion caused the gunman to panic, the finding concluded. The irony was that the explosion that averted Park Tai Jin's death took the lives of two hard-liners, assumed to have been behind the coup attempt. "Through Agent DeCovasi's decisive and heroic actions, a terrible disaster was no doubt averted—one that could have changed modern Asian history," the report concluded.

DeCovasi was presented an FBI medal for outstanding service. Shortly afterward, in a meeting with the FBI director and the secretary of state, DeCovasi supplied the material he had been able to procure on Kenzo Tanemura. Three months later, Joseph Pipe resigned as director of SIG; however, John DeCovasi was never named to replace him. Certain aspects of his character that had come to light well after the Niigata incident were not regarded as consistent with FBI leadership. He had been questioned about Helim Kim's disappearance, which was never satisfactorily explained. DeCovasi resigned after another year and accepted his fate calmly; he'd known that being right would have its price. He was hired by a security firm, with which he found a satisfactory sinecure.

As for media coverage of events of that day, Japanese TV news neglected to mention the blast except as an afterthought. Of greater interest was a fire reported aboard a North Korean ship berthed in the outer harbor. But since the blaze had been quickly extinguished, the main focus of all Tokyo channel coverage had been the meeting of Kenzo Tanemura and Park Tai Jin. Since the speeches had run overtime, live TV coverage had been terminated before the fracas at the end of the ceremony. Though some international press agencies released reports of an assassination attempt, this was strongly denied by Japanese officials and the story was quietly killed.

By morning, when the North Korean ship was allowed to sail, news of the explosion was also relegated to the third page of most Japanese newspapers.

No obituaries appeared in any papers, although it was rumored that several high-ranking North Koreans who were escaping the ship fire went up with the launch. As well as a German national. The German embassy offered no comment.

Ron Uemura's remains were flown back to the United States, where he was given a hero's burial.

Tomás Velaquez was released and allowed to return to Vienna, all expenses paid by the U.S. government. A letter clearing him of all accusations was subsequently provided to his chief at the IAEA. However, shortly after his return, Velaquez handed in his resignation, stating an intention to enter business for himself in Asia. In fact, he ended up working for someone else, at a newly established venture capital firm.

Several days after the events in Niigata, the Treasury Department visited the offices of the Korean Merchant Bank in Los Angeles and obtained financial statements dating back five years. Shortly thereafter, Chul Kim, managing director of the bank, was called in to explain a number of disturbing transactions: money transfers to politicians from both parties at the local, state, and national level sourced from offshore accounts that could not be traced to origins. Mr. Kim was unable to explain these transactions to the satisfaction of the Treasury officials, and in subsequent questioning by FBI officers, admitted he occasionally had contact with Finance Ministry officials in Pyongyang. After a two-month hearing, Mr. Kim was charged with failing to report he was an agent of a foreign government. He was deported.

Kenzo Tanemura was elected president of the Japan Democratic Party. The next day, he was invited to the emperor's palace and officially appointed the new prime minister of Japan.

Three days after his election, Tanemura withdrew his support for the Asia Tomorrow Project, which exclusively united Japan with North Korea, China, and Russia. He cited irreconcilable differences among the partner. He suggested the United States be included in all future discussions. A month later, after Hideo Katano had aired Helim Kim's pachinko interview and launched a scathing attack on the Japanese stock exchanges, their boards relented and approved all pachinko company listing applications.

SHERMAN WHITLOW RETURNED to the United States amid praise for a job well done. Soon afterward he received a request from a friend in the State Department to visit him in Washington to discuss a curious coincidence. It had been noted that he had voted to assassinate the North Korean leader at the Sierra Golf Club convocation with Jeff Archer. It had also surfaced that he had once had a relationship with a former Soviet KGB agent who was known for her sympathy with North Korean hardliners and was rumored to have been part of the plot to assassinate the North Korean leader. She had since disappeared. While nothing was ever proved, Whitlow's friends in Washington gradually stopped phoning. He received no further invitations to attend Washington conferences or seminars or to lunch with former influential congressional friends. Embittered, he retired to Colorado.

WHILE ON SADO Island, Helim wrote a detailed and personal letter to Park Tai Jin. Return address was a taiko drum school. Six weeks later, as she was about to leave the island, a reply arrived from Pyongyang. It requested her to be in a certain northeastern village of China on a specific date. Only a river separated the village from North Korea. There, her mother was delivered into Helim's arms with a small keepsake from Park Tai Jin: a single rose.

HELIM'S WHEREABOUTS ALWAYS remained a mystery. She was sighted at times in various Asian countries and was reported to have married. Steve Juric, after returning to L.A. to close his business there, returned to Asia, where he ran a successful venture consulting firm that eventually opened offices in five Asian countries. There were rumors he had married a woman in Taiwan; however, since this was not a legal marriage under United States law, the maiden name of the woman could never be confirmed. It was known only that she was Asian.

WHEN BUSINESS BROUGHT Mori to Niigata again, Captain Homma invited him to revisit the site where the launch blew up. The inspector accepted, and they reconstructed events, surveying the spot where it had all taken place.

Divers had given up the search for any remains long ago. Only small unidentifiable pieces of debris had been recovered.

The Niigata City police chief stood next to Mori.

"Hated to let them go, but we had no grounds, you see. They claimed the cars were bought free and clear. Had documentation to prove it. When they found the smoke was caused mainly by canisters, the captain was really angry. Said we had set the fire too. Couldn't prove a thing, though. All they found was an old charred shirt. Claimed territorial integrity had been violated. Threatened to make an international stink. Meanwhile, their leader and that former American president had come to terms. The Americans strongly suggested I let it pass. There was a rumor of an assassination attempt, which was quickly suppressed."

"Then it turned out well," Mori said. "And I think the girl was misunderstood."

"The one we took to Sado? She was some kind of double agent, from what I heard. He ever call to explain why he helped her?"

"No. Don't think it was out of charity. She probably knew too much. Jeopardized DeCovasi or somebody else. Guess we'll never know." Mori paused. "So you didn't get your cars after all."

"No. The Korean purchase documents were obviously false, but I decided not to pursue it. Anyway, the Koreans will never risk bringing cars through here again, I'm sure of that. Guess it solves the problem for us, don't you agree?"

Mori saw it differently. The police chief had the ship's captain cornered on the car issue but for reasons of his own had chosen not to press his advantage. Mori realized he would never know what the real reasons were.

"I think they suspected us, all right," Homma continued, as if reading Mori's doubts. "Of course, they were furious when the captain's launch went up. I told them what everyone else was saying later. Gas leak."

Mori chuckled. "Bastard calmly watched while that launch tore away for points unknown. Barely blinked when it exploded too."

"Who?"

"That American diver," Mori said. "DeCovasi. Right under everyone's nose. Radio-controlled magnetic bomb on the launch's hull, I'd guess now from the looks of the blast. Not enough evidence to fill a thimble. So we give the press an accident. Not that I'm disappointed. Bastards got what they deserved. Only thing that bothers me is, I should have figured it out beforehand, I suppose. Do you understand what I'm saying, Chief? They were in it too, you know."

"Whoever 'they' are, I suppose."

"The Americans. Anything that destabilizes the current North Korean government jeopardizes the Geneva peace accord between the North Koreans and the United States. A few deaths accomplished what diplomacy could not."

"Mori, we'll get you a medal for insight." The Niigata police chief stretched. "It's for the better. Trials are time-consuming, uncertain, and expensive, hey? I'm all for democratic legal process, but not when the keys to the kingdom are at stake. Let's get on with it then. Put the past behind us."

"You're right. There's more enjoyment in hope than in knowledge," Mori said. He spat over the rail into the water and looked off at the horizon toward North Korea. "Tonight, the drinks are on me."